PRIVATE
SECTOR

WARNER BOOKS

An AOL Time Warner Company

Copyright © 2003 by Brian Haig
All rights reserved.

Warner Books, Inc., 1271 Avenue of the Americas, New York, NY 10020

Visit our Web site at www.twbookmark.com.

 An AOL Time Warner Company

Printed in the United States of America

First Printing: September 2003
10 9 8 7 6 5 4 3 2 1

Library of Congress Control Number: 2003106119
ISBN: 0-446-53178-2

To Lisa
Brian, Pat, Donnie, and Annie

Acknowledgments

Books are the products of many hands and talents. For example, Alexander Haig, my brother, a crackerjack lawyer who gave me expert advice on law firms, telecommunications, and many lessons in sibling rivalries.

Or my agent and good friend, Luke Janklow, who handles everything with extraordinary grace, integrity, and humor.

Or my editor and also friend, Rick Horgan, a man with a remarkable eye, a brilliant mind, and patience.

Or Mari Okuda and Roland Ottewell, copy editors, but more than that, friends—and nearly coauthors, in my case.

I owe them all, and the rest of the remarkable crews at Janklow, Nesbitt, and Warner Books, a huge debt.

CHAPTER ONE

I BELIEVE YOU CALLED ME," I INFORMED THE VERY ATTRACTIVE YOUNG LADY seated at the desk.

She appeared not to have heard me.

"Excuse me, Miss. Major Sean Drummond . . . the phone, you called, right?"

She replied, sounding annoyed, "Yes. I was ordered to."

"You're angry."

"I'm not. You're not worth getting mad about."

"I honestly meant to call you."

"I'm glad you didn't."

"Really?"

"Yes. I was tired of you anyway."

She stared into her computer screen. And indeed, she was mad. It occurred to me that dating the boss's secretary might not have been a good idea. But she was quite good-looking, as I mentioned, with smoldering dark cycs, bewitching lips, and, I recalled, beneath that desk, a pair of splendid legs. Actually, why hadn't I called her?

I leaned across her desk. "Linda, I had a wonderful time."

"Of course *you* did. I didn't."

"I'm truly sorry it didn't work out."

"Good. I'm not."

I searched my mind for an appropriate sentiment and finally said, "So we beat on, boats against the current, borne back ceaselessly into the past."

"What?" She finally looked up.

"The Great Gatsby . . . the final line."

"Fuck off—that's Jackie Collins, if you're interested." She added, icily, "And take your hands off my desk. I just polished it."

Goodness. Now I recalled why I never called her after that first date. Actually, I never called her *before* the first date—she called me. But I learned long ago that what matters is not who starts it but who ends it.

I straightened up and asked, "So, why does the old man want to see me?"

"Ask him."

"I'd rather ask you."

"All right. Ask more nicely."

"Fine. Please, Linda . . . why am I here?"

"I'm not at liberty to tell you." She smiled.

Well, what more was there to say? She was being petty and unreasonable.

I backed away, far enough that she couldn't staple my hand to my crotch or something. That smile, however, bothered me. "Absit omen," I mumbled—*May it not be an omen.*

I suspected it was, however. So I spent a moment thinking about that. It occurred to me that nearly two months had passed since my last session with the boss. These are never pleasant meetings. In fact, they are never intended to be. The boss and I have a relationship that might be described as messy, and he has developed this really weird opinion that if he rides my butt hard enough, and often enough, it will fix itself. He calls them preemptive sessions. I call them a waste of time. They have not worked in the past, and we all know that persistent failure is not fertile ground for future success. But he stays at it. This must be what it's like to be married.

"I'll just wait here till he's ready," I informed Linda. It fit, I decided—General Clapper would toast my ears a little, and nosy, vindictive Linda would press her ear to the door and indulge in her vicarious retribution. I'd tune him out, as I always do, and I'd assure him at the end, also as I always do, that he'd made some very constructive points and had seen his last trouble from Sean Drummond.

No big deal. Right?

Wrong—ahead lay murder, scandal, and deeds so odious and foul they would turn my life, and this entire city, upside down. In fact, while I cooled my heels in this office, the murderer was already plotting the first of what would become many kills. And those who would become kills were going about their lives, unaware they were in the crosshairs of a monster.

But I don't think Linda foresaw that. I don't think she even wished it.

Incidentally, I don't work in the Pentagon, where this particular office was, and still is, located. I hang my hat in a small red-brick building inside a military base in Falls Church, Virginia, a tiny place with high fences, lots of guards, no signs, and no confusing room numbers. But if you're into confusing room numbers, Clapper's office is designated 2E535—2 connoting the second floor, E signifying the outer and most prestigious ring, and 535 indicating the same side of the building that got clobbered by Osama's boys. In the old days of the cold war, the courtyard in the middle of the Pentagon was called Ground Zero, the innermost A-Ring was Suicide Alley, and the outermost E-Ring was the place to be. But it's a new world and things change.

"He's ready for you now," announced Linda, again smiling.

I glanced at my watch: 1700 hours, or 5:00 P.M., the end of the official duty day, a warm early December evening to be precise. I love this season. I mean, between Thanksgiving and Christmas nobody in Washington even pretends they're working. How good is that? In fact, the last case in my in-box had just danced over to my out-box, and it was my turn.

Anyway, I stepped into Clapper's office, and he seemed so delighted to see me he even said, "Sean . . . I'm so delighted to see you." He waved at a pair of plush leather chairs and asked, "Well, my old friend, how are things?"

My old friend? "I'm fine, General. Thank you for asking."

"Well, good. You've been doing great work, and I'm very proud of you." His ass relaxed into a stuffed chair, and it struck me I was getting enough phony sunshine stuffed up my ass to be a health risk. He asked, "That Albioni case, has it been wrapped up yet?"

"Yes. This morning, in fact. We reached a plea agreement."

For some reason, I had the annoying sense he knew this already.

By the way, I'm what the Army calls a Special Actions attorney. If you want to know, I'm actually a defense counsel in a specialized compartment of lawyers and judges. We're specialized because we manage the legal issues of the Army's black operations, a menagerie of people and units so spooky nobody's supposed to know they even exist. It's all smoke and mirrors, and we're part of that circus.

In fact, my office supposedly doesn't exist, and neither do I, which often makes me wonder why in the hell I get out of bed in the morning. Just kidding. I love my job. Really. However, the sensitivity and seriousness of our work means we work directly for the Judge Advocate General, a line on Clapper's organizational chart he bitterly regrets, as we, and particularly me, are a royal pain in his ass.

So, what else? I'm 38 years old, single, have always been single, and the way things were looking, the past was lining up to be a prologue to the future. I regard myself as a fairly decent attorney, a master of the military legal code, clever, resourceful, and all that. My boss might object to any or all of those points, but what does he know? In my business, it's the clients who count, and I rarely get complaints.

But, back to my superficially perfect host. He inquired, "So tell me, Sean, what punishment did Albioni take in exchange for his guilty plea?"

"You know . . . it was fair and just."

"Good. Now describe for me please your idea of fair and just."

"All right. Two years in Leavenworth, honorable discharge, full benefits."

"I see." But he did not look happy.

The subject in question was Sergeant First Class Luigi Albioni, who was part of a unit that collects intelligence on foreign targets and who had been dispatched to Europe with an American Express card to shadow the dictator of a country that must remain anonymous. If you're curious, however, think of a large pisshole slowbaking between Egypt and Tunisia, a place we once bombed after it sent a terrorist to blow up a German disco filled with American GIs, and we still aren't invited to each other's barbecues. Yet it seems the dictator likes to don disguises on occasion and escape the stuffy Muslim ways of his country to partake in the decadent ways of the West, and Luigi's job was to skulk around and obtain photos of the camel-jockey as he shot craps in Monaco and cavorted in Amsterdam's brothels.

Exactly why our national leaders would want such disgusting pictures is, you can be sure, a question I would like answered. But in this business, don't ask. They usually won't answer. If they do, it's all lies.

Anyway, a week after Luigi departed from JFK International, he—and a hundred grand drawn on his charge card—disappeared into thin air, whatever the hell that cliché means. Six months passed before Luigi did something inexplicably stupid: He e-mailed an ex-wife. To inquire if there was a bounty on his ass, she called the Army's Criminal Investigation Division, who notified us; who swiftly arranged to have that same ass collected from a well-known

Swiss resort, which accounts for when and how I came into the picture.

Actually, Luigi turned out to be a pretty good guy for a scumbag who deserted his country. We bonded a little, and he confided that in order to protect his cover he had tried his hand at blackjack, got seriously carried away, lost ninety grand, then his luck turned and he won nine hundred grand. It was a fingertap from God, Luigi was sure—after seventeen years of loyal and courageous service, the time had come to pack it in on his own terms.

But back to Clapper. He logically asked, "And what happened to the money your client stole from the . . . from *our* government?"

I pointed out, "You mean the hundred grand he borrowed? He always intended to send a check with compounded interest. The rest were winnings—*his* winnings."

"Drummond . . . just don't." Well, it had worked with the prosecutor, but that's another story.

"The remainder's being donated to the Old Soldier's Home."

"Is that so?" He raised his eyebrows and suggested, I think skeptically, "A charitable gesture from a guilt-wrought man I take it?"

"In his own words, the least he could do, you know . . . considering his crimes, his love for the Army, and—"

"And the ten-year reduction played no role? None whatsoever?"

Well, he obviously knew more about the case than he had let on. And then he asked, "So what did *we* get for ten years of his life?"

"Seven hundred grand, give or take change. And be thankful— in the private sector, half that would be sitting in my checking account for services rendered."

"Yes, half would be about right." He chuckled and commented, "But then you wouldn't have the grand satisfaction of serving your country." This was an old joke that never goes down well, and he then added, "Actually, it's ironic you should mention it."

But he did not elaborate on that cryptic thought. Instead he asked, "Please remind me, Sean, how long have you been assigned to the Special Actions unit?"

"Oh, let's see . . . eight years, come next March."

"I think you mean since last September. Right? Four years prosecuting and four defending. Right?"

I nodded. Yes, that would be exactly right.

But regarding me, I believe wholeheartedly in the eleventh commandment: Thou shalt not fixeth that which is not brokeneth. The Army, however, was created to wreck things that aren't broken, a mindset that bleeds over into its personnel policies. Actually, nobody in the Army believes there are personnel policies, just a standing order that as soon as a soldier becomes acclimated to a certain place, masters a certain job, or appears happy where they're at, it's time to jerk their ass through some new knothole.

Professionally, I was very content where I was. Socially, I had serious problems.

But Clapper was explaining, "JAG officers have to be well-rounded. Contracts, negotiations, there's a whole world of law you've never touched."

"Good point. You're right. Let's keep it that way."

"I . . . I understand." He cleared his throat and continued, less tolerantly, "I also understand you're up for promotion this year." I nodded to acknowledge this fact before he added, "So, do I need to remind you that promotion boards tend to choose officers with more general knowledge and experience in the field of law?"

"Who cares?" Actually, I care. I'm as ambitious as the next guy, I just want to succeed on my own terms.

This, however, was neither the appropriate nor desired response. He got up, turned his back on me, and gazed out the window, across the highway at Arlington National Cemetery. He obviously had something up his sleeve, and I had the sense he was about to transfer it up my ass. That aside, you have to ponder the logic that placed the Pentagon and the cemetery next to each other—the living and dead, past and present, lucky and unlucky—right there. The sight of those endless rows of white stones tends not to promote those aspirations and ambitions that beget hard work, long hours, and diligence. But more sensibly, those markers do remind the powers who rule this building of the price of stupid blunders, which perhaps was what the designer intended.

I wondered if Clapper was staring across that road and pondering his mortality. How foolish—he was apparently pondering mine.

He asked, over his shoulder, "Have you ever heard of the WWIP?"

"Sure. I had a friend who caught it once. Very rough. His dick fell off."

He was not amused. "The full title is the Working With Industry Program, Sean. It's where we put an officer in a civilian company for a year. The officer learns what's new and state-of-the-art in the private sector, then brings that knowledge back into the military. It's a highly regarded program for our most promising officers—good for the individual and good for the Army."

"It does sound like a great program. I'll even name ten guys who'd love to do that." I then added, "But my name won't be on that list."

"In fact, yours is the only name on that list." He walked back in my direction and ordered, "Report for duty at Culper, Hutch, and Westin first thing in the morning. It's located here in D.C., and it's a damned fine firm."

I said nothing.

He said, "Don't give me that look. It'll do you good. You've worked a lot of hard cases, and you'll benefit from the break. Actually, I'm envious."

It's worth noting here that *who* needed the break was a debatable point. I had handled a few very sensitive cases, most recently one concerning a general officer accused of treason, where I'd stepped on a few very important, oversensitive toes.

Nor, I expect, did I do myself any favors when, in the afteraction report on that same espionage case, I referred to the JAG as a backstabbing ass who'd hung me out to dry. This was not news to him, of course. Still, this might not have been a good idea, I realized.

But concerning Clapper, he is, as I mentioned, the head of all the Army's lawyers, judges, and legal assistants, an attorney by trade, and a superb one in his day. The stars on his shoulders attest to his command of the legal arts and also his political moxie, as raw competence only gets you so many rungs up the pay ladder in this man's Army. He was raised in the South, where military virtues and selflessness were stamped into the young men of his generation from birth. He is tall, poster-boy handsome, and courtly in manner, except when someone irritates him, which, regrettably, I have a habit of doing.

Regarding me, I was raised as an Army brat, a lifestyle that leaves one rootless, with muddled habits and speech patterns and, oddly enough, with less reverence toward the grand institution than generational novices. We view it as a family business, and we tend to be a bit more alert to the Army's flaws and clumsy tendencies, and considerably more circumspect when it comes to entrusting our fates to professional whimsy.

"Please pick someone else," I replied.

"Sean, we all must do what we must do. Into the valley of death rode the six hundred, right?" Right. And none rode back out, he failed to mention.

He leaned back into his chair, possibly considering a new line of attack. After a moment, he suggested, "Captain Lisa Morrow, you and she are acquainted, I think. In fact, you're friends, aren't you?"

Did he really expect me to reply to this question? Understand that Clapper had, only two years before, personally assigned Morrow and me a very delicate Article 32, pre-court-martial investigation in Kosovo, after which she'd been transferred into my spooky unit. We had subsequently fenced in court many times, and I would prefer to say we were evenly matched and I gave as good as I got. But we weren't and I didn't. Frankly, it was a bit of a relief for me when she transferred back out. Not that I was keeping score or anything, but the Army does. She was blond, extremely attractive, and, as you might expect, clever, brilliant, and fiercely competitive. And also witty, well-mannered, and charming; however, let's not get too wrapped around the gratuitous footnotes.

She and I became professionally close, and I considered trying to become emotionally close, then physically close—perhaps I confused that order—but it never worked out. It could work, however. In fact, this conversation wasn't a complete waste of my time, as he'd just reminded me that I owed her a phone call.

When it became clear I wasn't going to reply, he said, "I want you to talk to her, Sean. You need to adjust your attitude, and I think the conversation will be helpful. Lisa's been with Culper, Hutch, and Westin this past year. She's had a wonderful time. She loves them and they love her."

No doubt we both recognized we could play this game for another hour, so to do us both a favor I cut to the chase and asked, "Is this negotiable?"

"No."

"Is your nonnegotiability negotiable?"

It appeared not. He replied, "You know your options."

Okay, my options.

One—tell him to stuff this opportunity up his butt, followed by my resignation. Among other problems with this course was the very pressing issue of who'd send me a check every month.

Option two—a good soldier does not question his orders; he snaps his heels and marches smartly off to his fate, at least pretending to believe that those who wear stars are celestially wise and all-knowing. Across the highway are several sections of monuments dedicated to this strangely popular option.

Oh, there was also, I suppose, a third option, though it is so disgraceful I hesitate to bring it up and, clearly, never gave it a second thought. But this would be the one where I reported to this firm, screwed up everything I touched—including a partner's wife—peed in the morning coffee, and got sent back to the Army labeled unfit for civilian duty.

As I said, though, I never gave it a second thought. What was the big deal anyway? I had caught a bad rap. Nobody goes the full three rounds of a military career who can't stand on their head for a year or two. And perhaps it would turn out to be fun, enlightening, and all the rest of that bullshit Clapper promised. For that matter, regarding Clapper, perhaps I misjudged his motives. He probably was concerned for me, my career, my chances of surviving the next promotion board.

So I contemplated this and said, "Perhaps I've been hasty." After a moment of further reflection, I added, "You're right. I could use . . . you know . . . professional growth, a chance to try something different . . . new horizons."

I smiled and he smiled back. He said, "Sean, I was really afraid you were going to be difficult about this. I'm glad you understand."

"I do understand." I looked him dead in the eye and promised, "And I assure you, General, I will do you and the Army proud."

P.S., see you in a week, two at the outside, big guy.

CHAPTER TWO

*T*he photo was a clean shot, revealing a face both lovely and angular. Full lips, pert nose, eyes that were deeply and memorably green. She was smiling when the picture was taken, a likable smile, effortless and without artifice. Eyes that festered with sympathy. No makeup. No jewelry. She was beautiful, yet tended to ignore or at least not amplify it. He liked this and so many other things about her.

She would be first.

He stole another glance at her bedroom window; the light was still on, and he returned to studying her photo, as though it could yield a clue he had somehow overlooked.

She appeared younger than thirty—no wrinkles, droopiness under her eyes, nor flab as best he could tell. Yet he knew for a fact that she had crossed that benchmark in May, was single, currently uninvolved, and had lived in the Washington suburbs the past three years.

He had unobtrusively edged into line behind her two days before at a nearby Starbucks, had sniffed her perfume and ap-

proved: expensive and tasteful. About five foot eight, possibly 115 pounds, and she carried herself well; poised, but with no hint of the conceit or brashness one expects from women with her looks and brains. She was courteous and friendly to the girl behind the counter and left a seventy-five-cent tip for a $1.25 coffee—overly generous by his reckoning—no sugar, no cream. She was not a health nut; he'd twice seen her eat meat, but she appeared mindful of bad habits.

Actually, she had to be the first.

He had batted it around inside his head three dozen times, chewed over the pros and cons, pondered it so hard that he nearly gave himself a splitting headache.

It had to be her.

Put her off and the whole thing could collapse.

But how?

By far, she was the riskiest of the group. He was methodical by necessity, and had actually devised a computer program to help him judge and assess these things. Plug in this factor and that vulnerability, and the algorithms worked their twisty magic and spit out a number. Ten was the level of most damnable difficulty. She was an eight, and anything above seven worried him—the program wasn't flawless, and there surely were factors he had overlooked, qualities he had failed to plumb, so the magnitude could be underestimated. He'd never done a nine or, God forbid, a ten. Over the years, he had considered a few and walked away. The odds of a blunder were simply too damned high and the penalty of failure unthinkable. A seven also happened to be on the list, edging toward eight, but the rest were sixes and below. His usual method was to save the hardest for last, as a mistake in the beginning could unravel the whole thing.

But it wasn't an option.

It had to be her.

So, back to how.

The top file on the car seat beside him was thick with details

*about her life and habits, acquired mostly with very little trou-
ble from public sources and several days of cautious snooping.
A few critical details had been obtained elsewhere.*

*She had clockwork habits. At 5:30 each and every morn-
ing her bedroom light flicked on. Fifteen minutes later she
came bolting out the front door in spandex running tights,
and she certainly had the figure for them: long, lean legs and
a bodacious ass. A dark runner's shirt that contrasted hand-
somely with her short blond hair and practical but expensive
running shoes completed her morning attire. She was fit and
very, very fast. He had clocked her twice—five miles in thirty-
two minutes over a course that was hilly and daunting, without ever varying her route or pace.*

*She had been a long-distance track star in high school and
college. Her college newspaper described her as a steady per-
former, consistently placing first against weak schools, but apt
to disappoint against the powerhouses. The rebuke struck him
as unfair. She ran in the East, where blacks dominated, and
did quite well for a white girl. Also, she'd managed a 3.9 GPA
as an undergrad at the University of Virginia and graduated
fifteenth in her class from Harvard Law. He regarded it as
shameful that they couldn't meet under less complicated conditions. He preferred intelligent, accomplished, athletic women
and felt certain they would hit it off.*

*She lived alone in a community of townhouse dwellers
whose homes, economic stations, and lifestyles were tedious
and ordinary. However, the neighborhood was clean, safe, and
a short commute from her office. She was sociable with her
neighbors, but that was as far as it went. Her close friends
were made at work and elsewhere.*

*Her townhouse was a two-story end unit, brick-fronted,
slat-sided, with a one-car garage tucked underneath the living
room. Thick woods were behind the complex, apparently left
standing by a thoughtful builder to afford a sense of privacy.
He appreciated the irony. Both nights he had scaled a tall tree*

and, using night-vision goggles, had observed her through a window.

After her runs she took thirty minutes to shower, dress, and breakfast. At 7:15 her garage door slid open and her shiny gray Nissan Maxima backed out. A brief stop at the Starbucks three blocks from her townhouse, then a straight scoot to her office. A Daytimer crammed with notes and appointments dictated her life. She lunched at her desk and shopped only on weekends. Her evenings were the only erratic and unpredictable part of her schedule. She tended to work late, occasionally past midnight.

She dated one man at a time, as best he could tell, and was finicky and old-fashioned about matters of romance. Spontaneous pickups and one-night stands weren't part of her style. Too bad, because he could picture scenarios where this would be a workable approach, but he could more easily picture a swift brush-off fraught with unacceptable complications.

She was cautious and had commendable security habits. With her looks she should be, in his view. She locked her car door every time she left it. Penetrating her workplace was out of the question. She had installed a security system in her townhouse that she meticulously activated every time she walked out the door. A fairly good system in his expert judgment: a battery backup; the windows and doors were wired; a motion detection system was installed in the living room; and he guessed there was at least one panic button, most likely positioned in her bedroom. She tended, however, to leave open the second-floor bathroom window, presumably to prevent odor and mildew.

That flaw, however, did him no good. His script was everything, and no matter how he jiggled, twisted, or warped it, that glaring oversight could not be made to fit.

He kneaded his neck, turned off the car's overhead light, and tossed the file back on the passenger's seat. His decision was made, and in every way he could consider it made sense.

He would take her where she least expected it. He would move in when her alertness and instincts were at their lowest ebb, and would approach her in such a manner that she would let down her defenses and allow him near.

She would be his calling card, and what a memorable one she would be.

CHAPTER THREE

T HE VERY GRATING VOICE ON THE PHONE SAID, "I'M SALLY WESTIN. I'VE BEEN assigned to welcome you to Culper, Hutch, and Westin." When I failed to reply, she prompted, "The firm you'll be working for."

The clock was still stuck on 4:30 A.M. I said, "Do you *know* what time it is?"

"Of course. Do *you* know where we're located?"

"I'm sure it's in the phone book."

"Fine," she replied. "Ask for me when you arrive. The partners are here by 8:00 A.M. and it's a good idea to arrive well ahead of them. There's no time clocks . . . but it's noticed. And I'm sure you want to make the right first impression."

Now that she mentioned it, yes, I did. I hung up, rolled over, and closed my eyes.

At 8:30, I flipped on the TV, let Katie and the gang bombard me with bubbly glee, allowed Diane her equal shot in the ratings war, showered, shaved, and so forth.

Understand why I didn't want to do this program. I love the Army. It's the life for me. FTA, as the troops say, which, depending on your day, either means Fun, Travel, and Adventure or Fuck The Army. On particular days, it means both. So what else—interesting work, simplicity in your wardrobe, a well-ordered universe, and the sense of serving a higher calling. I'm too horny to be a priest, so there it is.

Also, there's a wide chasm between the worlds of military and civilian law and, more particularly, the soft-heeled world of corporate law. We don't play the billings game, or scramble, or plead, or compete for customers, and, less fortunately, there's no fat bonus checks in our mailboxes at Christmas. Yet it has been my unfortunate experience that many big-firm lawyers look down their noses at us. They regard us as public dole idiots, soft, lazy, and lacking intellectual brawn. But I don't feel slighted; after all, they're all spoiled, arrogant, overpaid jerks.

Regarding Clapper's assurances about Lisa Morrow and her experience at the firm, generals don't lie, but truth can slip through their lips in fairly odd ways. I mean, do they say, "Three platoons that tried to take that hill just got the living shit kicked out of them and now, God bless you, boys, go on up there and take your ass kicking." No; they say silly things like, "You are the finest soldiers on earth and I've therefore elected you for the very prestigious honor of taking that small, lightly defended hill."

I'd be tucked in a corner office in the basement, where I'd spend my year counting how many paper clips it takes to run a law firm. I'd be handed a handsome plaque when the year ended, with my name misspelled, because, excluding the janitors, nobody in the friggin' firm had the slightest idea who the hell I was.

Last, Clapper is not as smart as he thinks he is. Like most generals, he is adroit at holding his cards close to his vest and, like most lawyers, at cloaking the truth. I actually was a little hurt that he didn't think I'd see through this. He obviously had a larger plan, and something told me it ended with Sean Drummond behind a desk in the Pentagon Contracts Office negotiating basing rights, weapons system agreements, and other things too appalling to mention.

Somebody has to do it, I guess. But, no sir, it wasn't going to be me.

Anyway, the firm in question turned out to be located on Connecticut Avenue, six blocks from the White House, a neighborhood renowned for power restaurants, sluggish traffic, and astonishing rents. I found an underground garage, parked, and made my way to the nine-story building, where a wall directory by the elevator indicated the firm took up the top three floors. This answered the first question. It was a big firm. Also the unasked question—money mill.

The elevator opened on the eighth floor, and that last point was underscored in impressive fashion—burnished mahogany walls, dimly lit sconces, and "Culper, Hutch, and Westin" obnoxiously scribbled in gold letters on the wall. I stepped out of the elevator and vomited on the carpet. Just kidding.

Also sprinkled about were a few brass-studded leather couches, side tables and lamps, paintings of sailing ships, and an attractive middle-aged lady with her well-dressed ass parked behind a long wooden desk, who instantly inquired, "Might I help you?" in one of those clipped, upper-class English accents that fit nicely with the ambience.

I replied, "You may. Sally Westin."

"Your name, sir?"

"Drummond."

She had one of those telephone microphone thingees, she pushed a button, she whispered into the mouthpiece, and she then informed me, "Have a seat. Miss Westin will be out shortly to retrieve you."

I smiled and asked her, "Hey, what's the difference between a corporate lawyer and a liar?" When she failed to reply, I said, "Spelling."

Appearing slightly annoyed, she informed me, "Really, I'm quite busy," pointed at a chair, then pushed a button and pretended to be talking to somebody else.

I sat. Clearly, this place needed to loosen up. There was a bit of foot traffic, men mostly, looking smug and self-important with their two-thousand-dollar suits and Gucci briefcases. I scrunched up my face and looked self-important, too. I was making a real effort to fit in. I wondered if I should get a Gucci briefcase. Probably not.

A young lady finally approached and said to me, "I'm Miss Westin. I was, well . . . I was expecting you earlier. Much earlier, actually."

So. Start with her physical appearance—thirtyish, wholesome, small but neat features, and I suppose pretty, yet groomed, wrapped, and coiffed in a manner that indicated some resentment about this. Brown hair wrapped in a tight bun, gold-rimmed glasses, no makeup; boobs, hips, and all the other female paraphernalia were present for duty, but tucked, shoved, and otherwise camouflaged to avoid prominence. The word "tightass" popped to mind, though perhaps I was being hasty.

Now her expression—puckered, reproachful, definitely guilt-inducing. So perhaps I wasn't being hasty.

"Well, as you can see," she said, after it was clear I wasn't going to explain my tardiness, "we have a great facility here. Electronically, we're the world's most advanced firm, we have top-caliber paralegals and secretarial staff, and our library is kept completely up-to-date with all the latest rulings on anything dealing with corporate law."

Without further ado she walked off, saying, "Let me show you the office allocated for your use. I'm sure you'll find it satisfactory."

So together she and I proceeded down a long hallway wallpapered in muted colors and carpeted with some kind of plush oriental runner. Very chez chic. She eventually hooked a left into a corner twenty-by-thirty-foot office with a few more sailing ships on the walls, a hand-carved wooden desk, and two leather sofas perched atop a gigantic oriental carpet. Two walls were windowed to offer a panoramic view of downtown.

My normal office, if you're interested, is a windowless ten-by-twenty-foot cell with a dented metal desk and a gray metal wall safe, and the Army's idea of artwork is reenlistment posters, which are an oxymoronic, even a moronic sight in a defense counsel's office, if you ask me. Yet it occurred to me that I might remain at the firm long enough for some of my Army pals to, you know, come over and check out how the other half lives. Disgusting . . . really disgusting.

She waved an arm around. "It belonged to a sixth-year associate who nearly made partner. He was discharged last week. It's yours until the next time our management committee meets."

As I looked around, she added, "My office down the hall isn't nearly this grand." She then asked, I think petulantly, "Well? Can you work out of here?"

"Is there a coffee machine?"

She rolled her eyes. "Cappuccino and espresso machines also. If that doesn't suit your tastes, one of our secretaries will be pleased to run out and get whatever you desire."

Boy, was this the life or what? If I told Sergeant First Class Imelda Pepperfield, my legal assistant, to run out and pick me up a little cup of that café latte crap, they'd have to dislodge her foot from my ass. But the Army, being a public institution, accountable to the public and all that, frowns upon the menialization of its females. As I mentioned, there are considerable differences between the public and private sectors; I didn't say they're all actually bad.

I sat on a leather sofa and bounced up and down a few times—good springs, soft leather, strong, resilient frame—a man could take damn fine naps on this couch.

"And what did you say you do for the firm?" I asked Miss Westin.

"I'm a third-year associate. I've just been moved to our largest corporate client." She asked me, "And what kind of law do you do in the Army?"

"Strictly criminal."

"Oh . . . I see." She shifted her weight from her left foot to her right. "Well, you've certainly come to the right place to learn corporate and contracts, Drummond. Culper, Hutch, and Westin has a top reputation in the field."

Before I could reply to that, a sudden cough shifted my attention to a figure in the doorway—male, mid-to-late sixties, wearing one of those aforementioned two-thousand-dollar suits, thick, wavy white hair, trimmed black eyebrows, pinched lips, and a ruddy, outdoorsy face. Every molecule of his being, bearing, and demeanor screamed white-shoe asshole, which, if you don't know, is how we refer to law firms that never enter the gutter of real law and therefore never get any shit on their shoes.

"I'm Harold Bronson, the managing partner," he announced, nodding at me. "And I think you must be Drummond?"

"Yes, I think I must be."

He did not offer his hand or in any other way offer the impression he was pleased with my presence. He said, "I dropped by to meet you. We've assigned Miss Westin here to work with you and guide you into our culture. She's quite well-schooled on the caseload you'll be working on." He regarded me more closely and asked, "And you?"

"And me?"

He shifted his glasses lower on his nose. "Of course you, Drummond. What's your experience in corporate law and litigation?"

"Oh . . . Well, I do strictly criminal stuff."

"Criminal cases?"

"Right."

Mr. Bronson sniffed the air once or twice, no doubt to detect whether I'd tracked any dog crap onto his expensive carpets. He informed me, "We don't touch criminal law, Drummond. Neither we nor our clients want any association with that side of law." He added, "And our work, as you'll surely discover, is more . . . intellectually challenging."

You see what I mean about these white-shoe guys? Get me out of here.

But Mr. White Shoes was on a roll, and he continued, "We handle litigation, corporate, M&A, contracts, SEC and FCC, libel, and, like any big capital firm, political lobbying on behalf of our clients. The past several years, given the deteriorating state of the economy, we've experienced a great expansion in our bankruptcy work. In fact, my background is in bankruptcy. It now represents over half our work."

I stretched and yawned. I might have been more attentive, and even cordial, except Mr. Bronson had one of those pinched, disagreeable faces, and I had the impression it wasn't just me, but his general outlook and overbearing arrogance. Also he had this clipped, condescending manner of speaking I was sure worked well with his clients, but it got on my nerves.

As if all that wasn't enough, Miss Weston's eyes were locked on his every move and gesture. I mean, you could smell her fear, apprehension, and discomfort.

Mr. Bronson shoved his glasses back up and added, "But how unfortunate it is for us that you lack any experience in our fields. You're going to be involved in issues that are quite delicate and important to this firm, Drummond . . ." and blah, blah, blah. More about my obvious lack of qualifications. About my need to unlearn and overcome the sloppy habits of military law. About what a great honor it was for me to learn at the knees of the great masters of the legal arts, and so forth.

I sat through his long lecture nonchalantly, listened politely, and subordinated my nearly overwhelming instinct to tell him to go fuck himself. I really wished Clapper were around. He would be really proud of me. I wondered what the lovely Captain Morrow was doing at that moment—I needed to call her, I reminded myself . . . also, I had dry cleaning to pick up, an overdue book from the library, and . . .

"Drummond, are you *listening* to me?"

Oops.

Mr. Bronson said, "I'm very busy, young man. And if you're too bored to listen . . . Did you hear a word I said?"

I felt really bad. It was time to look sheepish and assure him that his words were both instructive and inspirational.

"I'm sorry," I said very sincerely. "I thought you were finished about ten sentences ago."

He began twisting his necktie. But wouldn't it stink if this guy got the stupid impression I was some junior associate he could bully around? No, it would be best for both he and me for him to swiftly conclude that there wasn't enough room in this firm for the two of us and throw my ass out. I wasn't expecting this to happen on the first meeting or anything. Still, one should always try.

But apparently he'd had enough of me. He nodded curtly at Miss Westin and abruptly departed.

A roomful of air poured from her lungs. She frowned at me and said, "That was really stupid."

"Don't worry about it. He's just another lawyer."

"He's not *another* lawyer. He's God in this firm, you idiot."

"Can he stamp my parking pass?"

"What is your problem?" She crossed her arms, appeared supremely frustrated, and advised me, "When you meet the other partners, you'd better make a better impression. You rub off on me."

"I . . . *what?*"

"Just what I said. I'm responsible for you during your time here."

"Explain that, please."

"The firm's management committee recognizes there could be cultural and educational issues for an Army attorney in our ranks. It's my role to smooth them out."

"Meaning what, precisely?" Actually, I knew what it meant.

"Listen, Drummond—"

"My name's Sean."

"All right. Let me—"

"And I can call you Sally, right?"

"If that's important to you. Look, Drummond, you're obviously incompetent—"

"Please have a seat," I interrupted. I pointed at the opposite couch. I smiled. "Let's start over. I'm Sean and you're Sally. You're not my mentor or my baby-sitter—you're my colleague. We should treat each other respectfully, like friends even, and—"

Another figure had appeared in the doorway, who said, "Good morning, Major." He cracked a faint smile and added, "I'm Cy Berger . . . one of the senior partners around here."

I actually knew that.

In a city packed with recognizable faces, Seymour, aka "Cy," Berger had one of the better known. He'd been a two-term congressman and two-term senator who ruled the Hill before this embarrassing thing with a Senate page—actually, it was a flock of Senate pages, other senators' wives, and assorted other ladies—had toppled him. Such was the scope of Cy's political skill and influence, in fact, that he was known as the King of the Hill before one and then hordes of tearful women came out of the woodwork to testify that Cy had messed around in their panties. I recalled a few televised hearings, news of covered-up paternity suits, a second divorce from a cuckolded bride, and, finally, Senator Berger at a press conference announcing he was dropping out of his reelection race to "pursue private affairs."

He might've worded it a bit differently, if you ask me.

In any case, Washington is a weird town with a different cultural take on political disgrace and professional ruin. So Cy did the D.C. thing: He retreated into a powerful law firm where he earned ten times his Senate salary and after Jay Leno ran out of jokes about him, progressed into a sort of senior statesman, doing the Sunday morning talk-show circuit, backslapping his former colleagues for favors, and his private life became his *private* life once more.

But understand that Washington loves nothing more than a splashy political scandal, and for those two months Cy Berger had been *it*, the talk of the town.

The King of the Hill was retagged the Cock of the Walk, and the big joke making the rounds concerned this farmer who paid a fortune for a barnyard cock named Cy, a bird reputed to have miraculous prowess and endurance. The farmer brought Cy to his farm, placed him in the barnyard, and watched him go to work. He was astonished—Cy was not only tireless, he was indiscriminate.

He schtupped all 300 hens before lunch, then ran into the cow pasture, nailed 400 head of cattle, and had just leaped into the pigpen when the farmer got tired of watching. But the next morning, when the farmer returned to the barnyard, to his dismay he found his prized cock on its back, legs stiffly pointed skyward, apparently dead from exhaustion. A flock of buzzards was circling overhead. Furious about being cheated, the farmer began loudly cursing, until Cy cracked an eye and whispered, "Hey, shut up, would ya. I've almost got the buzzards sucked in."

Back to the situation, however. I said, "Good morning, Senator."

"Drop the Senator shit. Cy's fine." Never seen him face-to-face, Cy was taller than I expected, heavyset, with a florid, ravaged face, salt-and-pepper hair, and a thick nose, migrating toward a bulbous nose. He was not handsome, not even attractive, almost ugly, actually. Yet something in his pheromones exuded the essence of power, and in Washington, this is the ticket to the goodies.

"May I come in?" he asked me.

I nodded.

He looked at Miss Weston, smiled warmly, and said to her, "Good morning, Sally. How are you today?"

"Fine, Cy. Thank you for asking."

Back to me. He asked, "Did I interrupt something?"

"Miss Westin was just explaining that she's my minder."

"And do you have a problem with that?"

"Wouldn't you?"

"Yes, I suppose I would." He contemplated this and me, then said, "I'm the partner assigned to oversee the legal work you two will be doing. I'm also the one who persuaded the firm to participate in this Army program."

So this was the guy. Naturally, I asked, "Why?"

"I thought it would be good for the firm's image."

"I'm not even good for my own image."

He chuckled. "I'm sure you'll have a lot to offer us."

Wrong. But Cy casually picked a piece of lint off his trousers and mentioned to Miss Westin, "Sally, do me a favor and go inform Hal that Major Drummond's here." He explained for my benefit, "Hal Merriweather. He handles our personnel issues and has a tendency to be territorial and temperamental."

It was slickly done, but experience gives you a certain sense for these things. And in fact, the instant she was gone, he closed the door, leaned against it, and examined me from head to toe, "Sean, right?"

"Right."

"Well, Sean . . . We're going to have to make a few adjustments here. Harry Bronson just spoke to me. And poor Sally looks fit to be tied."

I was not expected to respond to this, and I didn't. After a moment he went on, "See this office?" It was obvious I saw the office, so he continued, "Jimmy Barber was the best associate we'd seen in years. Yale Law, head of his class, law review, our top pick that year. He was fast-tracked to make partner in six years. Anyway, last summer one of those *60 Minutes* knockoffs slammed a cabinet secretary, how he'd taken free flights from a political donor who'd also paid his kid's college bills and the rent for his mistress's condominium."

"The one with—"

"Yeah . . . same guy. In fact, I talked him into launching a libel suit. And I persuaded the management committee to assign it to Jimmy, as a final test, if you will, before partnership. Jimmy began with a thorough search through the cabinet officer's financial records. He found receipts for the airfares and the tuition payments for their son. The mistress turned out to be a Peruvian girl the man's wife sponsored for citizenship and was helping with her rent. His wife even signed the checks. So tell me, Sean, would you work it that way with a mistress?"

"Would you?"

That impertinent question just slipped through my lips. He stared at me for a long moment. But this guy had obviously been dispatched to administer a bureaucratic spanking, and he was my new boss, and attitude adjustment works best when it's a two-way street. He was the authority figure and I was the wiseass, and somewhere in between we had to find a workable middle ground. I did add, however, "The question was theoretical of course."

He laughed. "Well, I'll be damned." Then he observed, "No, I signed the checks myself. Waste of effort, though. My wives found out about my affairs on the evening news."

"I'll bet that was annoying."

"Yes . . . it really was." He then said, "But back to Jimmy, it turned out the network got its whole story from an ex-con. It further turned out that in his previous life, the cabinet member was the district attorney who got the source ten years without parole. More incriminating still, the network never verified the details, never even offered the cabinet member a chance to refute it."

"So you had a strong case."

"It did appear that way, yes."

He then studied the carpet pattern a moment, as though it was too painful to continue. But of course he did continue, saying, "Fields, Jason, and Morgantheau handled the defense with Silas Jackler, their top gun. You're probably aware, the hard part with libel of a public figure is the requirement to prove malicious intent. After weeks of footwork, Jimmy told us he'd located an inside source who participated in the production and said he was present when a junior editor asked his bosses if they shouldn't at least verify the story. He was told to shut up. In fact, Jimmy's source overheard one senior editor boast that he'd already bagged one congressman and wanted a new scalp to hang off his bedpost. Malicious intent, right?"

"Right. But I sure hope you carefully vetted this source."

"Yes, you always should, shouldn't you?" An eyebrow raised. "In fact, seconds after Jimmy examined our witness in court, Jackler introduced a ream of evidence showing the man had been fired by the network for cheating on his expense accounts, as well as statements from several witnesses who heard him swear he'd get revenge. Under Jackler's cross, the witness crumbled and admitted every bit of it."

"Always a cinematic moment."

"Indeed." After a moment, he added, "Jimmy later confessed that he'd lied to us. He wanted to impress us with his detective work. Actually, his source found him, claimed he'd read about the suit in the papers and tracked down our firm to offer his services."

"A plant?"

"Probably."

"But so what, right?"

"Right. Our case was dismissed. We were even ordered to restitute the legal costs of the defendants. Word spreads pretty quickly around the industry—it was a great humiliation for the firm, and Jackler charges six hundred an hour. The greedy bastard hit us for ten million."

Surely there was a point to this story, and I guessed, "This is the same firm I'll be facing?"

"Same firm."

"And you're looking for blood?"

"Absolutely not." He looked me in the eye and insisted, "We're all professionals here, Sean. We *never* take it personally."

We both chuckled at this little lie. I was starting to like this guy.

He then said, "But our cases are worth big money. The great corporations, the GEs and Pepsis of the world, they hire the best, pay a fortune for the service, and demand excellence. We don't pick cherries off trees."

Which was obviously the real point of our discussion. Motivational psychology 101: Cy was equating the stakes of corporate law with those of criminal law—money and reputations versus lives and fates.

Of course, one did not get where Cy had gotten without having a persuasive, even charismatic manner. I therefore spent a long and respectful moment contemplating his point. Nope—still bullshit.

But I decided it was my turn, and I leaned against my desk and asked Cy, "Sally Westin? Why's her name on your masthead?"

He sighed. "Sally's story is . . . intriguing. Her grandfather was one of our founders. He died about twenty years ago but remains legendary. His fingerprints are all over the firm, the secret to our success, we believe. He was an eccentric old coot who believed in winning at all costs. He drove the other partners crazy, and from what I hear drove the associates even crazier. Every firm likes to brag about what it puts its associates through. Frankly, we make the others look like daycare centers. We work them twice as hard, put more pressure on their shoulders, and are less forgiving than any firm we know. We tell our aspirants their chances of making partner are one in seven, and law students being the perversely competitive creatures they naturally are, it draws them like flies."

"And the connection to Sally Westin . . . ?"

"I'm getting to that. Sally graduated from Duke Law, barely in the top half of her class. We can afford to be very picky and we are. In practice we don't interview at Duke—we draw only the top ten percent from the top five. We made an exception for her."

The moment seemed appropriate to ask, "Why?"

"Guilt."

"Guilt?"

"Yes. Sally's father had also been an associate in this firm, back when old man Westin was our managing partner. It was one of those perverse instances of counter-nepotism. The old man nearly worked his son to death, gave him three times the workload of other associates, and hounded him relentlessly. This went on for seven years. Then he fired him."

"Sounds like a lovely guy."

"Last of the real coldhearted bastards." After a moment, he added, "It was long before my time, but I'm told he was also a very shrewd and talented lawyer. The son moved to another firm but was a shattered man. Five years later, when Sally was two, her father was again rejected for a partnership."

"Time to consider another profession."

"Perhaps he did. But instead he killed himself." He allowed me a moment to think about that, then explained, "But Sally works like a demon. I doubt if she's gotten more than four hours of sleep any night since she started. Nor have we gone easy on her. That's just not our way. All associates have to prove themselves."

"And how's she doing?"

He waggled a hand. "In a few months, we'll decide which three of seven associates in her year group we'll keep. Two are golden children . . . true prodigies. Also, since bankruptcy is now over half our business, we prefer our associates to possess both legal *and* accounting degrees. Sally lacks an accounting degree and, frankly, if she has a knack with numbers, she keeps it well hidden."

He appeared to have more to say, and after a moment, he added, "I was the one who persuaded the management committee to assign her to work for me. If she strikes you as a bit stiff and intense, I thought it fair to explain why."

Well, there are many motives for entering the field of law, intellectual or moral fascination, parental expectations, greed, and outright confusion heading the list. Miss Westin was apparently driven by ghosts. I wasn't sure that was altogether healthy. Actually, were I running this firm, there'd be a bomb-sniffing dog and a metal detector by the door on the off chance Miss Westin wanted to even up the score a bit. But that's just me.

Cy then said, "Don't mention this to Sally. Or, for that matter, to anybody. We try to respect one another's privacy, and only a very few of our senior partners know the tale. Our associates are bred to be competitive, and some would no doubt find ways to employ it as a weapon." His expression turned grave and he added, "But you're not in the hunt for a partnership, and you need to be aware that your behavior can affect her future."

"I'll try to be responsible for my own screwups."

"Always a commendable attitude." He shoved off from the door, flashed a smile, and placed a chummy hand on my shoulder.

He suggested, "And I'll bet you're wondering why the Army agreed to use this firm."

"Actually, I'm not."

"Sure you are." He gave me a knowing look and added, "I went to law school as a route into politics . . . Catholic University Law, in fact. A young Army officer named Tommy Clapper was in my studygroup. We got to be pretty good friends."

"Is that right?"

As he walked out, he remarked, "We talk all the time."

That aside, I found myself liking Cy, and I think he sort of liked me. I don't mean we were butter and toast, but I was marooned here because I pissed off my boss, and he was stranded here because he pissed off the American people. Set aside that order of magnitude and it did strike me that we had a bond of fellowship. Also, there was something of the charming rogue in him. I like a man with a few serious flaws. I can relate.

Further, it's an admirable skill to deliver a threat with panache, velvet gloves, and all that. Any idiot can say, "Cross me, mother-fucker, and I'll lump you up good." A diplomat smiles and says, "Here, doggie, doggie," with a big rock held behind his back.

The more impressive feat was that Sally Westin story. Talk about motivational force—how do you ignore that? The poor girl had all those awful demons in her head, and now it was up to little ol' me to see her that ass didn't end up on the street.

CHAPTER FOUR

SALLY RETURNED TO THE OFFICE MERE SECONDS AFTER CY DEPARTED. NEXT came a tour of the facilities, starting with the library, which occupied a quarter of the seventh floor. This entailed miles of expensive carpet, wood tables, leather lounge chairs, and sturdy shelves filled with thick books. Some thoughtful soul had arranged the interior decor to remind one of an English gentlemen's club. The smell reminded me of a men's locker room. I was getting nauseous.

"Most firms," Sally was saying, "use electronic services or books on CDs. It saves space and money. We took a vote and decided to retain a real library."

"Why?"

"Time. The electronic services are extensive and up-to-date, but you lose so much time logging on and waiting for your searches to find a match. The partners don't care, of course. But we associates care a great deal."

Actually, I didn't care either. "Next, please."

Next turned out to be an elevator ride to the ninth floor, where the partners were housed. It turned out that a key controlled by the English lady behind the front desk was required to coax the elevator to take us to that floor. Do I need this bullshit? Anyway, I smiled and winked when we drew near, but she was too well-bred to acknowledge that. The brass embossed nameplate beside her right elbow indicated she was named Elizabeth. Best I can tell, nearly three-quarters of all English ladies are named Elizabeth, which I guess is really convenient for English gents because when they awake in the morning beside an unfamiliar face, they say, "Morning, Lizzie," and something like six out of ten times the rest of the morning works out okay.

"Seven senior partners and eighteen junior partners are here in the D.C. office," Sally explained to me in the elevator. "New York, Philadelphia, and Houston have twice that many. And L.A., which specializes in entertainment and sports, has three times as many. Boston is our real backwater, but we're considered the poor stepchild and are working hard to rectify that." Translation: The Washington associates wanted more partnerships and fatter paychecks.

The elevator door opened—no receptionist, more burnished wooden walls, sconces, and rich carpet. This was getting tedious, an upscale version of monochromatic. The hallway formed a long rectangle. Doors were on the outer walls, none on the inner walls. The partners' names were inscribed in stylized gold letters on their doors. There's something very cool about having your name embossed on the door, an indication of stature, permanence, and job security. Also, nobody mistakes your office for the men's room and pees on your wall.

"The offices face outward," Sally explained. "Senior partners are on the east, newer partners on the west. The middle section contains a conference room and dining room. Only partners and clients are allowed to use the dining room."

We continued walking down the senior partners' hallway, and she pointed at more doorways. "That's Cy's. Next door is Harold Bronson's." After a bit more walking, with Sally pointing at more doors and repeating more names I made a point to immediately forget, we ended up back where we started, at the elevator.

I asked, "What's this case we'll be working on?"

"You'll find out in a moment. Senior associates are largely in charge of the cases and report directly to the partners." She looked at me and added, "You and I will report to Barry Bosworth. He reports to Cy. Like the military, isn't it?"

I nodded. But in fact, that's the way civilians think the military works, the way Hollywood portrays that it works, and not at all how it really works. Nobody butts into my business, as long as I don't give them cause. In fact, I was weeping with nostalgia.

We passed by Elizabeth again, and I got another flinty look. Probably she wanted to ball my lights out and was too reticent to admit it. The English are known for their reserve about these things.

But evidenced by the three steaming cups of java already positioned on his coffee table, Barry Bosworth appeared to be expecting us. He was straining to make a hospitable impression and, in fact, was coming around his desk, beaming idiotically and saying, "Welcome, welcome, Sean. Hey, I can call you Sean, can't I?"

"You already did," I noted.

He chuckled. It wasn't the least bit funny, but he chuckled. Word spreads fast when you're a pain in the ass.

Incidentally, I hate it when people get all obsequiously friendly at opening meetings. From my experience, they're usually the first ones to slide you the greased weenie when the chips are down.

Anyway, he was moving toward the couches, asking, "Well, why don't we sit down and get acquainted?"

A few observations about my new supervisor, Barry Bosworth: early-thirtyish, lean, handsome, dark-haired, with one of those silly three-day-growth beards. His most notable feature was a pair of dark eyes that squinted with cold intelligence and colder ambition. He wore a shiny, expensive suit and, I guessed, had a BMW 760 parked in the garage, a wife and 1.3 kids in the shiniest suburb, and a car payment and mortgage that screamed he make partner or pack up the family and find a lousier neighborhood. But that's a lot to surmise about someone you've only just met. Probably I missed a detail or two; like the mistress in the high-rise, and the BMW in the garage might be a 5 series wishing it were a 7 series.

Anyway, he leaned toward me and said, "I hope Sally has shown you around?"

"She did." I asked, "So what's this case I'm supposed to work on?"

He smiled and asked, "Right down to business, eh? Time is money, right?"

"Your time is money, Barry. At this moment, mine's a waste of taxpayers' money."

He giggled, like I was making a big joke. I wasn't. He picked up his coffee cup, took a few measured sips, studied me, and said, "Have you ever heard of Morris Networks?"

It can sometimes be a good idea to confirm misimpressions, but in the event he hadn't already concluded I was every bit the asshole he'd been led to expect, I shook my head. He, in turn, responded with a polite nod, as if it were perfectly natural for any grown-up with a television and access to newspapers not to have heard of Morris Networks. As I said, big-firm lawyers think we, their military brethren, are idiots.

"Well . . . right." He then suggested, "Why don't we start at the beginning then? Twenty years ago, midway through his sophomore year, Jason Morris walked up to the dean of Stanford University and said he was quitting because the college had nothing valuable to teach him. I'm a Stanford man myself . . . undergrad and law. Imagine how the school perceived that, right?"

"Right."

"This wasn't just any college, Sean, this was *Stanford,* right?" Having made that point, he continued, "He took a job with AT&T, and by twenty-six, was a senior vice president. But he left for WorldCom, who were grooming him to become CEO. Then one day, Jason just walked in and quit because WorldCom had nothing to challenge or teach him."

"Sounds like Jason has perseverance issues."

Barry replied, "That's very funny." But he didn't laugh.

He continued, "Next, he went to a private venture capital group in New York City, was very good at it, and by thirty-three was worth around a billion dollars. He cashed out in 1995 and started his own enterprise. He had two very good ideas: that broadband was the future of telecommunications, and that fiber optics was the future of broadband. Others were investing in satellites or ways to squeeze more gigabits of information across copper wires. Jason believed they were idiots. His idea was to build a global fiber-optic network that would revolutionize the industry. His reputation drew investors like lemmings."

"Morris Networks," I quickly suggested.

"Same guy, same company. We've been representing him for several years. Outside our bankruptcy work, which now accounts for over half the firm's annual billings, he's our biggest client. We do nearly all the outsourced legal work for Morris Networks, and take my word, it has put the D.C. office on the map within our firm." He dipped his head and added, "For instance, last year's annual billings were in excess of fifty million dollars."

Geez. So, okay . . . divide fifty million big buckos by the twenty-five partners upstairs, and last year's job security was in the bag. And if that spout kept pumping, they'd soon increase the number of D.C. partners, which gave motive, clarity, and intensity to that hungry look in Barry's eyes.

"And the types of work your firm does for Morris?" I asked.

"*Our* firm, Sean." He fixed me with a resolute look and informed me, "We're all one team here."

Yeah? Then let's compare paychecks, pal—but I didn't say that. I said, "Okay . . . what do *we* do for this company?"

"They've done twenty mergers and acquisitions to get their hands on technologies Jason felt he needed for his network. We handled all that. Also the work to get them patents, contracts, licenses, FCC and SEC work, overseas work, general corporate matters and financings, frequencies, and right-of-ways, and we manage their D.C. and state lobbying."

"What don't we do?"

"Not much—their in-house counsel handles internal legal issues, we handle external issues. They keep five partners and an army of associates laboring furiously on their behalf, and we have three foreign firms on retainer."

"And what case will I be working on?"

"No need to get nervous, Sean."

"I'm not nervous, Barry."

"No . . . of course you're not," he replied dismissively. We regarded each other a moment. Clearly we did not like each other, and clearly ours was going to be a difficult relationship.

But he continued, "Morris has a number of contracts to provide telecommunications services for government agencies, including HEW, the Labor Department, the FBI, and three or four Defense Department contracts. It just won another contract for a government agency called DARPA."

"The Defense Advanced Research Program Agency."

"Good. So you're aware it's where a lot of the top-secret programs emanate. The Department of Defense put out a bid for someone to provide backbone services for DARPA, to connect all its scientists and researchers on a secure videoconferencing network so they can share ideas and advances. Morris won, and two of the failed bidders have sour grapes. AT&T and Sprint launched protests, which is de rigueur in these things. The last hope for thwarted bidders is to try to get the decision overturned. It's worth one point two billion over ten years."

I contemplated this, then asked, "And you're—" He started to interrupt. "Right. *We're* doing what?"

"Defending against the protest. Partly working with the Defense Department, and partly doing missionary work with Congress, which funds these projects."

Everything he'd said up to this point made sense. It's what makes this such a great country, and what makes Washington such a great city for lawyers. The Feds collect some two trillion per annum in tax revenue, it has to be spent, and lawyers are up front, writing the contracts, and at the back, suing everybody for breach of contract. It's all one big foodfight, and the lawyers are the crumb snatchers.

"Why me?" I asked.

"Good question. Lisa Morrow worked on this same issue. We found her knowledge of the Defense Department quite helpful, and she found it equally fruitful. She learned a great deal about how your procurement practices work." He added, "It's pretty pathetic."

"Why's that?"

"Well, you know . . . you're dealing with military and government people."

"I see." Which was shorthand for, You're an asshole.

"Also, when it's government money, the face of politics sticks its ugly nose in. AT&T and Sprint have a lot of clout."

"And I'm allowed to work on this? No conflict-of-interest issues?"

"We'll keep you out of those areas that pose a problem. No lobbying in the Pentagon or the Hill." He added, "But you can certainly meet with in-house counsel at Morris Networks to help prepare our case." He put down his coffee. "Any questions?"

He was assuming, of course, that I'd be around long enough to help out. Barry obviously wasn't as smart as he thought he was.

I said, "Not at this time."

"Good. Now, last point. That awful uniform has to go. And, yes, we're aware that can present a financial burden, so we're making the same arrangement we made for Lisa."

"And what arrangement would that be?"

"Be at Brooks Brothers at 4:00 P.M. You'll be fitted with everything you need. The firm pays the bill and leases you the wardrobe for twenty dollars a month. At the end of your year, it's yours to keep. Also, you may occasionally be required to drive around clients, so we've taken the liberty of leasing a Jaguar sedan for your use." He regarded me with a smug expression and added, "These are professional requirements that are unapproachable at your salary."

I stared at him, and he stared back at me. "I already have a few suits."

"I'm sure you do. And I'm sure they're, uh, nifty suits . . . just . . . well, not nearly up to our quality standards. We can't have a member of this firm walking around looking like a clown, can we?"

"How about like a gigolo?"

He laughed. "Don't be an idiot. The people we represent don't want to be seen with hungry lawyers. All new associates get this package."

Sally commented, "We've passed this by your inspector general's office. It's perfectly legal."

So what do I say? If I accepted, I was like a kept man, and I owed the firm something in return. But clearly I wasn't being asked. So I didn't say anything.

Sally deposited me back at my office, where some idiot had stacked a foot of thick manuals on my desk. "Those are our operating and ethics policies," Sally explained, and with a pointed look, added, "have them read by morning. A short test will be administered to ensure you understand the material."

"You're kidding, right?"

"No, I'm not. It's routine. Fail, and you'll have to sit through three days of instruction."

"And then?"

"Then you'll be retested. The firm is quite serious about its attorneys knowing its procedures and ethical standards."

"As it should be. And if I fail again?"

"Associates are fired. In your case, the firm would probably notify the Army you can't complete the program."

Well, this was suddenly interesting. I said, "Really . . . ?"

"Yes."

I shooed her out and used the number Clapper had provided to call Lisa Morrow. A secretary answered and said she'd get her.

After a moment a slightly put-out voice said, "Thank you for calling, but I'm happy with my current phone service and I'm not at all interested in a timeshare."

I laughed.

She said, "Weren't you supposed to call about six months ago? About a drink? A dinner? Something?"

"Look, if you'll please allow me to explain—"

"Sean, don't." I heard her draw a sharp breath. "Don't lie to me."

"Lisa, I'm . . . well, I'm hurt. I've never lied to you," I replied, very sincerely.

After a pregnant moment, she said, "You're right. That was unfair. I'm sorry."

"You should be." I added, "I was in a coma the past six months. They say I kept mumbling your name. It's the only reason they didn't turn off the life support system. I, well . . . Lisa, listen . . . I owe you my life."

After a tender pause, she said, "Try again."

"Again . . . Okay, I heard you were going out with somebody else and I didn't want to confuse you." Incidentally, this happened to be true.

She chuckled. "I was going out with somebody."

Note the verb tense. Also how easily I got that out of her. Boy, am I good at this game. I said, "Guess where I am?"

"I don't care where you are. You should've called. I can sort through confusion."

"Maybe I can't. I'm sitting in my new office at a tightassed firm called Culper, Hutch, and Westin."

"*You're* the new exchange student?"

"Lucky me. Clapper said the last one claimed she had such a great time, I'd love it here."

"He's lying. I haven't even debriefed him yet." She added, "But *you?* . . . What was Clapper thinking?"

"He hates me."

"He doesn't hate you. I think he hates them."

"Well, tomorrow, it's going to be a much smaller firm. I'm bringing a gun to work. I've compiled a list of people I'm going to cap."

"I might have some suggestions. What are you working on?"

"Morris Networks. Same thing you worked on, I've been told."

"Then you've met Cy?"

"Would he be the guy who counseled me on my lousy manners as he casually mentioned that Clapper and he are asshole buddies?"

She laughed. "Smooth as a baby's butt, isn't he? And Barry?"

"Yes, Barry. The top spot on my list to get capped."

"Good choice. But don't underestimate him, Sean. He's vicious. Also very, very smart. He was number one at Stanford Law. Did he mention that yet?"

"He was working up to it when I cut him off."

There was another long pause before she said, "I'm really glad you called. I have some things you might want to hear about Culper, Hutch, and Westin."

"No need. I'm supposed to take some ethics and procedures test, and if I fail, I'm back in Clapper's lap. I mean, this is too easy, you know?" But as a matter of interest, I asked, "Incidentally, did the firm bill your government-funded time to the clients?"

"Three hundred an hour."

"Can you fail because your morals are too high?"

"That's *how* you fail." She then suggested, "And actually, I'd recommend it. Can we meet tonight?"

"My place or yours?"

"Don't push your luck, Drummond." She laughed. "Drinks in a neutral corner."

"Oh . . . I see."

"Don't get huffy."

"I'm not . . . Look, for you, is this meeting business or plea-sure?"

"Strictly business."

"Oh . . . I see."

There was a long pause before she said, "But what happens after drinks is up for grabs."

I laughed.

She said, "Unfortunately, I have some work to finish up that concerns Culper, Hutch, and Westin. We'll discuss it. Pentagon, North Parking . . . is around nine okay?"

"Sure. Look for the suave, good-looking guy driving the Jaguar."

"I will." She asked, "And what will *you* be driving?"

Hah-hah.

She added, "But, Sean, really . . ."

"Yes?"

"Don't be stupid—do take their suits."

"Right."

We hung up, and I leaned back into my chair with a nice sappy smile. I should've made this call a long time ago. I liked her. I liked her voice. She had one of those throaty voices that send a nice tingle up your spine. It was a sexy, edgy voice, which was part of her almost hypnotic power over male jury members. And probably her gorgeous face, great legs, and primo ass played a role also. But I'm part of the new Army, so thoroughly politically corrected I never even notice a soldier's sex. Right.

In truth, I had fibbed—to her and perhaps to myself; my pro-tracted dillying and dallying had a very primitive and reasonable foundation: fear. Some women you go out with, you both have a great time, and maybe it will work and maybe it won't. Some women are just a great time—remember each other's names in the morning, don't complicate things, and everybody's happy. Lisa Morrow, you don't run into her type often, and you don't dive in without considerable forethought, because you know it will be a long, hard climb out of a very deep, dark pit if things don't work out. But perhaps I'd just reached that time of life, that level of maturity, that emotional plateau where I was ready for something more. I did recall a conversation I'd once had with Miss Morrow where she said she believed in monogamous relationships, long-term commitments, and legally sanctioned castrations for cheaters. That sounded to me like a warning. Was I really ready for this?

Whatever; we had both made it clear that our previously warm, collegial, professional relationship was about to become something more.

CHAPTER FIVE

He admired her ass for a long and pleasant moment as she bent down to inspect what he knew would be a flat tire.

Tuesday night, at 8:59. He had dawdled and meandered around a small corner of the gargantuan parking lot for nearly three hours. Less than two hundred cars were still sprinkled over the nearly two square miles of flat, black tarmac. Only hours before, the vast expanse had been cluttered, without an open space to be found. Thousands of cars. Amazing, really. And to think there were two other huge lots and three smaller ones on the other sides of the five-sided complex. Thousands of people had streamed past him on the way to their cars, gripping their briefcases, planning their evenings, scurrying to get their kids from childcare centers, and largely ignoring him.

The very few who had bothered to give him a second glance would recall a tall, blubbery man with dark hair, a thick, walruslike mustache, and eyes completely obscured behind a pair of oversized sunglasses. Let them take a picture for all he cared.

Later, he would remove the mustache, burn the wig, and remove the thick padding that made him appear chubby and unfit.

What would the police do when they responded to the call? Very little that night, he gauged. The following morning they would likely post a pair of officers by the sidewalk that led to the parking lot. They would flash their tin at passersby and ask if they had observed anything or anybody suspicious the evening before. Somebody who appeared out of place? A loiterer taking an untoward interest in the females who passed by?

They could ask all the questions they wanted for all he cared. Few witnesses would recall him specifically, and even those would discount him automatically.

He moved down the line of cars, checking locks, inspecting the interiors through windows—to all outward appearances, diligently performing his job. Between five and six the foot traffic had been torrential. Surge after surge had rushed by him. First came mobs of underpaid secretaries in running shoes, flapping their arms and complaining in flustered voices about the stupid things their bosses made them do. Then hordes of sour-faced civil servants wearing bored expressions and cheap, wrinkled suits. Last came the people in uniform, serious-looking, as though the weight of the world rested on their weary shoulders. Between six and seven the pace slackened like a body pumping out its final spurts of blood. After eight the foot traffic dwindled to a trickle. The only people who remained inside the huge office building were the night shift and fanatically dedicated. There were few enough of those.

He approached and beamed his flashlight at her face. "Problem, ma'am?"

She looked up with a jolt, then relaxed as her eyes took in his uniform. "Uh . . . yes, my tire went flat."

He shifted the beam toward the right rear tire. "Sure did. Damned shame, too. Looks new."

"It should. Couldn't have more than ten thousand miles on it."

He chuckled. "Nothing's made like it used to be, huh?" Espe-cially after it's been vigorously punctured a few times with a kobar blade, he failed to add.

"I'm not old enough to know," she replied, chuckling and crossing her arms, appearing not quite as upset as he'd expected and hoped she would be.

He moved closer. "You got Triple A?"

"I do."

"Yeah, but . . ."

"Right . . . but. They'll send a truck in an hour."

He saw her glance at her watch and knew she was regaming her options. He raised his eyebrows. "Ever done it yourself? You know, changed a flat?"

"Never."

"Ain't easy the first time. Let me give you a hand."

"Thanks, but it won't be necessary."

His smile got friendlier. "No problem. I gotta be out here all night anyway."

"Is that right?" She gave him a curious look. "I didn't realize they were posting security guards in the parking lot."

"You work here?" he asked.

"Temporarily."

"Guess that explains it, then."

"Explains what?"

"Ever since that September thing, we been out here. You know, keeping an eye out for ragheaded rascals with suitcases."

"Oh . . . of course."

"Waste of time, you ask me. In a year, I've caught two car thieves, a couple of punks from the District." He patted his ample stomach and chuckled. "Given out plenty of parking citations, but seems like the terrorists were warned that big bad John's in the lot."

She chuckled with him, then asked, "Were you here the day it happened? When the plane hit?"

"Off duty, thank God. Saw it on TV like everybody. Hell of a thing."

"An awful tragedy."

"Sure was. So, should we get started?"

She smiled. "Really, I won't need your help." She glanced again at her watch, then looked up. "I have a friend coming to pick me up. He should be here any minute."

He smiled back, though this surely was not what he had anticipated or desired to hear. A visitor would screw up everything, and she was proving to be mulish and uncooperative. She should already be tucked inside her own trunk, hands cuffed behind her back, shuddering with fear and imagining the dreadful things he had planned for her.

He glanced around, the painstaking security officer surveying his domain.

Nobody in any direction.

Not a soul.

He looked back at her. "Mind if I keep you company till your friend arrives? Gets boring out here, this hour."

"I'd appreciate it. I'll enjoy the company."

"Me too. So what do you do in the five-sided nuthouse?"

"I'm an attorney. JAG actually."

"No kidding." He nonchalantly fumbled with something on his belt. "I like that show."

She smiled. "That's not what it's really like."

"No?"

"Not at all. A JAG officer flying off a carrier deck is com—"

She froze. The very big gun he was pointing at her stomach had suddenly acquired her full attention. She looked at his face. He was no longer smiling, and her expression turned to one of befuddlement.

"Don't get excited now." He kept his voice cool and deliberately calm. "Just a simple robbery. No more, no less."

Her eyes darted around the parking lot, and he could sense

her exasperation that they were completely alone in the vast expanse. Nothing but empty cars and the nasty man with the gun.

With his free hand he reached out and removed her shoulder bag and the briefcase she clutched with her hand. Not a spot of resistance from her. He said, "Almost done. Just open your car and your glove box."

"I have nothing valuable in the car."

"Maybe not . . . I'd prefer to judge myself."

She studied his face and he was impressed with her coolness. Some women would be frantic by this point, on the verge of howling bloody murder and blowing the whole thing. He had scrapped his original plan, was working spontaneously, and was hugely pleased that he had pegged her correctly.

He waved the pistol. "Come on, open your door and the glove box."

"I can't."

He worked up a fierce scowl. "Don't push me, lady."

"You've got my keys."

"Oh . . . in the purse?"

"Exactly."

He held it out and allowed her to dig through the insides till she found the keys. She held them in front of his face. She was playing the odds and hoping for the best. They both relaxed.

She turned her back to him and unlocked her car door. He quietly set her purse and briefcase on the ground and holstered the pistol. She bent forward and leaned inside the car to reach her glove compartment. He took a step closer to her body, reached forward with both hands, seized the front of her throat with one hand, and wrapped the other tightly around her jaw. She began straightening up, pushing back toward him, trying to fight, but the advantages of surprise, size, and brawn were his.

He gave her jaw a fierce jerk to the right and felt the distinctive snap of her neck. A choked groan exploded from her throat. Her body immediately sagged forward—if not dead, surely on *the way to dead. He pulled her backward and let her drop natu- rally onto the tarmac.*

He closed her car door, relocked it, and threw the keys back into her purse. He withdrew a vial from his pocket, bent over for a few seconds, made a few minor adjustments to her body, retrieved her purse and briefcase, then calmly walked away. He had parked his car in South Parking, and he walked com- pletely around the gargantuan building and departed without incident.

Too bad he'd had to improvise and leave such an under- stated calling card that way. He'd just have to make it up with number two, and he knew just how to do it.

CHAPTER SIX

THE TAILOR AT BROOKS BROTHERS HAD AN AVARICIOUS SMILE, WITH SEVEN suits and five sports coats with matching slacks slung on a backroom rack. Apparently there's a standard array, like with military uniforms—a blue pinstripe, a gray pinstripe, a herringbone, and so on. Black and brown shoes, belts to match, twenty shirts, and three pairs of suspenders I wouldn't be caught dead in. It began, however, with an idiot's tutorial regarding which shirts and slacks and ties matched which coats and suits, and why did I suspect Barry had a hand in that? Twenty minutes of being pinned and chalked later, I told the tailor to hold the alterations for two days, without mentioning my wishy-washiness about the ethical propriety of taking $30,000 in fine clothes for only a few days' work.

But, actually, I wasn't ambivalent.

Having a few hours to kill, I wandered back to the firm and noodled through their manuals. The Army also has manuals, but primarily to explain things like how to point a directional claymore mine so it craps death and destruction on the other guy, instead of spoiling your day, or how to frantically clear a jammed M16 auto-

matic rifle while badasses are storming your position. The subject
matter possesses a certain, shall we say, puissance, that moves you
to ignore the drollness, read carefully, and remember the tiniest details. But you have to wonder about a firm that hires the best and
brightest from the nation's top law schools, and then feels the
need to explain in tedious detail how to prepare a business letter,
and under which conditions it's ethical to bill a client, and under
which it's most definitely not.

There was, in fact, an espresso machine on my floor, one of
those souped-up models you find in glitzy restaurants, with copper
tubing, and pressurized nodules, and thingees you turn and doo-
dads you push, and geez—what if I jabbed the wrong damned button and the whole f-ing building exploded? To be safe, I coaxed a
passing secretary into fixing me a cup, and then wandered to the
library. It was about 8:00 P.M. Some thirty associates were hunched
over texts or scrounging through the stacks for some obscure rul-
ing or other. This wasn't the late shift. Everybody looked tired and
glum. This place really sucked.

They were mostly young and attractive, late twenties, early
thirties, hungry, ambitious, and what they all needed was to go out,
get drunk, get laid, and get a life.

But one should always follow one's own advice, so I departed
at 8:30, affording myself a leisurely thirty minutes to get to the Pentagon. So there I am, driving happily through the streets of D.C. in
my shiny Jaguar sedan, radio blaring, hopeful, horny, eager, and I
guess a little too preoccupied, because suddenly there's this
swirling blue light behind me. I did not need this nonsense.

And so we had to go through the whole rigmarole—eight minutes waiting for the cop to run my plates, five minutes explaining
why the car was not registered in my name, two minutes playing
lawyer and trying to talk my way out of the speeding ticket, then
ten more minutes completing the basic transaction. Miss Morrow,
incidentally, was raised well, the type who always brings expensive
wines to a dinner, never misses a thank-you note, and is punctual

to a fault. I glanced at my watch—Ooops . . . Miss Right was about to become Miss Rightly Pissed Off.

I raced into the Pentagon's North Parking lot at 9:26. I saw a wash of blue and red lights. I was not really in the mood to see another cop, so I parked and began strolling toward the sidewalk that leads up to the towering guardian of Western civilization. Radios were crackling. Uniformed flatfoots were copying license numbers off cars. I counted three police cars, two unmarked cars, and a gaggle of cops clustered around a gray Nissan Maxima.

Eventually I picked out an Army uniform on a corpse that I assumed was some flabby colonel who'd just left the Pentagon Athletic Club. He'd ignored that gut overhang for years, and with that gung-ho gusto military men are so widely admired for, overtorqued his artery-hardened ticker. It was fairly common. In fact, maybe this was why the cemetery was across the road. Convenient for everybody, right?

A Pentagon security agent edged toward me, waving his arms. "Police investigation."

"Sorry." Still, I tried to snatch a closer peek at the corpse on the off chance it was Clapper. Maybe God had answered my prayers and slammed a lightning bolt up his ass. But maybe not. I had made it quite clear that I wanted to witness this heavenly feat.

My thoughts were disturbed by an ambulance hauling at high speed down the road toward the parking lot. I was walking past a young detective chattering into his radio: "—Caucasian female, approximately thirty years old, in an Army uniform. The name on her nametag is Morrow. That's M-O-R-R . . ."

I stopped walking. I stopped thinking. I froze.

The detective glared at me and said, "Keep moving, sir."

"You said Morrow, right?"

"Please, keep moving."

Feeling suddenly frantic, I said, "Not Lisa Morrow?"

He tossed the microphone back inside the car and walked warily toward me. "You know her?"

"Aren't you listening? If it's Lisa Morrow, I know her. I talked to her a few hours ago."

He waved at two uniformed cops, who rushed over. He whispered something to them and said to me, "Please remain here. I'll be right back."

The pair of cops repositioned themselves beside me, while the detective jogged over to the gaggle by the Maxima. He approached an older, much heavier detective, they conferred briefly, and then both men headed toward me. The older detective was black, with a heavy, puffy face and washed-out, bloodshot eyes that regarded me curiously.

He hesitated a moment, then said, "I'm Lieutenant Martin, Alexandria Police." He then added, "Detective Williams says you might know the victim."

My eyes were fixed on the gray car. "Yes. Maybe."

He and Williams exchanged looks. Martin said to me, "The only identification we've found is her nametag. If the victim had a purse, it was stolen. It could save us hours. You mind?"

I did mind. I wanted to cling to the faint possibility that it wasn't her, that this was a really uncanny coincidence, that any second Lisa would come bounding down the walkway with her gorgeous smile and she'd take my arm and off we'd go.

Instead, he took my arm and guided me. When we were fifty feet away I noticed her blond hair . . . then her slender body curled up on the tarmac, her arms flung sideways like she'd crashed down, legs splayed at an odd angle, as though they had simply buckled beneath her.

Her green eyes were locked open and she was staring up at me. I fought an impulse to take a knee and hold her. Shock and pain were etched on her lips. Her body lay on its left side and she was looking over her right shoulder at an impossible angle.

I didn't say anything because I couldn't. Martin's eyes also were fixed on her face. He asked me, "That her?"

I nodded.

He led me away as two uniformed cops started stringing yellow crime scene tape around the car and Lisa's body, and the ambulance crew began breaking out a stretcher. One detective was slipping plastic Baggies over Lisa's hands, another speaking dispassionately into a microphone, recording his initial impressions.

We ended up beside Lieutenant Martin's unmarked car. He allowed me a respectful moment before he asked, "Her full name, please?"

"Captain Lisa Morrow."

"How do you know her?"

"We're JAG officers. We worked together."

"As friends or associates?"

I stared at him.

He said, "I'm sorry." He was the decent type, and allowed another moment to pass, then added, "Williams said you talked to her a few hours ago."

I nodded. "I've just been assigned to the office where Lisa spent the past year. We were going to compare notes."

"At this hour?"

"She was working late."

His next question was interrupted by a dark Crown Victoria that raced down the aisle and screeched to a halt beside us. Two guys in cheap suits leaped out, flashing their tin. One pounced in our direction and yelled, "What the fuck's going on here?"

Martin approached the guy acting like an asshole and said, "I'm Lieutenant Phil Martin of the Alexandria Police. We got the call about a body."

From their short hair, bad suits, and worse manners, it struck me the new arrivals were from the Army's Criminal Investigation Division, or CID, the military equivalent of detectives.

"Spell federal territory, asshole," the older agent said to Martin. He waved impatiently at the other CID agent to go over to Lisa's body, presumably to inflict the same treatment on the cops over there.

Martin said to him, "I didn't catch your name."

"I didn't give you my fuckin' name. Your assholes are fucking up my crime scene."

Appearing quite annoyed, Martin replied, "I was the one who called your night shift at Fort Myer and asked them to dispatch some people."

The object of his annoyance was a runt—ugly, nasty-looking face, big hooked proboscis, fat lips, small, tight eyes, and an olive complexion marred by acne scars. He was not a likable-looking sort, nor did he appear to be the likable-type. At that instant in fact, his forefinger was positioned an inch from Martin's nose and he was demanding, "That right? If you knew we was coming, why are your assholes collectin' my evidence?"

I'd had enough. Lisa Morrow lay dead on the tarmac and this guy's playing territorial prick. I stepped between them, faced the CID agent, and ordered, "Identify yourself."

He backed off a step. "Chief Warrant Spinelli." But he swiftly recovered his lack of manners and said, "And your rank don't mean shit to me. Get in my way and I'll charge you with obstructin' a criminal investigation."

Okay, fine. I needed someone to be angry with, and he'd do nicely. I reminded him, very coldly, "Mr. Spinelli, is it not proper military etiquette for junior officers to salute their seniors?"

Well, his eyes narrowed, but his hand did slowly crawl through the air to his forehead. For about five seconds I let him keep it there before I returned it. Power is a funny thing—one minute you have it, and the next, a bigger dog comes loping into the neighborhood and craps on your favorite lawns.

"Lieutenant, how were you notified?" I asked Martin, who was barely concealing a smile.

"Somebody called 911 from a cell phone. It was transferred to my station."

"Do you know who?"

"No. They apparently didn't want to be involved."

"And what time did you notify the military police about Captain Morrow's body?"

"Right after the call. Nearly thirty minutes ago."

I let that revelation hang for a moment before I said to Spinelli, "Fort Myer is only five minutes away."

"I came when I got the call. It's none of your business, Major."

Back to Martin, I said, "Lieutenant, I'd like to express the heart-felt appreciation of the Armed Forces. Mr. Spinelli was tardy, and this kind of cooperation shows your professionalism." To Spinelli I added, "You will now try to act equally professional. You will con-duct a proper handoff of evidence and responsibilities. You will handle this task with courtesy and grace. Have I made myself clear?"

Lieutenant Martin tipped his head and left to inform his peo-ple.

My eyes stayed on Spinelli. I informed him, "The victim is Cap-tain Lisa Morrow, a personal friend. So listen closely, because I will only say this once—mess up this investigation, Spinelli, and I will fuck up your life. This is not an idle threat."

"You know the victim?"

"What did I just say?"

His eyes narrowed. "Are you a witness?"

"No. I overheard one of them mention her name and I offered to identify her."

"Ain't that a fuckin' coincidence." His eyes shifted in the direc-tion of Lisa's corpse. "What happened?"

"She was murdered."

"How do you know?"

"Because unlike you, I saw her body. Her head is twisted at an impossible angle. Somebody snapped her neck."

"Uh-huh." He turned back and studied me. "Wait here. Don't even think of leavin'."

I leaned up against a car. It had been an unseasonably tepid De-cember filled with clammy, rainy days and dull gray skies. But the warm snap had broken the day before; the night was cold and beautiful, a full moon, a star-filled sky, and I stared up at the heav-ens and cursed.

Guilt. The circumstances were irrelevant; the guilt was unavoidable and overwhelming. Had I arrived on time, I'd be sitting
with Lisa in a cozy bar swapping drinks and laughs and stories. I
wondered if she was standing around and waiting when it happened. I wondered how it would've turned out had I come twenty
minutes earlier.

Spinelli's voice echoed through the night, hazing and bullying
the local cops. Martin's people began leaving as more and more
MPs began showing up, establishing a cordon around the crime
scene, and proceeding through the paces of cataloging a murder. I
felt as though I had just swallowed broken glass. A woman of extraordinary talent and great beauty had been left dead on the wet
pavement like a piece of crumpled garbage.

I thought of Lisa's face, yet for some reason I could not recall
her as I always knew her, as I wanted to remember her: happy,
smiling, lively, and self-assured. Her death mask was inside my
head, and I could not drive it out. The eyes, they say, are the windows into the soul. I believe this to be true, and, in fact, the feature
that had struck me most profoundly the first time we met were her
eyes, a very deep, nearly unnatural green. They were striking eyes,
and I had observed on many occasions the powerful effect they
had on men, women, and often, to my chagrin, on juries.

I had an odd and sickening suspicion that her killer had posed
her body after her last breath. As I mentioned earlier, her body appeared to have simply collapsed, yet the killer may have twisted
her neck afterward, wrenched it a few more degrees so that ob-
servers of her corpse could not miss her eyes—eyes no longer
filled with life and tenderness but with shock and betrayal.

The shock I understood. Her death was probably sudden but
not pointless, and that was registered in her expression. It was the
look of betrayal that haunted me to my soul.

CHAPTER SEVEN

A VERY LONG AND CHILLY HOUR PASSED BEFORE SPINELLI GOT BACK TO ME. He approached with a nasty smirk, withdrew a small notebook from his pocket, flipped it open, and yet, I noticed, there was no pen or pencil poised in his other hand.

He asked, "How'd you say you knew the victim?"

"I told you . . . we worked together. I was meeting her here to discuss a new assignment."

He smiled. "Yeah, shit . . . you did tell me that." He saluted. "Well, you can go."

If I had had an ice pick in my pocket, I would've buried it in his forehead. But I had to settle for pouncing over to my car, climbing in, and peeling out of the parking lot with an angry squeal of rubber.

I went straight to the phone when I got to my apartment, called the Pentagon switch, and asked the operator to connect me to General Clapper's quarters at Fort McNair, a tiny base along the D.C. side of the Potomac that hosts the National Defense University and a number of quarters for general officers.

Clapper picked up on the third ring and I said, "General, it's Drummond."

Long pause. "This better be important, Drummond."

"It is. Lisa Morrow was murdered tonight."

He did not respond to this startling news.

"I just left the crime scene," I informed him.

Still he did not respond.

"The murder occurred around 9:00 P.M.," I continued. "Somebody broke her neck. Her body was found in North Parking, beside her car. Her purse was missing."

After a pause, when he finally did respond, it was a technical question. He asked, "Who's investigating?"

I did not perceive this as coldness on his part. I knew Clapper regarded Lisa very highly, that he had been cultivating her for a very bright future, and this news was a bitter shock. But in the Army, business comes before both pleasure and grief.

"The Alexandria police responded, then CID arrived and took over."

"Where's her body?"

"I don't know where they took her." I allowed him a moment to assimilate this news, before I said, "I'd like to ask a favor."

"What?"

"I want to notify her family. Also, I'd like you to assign me as their survival assistance officer."

"All right." Although he and I both knew this was hardly a favor.

As you might expect, few organizations match the Army on the issue of death. Practice makes perfect, and the Army has had several centuries and millions of opportunities to work through the kinks. The notification officer is the guy who shows up on the doorstep to notify parents and spouses that their loved one has just been shifted on Army rolls from "present for duty" to "deceased." The survival assistance officer comes along afterward to help arrange a proper military burial, to settle matters of the estate, insurance, death benefits, and so on.

These are not duties that draw volunteers. A notification officer gets to share in the family's look of shock, the onset of grief, the emotional outpouring that is always discomforting and that sometimes turns ugly. It can be a touchy situation, and the Army of course has a manual that instructs one how to inform a family to set one less dinner place setting next Christmas. You are advised to remain stoic, polite, and firm, to strictly limit the conversation to "I am sorry to inform you that your (husband, wife, child) was killed on duty on (fill in the date)." Just be sure to fill in the blanks correctly. You are further advised to bring along a chaplain in the event the situation turns sticky.

As soon as we hung up, I called the casualty office in the personnel directorate, explained my intentions, and was informed a duty officer would call shortly. An anonymous major did in fact call, arranged for a courier to bring me Lisa's personnel file, issued me a ticket number to book a flight to Boston, warned me to abide by the Army manual and customs on notification, and wished me luck.

After three troubled hours of sleep, interrupted by a cheerless courier, I boarded the 6:15 early bird at Ronald Reagan National Airport. I waved off coffee and opened Lisa's file. The Army personnel file is a compendium of a soldier's life, from religion, blood type, and past assignments to schooling, awards, and so forth. The way Army promotions work, officers who've never met you pick through your annual ratings and personnel file, and from that paper profile determine whether Uncle Sam needs your services at a higher level.

Soldiers are required to submit a fresh full-body photo once a year to certify you meet the Army's height and weight requirements, and aren't too moronic-looking to be promoted to the next grade. The official line is that good looks and military bearing are completely irrelevant, not even considered—and the remarkable lack of physically deformed or ugly people in the Army's top hierarchy is obviously an odd coincidence. The photos are antiseptic, black-and-white, stiffly posed at the stance of attention.

I took a moment and studied Lisa's photo. The Army cautions

its officers not to smile for these pictures, and Lisa Morrow was a good soldier, and wasn't smiling. Yet she was one of those people with a reservoir of inner joy the camera couldn't repress. She was extraordinarily beautiful, of course, and the camera could not conceal that either. Also, she had incredibly sympathetic eyes, slightly turned down at the edges, eyes that drew you in and soothed your troubled soul. I missed her already. I ripped her photo out of the jacket and stuffed it inside my wallet, a reminder of things to be done.

By eight I was in a rental car, cursing Boston traffic and making my way to the Beacon Hill section. I reviewed what I knew about Lisa and her family. Her father was also an attorney, she had three sisters, and an affluent upbringing. All four daughters were close in age and friendship. I knew Lisa had attended a tony girls' prep school in Boston, then the University of Virginia for undergrad, then Harvard Law, a school that contributes very few people to military service, as firms like Culper, Hutch, and Westin offer juicier paychecks and, apparently, nicer wardrobes.

I knew Lisa's mother had died when she was a teenager. As the eldest, she filled the familial vacuum. She and her father were extremely close in the way that only wifeless fathers and elder daughters can grow to be. All in all, this was going to really, really suck.

The house turned out to be an impressively wide brownstone set on the downslope of a hillside cluttered with similar homes. Nice neighborhood, and judging by the Mercedeses, Jags, and Beemers lining the curbs, an exclusive preserve for professionals who aren't looking for success—they've already landed there. I spent ten minutes hunting for a parking place and appeared on the Morrow doorstep at 8:45.

I drew a sharp breath and tried to compose myself. The notification officer ordinarily has no acquaintance with the deceased, and it's no great ordeal to remain calm and stoic. But I gathered my nerves and rang the bell, and half a minute passed before the door was opened by a gentleman in a dark business suit. On the far side of his sixties, I'd guess, trim and fit, with wispy silver hair and silver eyebrows perched atop two very green eyes. The face was leathery and lined, a face that had spent a lot of time outdoors, a warm face, etched with character and intelligence, that also looked like it could get tough if the situation warranted.

We stared at each other for a few seconds, and before I could get a word out of my lips, he sagged against the doorjamb and emitted a long, terrible sigh. Those with loved ones in the military know an unhappy moment is in the making when an anonymous officer in dress greens materializes on your doorstep.

I struggled unsuccessfully to contain my emotions. "Mr. Morrow, I'm Major Sean Drummond. Lisa and I were, uh, good friends." That "were" popped the cork prematurely, so I raced to say, "I'm sorry. Lisa died last night."

When I said "died" he nearly collapsed, and I reached out to steady him. Neither of us spoke. His eyes closed and tears began spilling down his cheeks. I tightened my grip.

A woman's voice inside said, "Daddy, who is it?"

A choking sound erupted in his throat. A young woman appeared, saw me, saw her father crumpled with grief, and yelled, "Oh God . . . not Lisa?"

Mr. Morrow pulled away from me and he and the younger woman collapsed into each other's arms. This lasted a minute or so, them moaning, me standing miserably, clueless about what to do, or say, or *not* do, or *not* say next.

I finally managed to say, "I am terribly sorry. Lisa and I worked together. We became close friends. She was a gifted lawyer and she was a, well, a great person."

Appropriate words. But to the ears of a father who had burped her, changed her diapers, shared in a lifetime of great triumphs and few failures, they inevitably sounded wooden, empty, and condensed.

He apparently sensed my discomfort and said, "Come in, won't you?"

He took his daughter's arm, and I followed them down a hallway to a study at the rear of the house. The house itself—spacious, high-ceilinged, furnished tastefully with heavy wooden pieces, leather chairs, and oriental carpets—was a masculine home muddied by occasional frilly touches, evidence of four daughters. Pictures were everywhere of four young girls, from infancy through adulthood—graduation shots, a wedding picture, four girls on a boat with Mr. Morrow, hair blown back, all laughing. Above the mantel in the study hung a portrait of a woman beautiful enough to make you gasp; Lisa's mother, I guessed, blond-haired, green-eyed, looking curiously at the painter through two large orbs that exuded sympathy, a resemblance eerie enough to give me a shock.

The father and daughter fell onto the couch, arms wrapped around each other. I fell into the worn leather chair across from them. I said nothing—the questions would come.

"How?" Mr. Morrow eventually asked.

I replied, "Sir, I am instructed to state that the results and circumstances have yet to be finalized. You'll be notified as soon as we're sure."

He tapped a finger on a knee. "How?"

"She was murdered. Her neck was broken. It was quick, and as painless as these things can be."

I watched their faces crumple with shock. Death is death, regardless of the cause. Yet car accidents, plane crashes, strokes, and lightning strikes offer enough haphazardness to at least afford a sense that God or the fates simply plucked somebody you loved. Murder is different. So is its aftertaste. No random, supernatural force dealt the hand; some rotten mortal bastard robbed you of something infinitely precious.

"Have they caught the killer?"

"No. Not yet." His eyes were boring into me, so I added, "Lisa had left the Pentagon and was getting into her car. Her purse was missing, so it may have been a robbery. But I don't believe the police have yet discovered any evidence leading to a culprit."

A stunned silence followed as he and his daughter tried to absorb the full ramifications. Mr. Morrow eventually informed his daughter, "I'm going to call Carol and Janet and ask them to come right over."

He left me with a daughter who was perhaps twenty-three, dark-haired, thin, almost waifish, pretty, and, at the moment, severely distraught. I recalled that we hadn't been introduced and said, "I'm Sean Drummond. I was a friend of Lisa's. She spoke about all of you quite often."

She suppressed a sniffle. "I'm sorry. I don't want to speak right now." She fled.

I went over to stare at book titles, the final resort in every unwieldy, distressing situation. Mr. Morrow was a fan of the classics, I noted, and the books on the shelves had their spines heavily creased. Every family has *a* room and this study had that feel.

The front door opened about twenty minutes later, then murmured voices, a wail of anguish, then crying. The door opened again five minutes later, and the ritual was repeated.

After a while, I heard footsteps, then they all filed through the door into the study. Mr. Morrow's eyes moved distractedly around the room, and I suspected he was reliving what only an hour before would've been a happy memory and was now a painful one, perhaps of Lisa doing homework at his desk or thumbing through Dickens by the fireplace.

He said to me, "Major, I'm . . . I forgot your first name."

I was starting to open my lips when one of the three daughters prompted, "Sean, Daddy . . . Sean Drummond."

He nodded. "Thank you, Janet. Uh . . . Sean, these are Lisa's sisters, Elizabeth, Carol, and Janet."

I glanced at Janet, who had recalled my name, which was weird, because I was positive we'd never met.

All three sisters were identical in height and . . . and, actually, just height. Elizabeth, whom I'd been left with earlier, was, as I mentioned, black-haired and slender, whereas Carol was brunette, curly-headed, stockier, also pretty, but with that frumpy, sterilized look of the professional academic.

But back to Janet. She was quite attractive, in fact, stunningly attractive, raven-haired and blue-eyed, arched eyebrows, swept-up nose, carved cheekbones, and two dimples that warmed her beauty. She was dressed in a simple business suit that showed a body similar to Lisa's—slender, curvy in the right places, athletic, alluring.

"Is there anything else?" Mr. Morrow suddenly asked me.

"There is." I explained, "I've also been appointed as your survival assistance officer. This means I'll handle estate matters."

Janet immediately said, "No, you won't. I'll handle the estate."

"That's not advisable. Lisa has military life insurance, and military survivor packages, and . . . look, please consider it. You'll find it beneficial to have a military attorney wade through those things." I looked at her father and added, "Mr. Morrow, you're listed in Lisa's records as her beneficiary. About her funeral, I assume you'd like her to be interred in Arlington National."

"I'm afraid . . . I never considered it."

"Of course. Take your time."

They all four stared down at the floor, the "funeral" word truly driving home the point that Lisa's death was for keeps.

I sensed I had outworn my welcome and therefore said, "I'll leave my phone number and address on the table by the door. If there's anything . . . please let me know."

Nobody suggested otherwise, so I showed myself out. In fact, I was at the bottom of the outdoor stoop when the door flew open and Janet stepped out onto the portico. She held out her business card, and I obediently walked back and took it.

She said, "Call me with questions or issues."

"Right."

"I don't want my father bothered."

"Of course."

She turned around to go back inside, paused, then spun around and said, "You told my father there were no clues."

"It was true last night. I don't know what progress they've made since then."

"Who's handling the investigation?"

"The Army Criminal Investigation Division."

"Who's in charge?"

"It's in good hands, Miss Morrow. Army CID is very competent."

This, of course, was the kind of reassurance the Army expects you to offer in these difficult situations. But it's also true. Army CID has a much higher case closure rate than most civilian police forces. Of course, the artificialities of military life account for much of that success, as CID deals with small, clannish communities, where nearly everybody eats apple pie for breakfast, lunch, and dinner. Committing crimes in military communities is akin to farting in church—don't expect sympathetic witnesses.

What I failed to mention was the unusual nature of this crime from a military perspective. Having occurred in a massive, open parking lot a few miles from one of the world's most crime-infested cities suspects were not in short supply. Nor that the manner of Lisa's murder—the absence of a knife, bullet, and so forth—made it a real mess. Possibly Lisa had left a note back in her apartment that said, "In the event of my murder, please arrest (fill in the blank)," but life, and death particularly, never work that way. Finding the perp was going to be a bitch.

Janet stared at me, then said, a bit curtly, "Don't treat me like a novice, Drummond. This was my sister. Her murderer is going to be found."

"Right. CID will catch the killer and bring him to justice."

I had the impression she did not like this response when I heard the door slam.

I studied her business card. The top line read, "Janet Morrow," and beneath that, "Assistant District Attorney, City of Boston, Mass."

Oh shit.

CHAPTER EIGHT

I RETURNED TO THE GREED MILL SHORTLY AFTER 4:00 P.M., WHERE A CURT note from Sally ordered me to see her the moment I arrived. Beneath it was a second note to call Clapper.

I am ordinarily a stickler for that ladies-before-gentlemen thing. Exceptions are made when the lady is a bitch and the gentleman signs my paycheck.

Clapper inquired how it went, and I replied, bluntly, that it sucked and I wished I hadn't flown up to Boston but was reluctantly glad I did. He said he understood perfectly. There actually are a few fleeting moments when Clapper and I are friendly and even see eye to eye. It feels really good to both of us, I think.

Anyway, I warned him to expect to hear from one of Lisa's sisters. He said she had already called, and he had politely attempted to coax her to stay out of it. We agreed that she would probably ignore us both, and he then updated me on what CID had learned, which amounted to nothing—no fibers, no fingerprints, and enough tire tracks in what was, after all, a public parking lot, to make it impossible to pinpoint an escape vehicle. I told him I'd work on arranging the funeral. He said fine, make it a good one, and stay in touch.

Sally next, and I was directed to a carrel in a massive cube farm. There was a fairly gaping gap between junior and senior associates at Culper, Hutch, and Westin I had learned. After also learning that junior associates started at $130,000 a year, my sympathy meter was stuck on don't give a shit.

I stuck my head in and coughed. In response, she frowned, pointed at her watch, and said, "Drummond, yesterday was bad enough. This . . . well, it's absurd. Cy and Barry both asked where you were a dozen times. You're in big trouble."

"Lisa Morrow was murdered last night. I flew to Boston to notify her family."

I wasn't sure she heard me. She continued to stare at her watch. "Murdered?"

"Yes. Somebody broke her neck."

"Do they know who?"

"No. Not yet. It appeared to be a robbery."

She briefly contemplated this, and then concluded, "You still should've called."

It struck me I was arranging the wrong funeral.

I informed her, "I've also been appointed her family's survival assistance representative. I'll need time over the next few days to arrange Lisa's funeral and handle her affairs."

She said, "Explain your problems to Barry and Cy."

"I will." *Bitch.*

She went back to studying whatever she was reading and sort of casually asked, "So did you or didn't you study for your test?"

Okay, here's the deal. She had all the proper affectations of the model junior attorney—ambitious, hardworking, buttoned-down, dedicated, and so forth. And yet she didn't strike me as overly bright—not dumb or brainless, just not bright. More obviously, she lacked a few human ingredients, like sympathy, a sense of humor, and compassion.

Anyway, my choices seemed to be continue this line of conversation and end up putting her in a chokehold or change the subject. "So what's that you're working on?" I asked.

"What you should be working on." She pointed at one stack. "That's the original proposal sent by Morris Networks for the DARPA bid." She pointed at another. "That's the protest filed by AT&T, and that's the one by Sprint."

"It takes two hundred pages to file a protest?"

"They were probably in a hurry."

A voice behind me chuckled and said, "It's an industry standard, thank God. You don't suspect reputable firms of padding bills?"

I spun around. Cy was smiling, though it was something short of his normal, gregarious smile. He remarked, "Perhaps Sally failed to mention that we like our attorneys to come in before noon."

"She did mention it. But Lisa Morrow was murdered."

"Oh . . . ?"

"Apparently a robbery gone wrong."

He, at least, had the decency not to stare at his watch. In fact, he appeared both stunned and upset. After a moment of hesitation, he said, "I'm, uh . . . I'm sorry, Sean. Were, uh, were you two close?"

"We were."

Again he appeared uncertain what to say next, a reaction that struck me as uncharacteristic. Silver-tongued types like Cy were never at a loss for the right sentiment, the right words. He finally said, "She was quite a woman. Truly, she was. She had spunk and smarts."

He saw the confused expression on my face and pulled me aside so Sally and the others couldn't overhear. "She made quite an impression on us," he informed me. "We offered to bring her in as a partner."

I suppose I looked surprised, because he swiftly added, "In fact, she accepted. She asked for a few weeks to put in her resignation and get things cleared up with the Army. We were expecting her to start next month."

"I don't believe it."

He acknowledged this with a nod. "A salary of three hundred and fifty thousand, a cut of the annual take, and the usual assortment of gratuities this firm generously provides its partners. We intended to move Lisa to our Boston office, where she'd be near her family."

Okay, I believed it. In fact, it did explain his sudden discomfort, and also why Lisa wanted to talk to me about the firm. The Army is where you came to be all you can be, but there comes a time for all of us to get all you can get, and I suppose Lisa had reached that point.

"Have you heard anything about her funeral?" he asked.

"I'm arranging it. I'm also supposed to settle her estate and help get her family through this."

"Take whatever time you need. She made a lot of friends here, so please be sure to let us know. And Sean . . . anything I can do . . . let me know."

I heard a grunt of disapproval from Sally. But I said I would, and Cy wandered off to notify the rest of the Washington office that there was still an opening in the Boston office for a new partner.

I returned to my office and immediately called the Fort Myer military police station to inquire if a certain prick named Chief Warrant Spinelli worked there. Indeed he was a prick of thoroughbred proportion, the duty officer confided, but he wouldn't be in until 5:00 P.M.

I assumed Spinelli had experienced a long night and an even longer morning. The murder of a female JAG officer on military property raises a lot of eyebrows—eyebrows of the wrong variety in the Military District of Washington, a sort of grazing pasture for general officers, some of whom have little better to do than stick their fingers up their posteriors, and their bossy noses into your business.

There was, of course, a television in my office, and I decided to catch the 5:00 P.M. local news. After fifteen minutes of chatter between a pair of overly jocular anchors, the male anchor said,

"And in other news, the body of Army captain Lisa Morrow was found dead in a Pentagon parking lot, apparently murdered. The police are investigating."

Other news? What the . . . ? My phone rang. I picked it up and a female voice said, "Major Drummond?"

"Do I have a choice?"

"This is Janet Morrow. We met this morning."

"Oh, right . . . what can I do for you?"

"I just checked into the Four Seasons in Georgetown. I was wondering if we could meet for dinner."

"I, uh—"

"Please. I'd like to go over a few details about Lisa's funeral and estate. You mentioned you were handling that."

No—I distinctly recalled her saying *she'd* handle the funeral and estate. So this was interesting.

However, she *sounded* perfectly sincere, and possibly she *was* perfectly sincere. I wasn't betting on it, of course.

But no wasn't even an option.

CHAPTER NINE

I RACED HOME AND SLIPPED INTO A BLUE BLAZER AND TAN SLACKS, APPROPRI-
ate attire for 1789, the Georgetown restaurant where Miss Morrow
had suggested we meet and eat. Among those in the know, 1789 is
a well-regarded D.C. powerplace. Though to be socially correct, it's
an *evening* powerplace, which I guess is different from a *midday*
powerplace, which I guess means only real schmucks eat breakfast
there. As long as nobody made me drink sherry.

When I was a kid, my father did a tour in the Pentagon, which
was my initiation to our capital and its weird and idiosyncratic
ways. We lived in the suburb of North Arlington, some four miles
from the city. Washington, back then, was a government town pop-
ulated mostly by impoverished blacks, penny-pinching bureaucrats, and a small coterie of political royalty. Even in those days it
was an expensive town, but my mother was a wizard with Green
Stamps, so we lived like kings. Just kidding—but my father's commute wasn't all that long.

More recently, Washington has become a roaring business
town, attracting a whole new breed of denizen; entrepreneurs,

wealthy executives, bankers, and, with the smell of money, corporate lawyers. Military people these days live in North Carolina and commute. The city never had any pretension of being an egalitarian melting pot, yet the sudden influx of money, and monied classes, has upset whatever precarious balance once existed.

Back to me, however. I returned to the city to attend Georgetown University undergrad, courtesy of Uncle Sam's ROTC scholarship program, and, five years later, was hauled, comatose, to the Walter Reed Army Medical Center after I learned the Army lied; I wasn't really faster than a speeding bullet. I was an infantry officer, the branch that handles the Army's dirtiest jobs, like killing bad guys in wartime, and painting rocks in peacetime.

A bullet had damaged an organ—a spleen, if you care to know—that needs to function effectively if you walk long distances with great weights on your back, a quality jackasses and infantry officers have in common, among others. I was already a captain, and the Army's personnel branch checked for shortages in my rank and years of service. The Army, you have to understand, views itself as a big machine, and when a nut can no longer be a nut, it can maybe become a washer, but not a screw or a bolt. Personal talents and desires are obviously secondary. In fact, I recall telling the personnel officer handling my case that as a wounded war hero, the service owed me a debt and should repay it by letting me choose. He thought that was hilarious.

So I was eventually informed I could become a chaplain, a supply guy, a lawyer, or a civilian. Wrong, wrong, maybe, wrong. As I mentioned previously, I'm Catholic, and while I'm drawn to fancy uniforms and elaborate ceremonies, that vow of chastity goes a bridge too far. A supply guy? . . . Get real. I wasn't ready for civilian life, and therefore defaulted into law and returned to my alma mater for a degree.

Which meant I'd lived in Washington nearly fifteen years, off and on. I love this city. I love the inspiring monuments to great deeds and great men, the monumental cathedrals of power, the everyday reminders that this city truly is the Shining Light on the

Hill. It's the people I can take or leave. The town has more than its share of oily scoundrels and the pompously high-minded, and it can be impossible to differentiate between the two, or which inflicts the most damage. Anyway, I passed through the portal into 1789 at 6:30 and the maître d' steered me to the table where Miss Morrow was coolly sipping a cocktail. I asked him to have a waiter bring me a beer and sat down.

So we studied each other a moment. She was smartly dressed in a red pantsuit, no makeup, no jewelry—to include, I idly noticed, no wedding or engagement bands. I could detect no physical resemblance between her and Lisa, excluding their sizes, and the not inconsequential fact that both were stunners, with all the requisite plumbing, bumps, and protuberances associated with their chromosome. It was salt and pepper, however—one blond and fair, the other raven-haired and darkly gorgeous. Plus, Lisa, as I mentioned, had the most sympathetic eyes I ever saw. Janet's were more . . . intolerant.

She awarded me what might be labeled a wan smile and said, "Thanks for joining me. I was brusque this morning, and I apologize. I was . . . upset."

"Perfectly understandable."

"It was very kind of you to fly up and tell us personally. Did you ask to do that?"

"I asked."

Her eyes strayed around the restaurant, and then back to me. "How long did you know Lisa?"

"A few years. We did an investigation together in Kosovo. Afterward, we tilted in court a number of times."

"That must have been interesting."

"It was. I got my ass kicked. Each time . . . every time."

She chuckled. "What was she like in court?"

"Devious, brilliant, and ruthless. She had a knack for coming up with the most wildassed defenses and making them stick."

"She was good, then?"

"No. She was the best."

She stared into her drink and seemed to contemplate, I don't know . . . something. For some reason she reminded me of Lisa. I had to think about it before I put my finger on it—it was that same throaty, edgy voice I previously mentioned. Similarities between the living and the dead can be eerie. Also, they can cause you to transfer a false sense of familiarity and affection. This can be misleading and, in the wrong circumstances, dangerous.

Eventually she said, "We're not certain about Arlington National Cemetery. Her family and friends are in Boston."

"I understand. Military honors come either way, but consider Arlington. The Army's Old Guard puts on a great show, it's a lovely setting, and she'll be in the best of company."

She replied politely, "You make a good argument. We'll think about it."

We then lapsed into a moment of friendly silence. We had gotten past the morning's rudeness, established that Lisa's death was emotionally affecting for us both, and some kind of unspoken bond had been forged. Miss Morrow was very deft at moving things along, I noted.

So we slowly drank our drinks and chatted amiably for a few more minutes. Nothing deep or really relevant; more in the nature of two strangers thrown together by a common grief and searching for some common ground. I learned she was twenty-nine years old, had attended Harvard Law, that she liked boating, was a big runner, preferred red wine, liked to read in her spare time . . . and so forth. She wasn't outwardly defensive, evasive, or anything. In fact, she remained impressively well-mannered, ladylike, expressive, great posture, and, if you're interested, had really great legs. Yet, she was not particularly talkative or open. Clearly, she had an agenda and did not intend to expose more of herself than necessary.

What she learned about me I wasn't sure. I did note that her questions were both more disarming and more penetrating than mine, and it struck me that she was probably quite adept at drawing out witnesses in a courtroom, or ascertaining if her blind date is a phony shit.

Also, her eyes were a sort of striking sea blue tone, which makes for a lovely contrast with black hair, and they had this almost foxlike quality to them, like she could see and detect things you might not want seen or detected.

In summary, she was getting up to speed on me, and I was learning about her hobbies. So I said, "Your business card mentioned you're an assistant DA."

"That's right. Five years now."

"Like it?"

"I like putting assholes behind bars."

"The Lord's work."

"Amen." She smiled and added, "Of course, the politics and bureaucracy I could do without."

I smiled back. I'd given her an opening.

Without pausing, she asked, "If you don't mind my asking, Sean, what's your take on why Lisa was murdered?" This was asked with disarming casualness, like, Could you please pass the salt? Very cool.

"And what makes you think it wasn't a simple robbery?"

"I've helped prosecute nearly thirty killings. I think I have a feel for the patterns."

"I'm listening."

"Start with the victim. Lisa was too street-smart. She would've handed over her purse."

"Perhaps she saw the robber's face and he wanted no witnesses. Or maybe he has a thing against women, or he was hopped up on something, or has a screw loose."

"Those are all possibilities. But consider the method. I had the taxi drive me by the Pentagon parking lot this afternoon. Lots of overhead lighting, cars coming and going . . . no thief with a brain in his head would pick such an exposed spot."

"Good point. Maybe he was an idiot."

She nodded, but said, "Also, her neck was broken from behind, hardly the direction a robber approaches his victim." We looked at each other awhile before she said, "It doesn't look like a robbery. It looks like something else."

"And what would that be?"

"Premeditated murder."

I pondered this, then said, "Motive, Counselor. Lisa wasn't involved in anything dangerous. She'd just finished a year working in a civilian firm where her work was both nonprovocative and mundane."

"She was a criminal lawyer before that. How many criminal cases did she work on?"

"A lot. Possibly hundreds."

"Last year, half a dozen lawyers were murdered for representing a party in a divorce case. I've had death threats, and I've been stalked. Isn't it possible she made enemies?"

"Let's not confuse possible with likely."

"But you have to consider it." She added, "Would your CID know what to look for?"

"She had six years' worth of cases. I wouldn't know what to look for."

"Yes, but wouldn't it make more sense to have a couple of experienced attorneys poking through her files than a warrant officer who has never tried a case and wouldn't know a tort from a tortilla?"

"What?"

"You get my point."

"Yes, I get your point." I twirled my finger in my beer suds. "And it's a bad one. Lawyers don't investigate murders, we prosecute and defend after the dust settles."

"I'm aware of the technicality."

"It's more than a technicality."

"Well . . . let's change the way it works." She added, "You claim she was your friend."

So we were down to this. Shame on her.

Appearances suggested that Miss Morrow was smart, disciplined, and, as the present setting indicated, stubborn, willful, and manipulative. Throw in her looks and "no" was a word I was willing to bet she did not hear often from the opposite sex. Her type don't play fair. They get those two male brains pitted against each other, and the lower one cheats by draining all the blood out of the higher one. You get suffocated into doing idiotic things that aren't in your best interest.

Actually, I fully intended to stick my nose into Lisa's murder investigation. I don't go gently into the night when you murder someone I care deeply about. Legal professionals, like me, and, I suppose, like Janet, are professionally and personally aware of the odds in these things. Less than a third of murders get solved and only half those lead to convictions. I wasn't expecting to solve the crime or anything, but I could and would prod, second-guess, and make myself a royal pain in the butt for the investigators.

Add to that, Warrant Officer Spinelli pissed me off and it was now my God-given obligation to piss him off back. Petty and vindictive, I know, but it's the regrettable code I live by.

In fact, my ulterior motive for offering my services as survival assistance officer was to afford me the legal authority to sniff through Lisa's personal effects and see if I found anything suspicious. Of all the thousands of people who walked out of the Pentagon that chilly evening, why her? Also the method of her death—it struck me as too personal. I thought the killer wanted to feel her, wanted to connect, wanted to make her murder an intimate experience.

Robbery? Maybe. Or maybe not.

So I briefly weighed the pros and cons of working with Miss Janet Morrow. On the plus side were her intimate knowledge of the deceased, her experience and expertise as a big-city criminal attorney, and she was obviously beautiful and sexy. Other men aren't as impervious to feminine wiles and charms as me, and her looks could open a lot of doors. Also, I liked her voice. And she had great legs.

Moving to the minus column, Janet Morrow lacked emotional

distance. The cardinal rule of murder investigations is to focus on the perp, not the victim. Also, a certain coldheartedness is needed to sort facts from fiction, and there are times when the victim's own faults or mistakes led directly or indirectly to their deaths. Dispassion is required and dispassion is impossible from a victim's sister.

"It's out of the question. Sorry," I informed her.

She studied my face. "You're wondering if I have the emotional mindset to handle this?"

"That thought crossed my mind."

"It won't be a problem."

"Of course it will."

"No . . . it won't."

"Nobody can shut down their emotions that way."

"I can." Trying to appear sincere, she added, "I shed my tears this morning. I won't cry again until this thing is finished."

"No . . . I'm sorry."

She waved an arm and the waiter rushed over. She looked up at him and said, "Check, please."

I said to Janet, "Please don't take this personally."

"I won't." She smiled at me and dropped a twenty on the table. She got to her feet and asked, "Where do we start?"

"*We* don't."

She took my arm and began leading me. "You drive. I took a taxi."

"Sure. What hotel did you say you were staying at?"

CHAPTER TEN

FORT MYER IS A SMALL BASE LOCATED ON ARLINGTON HEIGHTS, A BIG LUMP of earth with a commanding view of the majestic city of Washington, D.C. The land was once part of the ancestral estate of a certain Anna Washington Custis, who married a certain Robert E. Lee, whose southern sympathies made it suddenly difficult for him to appear in Washington to pay the land taxes. The property fell into arrears, the government promptly seized the homestead, and somebody in the federal government with a sense of humor and/or irony converted the family homestead into a Union military base and a cemetery. Not amused, Lee did his best to fill the cemetery.

The post has since become a quaint relic of Army times past, filled with ancient red-brick quarters for senior officers, horse stables, and ceremonial units. It was here where the Wright brothers launched the first military test flight; it crashed and burned, and on that oxymoronic note, the United States Air Force was born. On this same post, on a chilly December day, General George C. Marshall was interrupted from his horseback ride to be informed that the Japanese were kicking the crap out of Pearl Harbor. Much history, good, bad, and otherwise, has been written or buried inside its fences and accompanying cemetery.

The Post military police station is a deceptively small red-brick building located near the community center.

The young duty sergeant perked up as we entered and asked with rare enthusiasm, "Evening, ma'am. Can I help you?"

"Yes, please," Janet replied. "We're looking for Mr. Spinelli."

"I'll see if he's in." He pushed a button on his switch, had a brief conversation, then informed us, "He'll be out in a minute." He very politely asked, "Can I get you something, ma'am? Coffee? Soda?"

I've been in a lot of MP stations and never been offered so much as a seat. Thirty seconds later, Spinelli cruised out of a back hallway.

"Oh . . . you," he said to me, followed by a half-assed salute.

"Yeah . . . me." Usually, it's nice to be remembered; this obviously wasn't one of those occasions. I added, "Mr. Spinelli . . . Janet Morrow, the victim's sister."

Janet looked around the station as she asked him, "Could you spare a few minutes? In private?"

"Maybe." He jabbed a finger at me. "Why's he here?"

Good question. Why was he here? Could it be because he's a gutless ninny who couldn't stand by his convictions?

But Janet didn't say that. She said, "He's handling the estate. He offered to chauffeur me around and I accepted. Ignore him."

Spinelli smiled and appeared to like that answer. But we were here to gain his confidence and cooperation, and I thought to myself that if that meant I had to eat a little humble pie, I'd just play along. This made me feel good about myself, that I could, you know, swallow my pride and accommodate Janet's needs.

I'd get Spinelli back later, of course.

Nor had it escaped my notice how easily Janet picked up on the bad blood between us, nor how instinctively she exploited the mood. This was a woman with impressive situational awareness, and a good nose for male idiocy.

"Follow me," said Spinelli.

So we did, back to his tiny, cramped office in the back, where a menagerie of framed I-adore-myself things were hung floor-to-ceiling. I spied around for the Dear John letters from former girl-friends, late notices from mortgage companies, and so forth. But they somehow didn't make it to this wall. Well, probably they were hanging on another wall.

As we got settled, I did spend a moment examining what was present—commendation letters from various generals, case closure awards, certificates of graduation from various technical courses, including the FBI Academy. The former attested that he was good at his job, the latter that he wasn't quite the incompetent boob I had initially presumed. On paper.

"Somethin' particular you have in mind?" asked Spinelli as he fell back into his chair.

Janet handed him her business card and by way of introduction said, "I won't beat around the bush. I've taken thirty days off to find out who murdered my sister."

He studied her card for a moment. He asked, "And there's a reason I should find this acceptable?"

"A very good one, actually. You may need my help to solve this case."

"No shit?"

"I'm perfectly serious."

He replied, "You gotta be shittin' me."

Bad idea, Spinelli—the woman couldn't spell no. I might've warned him about this, except I actually wanted to witness this scene. I mean, all this male machismo crap aside, it would harm my frail, frail ego to discover I was the only one she could drag around by the scrotum.

But Spinelli was still shaking his head.

Janet said, "I don't want to play cop. I want to work with you. We have things to offer each other."

"I don't give a shit."

She smiled sweetly and asked, "But would you at least answer a few questions?"

He did not appear happy at this prospect, yet reluctantly said, "You bein' family, a few."

"Thank you." She paused a moment and then asked, "Did you return to the murder site and resweep the scene in daylight?"

"Yeah. We quarantined the site last night, then came back with a full forensics team. We even brought dogs."

"Was any new evidence discovered?"

"Not a thing. Sterile site."

"I called in permission this morning for an autopsy. Has it been conducted?"

"This afternoon. But toxicology and lab results won't be done till next week."

"You were present?"

He nodded. "Required to be."

"What were the results?"

"Hemorrhaging around the pupils, severe bruising on her left and right clavicles . . . the preliminary verdict, subject to the lab results, death by asphyxiation brought on by the fracture and dislocation of her vertebrae."

I watched Janet's face to see how she responded to the clinical description of her sister's death. Indeed, this was tough territory, and I found myself swallowing hard. But Janet nodded and suggested, cool as a pin, "Then allow me to reconstruct for a moment. One hand pinned her throat to keep her from screaming while the other twisted her head around to break her neck, right?"

"That seems to be the technique."

"And which direction was her head twisted?"

"The right."

"Indicating a right-handed killer, correct?"

"Most likely."

"Further indicating the murderer was a male, correct?"

"It takes great strength to snap a neck." In other words, yes.

She asked, "Any particles or skin in her fingernails?"

"Yeah. There was."

"Skin?"

"Deerskin."

"Then the killer wore gloves." He nodded again, and she then hypothesized, "The gloves were to protect against fingerprints." When he didn't respond to that, she suggested, "And from that, is it safe to assume the murder was premeditated?"

"From that, it's safe to assume it was cold. I wore gloves."

They stopped dueling for a moment to catch their breath.

Janet's courtroom experience and technique were evident and impressive. She understood the trail of evidence in a murder investigation, what questions to ask and which to avoid. Some lawyers are very good at this. Some lawyers should consider a different line of work.

Spinelli, no hump either, had stuck obstinately to the facts and displayed impressive restraint when she tried to prod or lead him into conclusions and conjecture. All in all, he was a tough egg to crack.

But I'm as competitive as the next guy. I searched my brain for what she'd left out, and then asked Spinelli, "Have you searched her car yet?"

"Yeah . . . her car. There was some nondescript smudge marks on the side, from the struggle probably. That's it."

"No fingerprints, no footprints, no hairs?"

"Didn't I just say only smudges?"

"Right." *Prick.* I asked, "And your best guess at motive?"

"Theft. A woman workin' late . . . comin' out into an empty parking lot . . . her purse stolen—"

"That's really your conclusion?" Janet interrupted.

"That's *really* my working hypothesis . . . and all that implies."

"But why would a thief kill her from behind?"

"Who says it was only one? There coulda been a backup man. In a public parking lot, breakin' her neck that way—no noise, no attention, no evidence . . . Makes sense, right?"

Yes, it did. And Janet replied, "Perhaps."

I said, "So what's next, Mr. Spinelli? What are you doing to find the killer?"

No cop likes to be asked this particular question. It's smacks of accountability, and public servants are allergic to the entire concept of responsibility and liability. But sometimes it's because they have good and well-thought-out plans and don't want them compromised. Other times it's because they haven't got a clue. They intend to tie all the proper procedural bows and knots, and wait breathlessly for the next crime so they can stuff this one in the unsolvable drawer.

Spinelli regarded me a moment, then replied, "If it's a robbery, the killer was probably some punk from D.C. or the suburbs. I've notified the local authorities and asked for lists of known felons who operate this way. I traced her charge cards and military ID and notified the Post Exchange and Commissary to be on the lookout. I notified her banks that if there's any attempts to charge on those cards, I'm to be informed."

In short, everything Spinelli's procedures required when the felony is robbery. He probably had a file reserved in the unsolvable drawer.

Janet asked, "And do you expect to get anything?"

"I'm optimistic."

I glanced at Janet and she glanced back at me. Bullshit.

I said to Spinelli, "Do you really expect him to be idiotic enough to use her charge cards?"

"Crooks do all kinds of stupid shit. It's why they're crooks." Spinelli then bent forward and asked, "We done yet?"

"Yes, thank you," Janet replied. "You've been very helpful."

He smiled. Then he stated, "Let me be even more helpful, then. I catch you or him stickin' your toes in this, I'll slap you both with charges for obstructin' my investigation. We clear on this point?"

She conceded, "It would be hard to be more clear."

His rodent eyes turned to me. "You clear on this point?"

"Oh . . . me? I'm the chauffeur, right?"

He gave me a nasty, distrustful squint, then looked at Janet and added, "Also, I'd get very pissed to discover you withholdin' relevant information or evidence. Should I explain the deep pile of shit that can get you into?"

"I'm aware of the penalties, Mr. Spinelli."

Before you knew it we were all shaking hands, pleased to have had the pleasure of one another's company we all agreed, which was, of course, bullshit. Nor did Spinelli offer to escort us out of the station, which struck me as perfectly in character. In fact, the session had gone pretty much as I had anticipated—a waste of time—and Spinelli had been every bit the unlikable asshole I recalled.

Outside, walking through the parking lot, I asked Janet, "Did you get what you wanted?"

"I got what I expected."

"Which was what?"

"Confirmation."

"Go on."

"They're headed in the wrong direction."

It struck me that Miss Morrow sounded more certain about this than me. If, in a day or two, some hophead was apprehended in D.C. for charging a stereo or something with Lisa's charge card, I could live with that. Eight years of trying criminal cases had taught me that first impressions are often wrong impressions, and clues that may appear very complex often turn out to have very simple solutions. But I detected no hint of doubt in Miss Janet Morrow and I obviously wondered why. Wanting to find out why, I asked her if she wanted a drink, but she begged off, claiming it had been a hard and emotionally draining day.

It had indeed.

And what I should have done at that moment was drop her off at her hotel, wish her all the best, and disappear. But I wanted Lisa's killer. And I enjoyed hearing Lisa's voice, even though it belonged to a different body and personality. So I took her back to her hotel and we agreed we would stay in close touch and share everything we learned.

CHAPTER ELEVEN

*H*e began tracking Julia Cuthburt as she pulled out of the parking garage underneath her Connecticut Avenue office building at 5:30. She drove a silver 2001 Toyota 4Runner with a six-cylinder engine and four-wheel drive that had probably never once, not since the day she'd bought it, ever been engaged. Her choice of automobile was in character with her general profile: practical, reliable, and best on the market for holding its value. The car conveyed an outdoorsy, rugged, and adventurous image, three qualities Julia Cuthburt roundly admired and sorely lacked. Poor Julia was a glorified clerk who wanted to be a princess in a Disney movie. Following her was too easy.

It was rush hour in Washington, and the traffic was dense and sluggish. She was a cautious, meticulous driver who rarely changed lanes and signaled far in advance of every maneuver. She drove like a snail.

At 6:15 she took a left off M Street in Georgetown, drove downhill half a block, and turned right into an underground garage. He waited fifteen seconds before he followed her in, just *in time to see her taillights turning to the right. She went down three levels. He went down three levels. She pulled into an open space and he parked twelve spaces away.*

He was quietly congratulating himself, when, suddenly, things went haywire. She locked her car and walked directly to the handicap elevator instead of the stairs. He was just stepping out of his car as the elevator doors closed and her guilty grin disappeared. The lazy bitch should've taken the stairs, instead of abusing the public trust.

He rushed for the stairwell, sprinted up three levels to the ground floor, and barged through a pair of heavy double doors just in time to knock a mother and her little children flat into a wall.

"Sorry," he mumbled, looking frantically around, as the mother glared nastily and one of the children wailed, bouncing up and down on a hurt foot. He found himself on the ground floor of a two-level indoor mall, filled with expensive and exclusive shops. Julia Cuthburt wore a dark blue business suit. The crowds were light, and spotting her should be easy. If she was there. For five minutes he searched with increasing despair.

He gritted his teeth and cursed as he rushed toward the M Street exit from the mall. He stormed out onto a street thick with pedestrians, mostly young people and college kids wandering in noisy swarms and lambapping. He looked both ways and Julia Cuthburt in her blue business suit was nowhere in sight.

He had not considered this. Not from her. His computer had rated her a three. Tiny children with their naive trust of strangers and frivolous ways were twos. Julia Cuthburt was barely two steps above a drooling paraplegic in a wheelchair, he thought, as he shrugged with bewilderment and pondered his options. The simplest solution would be to go back into the parking garage, linger beside her car till she returned, and try something different. That option was canned nearly the moment it popped into his head. Bad enough that Lisa Morrow had required a script revision. One, okay, but Julia's role was sacrosanct.

He racked his brain and tried to calculate what had brought her here.

Shopping, possibly, but as he looked up and down the street and studied the environment, it struck him as more and more unlikely. The array of expensive, upscale Georgetown shops was out of character for a tight-fisted bargain hunter who liked to brag to her friends about all the great deals she bagged at Wal-Mart and Kmart and Dollar stores. Her pretensions aside, Julia had an accountant's soul. Life for her was a never-ending tug-of-war over who got to keep the highest percentage of the margin.

She would be hungry at this hour. But he doubted she had driven forty minutes through rush-hour traffic to find an over-priced restaurant in the most crowded district of the city. Possibly she was meeting a date, and that eventuality unsettled him greatly. It would mess up everything. This was Julia's night to rise and shine.

He thought of all the other details and notations in her file and a hunch began to take shape. He looked both ways again, then swiftly crossed the street and walked into Clyde's. The bar was packed with young men and women, mostly wearing suits and business attire, hefting drinks, chattering and chuckling, ogling one another, and posturing in ways they hoped would attract the opposite sex. He wandered through the bar pretending to search for someone he was supposed to meet. But no Julia in her blue serge suit. Possibly she was in the ladies' room, so he loitered nearby, gave that five minutes, and then departed in a huff.

A block down was Nathans and he made a beeline for the entrance. An almost identical scene, another upscale meat market filled with horny young people willing to pay seven dollars per beer on the off chance they might get lucky. He searched the tables first on the possibility that she was having dinner with a date. No Julia in a blue suit at the tables. He progressed to the bar, where women aspiring to be picked up mostly congregated. After two minutes of fruitless searching, he caught a flash of dark blue at the far end of the bar, right below a pair of ancient rowing oars hung on the wall to give the utterly false sense of a sporting clubhouse. He moved across the floor and improved his angle. Bingo—it was indeed Julia in her blue serge suit, perched on a tall barstool, a mixed drink of some sort held daintily between two fingers of her left hand. A man stood beside her, gripping a longneck, bouncing nervously on the balls of his feet and chortling at something.

The man was in his late thirties, balding, chubby, with a long, pointed nose, and his posture and gestures suggested he was trying hard. Her posture and flat expression suggested he was trying much too hard.

He maneuvered through the thick crowd until he was directly behind the man chatting with his Julia. Was this a date going sour or merely a stranger attempting a pickup? That distinction mattered. It mattered greatly.

The man was waving his longneck through the air and saying to her, ". . . and the senator was all over me to get it fixed. I have lots of friends in the White House, and you know what? . . . If he hadn't pissed me off, I might've picked up the phone and handled everything."

Julia nodded and said, "Uh . . . okay."

"Know what I did?"

"No."

"What I did was tell the senator I didn't like the way he approached me. I told him I wouldn't lift a finger. You should've seen him. Guy's got hair transplants, you know. I swear to God, his face went red from here to here."

He rocked back on his heels and chortled loudly. Julia took a long and serious sip from her drink.

"So, anyway," the guy asked, "what did you say your name was?"

"Julia."

"Uh-huh. Ever been up on the Hill, Julia? I could get you in, show you the corridors of power, introduce you to a few senators."

"What a thrill," Julia replied. Funny, she didn't sound the least bit thrilled.

The important question was answered. He leaned across the bar and used his elbow to push back the man hitting on Julia as he yelled, "Julia? My God, it's been what? Ten years?"

Her eyes shifted to him and she blinked a few times. He winked at her and said, "You don't remember me? The prom? Senior year in high school?"

Julia's expression became even more confused, so he widened his smile and added, "Gosh . . . Tom Melborne? Maybe you don't recognize me without my tuxedo."

Julia seemed to catch on. "Tom? Oh God. Please, I'm sorry."

He edged closer to her, using his body to force the Senate staffer to back away a few more steps. He said to Julia, "What are you doing in Washington? Last I heard, you were going to . . . oh, gosh . . . I'm embarrassed—"

"University of Delaware," she answered, smiling.

"Of course." He looked at the staffer. "I'm really sorry, I didn't mean to intrude. Are you Julia's boyfriend? Husband? Date?"

"Uh, no. We just met."

He put a hand on the staffer's shoulder. "We went to high school together, until my mom and dad died in a car accident . . . right after the prom." He glanced at Julia and said, "That's why I dropped out. I'm sure you wondered, and . . . I guess I should've told you, but I . . . Hey, look, I didn't want your sympathy. You had your life, your great future, and I had to raise and care for my four younger sisters. You didn't need that. They're all doing great, by the way. Jessie, the youngest, remember her? The one in the wheelchair? She just started college."

Julia had her face stuffed inside her drink. She bit her lip, glanced up, and said, "I always wondered what happened to poor, sweet little Jessie."

Uncomfortably shuffling his feet, the staffer was looking like the deflated third wheel he had tacitly become. He studied the intruder, his competition, and realized without a doubt that he *was dealing with a number one draft pick. He saw a tall, broad-shouldered, blond-haired man, slightly older than Julia, with a square jaw, blue eyes, and the kind of sculpted looks that could get him any woman in this bar, or any other.*

The staffer backed away, saying, "Well, uh, it was nice to meet you, Julia. That offer to show you the Hill is still open."

She looked down at the floor and mumbled, "Thanks . . . honest."

The staffer melted back into the crowd and they erupted in chuckles.

"The name really is Tom," he said. "Tom Melborne."

"And I'm really Julia . . . Julia Cuthburt."

They giggled some more.

He said, "You owe me. Another three minutes and he would've been pelting you with stories about how he and the Speaker of the House play golf together every Sunday. That's where he advises the Speaker on how to run the country."

She chuckled. "Did you really have four little sisters?"

"Of course. And do you really plan to go visit him on the Hill?"

She stole another sip from her drink and he could see her eyes studying him, liking what she saw, and wondering if this was all there was. A white knight saves her from a horny dragon and then drifts off into the night, leaving her to the next hungry Hill staffer, or lawyer, or civil servant. The city was filled to its bowels with all three and she was long past the point where she found them entertaining.

He smiled at her and asked, "Would you care for another drink? Perhaps you'd like to hear how poor Jessie is really doing."

She gave him a smile that was half yes, and half bald relief. "Rum and Coke would be great."

He waved at the bartender, ordered hers, and a scotch on the rocks for himself. As the harried bartender rushed off, he asked her, "So, what do you do?"

"I'm an accountant at a firm here in Washington. Johnson and Smathers. Maybe you've heard of it."

"Never. But I'm not in business."

"Are you in government?"

"Sort of."

When he failed to elaborate, she said, *"I'm baffled. Where do you work?"*

He took the drinks from the bartender, handed her one, and shrugged. *"Across the river."*

"Where across the river?"

"That big outfit located in a big building down the GW Parkway. I don't actually work in that building, but I keep a townhouse nearby for when I'm in town."

"Oh, you're with the CIA?"

"Yes. But we're not really supposed to admit more than that."

"What do we talk about then?"

"At the moment, I'm posing as a college professor on sabbatical who travels overseas and does research on public health systems. If you happen to have a keen interest in matters of public health, ask away."

A look of dread crossed her face. *"Public health?"*

"I know." He chuckled. *"I hate my cover."*

"It's a bad choice anyway. You don't look like a college professor."

"No?"

"Nor do you dress like a college professor."

"I have a closet filled with worn tweed jackets. Also a pair of tortoiseshell glasses. You'd be surprised how a few minor touches can alter an appearance." And truly she would, he thought.

She licked her lips. *"That's exciting."*

"Sometimes. But like I said, we're not supposed to talk about our jobs."

"Are you supposed to lie?"

"If need be, yes."

She coyly stirred her drink with her forefinger. *"You mean like you went to the prom with somebody, dropped out of school, and raised four orphaned sisters?"*

"Touché."

She chuckled and twisted her ankles together. Julia Cuthburt was everything his file and research projected her to be—a bored woman in a tedious job she could barely stand, past the age when she had hoped to be married and raising three kids, a living parody of Looking for Mr. Goodbar, prowling through singles bars in search of a jolt of excitement.

A tall, muscular, absurdly handsome CIA agent just in from the trenches was exactly what the doctor ordered.

She licked her lips again and asked, "You're not joking, are you? You're really a spy?"

"It's what I do."

"Are you working now?"

"I'm back for a debriefing."

She felt a flip-flop in her stomach. No more Hill clerks, two-bit lawyers, and civil servant jerks for her. A real-life James Bond type had his feet perched on her barstool, his briefcase parked at her feet, and was buying her drinks.

What was in that big briefcase anyway? Plans for the defense of Pyongyang, maybe. A termination order for the greedy, evil prime minister of Botswana who'd been dealing under the table with terrorists.

"I've never met anyone who works at the—" She caught the frown forming on his face, and swiftly said, "Well, that place."

"How do you know?"

"Oh . . . of course." She nodded, as though this made sense.

After a moment, he said, "But enough about me, I'd rather talk about you. For instance, where are you from?"

"A small town in Kansas. But I left a long time ago."

He knew this, of course. And that she hadn't merely left Kansas, but fled at the first chance. He knew she was a math genius, had two little sisters, left Kansas at seventeen, and after majoring in mathematics at the University of Delaware, had *picked up a master's in accounting at Boston College. She'd done well. Offers had poured in from the top firms. Her specialty was corporate taxation, and setting up tricky offshore accounts was her particular talent. She billed out at $350 per hour, high for an associate, but her firm described her to interested customers as a wizard at loopholes. The bookshelves in her apartment were crammed with thick accounting texts, intermixed with romance paperbacks with those corny covers depicting forlorn women being crushed in the arms of bronzed, muscular men. He assumed she had taken the job in Washington because it was filled with powerful men with interesting lives she wanted to marry into.*

Over the next hour he walked her back through her history, posing a succession of perfectly timed questions that allowed her to portray herself in the most favorable light, no easy task with an accountant. She liked talking about herself and was thrilled to the core that such a man would be so fascinated with her.

She was merrily chattering away when at 8:30 he absently glanced down at his watch. "Oh . . . my God . . . Julia, look what you've done."

"What?"

"I never lose track of time. Never."

"It's only eight-thirty," she protested.

He looked embarrassed. "I have a 6:00 A.M. debriefing scheduled. My mind has to be sharp. I should walk you to your car. Where are you parked?"

The invitation was a test, she was sure. Say no, thanks, and he would conclude she was still on the prowl. There would be an awkward moment, then sayonara, and she'd never see her CIA man again.

A toothy grin and she grabbed her handbag. "In the underground garage across the street."

"Me too." He dropped a fifty on the bar to cover their drinks with a hefty tip, hefted up his briefcase, took her elbow and helped her up.

They chatted amiably until they reached her car in the garage. He opened her door, then shuffled his feet and said, somewhat awkwardly, "Julia, I . . . I've really enjoyed this evening. I mean, really."

"Me too."

The ball was back in his court, and he appeared suddenly tentative and nervous about what to do or say next. How beguiling. This fearless man who could face the most daunting dangers had melted into a shy puppy. He said, "I'd invite you back to my apartment for a nightcap, but . . . not tonight."

"Why's that?"

"Two other agents are crashing there. Most guys don't keep apartments here. When they return for a debrief, I let them use my place." He gave her a sad smile, and added, "In the field, we all live in a state of constant fear and anxiety. Sometimes . . . well, it's nice to cook your own meals, be with friends, people you trust."

Her stomach did another flip-flop. She'd been so obsessed talking about herself, and so selfishly concerned with her own romantic needs, she'd nearly forgotten how hazardous his life was. The man could be killed at the drop of a hat.

She clutched his arm and stared deeply into the contacts that gave his eyes that wonderful sea blue glaze. She said, "My apartment's not far. I know it's late for you . . . but a nightcap?"

She felt exuberantly guilty. So selfish of her.

He smiled. "A quick one. I'll follow you."

"Maybe you'd feel more comfortable talking about yourself in my apartment. You're so mysterious. I'm dying to know the real you."

He grinned. "It's a promise."

CHAPTER TWELVE

I RETURNED TO MY APARTMENT AND FOUND A MESSAGE ON MY ANSWERING machine from a ceremonies officer of the Army's Old Guard who wanted to finalize the funeral details; how many guests, the denomination of the chapel ceremony, who'd get her flag, the normal menu items regarding military funerals. The Army was moving with its usual selective efficiency. It's astonishing how differently the Army treats the living and the dead. Have a problem getting paid correctly and you'll be retired before it's fixed; die, and clods of dirt are bouncing off your coffin before the obituary's dried.

Message two was from Clapper and said, "Cy Berger called about some damned exam you're supposed to take. Don't screw with me, Drummond. Fail and I *will* make you the legal officer on Johnston Island Atoll. The orders are sitting on my—"

Wow! My answering machine suddenly leaped off the side table and crashed into the wall.

I mean, you think you've got it all figured out, some smartass reads your mind, and life turns to shit. It was past ten. The manuals in question were gathering dust on my desk at the firm.

Forty minutes later, I was seated behind said desk, studying a thick binder titled "Preparing and Processing Billings," aka "Keeping the Juices Flowing." By 4:00 A.M., knowing more than I ever wanted about the ethical and administrative policies of big law firms, I crawled over to the comfy leather couch.

A very irritating hand was soon shaking my shoulder and I looked up into the gloating face of Sally Westin. She said, "It's about time that you got into the swing of things."

"You ratted me out."

"Yes, I did. For your own good."

We exchanged brief stares of mutual animosity, then I said, "These two guys, Sam and Bill, end up seated side by side on a plane, and Bill can't help noticing that Sam has a black eye. So Bill says to Sam, 'Hey what happened to your eye?' Sam says, 'Well, I had a slight verbal accident,' and Bill curiously asks, 'How's that?' Sam says, 'I was having breakfast with my wife, and I was trying to say, "Hey honey, could you please pour me a bowl of those delicious-looking Frosties." Only it came out, "You ruined my life you fatassed, evil, self-centered bitch." ' "

She stared for a moment, then remarked, "That's not funny." She crossed her arms and contemplated me. "You don't like it here, do you?"

"What gave away my secret?"

"What didn't?" She asked, "Why?"

"You don't want to hear it."

"Play your cards right and you could get an offer to join the firm. I hear Morrow got an offer. Most lawyers would love to be in your shoes."

"You mean, isn't it the ambition of all public-sector lawyers to join big firms?"

"I didn't put it like that." But it was certainly what she meant. The third-year scramble at law schools is all about a certain pecking order, starting with prestigious big firms, then smaller, less prestigious ones, then your mother's brother with that small real estate titles business.

The lucky few who make it to prestigious big firms assume that we who don't are envious swine who'd do anything to escape our dreary jobs and Lilliputian paychecks. There is a modicum of truth in that, somewhere; I, however, count myself as an exception. Near-poverty suits me fine. It relieves me of so many burdens, temptations, and difficult choices.

I threw my legs off the couch and the momentum brought me to my feet. But regarding her point, I said, "Law isn't all about making money or prestigious titles."

Whoops—I looked around to be sure the walls were still standing. But it appeared the building's pilings were sunk deep enough in the muck of greed and avarice to keep it upright.

"Why do you practice law?" I asked Sally.

"What does that mean?"

"This firm, twenty-hour days, overbearing partners, the race to bill . . . why?" Note how cleverly I sidestepped her father and grandfather.

"I love law."

"*What* do you love about law?"

"I . . . I haven't really thought about it."

"Think now, Sally." She looked away, and I added, "You don't look like you're having fun."

"Really?"

"You look overworked, miserable, and empty."

Her nostrils flared. "Thank you." Anytime, Sally.

I stretched and yawned. I had arrived the night before dressed comfortably in jeans and a sweatshirt, so I slipped out of my sweatshirt and reached for one of my new oxford button-downs. She pointed at three or four round scars on my torso and asked, "How did you get those?"

"Poor timing, bad luck . . . the usual way."

"Is Army law that dangerous?"

"Before my life turned to crap, I was an infantryman."

"You sound like you enjoyed that."

"Yes . . . well." I rubbed my forehead and confessed, "Infantrymen kill people. You know, people piss you off, and . . . Look, I know this sounds sick . . . you'd be surprised how gratifying . . . not that I think about it all the time . . . "

She edged away from me. "You're serious?"

"My . . . well, my counselor . . . I mean, surely you've heard of post-traumatic stress . . . I'm making swell progress, she says. As long as . . . you know, nothing exacerbates my condition. Please, don't mention it to anyone. It's kind of embarrassing."

She was staring at a blank wall, and I suggested, "Perhaps you can leave, so I can change."

"Yes . . . of course." She left and returned a few minutes later, placed the exam on my blotter, and said with newfound courtesy, "Incidentally, we have a flight at nine."

"Who has a flight?"

"The protest team. You'll want to shave and clean up. Jason Morris is sending his private jet. I . . . I know this is hard for you, but a good impression is important."

"Just don't tell him about . . . well, my condition, okay?"

She gave me a long stare before she left me to ponder this new possibility. Of course, it was only a matter of time before the whole firm learned the Army had sent a homicidal idiot into its midst.

Still, it certainly couldn't hurt to piss on the shoe of the firm's biggest rainmaker.

CHAPTER THIRTEEN

Cy, Barry, Sally, and I congregated at the private-plane terminal at Dulles International and were promptly ushered aboard a twin-engine Learjet. The plane's interior was specially outfitted for the rich and pampered, with four plush leather chairs collected around a conference table, and a pert young stewardess named Jenny who sported a fab tan, great legs, a rock-hard fanny, and the perky, upbeat manners of an aerobics instructor. "Come on, everybody, let's get those seatbelts buckled now." Big smile, clapped hands, the works. Save me, please.

But the lovely Miss Jenny jibed with something else I had heard and read about her employer. Mr. Jason Morris was reputedly a cocksman of renown, rumored to have balled half the eye candy in Hollywood and assorted other famous ladies. If those tabloids with splashy headlines about who's been sneaking in and out of whose boudoir were to be believed, Mr. Morris was quite the little sneak.

But exactly how poor Jason managed to scrape together all that moolah, between dashing off to Bimini with this bimbo this week, and the Hamptons with that hottie the next, was, you can bet, a question I'd like to know the answer to. There was even, reportedly, a mile-high club among his formers. I idly wondered how the striking Miss Jenny occupied herself while her boss screwed his lovely guests into the fine leather of my seat. The onboard breakfast: eggs benedict, side orders of kippers and bacon, brioches, and orange juice with a hefty jolt of gin. Was this the life, or what?

And in fact, Cy and Barry were stuffing their greedy faces, knocking back loaded juices, and mumbling joyfully between themselves as Sally and I played ambitious junior associates and perused the same legal packets that had been stacked on her desk the day before. The documents were wordy and composed in that murderous syntax lawyers employ to confuse their clients and justify high fees, but the matter at hand was fairly simple. It boiled down to this:

The DARPA original request for bid was built around three essential requirements. One—the network, or pipeline, in techie lexicon, had to be capable of transmitting streaming video on sixteen channels simultaneously, so the scientists of DARPA could work collaboratively. This is something like cramming sixteen different television stations across one wire and onto one TV screen. Two—the network had to be completely secure, impervious to jamming, eavesdropping, hackage, or leakage. Three—the personnel administering the network had to possess Top Secret clearances.

I browsed swiftly through the technical malarkey regarding gigabits, frequencies, routers, switches, and so forth, then dozens of spreadsheets, business plans, and financial estimates, the sum of which made it clear that Jason's boys had creamed the contenders. The next best bid was 25 percent above Morris's. Ticket prices rose steadily from there.

On November 15, the Department of Defense had publicly declared Morris Networks the victor. A day later, an attorney representing AT&T visited the Pentagon Contracts office and posed a number of due diligence queries. He learned that a baffling exception had been granted to Morris Networks. The requirement for employees with Top Secret clearances had been waived.

Thus, the basis for contention number one in both AT&T's and Sprint's protests. Why had said waiver been granted?

Contention two was more open-ended, and long-winded, the long and short of it challenging how Morris Networks could conceivably perform the work at the price it had bid.

I closed the last document and looked up. Sally, beside me, was still thumbing through the pages. She had started at least the day before and still hadn't finished. Good lawyers read fast—it's a fact. I recalled Cy informing me she had barely made the top half of her law school class, and I found myself wondering how she had made any half.

I looked at Cy and commented, "This is very interesting."

He laughed. "We deserve six hundred an hour just for reading through that verbose horseshit."

"Six hundred an hour?"

"That's my going rate."

Wow. I mean, wow. Cy made more in a morning than my monthly salary. I asked, "Could I pose a few questions?"

Barry smiled in his unctuous way and replied, "Sure. What part confuses you, Sean?"

"Barry, did I say I was confused?"

"Uh . . . no. Sorry if I offended you."

He wasn't sorry, and I was contemplating the precise manner of his death when Cy shot me a black look.

I wasn't really in the mood for another lecture about how we should all be big pals, and share jockstraps and so forth, so I asked, "Why did Defense waive the clearance requirement?"

"It was unnecessary," replied Barry. "Whoever wrote the bid apparently didn't understand how networks are run. Typical for government and military people, really."

Perhaps a garrote for Mr. Bosworth. Gradually tightened, exquisitely painful . . . But I asked, "Did Morris approach the Department to have it waived?"

"Did you read the whole requirement?" Cy asked me.

"I did."

"You saw it's a twenty-four/seven network that extends to fifteen hundred sites?"

"Yes."

"And do you recall the manpower requirements?"

"It varied by bid. Between a hundred and fifty and five hundred network managers and administrators."

"Very good," Barry commented. Just for the record, I needed neither his approval nor his condescension, and I rejected the garrote. He should hang by his Gucci necktie, I decided. In fact, his feet were kicking and his eyes were bulging as he added, "Top Secret clearances cost approximately two hundred and fifty thousand per head, *and* take a year or longer to obtain. That adds tens of millions to the cost of the program."

"So?"

"So Morris simply pointed out that the requirement was unreasonable. An absurd waste of taxpayer dollars."

"That was it?"

Barry replied, "Procedures are built into the contract that allow the Defense Department to check Morris's security, so it's also superfluous. It didn't hurt that the contracting people wanted the low bid."

Sally peeked up and said, "That makes sense to me."

But it still didn't make sense to me, and I asked, "Then why are AT&T and Sprint protesting?"

The two men exchanged intriguing glances. After a brief pause, Cy informed me, "About a year ago, Jason hired Daniel Nash as a board member."

"I see."

"But Danny had nothing to do with this," he swiftly added. "Danny's not stupid. Nor is Jason, who well appreciates the need for firewalls between Danny and the Department."

Incidentally, the Daniel Nash who'd just entered the conversation had spent two years as Secretary of Defense under the previous administration, a former congressman whose most remarkable quality turned out to be his utter lack of remarkable qualities. After a long career on the Hill poking his nose into defense issues and spouting off like a defense expert, he had, to put it generously, been a big flop as Secretary of Defense. Mr. Nash turned out to be great at throwing barbs and javelins at the Pentagon, and not quite so good at dodging them.

Yet he was not entirely without talents. In fact, he turned out to be quite good at wallowing in a lifestyle money can't buy: traveling in his luxuriously outfitted 747, staying at five-star hotels, and hobnobbing in regal milieus with an assortment of corporate leaders and foreign bigwigs. His deputy was reputed to be the most overworked man in Washington.

Were one possessed by a cynical nature, one might even suspect Mr. Nash was feathering his nest for a prosperous afterlife, stuffing his Rolodex to exploit after he returned to the private sector; for instance, as a board member of Morris Networks, which clearly hadn't hired him for his managerial competence.

I allotted a respectful silence to contemplate Cy's assurance before suggesting, "However, it's possible we have at *least* the *appearance* of a serious violation, right? There's what? . . . a two-year ban on Nash trying to influence his former department?"

Cy chuckled. After a moment, he replied, "They'll damn sure make that case. But Danny swears he kept away from the whole damn thing."

"No doubt."

Slightly put out that I didn't seem to be swallowing the assurance of an esteemed firm partner, Barry said, "Daniel even volunteered to take a lie detector test. We've advised him against it, but the offer's still on the table. Would a guilty man do that?"

I always love that question. And why did I suspect that if the government actually said, Okay, Danny boy, let's go ahead and hook your ass to the dirty liar meter, the boys and girls from Culper, Hutch, and Westin would prevail and the offer would be abruptly withdrawn?

I muffled that suspicion, however. For the time being, I was one of those boys and girls, and therefore was expected to know where my bread was buttered. Though it was their bread being buttered. And the department I worked for getting screwed. I can't tell you how much I love being thrust into situations where I have conflicting loyalties.

It was time to move past this point, however, so I asked, "Exactly how does Morris Networks come in so much cheaper than the competition?"

"A number of factors," Barry explained. "For starters, Morris Networks is a much newer company."

"Oh . . . newer."

Barry smiled coolly. "Its entire network is state-of-the-art and not bogged down with old legacy systems, like Sprint and AT&T. Newer systems are more reliable, less manpower intensive, cheaper to operate and maintain."

"And that accounts for a twenty-five percent advantage over the next nearest competitor?"

"Partly. Jason also runs a flatter, leaner organization. He's a more efficient manager, without the huge overhead of the bigger companies. Trim off that fat and you don't have to spread the costs as far." He smiled and added, "But you obviously lack business experience, so this is probably over your head."

Cy apparently decided to head off a murder and swiftly said, "But these are good questions, Sean. Spend some time with Jason's people. You'll end up a believer."

I said, "I'll bet you're right." But I was lying.

I mean, having a key requirement waived for a company with a former Secretary of Defense in its pocket does tend to stretch the imagination in certain directions.

When it comes to Defense Department contracts, industry loves this little game that kicks off with the lowball bid. A few years later, the winner returns to the Department and says, "Whoops, hey, boy, this is embarrassing, but a funny thing happened on the way to fulfilling the bid. There were . . . well, a few unforeseeable problems . . . cost overruns . . . adjustments for things you guys failed to clarify in your request for bid . . . one or two acts of God, and, uh . . . we mentioned this is embarrassing, right? . . . Could you guys wrench that money spigot a bit more to the right?"

Sometimes, the Department tells them to shove it and cancels the contract, or, when it's really smelly, sics a squad of federal fraud investigators on their asses. I think there was once even a conviction. Nearly always, the government considers the near impossibility of proving fraud, and then says, "You're right, this is embarrassing . . . only it concerns a real vital program and an interruption or, God forbid, outright termination will be disastrous to national security. But, uh . . . let's see if we can keep this off the front pages, shall we?"

A gleaming black stretch limo that awaited us at the Palm Beach airport sped us through town, down a highway, and across a bridge to Jupiter Island, which, from the size and grandeur of the homes, would more aptly have been named Olympus Island, as this appeared to be where the Gods of Commerce came to recuperate from the sweat and toil of shoveling the big buckos into their vaults.

We pulled into a gated driveway and drove a hundred yards to a massive, sparkling pink monstrosity perched some twenty yards from the ocean. Half of El Salvador were trimming shrubs and hedges, and tending flower beds, and one had the sense of entering another world, of a southern plantation with Massa inside slamming down mint juleps while the "boys" kept the old ranchero looking all rich and sparkly.

Sometimes I think I am a Republican, and other times I think I'm a Democrat. At that moment, I was battling fits of Marxist passions. I actually had this weird impulse to leap out of the limo and scream, "Juan, Paco, José, grab those machetes and shears . . . Viva la Revolución!"

But before I could act on that urge, a very large man opened the front door and walked out to greet us. His pitch-dark suit marked him as hired help, and the mysterious bulge under his left armpit as a particular kind of hired help. Wasn't this odd?

The guy grinned at Cy, and it was obvious he knew him, because he said, "Mornin', Senator. Good to see ya again." His eyes roved over the rest of us, and I guess we looked harmless enough, because he then said, "Mr. Morris is out back. You're three minutes late, so please hurry along." He was really courteous.

So we stepped it up a little, as we were led through the entry, and the living room, and through a pair of very tall French doors, a journey that lasted nearly two hours as the frigging living room was slightly larger than Europe. I counted twenty different couches clustered in various clumps. Mr. Morris either liked to throw really big parties, or had this really weird thing for couches.

I ordinarily try to avoid judging a book by the cover, but jam it up my ass and twist it around a few times and I succumb to the temptation. I mean, private jets and stretch limos and beachside mansions do tend to rub salt in the wound of lower-middle-class poverty. And just as I was telling myself, Grow up Drummond, don't be so petty, I spotted the frigging *Queen Mary* parked along the dock out back—about 150 feet long, three sparkling decks of pure, shimmering, up-your-ass wealth.

Having seen the richboy's face plastered on any number of magazine covers, I recognized the figure seated in a lounge chair by the pool, staring off at the ocean, chatting on a cell phone, sipping coffee, finger tracing down a spreadsheet on his lap—multitasking gone berserk.

He punched off the phone and approached. The papers listed Jason Morris's age at thirty-nine years, and he looked every bit of eighteen: muscular, bronzed, sandy-haired, with pale blue eyes and a glistening smile, not to mention a checkbook that would have the ladies leaping out of their undies in about ten seconds. He did not look at all like a business mogul, more like a Ralph Lauren model, down to the square jaw and bony face, Bermuda shorts, faded polo shirt, and beach sandals. We looked like idiots in our business suits.

He threw out his very famous hand and said, "Cy, thanks for coming on such notice. I hope this isn't an inconvenience?"

Cy's equally famous hand shot out. "Inconvenience? Jason, I love that damned jet of yours. And that Jenny . . . she rent by the hour?"

It struck me that Mr. Berger and Mr. Morris shared a passion for the ladies, and I briefly wondered if the question was serious. But Jason chuckled. "You are an unreformed devil, Cy. Jenny makes her own arrangements. As for that jet, ostentatious as it might be, my board of directors insists it's needed to make the right impression. Am I going to argue?" Now everybody was laughing, though in my view the joke wasn't really funny. It struck me that when you're really rich, you can never be sure whether you're truly charming, sexy, or funny. I'll bet the rich lose a lot of sleep over that. Right. Then Mr. Morris turned to Mr. Bosworth and asked, "How you doing, Barry?"

"Just fine, Jason."

"Fine my ass." Jason regarded Cy and said, "Look at those bags under his eyes. Jesus, Cy, give the poor guy that partnership before you kill him."

"It's under advisement," Cy assured him. "Barry's in very good standing."

"He damn well better be. Seriously, Cy . . . Barry's made me a lot of money. I expect you guys to recognize and reward it."

Well, Mr. Bosworth beamed like a poodle that just got its ass sniffed by a well-hung Great Dane; Cy awarded a supple nod to the firm's rainmaker; and Ms. Westin stared at her shoes, no doubt contemplating the possibility that an end run to an instant partnership was standing a mere two feet away.

I stared at that big damn boat and wondered how hard it would be to sink.

But Morris interrupted my destructive musings, saying, "And I'm afraid I haven't met you two yet."

"I'm Sally Westin," chirped my associate. She added, "The firm just switched me to this case. I'm very, very pleased about it. I really admire you and all you've accomplished."

She hadn't actually dropped to her knees or anything, but geez.

Cy said, "And this is Sean Drummond, on loan from the Army. He joined us only two days ago."

"The Army? . . . Oh, like Lisa Morrow?"

"Same program." Cy paused, and then said, "Incidentally, poor Lisa is, well, this is bad news, Jason . . . Lisa was murdered."

Morris stepped back. "Murdered?"

"A robbery gone bad. Right, Sean?"

"That's what the police think," I replied.

Morris was shaking his head. He said to me, "What a terrifically sad world we live in. Is there anything I can do?"

"Sure. Can you dig holes?"

He stared at me. I slapped him on the arm and chuckled. Then he chuckled. Then he stopped chuckling, realizing, belatedly, that he'd just failed the authentic sympathy test.

He said, quite quickly, "Look . . . I didn't know Lisa well, but she seemed . . . well, like a lovely person. And very smart and competent."

"She was all that, and then some."

So, I'd been caught being rude. Introductory chitchats are only fun when everybody plays by the rules, and I had broken the taboo, so we all trooped over and sat in lounge chairs. We lawyers skillfully flopped our briefcases on our laps and arranged ourselves in a circle, like bloodsucking leeches surrounding our meal. A truly stunning Hispanic maid appeared out of nowhere, took our drink orders, and silently sashayed into a cabana expansive enough for a family of ten.

Morris allowed us enough time to get composed, and then said, "Concerning the case, any opening thoughts?"

Never one to lose the moment, Barry said, "I don't anticipate problems. The protests are based on an implied accusation of insider influence and the considerable gap between your bids."

"I agree," said Sally, slapping a point of her own on the board. "I really see no great problems."

Jason nodded at this display of blunt confidence. "And how do you intend to handle it?"

"Concerning the first charge," Barry replied, "we'll discuss that with your legal department and come up with a strategy. On the second, for starters, we recommend that you reaffirm that the bid price is genuine."

"It *is* genuine," Morris responded.

Cy asked, "You're sure, Jason?"

"Cy, I could've bid a fifth lower and still made a fat profit. Those old telecoms are so damned inefficient it's a scandal they're still in business."

Cy gave me a sideways glance and asked Jason, "No chance your people fudged it and it might bump up in a few years?"

"That's nonsense." He chopped an arm through the air. "Look, if it would move this thing along, tell them I'll even accept a penalty clause if there's any upward slippage."

"That would help," commented Barry. "It shows you're sincere. And confident."

"I *am* confident, damn it. As for inside influence, for Godsakes, the guys accusing me are the ones who've been picking Defense's pocket for generations. It's their game, right? How in the hell can they accuse me of foul play?"

And everybody was nodding along nicely, like Jason was making some real ironclad points, and what a rotten, rotten world it is when such transparently trumped-up accusations can even see the light of day. Although to be perfectly accurate, not everybody was nodding. I suggested to Jason, "Perhaps suspicion arises because you have a former Secretary of Defense in your pocket."

Cy, Sally, and Barry had been collectively stuffing their noses so far up his ass, he focused on me for the first time. "Yeah, yeah, you're right, Sean. I'm painfully aware of it. I regret that I hired him."

"Yeah? Why's that?"

"It's double jeopardy. We can't use him for Defense work, but everybody thinks we do."

"But you're certain he made no phone calls, didn't call in any chits?"

"How can you be sure about anything?" Obviously that was an honest response, and he added, "Look, Dan wasn't even aware we were bidding. He's a board member, not part of the company. I pay him a hundred fifty grand a year to come to meetings and listen to accountants talk about our financial health." He shook his head. "The son of a bitch slept through the past two meetings."

Cy chuckled. "Count your blessings. He's more impressive asleep than awake."

"Hey, aren't you the one who recommended him?"

"Yes. And didn't I warn you he was an overrated idiot?"

Morris chuckled. "Yeah, you did."

Well, they were all yucking it up, and while I don't regard myself as naive or anything, listening to these guys chat about buying and selling a former Secretary of Defense like a used toaster oven did get a little under my skin.

Anyway, Jason stood up and walked around for a moment, apparently collecting his thoughts. He ended up with his back to the big damn boat, creating a photogenic pose, him in the foreground with his muscular arms crossed, the ultimate monument to staggering wealth bobbing gently in the background. Possibly the pose was coincidental; possibly not.

He studied each of our faces very briefly, then said, "Look, I asked you all down here to inform you that this case is damned important. There's a reason AT&T and Sprint decided to launch this particular protest. My sources tell me Defense's releasing three more requests for bids this year. I think my competition's sources are telling them the same thing. If we get bumped on this one, it could create a chain effect. The combined value of all four bids is about four billion a year."

"That's big money," remarked Barry, quite needlessly.

"It really is," said Sally, equally needlessly—unless you considered her need for a partnership also.

"Yeah, it is." Morris again studied each of our faces and explained, "Look, I'm a simple businessman. I build a great product and sell it at a great price. That's why these dinosaurs are coming after me. I'm a threat to their existence, and they're going all out to destroy me. I need you guys to stop them. I have eight thousand hardworking people on my payroll who depend on your firm to keep the game fair. If we get nudged out of the Defense market, we'll survive, but Wall Street demands unceasing growth, and for the next few years, until the economy recovers, we need to be in the defense game. Bill me till I bleed . . . just don't lose this one."

The part about "bill me till I bleed" was intended for Cy, who nodded very enthusiastically. Barry, of course, was already fully on board, baggy-eyed, hungry, a hop, skip, and a jump from partnership, and was in need of no further prodding or inducement. So the bulk of the speech, I suspect, was aimed at Sally and me, the junior members of the team, if you will, who would perform most of the scut work. I glanced at Sally. She was nodding fiercely, like, Right, Jason, with you all the way—I'll work my ass into the ground for you, big guy. P.S., like my buddy Barry, I yearn for a partnership . . . oh . . . and P.S. to my P.S. . . . that mile-high club thing . . . I love to fly.

To his credit, Morris appeared to sense that her enthusiasm was, shall we say, over the top, shot me an apologetic grin, patted her shoulder, and then looked down at his watch. He said, "Cy, I'm afraid I have an appointment with some investors. I have to dash off. I hope you don't mind."

We agreed that we didn't mind, and he came over and gave us all hearty handshakes, pumping up the troops for battle, looking meaningfully into our eyes and checking our give-a-shit meters.

When he got to me, I gripped his hand and asked, "Time for one more question?"

"Sure."

"Why the armed guard at the door?"

"Him? He's just precautionary."

"I see. Is there a specific need for that kind of precaution?"

Instead of telling me to screw myself, he explained, "I'm sure you're aware I have a very high public profile. It's not something I like, but the company has been built around me, and every story the press does benefits my stockholders and employees. It's a fortune in free advertising. Unfortunately, my wealth is reported in many of the stories."

"So, nothing specific?"

"A few threatening letters." He added, "Once you're known for having money, the nuts and freaks line up. I'd be foolish to leave myself vulnerable."

"Gee, it sucks being rich, doesn't it?"

"No, Sean." He winked. "I wouldn't have it any other way."

Less than five minutes had elapsed since the guy with the lump under his armpit had deposited us in the backyard and we found ourselves ushered right back into the lush seats of the stretch limo. Figure—between the plane, the car, and the billable hours for four lawyers—our little three-minute chitchat had just cost Mr. Morris somewhere in the neighborhood of five times my annual salary. The rich do indeed have queer ways.

The moment the plane took off I shut my eyes and pretended to sleep. This, of course, is a polite way to avoid conversation. I had nothing in common with my colleagues; Sally was a heartless, manipulative bitch; Barry was an idiot; and Cy, whom I actually liked, was preoccupied with spiked orange juices and with Miss Jenny.

Also I wanted to mull over Jason Morris and his problems. Actually, it was my problem with his problems. For starters, he was rich and famous and got to ball nearly every babe in Hollywood—an impressive list of haves I regrettably have not. Well, life isn't fair and get over it, Drummond. *Forbes* magazine had recently pegged his worth at four billion big ones, and, looking deeply into my soul, anybody with that much self-made goulash has earned enough capitalist's merit badges to indulge in a few baubles and palaces. And if it would benefit my employees, I too could scale the heights of self-sacrifice and stomach a weekend on an exotic island with Jolie What's-her-name scampering around in a skimpy bikini. Noblesse oblige, right?

So ignore his wealth, and he seemed fairly down-to-earth and unpretentious, like he got the joke about his wealth, and if *you* wanted to take it too seriously—like Sally, who was squirming with restless ambition beside me—fine. But *he* didn't take it that seriously. I find that appealing. A bumper sticker that's very popular on Wall Street proclaims, "He who dies with the most toys wins." Au contraire—in the immortal words of Napoleon Bonaparte, he who possesses the biggest battalions wins. Capitalist pigs are well-advised to remember that.

About Nash, it would surpass the bounds of corporate idiocy to employ a former Secretary of Defense to bag a Defense contract. Everybody *expects* you to. Right? Contrarian logic would argue that you use him for exactly that reason, since stupidity can be the best camouflage. However, people are rarely that devious.

Finally, I had to ponder the tricky ethical territory involved in this mess. The American Bar Association would spank me for confessing this, but I have this simpleminded need for moral clarity. It's what I love about criminal law—the lawyers enter the fray *after* the crime has been committed, when we're only arguing about who gets the final credit. With corporate law, if your client decides to slide over that line that separates the legal from the less than legal, you can end up along for the ride. The textbook calls this abetting and assisting a crime. Added to that, it's all white-collar stuff, where the laws are vague and mushy, and it's all about greedy bastards fighting other greedy bastards over a nickel.

So where was the moral clarity in Jason's charge? Was there moral clarity? After several minutes of tossing the proverbial pros and cons into the ethereal air, I concluded that Morris Networks was offering a needed service at a fraction of what its competitors wanted to gouge. If that freed up an extra shekel or two to, say, buy more tanks and planes for our fighting boys and girls in the field, well, that's good for the goose and the gander. Right?

That issue settled, my mind drifted to another muddled order of business. Janet had called that morning, and I had agreed to spend my evening with her going through Lisa's apartment. I had no idea what she expected to find, even if there was anything worth finding. However, she had sounded unusually eager to look—quickly—which gave me an odd sense she had some specific knowledge I didn't.

Ask that question and you invariably end up asking yourself: Where and how does Sean Drummond fit into her plans?

CHAPTER FOURTEEN

THE LAST PERSON I EXPECTED, NEEDED, OR INDEED WANTED TO FIND IN MY new office was lounging on the plush leather couch, sipping an espresso, feet on the coffee table, watching Judge Judy on my office TV.

Chief Warrant Daniel Spinelli glanced up and asked, "Hey, how was Florida?"

"Warm, overpriced, and full of old farts. What are you doing here?"

He punched off the TV, and his eyes shifted around. "Nice place, ain't it?"

"Actually, the place sucks. But it's nicely furnished."

"They're spoilin' the shit out of you."

"Well, I'm the best. I deserve it."

He chuckled. "You gonna be able to come back home when this is done?"

Spinelli's idea of inconsequential chatter was wearing thin. I replied, "I'm sure I asked, why are you here?"

He shrugged and set down his espresso. "Ever hear of Julia Cuthburt?"

"Never."

"You're sure?"

"I'm sure."

He stood and walked to the window. He said to me, "Nice view, ain't it?"

"Great view. Incidentally, if I have to ask why you're here again, we'll do it with my foot up your ass."

He continued to stare out the window. "The body of Miss Julia Cuthburt was found in her apartment this mornin' by the Alexandria Police. Sexually molested, robbed, and dead."

"I didn't do it. I've got witnesses."

He faced me. "The victim was twenty-eight, single, a CPA with Johnson and Smathers, some big accounting outfit in the city. She had a long, ugly hour before her neck was broke."

"Her— What direction was her head twisted?"

"Same as Morrow's."

I asked, "And you're here to ask me if there was a connection between her and Lisa?"

"Was there?"

"I have no idea."

He thought about this a moment, then said, "Two women, roughly the same age, single professionals, attractive. Similar victim profiles . . . same manner of death . . ."

"But what about the sexual molestation?"

"Yeah. I thought about that. Try this scenario. He's waitin' for Morrow in the parkin' lot, he tries to drag her into a car, she tries to fight him off, threatens to expose him, and he decides she's too much trouble."

I nodded, but said nothing. Spinelli was playing games, and he annoyed me. CID people are all sneaky little bastards anyway. For some, that's part of the job, a suit they have to wear to work, and if you put enough beers in them, they'll even admit they find it distasteful. Spinelli was the other type. Also, this news came as a bit of a surprise, and a shock, and emotionally I needed a moment to absorb it, and intellectually, to fit Lisa's death into this fresh context and perspective. I had imagined any number of scenarios and likely motives—vengeance, theft, and jealousy leading the list, none of which involved a complete stranger. I had not considered that she was a number pulled out of a hat by a maniac.

The manner and style of her death, however, comported with the little I understood about serial killers who actually prey on complete strangers, and the whole concept of murder as something ritualized, personalized, and even illogical. Also Lisa had the kind of fetching looks that stand out from the crowd, and the more I thought about it, the more sense it made. She was a poster child for serial killers and their odd hungers—attractive single women who travel alone, live alone, shop alone, all of which left them available to be raped and die alone.

"All right, I see it," I informed him. "But it needs refinement."

"How's that?"

"You didn't know the victim. I did. Lisa was a champion runner. Also, she was very smart and alert, not the type to let down her guard. How did he get close enough? How did he keep her from bolting?"

He suggested, "She trusted him."

We both considered this a moment. I suggested, "Maybe he wore a uniform."

"Maybe."

Well, I suppose neither of us wanted to stipulate the next ugly stride in that progression. The military uniform, particularly an officer's uniform, inspires trust and respect. Fellow officers, like Lisa, regard it as an emblem of comradeship and brotherhood. Even civilians, like Julia Cuthburt, consider it a mark of virtue, integrity, and professionalism. But what is true for military uniforms holds water in varying degrees for other uniforms, including cops, FedEx employees, and garbagemen. A uniform signifies membership in an organization, which implies selectivity and screening, all of which confers trust, or, at least, familiarity and acceptance.

"Have you talked to her sister yet?" I asked him.

"I intend to," he replied. "I was wonderin' if you knew how to find her."

I checked my watch. "I'm supposed to meet her in thirty minutes. Come along, if you wish."

I offered only to be polite. But the rotten bastard took me up on it. We drove in silence because the only question I could think to ask was how he became such an asshole. If I asked, he might answer.

Janet was waiting in front of the hotel, a convenience I appreciated greatly as it saved me a six-dollar parking fee. And while I was working in a rich firm, driving rich, and even dressing rich, I was all wrapping without the flavor.

Surmise from this that I had decided to remain with the cutthroats of Culper, Hutch, and Westin a while longer. I wanted to pursue Lisa's killer, and if I was ejected for misbehavior, Clapper would banish me to a job that sucked, in a place that sucked, two commodities the Army has no shortage of. Regarding the firm, handling a few protests couldn't be that time-consuming, and anyway, Barry and Sally would shove shivs in each other's backs to solve Jason's crisis, and battle for credit, partnership, and a cut of the annual take. Sly little Sean would coast on their coattails right to the finish line.

Also, I was getting a lot of compliments on my new wardrobe.

Anyway, Janet peeked in the car, saw Spinelli, and climbed into the backseat. As though they were lifelong pals, she said, "Hi, Danny. How are you?"

He grinned. "Busy as shit. We got a new development on your sister."

He then proceeded to detail the particulars and question her on the newest deceased—Janet replied that she had never heard of Miss Julia Cuthburt, but yes, the connection to her sister's death appeared both plausible and taunting.

Then Spinelli turned his eyes back to me and asked, "Remember that asshole Martin you met in the parking lot?"

"An asshole in the parking lot?" I looked at him. "Oh . . . yeah. I'm sure his name wasn't Martin, though."

He mumbled something under his breath that wasn't very clear. He then said, "He wants words with you. You know the way to the Alexandria station?"

I did. And the drive over was fairly pleasant, as Janet kept Spinelli occupied, chatting about his life as a CID agent, him boasting about how many bad guys he'd busted and bagged, her filling his ears with admiring things that fed the little prick's ego.

Incidentally, I lied about the drive being pleasant.

However, it was both illuminating and edifying to watch a pro at work—her, I mean. It is not uncommon for runts, or, these days, altitudinally challenged males, to develop ego complexes, from insecurity to Napoleonic. Clearly Spinelli's I-love-me wall intimated a man who landed somewhere along that spectrum. I had the sense that Miss Morrow had given him some thought after our first testy session, and settled on a strategy to win his heart and mind. I love scheming, manipulative women, incidentally. And, again, she had great legs.

Anyway, we finally arrived, and Spinelli seemed to know his way around the police station. We ended up inside a big room that looked just like a detective office, with about twenty wooden desks, half of which were manned by guys, some of whom were interviewing people, some of whom were talking on the phone, and some of whom were eating bag dinners.

I pointed out to Spinelli that there were no donuts anywhere in sight, and perhaps we'd come to the wrong place. He didn't think that was funny. Perhaps it wasn't.

We entered a glass-enclosed office in the rear of the room, and Lieutenant Martin shooed out two detectives. Spinelli and he eyed each other apprehensively a moment, as Martin pointedly said to me, "Major . . . good to see you again. And you must be Miss Morrow?"

"Janet, please." She handed him her card, which he quickly read and then stuffed into a pocket.

He then asked if we knew why we were there. We indicated
we did, so he said, "Okay, good. Please, everybody be seated." He
lifted a photograph off his desk and handed it to Spinelli, who
handed it to me, who, after a quick peek, handed it to Janet. She
handed it to nobody, but studied it intently for nearly half a minute.
Her eyes narrowed, but to the best I could tell, she was emotionally detached. I hadn't expected her to vomit or anything, but a
slight groan or twitch of disgust would've been in order.

The photo—black-and-white, a naked corpse resting on her elbows and knees with her bare rump up in the air, hands and feet
trussed together, head turned gruesomely back so that her face actually peered over her right shoulder. The floor beneath her was
carpeted, and a side table with a stack of magazines was beside her
body. This was obviously not the position in which Miss Cuthburt
had been murdered, and it occurred to me again that her corpse
had been posed in this obscene manner by her killer, an in-your-
face message to the police, a vicarious way of shooting the moon.
The victim herself—brunette, young, bruised in a number of
places, and her facial expression was a study in terror.

"I don't know her," Janet informed Lieutenant Martin. She
tossed the photo back on his desk.

I said, "Likewise."

"Please take another look." He handed us another picture, a
color shot, enclosed in a brass frame, showing a young lady in a
graduation gown, gripping a diploma, standing between a Mom
and Pop bursting with pride and hope. Martin had filched it from
Miss Cuthburt's apartment, obviously. But who cared? She didn't.

Not a knockout, but Julia Cuthburt had been pretty enough,
slender, creamy-skinned, though a bit dreamy and gullible-looking
in my view. She had that fresh-off-the-farm look pimps hunt for in
young runaways at bus stations, and the next stop was a nightmare. Why is it a look of innocence is nearly always an invitation
to evil?

"No, I don't know her," Janet informed Martin, and I nodded
likewise.

Martin said, "Well, I apologize for dragging you in here. And for this." He indicated the police photo, and added, "I had to be sure."

"It's not an inconvenience," Janet replied. "I'm here to help in any way I can. When was she killed?"

"Approximately nine o'clock last night." He stared down at Miss Cuthburt's photograph. "She was having plumbing problems, and her landlord let himself into her apartment this morning."

Janet suggested to him, "Implying the killer knew where she lived. Just as he knew Lisa's car?"

"Don't assume it's the same killer."

"But you obviously think it's the same man?"

"Don't stretch the similarities." He sighed, rubbed his forehead, and insisted, "*Any* conclusions would be premature at this point."

Which was copspeak for, Yes, same guy. Martin struck me as decent and honest, and his studied reticence, or, in civilian parlance, his bald-faced lie, was understandable. If the general public learned a murderous sex maniac was on the loose, his job would get a hundred times harder.

"Evidence in her apartment?" Janet asked.

"That's the odd thing," Martin commented. "He cleaned up after himself. He wiped down the tables and even vacuumed the floor. But the forensics people did find some clothing fibers, some rape debris—semen, to be specific—and leather in her fingernails. The lab's doing a workup. We'll have his DNA type in a few days, then we'll look for a match."

Janet glanced in Spinelli's direction and said, "So he wore gloves?"

Martin said, "Yes. Deerskin gloves." Bingo—same guy.

I said, "And you'll obviously forward the lab results to the FBI?"

"Standard procedure in cases of this nature."

"The rape?" Janet asked. "Just vaginal?"

"We're not sure. Swabs from her orifices are at the lab." He pointed down at her photo and added, "There was semen on her back. Right there."

Janet suggested, "Indicating that the rapist may have mastur-bated on her? Or perhaps had an involuntary ejaculation?"

"Or dripped, or missed. You could manufacture many possible explanations. We'll know when the lab's finished."

I said, "In the meantime, you've got two murders in three nights. The attacks occurred at roughly the same time, and the bro-ken necks and deerskin gloves suggest it's our guy."

Martin replied, "That's circumstantial. It's still too early to draw conclusions."

"Indicating," I persisted, "a pattern with ugly possibilities. Our killer could be on a spree. He might have a number of victims lined up in advance—"

"There's no reason to—" Martin said.

"And," I said over him, "if he's a creature of habit, and 9:00 P.M. is his witching hour, in thirty minutes or so, a repeat performance could be in the offing."

Spinelli, who'd been uncharacteristically quiet, stated, "That stays in here."

"Unless he decides otherwise," I pointed out.

From the looks Spinelli and Martin exchanged, they'd already had this conversation. If another female was murdered, the public would have to be informed and the fun would begin—single women freaking out, politicians banging the drums, Feds rushing in, task forces forming, hourly press conferences, and a bunch of befuddled cops trying to look and sound confident, which is nearly always a mask for cluelessness.

Janet walked over to the desk, picked up the picture, and stud-ied it again. She asked, "How did he get into her apartment?"

Spinelli scratched his nose. "He picked her locks."

"Can you be more detailed?"

"Miss Cuthburt had two locks. He employed a special tool to get past the tumbler lock . . . a bolt cutter to get past the chain."

"Thank you." She very insightfully asked, "And how did he keep her silent?"

Martin explained, "A halter . . . like a modified dog halter with a strap for her throat and a bit that went into her mouth. The killer seems to be into bondage, humiliation, and possibly sadism." After a moment, he added, "An FBI profiler will be studying the case in the morning."

Janet threw the photo back on the desk and concluded, "You've got the worst nightmare possible."

"Why's that?" asked Spinelli. But I suspected he already knew.

"At both murder scenes he left a paucity of evidence. He wore gloves so you couldn't match his prints, indicating this was a matter of concern to him. But he knew you'd get his DNA, indicating confidence that he's not in your, or the FBI's, DNA database. Nor will he likely be found in your sex offender databases. But his fingerprints could be on file. You should think about what that means."

"Maybe he's just stupid," Spinelli replied.

"You know he's not."

"Do I?"

"Danny, the man's a planner. He studies his targets and prepares. He somehow manages to get close to them. He brings along a rape kit, all the right tools, and he knows how to use them. He's a sexual predator, but when his prey bucks his scenario, he shuts down his sexual impulses and coldly terminates the problem."

"Meaning what?"

"He's done this before. And his ability to control his urges and rages is worrisome." She observed, "You don't see many like that."

It was a very impressive display of conjecture. Both cops nodded appreciatively. I also was impressed. But I was even more mystified. In case you haven't noticed, her sister was murdered three days before, and she shows up, cool and icy calm, and insinuates herself into the investigation. Now she's professionally hypothesizing about the guy who may have brutally murdered her sister, her emotions completely in check, her brain firing on all cylinders.

Weird? Right.

But a knock on Martin's door showed three impatient detectives waiting for us to exit so they could enter. We had fulfilled our purpose, and aside from the normal troubles and nightmares the Alexandria Police Department had on its hands that chilly evening, with two women murdered by a maniac, clearly Martin and Spinelli were busy staring off the edge of a cliff.

Janet and I found our own way out, leaving Martin with Spinelli, which I regarded as less than a favor.

Outside, I asked Janet, "You eat yet?"

"No. And I'm famished." She was shivering and had her coat pulled tightly around her body. It was cold, but not that cold.

I said, "Me, too. And I know the perfect place."

In truth, Julia Cuthburt's photo had ruined my appetite. When you're in a cop station everybody's working hard to keep it light and insensitive. Part of that's just macho horseshit, but also passion and emotion cloud up logic, logic solves crimes, and there's this forced, almost competitive effort by all parties to treat the whole thing like a clinical discussion. It's all phony. Under the surface, I think we were all picturing the final hour of Julia Cuthburt's life and feeling a bit green in the gills. The killer had turned a living, breathing human being into a vulgar calling card to say, Fuck you, I'm here, I'm very good at this, and I'm not through.

So we needed to decompress and clear our minds, and I knew a great place with brick ovens, genuine pan-baked pizza pies, and a nice mix of artery-cloggers you could pile on. We both kept it light on the short drive over.

Bertolucci's, by the way, is a popular establishment, very thematic, though some of the locals seem to feel it goes a little overboard; in fact, the walls are painted with guys in funny clothes shoving around gondolas, and Venetian palaces, and spewing volcanoes, a collage of another world and another place, so wildly ridiculous that it almost works. But, like everything in the suburbs, it is part of a strip mall. Also, the waiters and waitresses speak with these goofy, half-baked Italian accents and call one another Dom This and Dom That, which adds to the hilarity because they're all local teenagers with names like O'Donnell and Smith. Only in America. But it was late and the usual family crowd had thinned out, so no line, and no squalling kids, and we ended up at a nice quiet table by the roaring fireplace.

I ordered a bottle of vino as we got settled. A kid showed up, said, "Buon giorno, signores, my name is Dom Jimmy Jones, and I'll be your sommelier and waiter this evening," uncorked our bottle, poured our glasses, and took his Disney act somewhere else. At least the pizza's real.

Janet took a few deep sips of wine, then asked me, "What do you think about Julia Cuthburt?"

"There's no dignity in death."

In a sort of rushed tone, she said, "I know this sounds odd, but maybe Lisa was lucky. If she hadn't forced his hand—"

"I know."

"I couldn't have stood it if she died like that."

"Amen."

"A bunch of strangers sitting around . . . studying her photo . . . naked . . . that way Julia Cuthburt was posed—"

"Drink some wine. Dream you're in Italy."

She drank some wine. After a moment, she asked, "Did you ever try a case like this?"

"No. Our serial killers have chests filled with ribbons and are called heroes. Some of our graduates make a big name for themselves after they leave the service, but Army life tends to discourage them from acting out their fantasies."

"But you've handled rapes, sex crimes?"

"Yes. A few."

"What about Lisa?"

"Probably. The JAG Corps likes us to be well-rounded. Great efforts are expended to round out our trial experience."

"Could she have been involved in a case with her killer?"

It was an insightful question, one I should've thought of. I replied, "I wouldn't rule it out. She couldn't have handled many violent sex crimes, because we do generalize. It shouldn't be too difficult to back-check her case records."

"That would be helpful."

"Maybe not. Even if Lisa and the killer met in connection with her legal duties, it wasn't necessarily a sex crime."

"What do you mean?"

"You're familiar with criminal profiles. Those who would commit murder and rape have a disdain for all laws. He's as apt to have been prosecuted for DUI, shoplifting, military disciplinary problems." I added, "I'll check her record on sex crimes, but don't hold false hopes."

But since she'd raised the subject, I also suggested, "You know, now that it appears Lisa's murder was at the hands of a serial killer, there's not much you and I can do."

"What do you mean?"

"You know what I mean. The customary motives of jealousy, greed, revenge, and cover-up have just been eliminated. *Why* she was killed is no longer the mystery. Catching serial killers requires strong procedural police work."

"Are you suggesting I should go home?"

"Yes. Grieve with your family. Wait for the cops to find this guy."

She stared at me for a few seconds, then said, "And if it wasn't a serial killer?"

"If it . . . Didn't I just hear you tossing theories at Martin and Spinelli about this guy?"

"What if they're wrong?"

"But you agreed with them."

"You didn't listen carefully. I neither agreed nor disagreed. I speculated."

"All right. Do you have a reason to suspect something else?"

"I'm keeping an open mind."

When I said nothing in reply, she added, "Consider the differences between Cuthburt's and Lisa's murders. Cuthburt's was inarguably a sexual assault. We're *presuming* that was the motive with Lisa. Cuthburt was attacked in her home, Lisa in a public parking lot. I could go on." She paused, and then added, "In fact, the only similarities were pieces of the victim profile and the broken neck. That could be coincidental."

She was right. But she was not convincing. I said, "I would think an assistant DA would have confidence in cops."

"Really? I thought it made us experts in their mistakes. I've lost more cases off their blunders. Also, they're human. When a live person is around every day checking on their progress, they keep the case on the front burner and pay attention to the details."

Okay, I appreciated her logic. Spend a few years as a defense attorney exploiting cop screwups, or as a prosecutor trying to wallpaper over them, and you'll be damned sure to lock your doors and sleep with a gun under your pillow. Truth and sincerity, however, are different things.

But Dom Jimmy Jones arrived with our pizza pie and the awful Italian accent he had lifted from *The Godfather* or something, and I said, "Grazie," and he looked back with a dumbfounded look until I clarified, "Thank you." Mamma mia—welcome to the suburbs.

Janet laughed and commented, "Maybe it's your pronunciation."

"No wonder I had such a lousy time in Italy. I was there with your sister, in fact."

"I don't think she ever mentioned it."

"A few years ago. We were taking statements from some soldiers who were being kept in a jail there."

"Oh, the Kosovo thing. She did tell me about that. She called right after you returned, in fact. She was smitten with you."

"Smitten?"

"It's how we say it in polite Boston society. It means—"

"I know what it means. What else did she tell you about me?"

"All of it? The good, the bad, and the ugly?"

I smiled. "I have a strong ego."

"Funny, that's the first thing she mentioned—no, she mentioned a *big* ego."

"The good, the bad, and the ugly. You start with the good."

"I did." She laughed, her first genuine laugh since we'd met. I don't mean she'd been dour or bitchy or anything—the woman could frown and look pleasant. But she'd been concealing her feelings, smothering her grief, trying to accomplish the task she'd set for herself; but you had to know things were a little brittle underneath. I was glad I'd brought her here. I was glad I was diverting her mind for the time being. I liked her laugh. I was pretty sure I liked her.

She said, "Actually, Lisa described you as this big manly hunk who snorts testosterone at breakfast . . . bullheaded . . . trouble with authority figures . . . Should I go on?"

"I thought you said she was . . . what was that word again?"

"Smitten. She was. She also said you were smart, clever, sexy, and very funny without meaning to be funny."

"What's that mean?"

"That's hard to explain." She added, "But I think I see what she means." Then she looked at me pointedly and asked, "Why didn't you ask her out?"

"A lot of reasons."

"All right. Give me one good one."

"After Bosnia, a long case in Korea, three cases in Europe, a long case that kept me in Russia, and so on. I know this is difficult to understand, but Army life's not conducive to starting relationships."

"Of course." After a moment, she said, "Have you thought of a good one yet?"

Right. I allowed a few seconds to pass, then said, "Your sister scared the hell out of me."

She put down her wineglass and studied me. "Why?"

"You know why."

"I want to hear it." But she already knew, and she chuckled. "Maybe you're not as brave as she claimed."

"I don't see any engagement rings on your finger, sister."

"I have an excuse."

"What's your excuse?"

"I'm much younger than you." She laughed. Again. She then said, "You should have asked her out. She got involved with another man. We weren't all that happy about it."

"What was his problem?"

"*Problems.* Older, married twice before . . . a charming, successful guy, just definitely not right for her. My father lost a lot of sleep over it."

Well, for some reason, perhaps guilt or perhaps a need to change the topic from the dead to the living, I asked her, "Well, what's your life story?"

She appeared amused by this question. "The same as Lisa's."

"I know you were sisters, but—"

"No, Sean. Literally almost identical. We were eleven months apart, Irish twins. Still, you'd swear we sprang from the same egg. Same height, clothing size, tastes, grades in the same courses . . . perhaps you've noticed we even sound alike? We did everything together. She was a track star, I was a track star. She went to a girls' prep, I went with her, then to UVA, then to Harvard Law."

"No kidding."

"Because I'm darker, and she was a year ahead of me, they called me her shadow. I know this sounds strange. We were sisters, but more than sisters."

"You miss her."

"He cut out my heart. It's like he killed *me.*"

I didn't respond to that, but it brought some clarity to why she was here, and the scale of her emotional stake in this case.

But recalling that the purpose of this dinner was to take our mind off more serious matters, I asked, "And did you like the same men?"

"No. Poor Lisa was always attracted to creeps and jerks." She laughed.

Interesting.

"So you never fought over boys?"

"Actually, I was seriously involved until recently."

"What happened?"

"Old story. Business mixed with pleasure, and it didn't work out."

"Another lawyer?"

"He has a law degree, but wasn't practicing. He was in the FBI. I met him on a case a few years ago, we moved in together, got engaged, and . . ." She brushed some hair off her forehead and said, "You don't want to hear about this."

"Am I getting too personal?"

"No. It's just such a common tale."

"These things are never common. What happened?"

"George was a real hotshot in the Boston Field Office. Early promotions, a drawerful of citations, a real up-and-comer. We worked a case together, some mob murders actually, that he had broken and developed. I had just moved into the felonies section, it was my first big case, I needed help, and he got me through it."

"Go on."

"I was madly in love with him. We lived together three years." She looked away and said, "I broke it off."

"Why?"

"We worked another case, and it didn't work out."

"His problem, or yours?"

She paused a moment, then said, "George was very ambitious. The more successful he became, the more ambitious he got. You know how that happens?"

"It happens to some people."

"George had been working this case for a year. He was under unbearable pressure from the mayor's office and his bosses to break it. Car theft is a major problem in Boston, everybody pays for it in high insurance rates, and the case involved a massive interstate auto theft ring. Whoever brought it down and got the convictions was going to be a hero. George somehow got to some people on the inside, treated it like a conspiracy, used one source to roll up another, and a number of the indictments landed on my desk to take to the grand jury."

I nodded but wasn't expected to comment, so I didn't.

"The ring was large, several hundred people, from street kids who collected the cars, to chop shops, to the millionaires who controlled it. A few of the defense attorneys approached me. They said George had broken the rules, and complained that the discovery elements that had been turned over to them were partial, that certain critical pieces of evidence were withheld. They were talking about witness coercion, some strong-arming, and perhaps unauthorized wiretaps. There was enough there that I went to George and asked him. He insisted they were lying. But I knew George. He was lying. The next day his office approached the DA and asked to have me removed from the case on the pretext that I hadn't shown sufficient enthusiasm and dedication."

"And your boss bought that?"

"The part he bought was that no DA is successful without the full and friendly support of your local FBI office. Also, this was your basic checkbook case. He also wanted credit for bringing down insurance rates."

"I'm sorry."

"Well, George got his grand jury indictments, his promotion, and his reassignment to FBI headquarters."

"When was this?"

"About six months ago."

"What did you say to him afterward?"

"I didn't. Oddly enough, I was still in love with him, and I wasn't sure how I'd do in a confrontation. I left him a note, moved out, and took a thirty-day vacation. When he tried calling, I hung up."

"The cathartic solution in these things is to look them in the eye and tell them to screw off."

She smiled and said, "Next time, I'll call you and ask how to handle it."

I didn't seem to be having much luck staying on cheerier topics, so I tried again. "Why didn't you follow Lisa into the JAG Corps?"

"I actually considered it. But my father's getting older, my youngest sister was just starting high school, my mother's dead . . . you understand? . . . Somebody had to stay nearby. Lisa did the heavy lifting when we grew up. It was her turn to go into the world and follow her dream."

Sometimes in the midst of a pleasant conversation, something perfectly innocuous gets said, but it isn't at all innocuous. We both, I think, experienced the same jarring, nasty realization that Lisa's dream had just ended in a nightmare. And like that, the mood was killed.

She took a few more sips of wine. I took a few more sips of wine. We avoided each other's eyes.

Then I said, "Janet, be honest. What's your interest in catching this guy?"

"As in, justice or revenge?" I nodded, and she said, "I'm a law enforcement officer. I work inside the system and believe in it, for all it's worth."

"I'm relieved to hear that. I wouldn't have it any other way."

So we'd both said the right words. Actually, for me, justice was revenge, especially if the killer got to squat on the hot seat. But I wasn't sure she wanted that same order. We returned to the task of eating our pizza, and trading small talk, but the mood was irretrievably dead, and then the tray was empty and Dom Jimmy Jones was clearing the dirty dishes, and presenting our bill.

On the way out, I said to Janet, "I'll drive you back to the hotel."

She replied, "Not yet. I thought we'd go search Lisa's apartment now."

"What?"

"It's not far. I'd like to search it now."

"I thought we agreed we're facing a serial killer."

"And I thought we agreed that's speculative. Martin and Spinelli can work that angle."

"Translate that for me."

"We've taking precautionary measures."

"Precautionary?"

"Yes. At least, somebody should consider other motives and possibilities."

This was very obtuse and I found myself wondering if Janet

Morrow knew something she hadn't yet shared, that she had some tangible reason to suspect that the facts, as we currently understood them, had a few holes.

If so, for some reason she had not shared those reasons with me. Which was odd, but I'd also spent enough time with this lady to appreciate that she played by her own rules. In short, the only way I was going to get to the bottom of this was to go along for the ride, which brought to mind that ancient warning—curiosity killed the cat.

But I'm a dog person. Surely I was safe.

CHAPTER FIFTEEN

SPEAKING OF CATS, THE MANAGER OF LISA'S APARTMENT COMPLEX WAS actually named Felix. Lisa had lived in a pleasant yet sprawling maze of cookie-cutter townhouses in Alexandria, a few turns after the Duke Street exit off I-395. The complex appeared modern, perhaps fifteen years old, was spacious, clean, and well-tended; a nice starter village for upwardly mobile professionals. There were plentiful Saabs and Volvos, and also trees, shrubs, and flower beds, and had it not been December, the place would've been bursting with manicured prettiness and gleeful yuppies flipping burgers on backyard grills.

After I showed my military orders appointing me as survival assistance officer, and Janet flashed the ID that verified she was the victim's sister, Felix, who seemed friendly enough, agreed to let us into her apartment. Felix, incidentally, was built like an old spark plug, and had the appearance of a former fighter, with the shambling, disjointed movements of a guy who got better than he gave.

We walked a few yards with Felix in the direction of Lisa's

townhouse before he said to Janet, "Listen, yer sister, she was somethin' special. A real sweetie, that one."

Janet replied, "Thank you."

He seemed uncomfortable. "I, uh, well, we were pals."

"Oh . . . I didn't know. We didn't know a lot about her life down here. She usually traveled up to see us."

"Yeah, I know that. I always kept an eye on the place when she left." After a moment, he added, "Everybody 'round here liked her, y'know. Real popular, that girl." After another moment, he asked, "Hey, there gonna be a funeral?"

"Yes. We just haven't decided where yet."

"Keep me in mind, would ya?"

"I will, Felix."

We walked on in silence for a while. He finally said, "She used to have me over for barbecues, when the weather was decent. Most folks here . . . I hear from 'em when they got complaints, y'know. Always appreciated that about Lisa. She was real special."

Janet smiled warmly. "You must've been very special to her, too."

He grinned, stared down at his big feet, and led us up the path to her townhouse door. He dug a ring of keys out of his pocket, studied them, then selected one. He stuck it in the keyhole and tried turning it. Nothing.

He bent over and studied the key. "I don't get it. It's the right key."

I suggested, "Maybe she changed her lock."

He shook his head. "I used it to get in, y'know, the day she died, to shut off the heat and gas, so the bill don't run up."

He reached down to his toolman belt, withdrew a flashlight from a loop, flipped it on, and directed the beam through a side window. He stuck his face to the pane of glass and then muttered, "Ah, Christ . . . would ya look at that."

I peeked over his shoulder. Coats were littered on the floor, some chairs tipped over, and I remarked, "I take it this wasn't like that when you went in?"

"Lisa kept the place real neat. Good tenant that way."

My question had obviously been misconstrued, but his reply placed the timing of the break-in somewhere between the day of Lisa's death and this moment.

I asked him, "Can you replace windows?"

"I'll do it," he insisted, "No charge to you."

He pulled a wrench off his toolman belt, crashed it into the living room window, then swung it around, enlarging the hole, proving himself to be a man of deed and little thought. A line of smaller windows was beside the door; knock in one of them, reach through, unlock the door, and voilà. He climbed over the sill and worked his way to the front door, unlocked it, and allowed us to enter. Janet flipped the light switch that illuminated the hallway. Felix flipped the switch for the living room and kitchen.

The sight was a combination of mayhem and efficiency. Janet wandered around, stepping over broken pictures and toppled furniture.

I said, "What were they looking for?"

Janet said, "I . . . oh my God . . . let's check Lisa's bedroom."

We rushed down a short hallway to the bedroom at the end. As with the rest of the apartment, it had been violently tossed. The mattress had been yanked off the bed, a bookshelf flung over, pictures torn off the walls. A jewelry box lay on the floor. I used a foot to flip it on its side—empty.

"Don't worry about that There should've been a computer in here," said Janet, pointing at a small desk in the corner.

We returned to the living room. I asked, "Did Lisa have a stereo, a television, a microwave?"

"Of course."

"They're all gone." My eyes caught on a family photo of Lisa, her father, and her sisters; the same one I'd seen in her father's home, the five of them laughing and sailing, their hair whipped by the wind. The picture lay on the floor, covered by shards of broken glass. Janet caught my eye and noticed it also. We both froze for a moment.

I suggested to Janet, "Lisa's address is in the phone book. Her murder was announced on the news. There are thieves who listen for those kinds of things."

"Or maybe it was arranged to appear that way."

"Maybe." She looked at me and I asked, "Do you have reason to suspect that?"

She didn't reply.

Felix was shuffling his feet. He said to Janet, "I'm real sorry. Shoulda kept an eye on the place."

I said, "Happens all the time, Felix. Nothing you could do."

He shuffled his feet some more, but did not appear mollified.

Janet wandered around a minute more, then faced us and said, "I'd like you two to leave me alone for a minute."

"I don't think that's a good idea," I replied. "This is a crime scene."

"It's my sister's apartment, for Godsakes."

"*And* a crime scene. You shouldn't touch anything, and we should call the police."

"Spare me the lecture. I just . . . She was my sister. These are her things, all I have left to remember her by. Please . . . a moment of privacy?"

So, what do I say? Look, I suspect you're up to something, and I'd like to know what it is, but if I step outside I'll lose that chance? But one has to know it's time to retreat.

I looked at Felix, and he looked at me, and then the two of us were outside. We contemplated the sky awhile. I finally asked, "You were a boxer?"

"Long time ago. Used to be pretty good, too."

"Fight anybody I ever heard of?"

"Not that good."

I shrugged. "Miss it?"

"Nah. Like I said, I wasn't never that good. Took some awful beatings near the end." He pondered the pavement and asked me, "You, uh, you were pals with Lisa?"

"Good pals."

"Uh-huh. She was special, y'know?"

"I know." When you have extended discussions with former boxers, go with the flow. Too many hard shots in the noggin get the circuits a little scrambled.

That was his excuse.

My dog ate my excuse.

"She did me favors," Felix informed me. "She was a lawyer, y'know."

"Yeah, I went against her a few times. Those were my bad beatings." He chuckled.

After a moment, I asked him, "What kinds of favors, Felix?"

"Legal things. I don't read so good. My eyes . . . I probably got hit hard too many times. She filed some papers with the VA so I could get medical benefits . . . invested some cash for me. I don't got much, only she made sure it was safe. Never was too good about those things."

"You're a vet?"

"Yeah. Korean War."

I dug into my pocket and withdrew a business card. "I'm a lawyer, too. You need anything, I'm available."

"Appreciate that." He stuffed the card in a pocket.

We stared at the sky awhile longer. The night was clear, the normal fumes and pollution banished by a cold snap. Bright stars, a chalk white half-moon, a full and unencumbered view of a spectacular universe. Yet I think Felix and I felt a common twinge of guilt, even remorse, relaxing in front of Lisa's townhouse, stargazing, while her body was reposing in a morgue.

Janet finally emerged, eyes red and puffy, as though she'd been crying. We walked back to the management office. None of us said anything.

But Janet remarked to Felix as we got in the car, "Don't call the police until we tell you to." She placed a hand on his arm. "Can you do that?"

"I gotta repair that window."

"Please do. But nothing to the police yet, okay?"

"Uh . . . okay."

Anyway, Felix dug my card out of his pocket and peered at it, until I recalled that he couldn't read. I said to him, "My name's Sean Drummond. I'll call in a few days, okay?"

"Uh, okay."

We departed. Possibly it was, as I mentioned to Janet, a case of bottom-feeding crooks tossing the home of a deceased person. The world is filled with foul sorts who profit in the misery of others. Or possibly the robbers were hopheads who trashed the place in a dope-induced frenzy.

A more dubious mind, however, might suspect that the chaotic tossing was in the nature of a ruse to disguise a more calculated and painstaking search of Lisa's belongings. But why the sheer disorder and destruction? Far safer to put everything back in place, neat and tidy, exactly as Lisa Morrow lived her life, right?

Unless.

Unless something needed to be taken away, something that had to be studied, something that had to be examined in privacy. Lisa's personal computer, for example. Army lawyers are notoriously overworked, and Lisa probably brought work home, and she would've been careful to have all the modern software protections, like a password entry that would require time and a skilled nerd to get past. Under that scenario, the TV, microwave, jewelry, and so forth were lifted to disguise the true purpose of the break-in.

The law breeds lawyers to respect facts and exercise skepticism about conjecture, hunches, and so forth. A leads to B, which leads to C, but A doesn't leap to Z. And I might have considered it far-fetched had Janet not just persuaded Felix to withhold reporting the robbery. A to Z, right? She had just involved Felix in a crime, not to mention me, and, incidentally, herself.

So we sat together in my elegant leased Jaguar, her having certain suspicions, and me entertaining certain suspicions, neither of us sharing, so to speak. I didn't like this silly game, but I was forced to play along—for the time being.

But Janet Morrow struck me as smarter than this. When we walked through that apartment, she had bypassed the other thefts and damage, headed straight for the bedroom, and noted only that the computer was stolen. Arbitrary? I think not. Dropping breadcrumbs for clueless Sean Drummond? Possibly.

But if Lisa had been murdered by a garden-variety serial killer, why would he break into her apartment and steal her things? Trophies? Or did someone else do the theft? Was there a relationship to her murder? I was getting a headache.

Also, I was getting a better bead on Miss Janet Morrow. That ladylike exterior, those lovely Boston manners, and those oh so properly reasoned responses concealed a truly conniving mind. Her sister Lisa once informed me that my approach to life was bullheaded. I took it as a compliment, though I'm not sure it was intended as such. Janet Morrow was a spider, building a web, and slyly collecting the men and pieces she felt she needed to solve this crime.

But another thought struck me. I had thought I knew Lisa fairly well. We had worked together for long days and nights on an investigation that was dangerous, tense, and in the end forced us both to search deeply into our souls about who we were and what we believed. I had seen her in court and around the office countless times, flirted with her intermittently for two years, and yet, I was quickly realizing, I had only scratched the surface.

Since her death, I had met her family, learned she had the big-time hots for me, that she was planning on leaving the Army to join a civilian firm, and that she was the type to take a duckling with broken wings under her care.

I was falling in love with Lisa Morrow, after the fact.

CHAPTER SIXTEEN

ON MY DESK THE NEXT MORNING WAS A MESSAGE FROM BARRY INFORMING me of a ten o'clock meeting in his office. Also a long manila envelope, containing an aerial photo of a few tiny specks in the middle of a big, blue ocean. A sidebar note said, "Johnston Island Atoll, look it up on the Internet: Behave. Clapper."

Has that guy got a sense of humor or what? Actually he doesn't, so I looked it up on the Internet. Average population around 100, all but a tiny handful being civilian contractors who rotate through on two- or three-day stints. The atoll contained a facility for the destruction of chemical weapons, a process with so many safeguards and catch-alls that the Army guaranteed it to be, like 99.999 percent accident-proof. That other .001 was, I presumed, why it wasn't next to New York City. After the last chemical weapon was destroyed, the article continued, the atoll was slated to become a bird sanctuary for whatever kind of idiot bird wanted a perch on the highly prestigious endangered species list.

Clapper can be very annoying.

However, that reminded me, and I called his office and asked his executive assistant to run down Lisa's previous assignments and task her former offices to conduct a file search for all sex cases she had handled or been involved with. I implied I was doing this at the behest of the Army's Criminal Investigation Division.

What was interesting was that the executive assistant did not say he had already received such a request—ten demerits for Spinelli.

As it was, I was fairly certain the whole drill was a complete waste of time. But in murder investigations the most unlikely routes sometimes turn out to be the path to a killer.

Speaking of a waste of time, the Pentagon naturally has a manual that details its procurement and protest procedures, and I spent the three hours before Barry's meeting reading it cover-to-cover. I was a little tired of Mr. Bosworth rubbing my nose in shit, and if you want to beat the home team on their own turf, you have to work at it a little.

I entered Barry's office at ten on the dot, and he looked up and said, "Well, well . . . look who's *finally* shown up."

What the . . . ? Four people were already seated around his conference table, jackets on the backs of chairs, empty coffee cups and water bottles strewn about.

Of all the lousy, crappy stunts—the little prick had purposely given me the wrong time. I don't mind looking like an idiot, but I prefer to do it on my own terms,

I smiled and said to the group, "Okay, this guy walks into a bar and takes a stool next to a beautiful woman. He orders a drink, and pretty soon the woman leans over and whispers into his ear, 'Hey, you big stud, I'll screw you anywhere, anytime, any way you wish.' He ponders her offer, then turns to her and replies, 'I'm sorry, what law firm did you say you were from?' "

Barry and Sally nearly vomited. The other two laughed so hard they nearly cried. Boy, I'm good at this game. I'd already identified the other two—clients.

The large woman at the end of the table said, "I'm Jessica Moner from Morris Networks legal. You've gotta be Drummond."

"I've gotta be." Regarding Miss Jessica Moner: mid-fortyish, platinum hair with brown roots, and fleshy, not really attractive features, made less attractive by a few gallons of rouge and this really tacky, orangey lipstick. Also, she was stuffed into a blue business suit that was either three sizes too small or she was a blowfish imitating a human. Given Morris's fetish for the babes, I was a little mystified about where Miss Moner sat in his harem. But perhaps she was hired for her competence. What a novel concept.

Anyway, she pointed at the guy beside her and said, "Marshall Wyatt, from corporate accounting." Marshall was skinny to the point of cadaverous, balding, wore a cheap gray pinstripe suit, an unpressed white shirt, and, as you might expect, peeking out of his pocket was a pencil holder. Really, not in a million years would I have guessed he was an accountant.

Anyway, I sat and informed them, "Sorry I'm late, but Barry begged me to come a little after the meeting started so he can look like the smartest guy in the room for at least a few minutes."

Even Sally chuckled. Barry, however, chose to turn slightly pink and reply, "Since you've already missed an hour's worth of discussion, Drummond, we're not going to rehash it for you."

Boy, Barry really knew how to punish a guy. Better yet, as time literally was our client's money, they did not object, so he picked up where he had apparently left off, saying to them, "The point is, Cy will work the military appropriations committees on the Hill. Believe me, Jessica, you couldn't find better. He used to sit on that committee and—"

"We know what Cy can accomplish, Bosworth," Jessica informed him. "We came to your firm for his grease. That's just not where we see the goddamn problem."

"Where do you see the problem?" I asked.

"Your guys." She was looking at me, I think.

"My guys?"

"Yeah." She explained, "When it comes to Congress, it's about who hires the biggest guns. Had Cy kept his dick in his pants, he'd still be running the place. A hundred guys up there still rush in to kiss his ass every time he shows up. Don't take this personally, Drummond, it's your fucking Pentagon giving us gas."

I actually like women who don't play games and lay it on the line. Also she obviously disliked Barry, so I was half in love already. I said to her, "Explain that."

"Clearly, we won the contract on merit. But protests change the rules."

"How?"

"Now it's a matter of who can reach under the table and squeeze the hardest."

"It's crooked?"

"Not crooked. Bendable. Susceptible."

"How?"

"Because this charge about Danny Nash can cause a shitstorm. The Pentagon doesn't want the appearance of a problem. Pretty soon, Congress starts talking about investigations and everybody's screwed."

I said, "So the issue is how to shape our response so it does not appear there was any dirty dealing?"

"You think that's easy? The press, the public, everybody believes the game is rigged anyway. This just feeds a preconception. Sprint and AT&T knew what they were doing."

Barry nodded as though he shared that thought, and then he asked, "Does anybody have any ideas how to handle that?"

"I do," I replied. In response to their astonished looks, I said, "Ignore it."

Now everybody looked like I just farted. Everybody but Marshall that is, who had whipped out a pocket calculator and was vigorously punching in numbers, trying to ignore *us*.

Barry commented, "That's the stupidest thing I ever heard."

Sally added, "That won't work."

Jessica said, "I'll assume you're not a fucking moron and ask you to explain that."

So I asked them, "Did AT&T or Sprint mention Nash in their protests? Specifically, *him?*"

Barry replied, "Perhaps it was too subtle for you, Drummond, but it was very strongly implied."

"To who?"

"You mean whom," Sally said, contributing hugely to the issue.

"Oh . . ." Jessica muttered.

I explained, "John Q. Public hasn't got the slightest idea Nash is on the board. We should not define their charge of impropriety and eliminate their risks."

Sally asked, "What risks?"

Obviously the quick study of the group, Jessica replied, "You're right, Drummond. They could step into a big pile of legal shit."

Sally, appearing even more confused, asked, "What pile?"

I said, "Ask yourself why they didn't specify Nash's name."

Jessica explained to Barry and Sally, "They're worried about slander, leading to libel."

I added, "Further implying a lack of substantiation. They're praying we'll respond with a specific defense. If we raise Nash's name, *we* make him the topic of discussion, which frees them to publicly trash him."

Barry, nodding his head also, commented, "Exactly what I was thinking."

Jessica ignored the idiot and said to me, "But in one way or another it's bound to come up."

"Probably. Force them to do it. If they overstep, slap an injunction on their asses for slander. That'll force them to disclose how little or how much they know."

Jessica pondered this advice for a moment, then said, "Drummond, you're good."

Barry said, "That's why you come to this firm, Jessica. We know how to tackle the hard ones."

I think this meant I was becoming part of the team. I actually thought about reaching over and exchanging high fives with Barry. I felt really bad about wanting to strangle him.

Barry then said to Jessica, "Last issue—the resubmission of

your financials. We'll just send the old one and the problem's settled."

Unfortunately, the word "financial" prompted Marshall to glance up from his calculator and mutter, "Nope."

"What?" Barry replied.

"Won't work. The original was based on an in-house audit."

"So what?"

"Before the Pentagon awards a multiyear contract like this, it's required to ensure that the winner possesses the financial fundamentals to stay in business long enough to perform the work. Now that it's been challenged, we have to produce a much more in-depth audit and cash flow analysis . . ." and so forth, and so on.

I was stretching and yawning, and in fact, my forehead was slamming off the table as Marshall began discussing EBIDTA and amortization and a host of other appalling issues. Well, this went on awhile, and all four lawyers began dozing off.

Suddenly, Marshall was loudly asking, "Excuse me . . . excuse me . . . once again . . . are there any questions?"

Well, there were a few nervous coughs and we all four exchanged wary glances. This could be fatal.

I finally said, "In shorthand, Marshall, this means, what?"

"Well, based on—"

"In English."

He studied our three faces and, I think, grasped the risks. Another word of that financial mumbo-jumbo and we'd rip his lips off. He said, "Uh . . . well, an external audit."

"Please explain that."

"Yes, I'm afraid so. An outside accounting firm needs to confirm that we're profitable and likely to remain that way for the foreseeable future."

Barry asked him, "And how long will that take?"

"Well, you know, we were expecting this, and therefore have everything organized for a speedy audit. Assuming we get—"

"How long?" I asked menacingly.

"Uh . . . perhaps two weeks."

Barry said, "Next week at the latest."

"Oh my. I . . . well, I don't think that will be . . ." He fingered his calculator, then suggested, "Maybe, if we double the number of auditors and work twenty-four/seven. Then . . . maybe . . . I don't know, maybe ten days."

Barry said, "Drummond, you're in charge of the audit. You get seven days."

"What?"

He said, "Sally and I will handle this matter about Nash."

"No. For one thing, I am legally incompetent to handle an audit. Second, I'm going to remain that way."

Sally said, "Neither you, nor we, have a choice. It's the only thing you can work on that's not a conflict of interest."

Jessica, smiling, said, "Don't be such a pussy, Drummond. The real work's done by the green eyeshades. If a legal issue arises that's beyond your competence, refer it to Barry."

Boy, it sure looked like I missed a major agreement being late.

Barry gave me a nice screw-you smile and said, "Sink or swim around here, Drummond. This is the big leagues. But if you're scared, I'll find another junior associate to handle it."

No smart lawyer accepts a task that exceeds his legal competence. Nor did I have the slightest doubt *why* Barry wanted to stuff this audit down my throat. But the proper response was both obvious and irrefutable. Ignore his infantile goading, and tell him to stuff this job.

So I got up, grabbed my legal pad, looked them all dead in the eye and said, "Sure, no problem."

CHAPTER SEVENTEEN

*H*e had watched with amused detachment the news coverage of *his murders. Two brief articles on page 3 of the metro section of the* Post, *and a couple of oddly casual mentions by the local TV stations was all.*

The police were working overtime to avoid a frenzy. They had withheld the connection between his murders, not to mention a few very glaring and meaningful details. This amused him more than anything.

They were hoping he'd fled, or had fed his craving and stopped. They were telling themselves that staying mum about those details was in the best public interest—the only responsible thing to do, really. Getting the locals all worked up would serve no good purpose. Besides, release everything, every last dirty detail, and the copycatters would make careful notes and regard it as an invitation for a free-for-all. Bodies would start popping up all over, and after exposing all the trademark secrets you can't tell the real deals from the fakers. Couldn't have that, they were persuading themselves.

Truth was, they'd invent all sorts of silly excuses and theories, and hang with them as long as circumstances permitted. Human nature and bureaucratic instinct was what it was.

Their luck was about to crash. He assumed they'd already formed a task force to dissect his methods and catch him. They always do. As yet, the cell would be small, a group of local flatfoots scrumming and doing their best, though their expertise in such matters was pathetically limited. They'd likely made a few phone calls to the FBI but weren't yet on their knees begging for help. Nor were they getting much, he guessed.

Odd how it always took the third. The first nearly always was regarded as an everyday thing or an aberration unlikely to be repeated. Too bad, tragic and all that, but hey, shit happens. Standing over that second corpse, they stroked their chins a bit more doggedly and gave consideration to going frantic, but somehow they always reined back the urge. Three just was the golden number that kicked the scaffold from under their feet.

And what a memorable third she'd be. By afternoon, the local cops would feel hopelessly out of their depth and like all mortals would turn to a higher authority, for guidance, for expertise, for someone else to share the blame. The calls would be frenzied and the Fibbies would start crawling over everything. Their Director lived here. He likely got the Washington Post *delivered to his house each and every morning. Right there, on his front doorstep, before he even had that first sip from his morning coffee, it would be rubbed in his nose—a sexually perverted murdering maniac was performing his filthy deeds in his backyard. His wife and kids would see it on TV, for Godsakes.*

Truth was, the sooner the FBI got into this thing the better. According to his script their time had come.

Carolyn Fiorio—she'd bring them, stampeding and tripping all over themselves. She would remove any last vestige of doubt that a depraved monster was tormenting Washington.

At that very moment, in fact, he was admiring her cool poise on the tiny TV screen in the back of the big stretch limo. The death sentence was the issue and the debate was passionate and fierce. Only twenty-nine years old, and there she sat with two silver-tongued senators and a fat, tart-mouthed Republican tout, holding her own quite nicely.

The fat Republican was rude and obnoxious, an advocate who interrupted frequently and howled every point. One of the senators, another dyed-in-the-wool advocate, kept trying to exploit his age and prestigious title to condescend to Carolyn, a slyer but similarly poisonous form of rudeness. The other senator was a fence-sitter, too weaselly to take a stand, his head and eyes swiveling back and forth, leaving Carolyn to tote the position of opposition on her own. No problem—she required no help, as best he could tell.

She was lovely and angelic-looking, and the ruder the Republican tout got, the better she looked. Hers was the power of contrast, and every time he got to loudly spouting his crap, the camera veered between them, making him appear somehow fatter, and meaner, and his position became not the one you'd want to associate with. Every time the condescending senator said "Wellll, miss," in that languorous way he did, she peered into the camera, and somehow, the audience couldn't help but see him for a pompous, bullying idiot.

She was cunning and her opponents paid savagely for underrating her. CNN tossed her six million big ones a year to orchestrate the most watched talk show on TV, the liberals' version of that O'Reilly Factor, *and she was worth every penny. She banged the Nielsen ratings right out of the park and advertisers lined up and threw in the big dough. She was bunnylike perky, had a fly-trap mind, and murdered her guests with a patina of innocence assassins would die for.*

America's Girl, they called her on the ads. Newsweek, TIME, People, *and an assortment of lesser rags had splashed her on their covers, the smart girl everybody just loved to love. She had come out of nowhere and taken the journalistic world by storm. She was some phenomenon, that girl.*

He watched her close the show, turning to the camera with those pleading blue eyes and a rueful smile. "The issue is the death sentence. Is it right for a civilized nation to kill as revenge? Remember, when that executioner pulls the lever that sends fifty thousand volts coursing through another human being, he represents you and me. If what he does is wrong, aren't we all guilty?"

He shook his head, reached forward, and shut off the five-inch screen. Oh yeah, she was good—had the golden touch, that girl. He lifted the black hat off the seat beside him, shoved it over his wig, and climbed out of the backseat. Two minutes later, he was standing attentively in a pitch-dark suit beside the long black car outside the studio.

Carolyn Fiorio was being honored as Newsperson of the Year at a big, fancy dinner at the National Press Club. The royalty of American journalism had flown in from far and wide for the big bash, to bask in the glow of her lovable glory. Her show ended at 7:00, and the dinner kicked off at 7:15, so she frantically dodged out the studio entrance and jogged straight toward the rear door of the shiny black stretch limo.

He held open the door and very politely said, "Evening, Miss Fiorio. Fine show this evening."

"Thanks," she murmured and climbed inside. Never gave him a second look. None of them ever did. The limo came from a service that shuttled lookalike cars and anonymous drivers to rich customers throughout the city.

He gently shut the door, admired his own reflection in the blackened windows, then walked swiftly around and got into the driver's seat, turned the ignition key, and pulled smoothly away from the curb. Miguel Martinez, the service driver, was stuffed on the floor by his feet, a bullet hole in his forehead.

He briefly glanced back and said, "National Press Club, right, miss?"

"That's right. And I really need to be there in ten minutes."

He chuckled. "So I gotta hurry, huh?"

"Yes, I'd appreciate it." She dug into her purse and began pulling things out. "There's a welcoming party, and some camera crews waiting for my entrance."

He allowed a respectable minute to pass before he said over his right shoulder, "Tough life you got."

Her laugh sounded more melodic than on TV. "I'm sitting in the back of a big stretch limo, raking in a fortune, and you think my life's tough?"

"Yeah. Guess you're right."

He allowed another moment of silence to pass, one of those perfectly natural pauses between the hired help and the fat wallet in the backseat.

He said, "I, uh, I watched your show on the TV back there while I was waitin'."

An alcohol pad was pinched between her fingers and she was furiously scrubbing off the thick studio makeup. She glanced up at him briefly, then returned to staring into the small mirror gripped in her other hand.

He said, "You really believe that? 'Bout the death sentence being immoral and all that?"

"Yes, I do. I never take a stance I don't believe in."

"Reason I asked is, I like the death sentence."

"A lot of people do. That's why it's law."

"I guess." He adjusted his rearview mirror and studied her. "But see, I come at it different from you."

She was applying liner around her eyes and still focusing on the mirror. "How's that?"

"Figure it this way. Say you got caught doin' somethin' real bad and they give you a choice—life or the death sentence. What would you pick?"

"Life," she answered.

"Too quick, Miss Fiorio. Some things are worse than death."

"Like what?" she asked, not really focused on the conversation, painting her face and going through the motions of accommodating an overly opinionated and talkative driver. She

was paid the big bucks to debate these things with big-time pros on the tube and wasn't all that enthused about giving freebies to rookies.

"Well, like bein' in a cage where your only company for the rest of your life is a buncha murderers, crooks, and street scum. You read these books . . . Christ, the things some of them criminals do behind those bars." He glanced into the rearview mirror again. "Sickening stuff, you know? A painless death's gotta be better'n that, ain't it?"

"I don't look at it from the criminal's perspective," she replied, swiping a tube of cherry-red lipstick across her lips.

"Well maybe you should."

"No. They're responsible for their actions, and I'm responsible for mine. If I support the death penalty, then I bear the burden of guilt."

"Yeah," he replied. "Heard you say that at the closing. Real eloquent."

Another long pause, then he said, "Thing is, you ever get to thinking there might be some people that just are addicted to killing? I mean, like, it's what they do. Over and over. Only way to stop 'em is to kill 'em."

"You mean sociopathic individuals?"

"Well, I don't know the right educated word for it, but I guess, yeah."

"They're mentally disturbed. They should be treated, not killed."

She had obviously been through these points before and had a glib response to every twist and angle. Like on the tube, there wasn't the slightest glimmer of self-doubt when she spoke.

She had finished applying her makeup, and was studying her handiwork in the tiny mirror, oblivious to the fact that they were now twenty blocks away from the National Press Club. Or that the limo had just entered a section of D.C. that big shiny cars without drug dealers and pimps behind the steering wheels don't often visit.

Other parts of the town were experiencing the final squirts of rush-hour traffic. This part of the city, few people had jobs, at least taxpaying jobs, and traffic was consequently sparse. A few kids were hanging out by corner bodegas, swigging bottles of Colt 45 and looking to score a few joints, though most folks were huddled in front of the TVs in their homes, wisely staying off the dangerous streets.

He said, "You know, I bet if I had like, say, two hours with you, I bet I could change your mind. I bet I could have you believin' with your heart 'n' soul in the death sentence."

"No way." She chuckled. "My view is rock-hard."

He took a sudden left and carefully maneuvered the limo into the very narrow alley he had scoped out three days before. He shifted into neutral, spun around, and began climbing over the seat. She looked up in surprise, dropped her mirror, then sat stunned and frozen for a moment, saying, "Hey, what the—" then she saw the expression on his face. She tried desperately to open her door, only to discover that the alley walls were too close.

CHAPTER EIGHTEEN

IT WAS 11:30 A.M., MY FIRST DAY, WHEN THE GODS SENT A MESSENGER TO save my ass. The headquarters of Morris Networks, incidentally, is situated in a tower that resembles a thirty-story scotch bottle, one block off Route 123 in a Virginia suburb known as Tysons Corner.

Some thirty years ago, a gang of farsighted investors built a big shopping mall on this spot because it was twelve miles from the city, all farmland, and the acreage was cheap. A few years later, a few business towers went up beside that mall, then a second mall, then hotels, and more glass towers shot up, and pretty soon everybody went berserk, and what began as a mall turned into a full-fledged city with every urban inconvenience that a stunning lack of planning and idiotic growth can bring. It was a real nice place when it was farm country.

Anyway, I was trapped inside a huge conference room at a long table crowded with geeks and geekesses who mostly wore thick glasses and spoke in some strange foreign tongue. They were all fiercely pounding keys on calculators, tossing spreadsheets around like confetti, chattering about write-downs and hedged sales and amortizing assets, and if I had had a gun I would've popped every last one of them.

If I had only one bullet, I would've shot myself.

The door swung open and a young lady stepped inside, smiled brightly, and said, "Could somebody please help me? I'm looking for Sean Drummond."

I actually felt a little insulted that she had to ask. But somebody pointed a finger at the miserable idiot seated in the corner with his right finger pointed at his forehead, practicing Russian roulette.

Regarding her, she was around twenty-five, blond, blue-eyed, in fact was so absurdly perfect, I wondered if she breathed.

She and I stepped out into the hallway, and she held out her hand. "I'm Tiffany Allison, Jason's executive assistant."

"Right. And I'm Sean Drummond."

She smiled. "Yes, I guessed that. Jason was wondering if you had time to join him for lunch."

Her hair and eyes I already covered; she was about my height, dark blue business suit, tight at the hips, tight at the bust, and I was sure she was on page 33 of the most recent Victoria's Secret catalog. So the rest of her was coming back to me . . .

"Major Drummond?"

"What?"

"Lunch?"

"Uh . . . sure."

"Good. Then let me show you the way."

As we walked, I asked, "What's the occasion?"

"Occasion?" She rolled her eyes. "Oh . . . you mean, why does Jason wish to dine with you?"

"Exactly."

"He mentioned that he met you at his Florida home. You made a good impression."

I recalled that I had made anything but a good impression, and replied, "No kidding?"

"Oh, he was quite impressed with you. He called you a straight shooter. Jason places a high premium on honesty and character."

"I see." Actually, I didn't see. But I was determined to be congenial, because I wanted Miss Allison to see I was a perfect gentleman.

She said, "It's only three floors to Jason's office. Would you prefer the stairs or the elevator?"

"Stairs. Keeps you fit, right?"

"I prefer stairs, too." She smiled.

So I opened the door and, being a gentleman, said, "After you." I prefer elevators actually. But I really wanted to check out her butt, and that's hard to do in an elevator.

Over her shoulder, she said, " 'Refreshing' was the word Jason used to describe you." She paused before she confided, "Allow me to let you in on a secret. The bane of Jason's existence is that people are always telling him what they think he wants to hear."

"You mean kissing his ass because he's worth three or four billion dollars?"

"That's a way of putting it, yes." In addition to her more apparent perfections, Tiffany appeared to be highly educated, had great elocution and diction, was impressively well-mannered and -behaved. She was like the human version of a French poodle. Her butt, incidentally, was definitely worth three flights of stairs. She added, "The truth is, Jason Morris is a very normal guy. People don't think of a billionaire being just a regular Joe, but he is."

"Boy, life's really unfair, isn't it?" I shook my head and she shook her head. I said, "Hey, what's Jason's favorite football team?"

"I . . . well, I'm not sure he has . . . Actually, Jason doesn't watch sports on TV."

"His favorite beer?"

"Jason's quite health conscious and abstains from beer." She peered back over her shoulder and said, "But if you're implying he's a stuffed shirt, he's not."

"No?"

"He is actually a fairly well-known wine aficionado. *Wine and Cheese* magazine did a recent spread on his collection . . . Perhaps you saw it?"

"No. But thanks for reminding me to renew my subscription."

She was shaking her head and chuckling as we left the stairwell and crossed a hallway. Then we were passing through a complex with seven or eight desks manned by secretaries, most of whom had two or three computer screens positioned in front of them, and all of whom were talking into phones or furiously tapping on keyboards. One couldn't help but be astonished by any guy who kept a whole squad of secretaries and twenty or thirty computers busy. I have one legal assistant, and she spends half her time chatting on the phone with her buddies. I haven't got a clue what she does the rest of the time.

We walked down a short hall that led to a pair of shiny black doors. Tiffany shoved them open and shoved me inside.

The room was mammoth. Jason Morris was seated at the far, far end behind a huge, huge circular white desk. Ten computer monitors cluttered the surface. He glanced in my direction, shot a finger in the air, then went back to typing and talking at a staccato pace into a speakerphone, saying something about derivatives being overpriced, market curves being off, and so forth. I got dizzy watching him. Everything in the room was high tech. The chairs looked like carved bowls. The three or four large paintings hung on the walls looked like an elephant puked colors on a canvas. The carpet was striped black and white in a swirling pattern, matching the colors of the furniture, like some monster zebra crawled in here and died.

My personal tastes run toward the traditional, but the room made a statement in a sort of hyper-modernist way that I guess was appropriate for a leading-edge company. Jason hung up and popped out from around his desk. He wore jeans and a sweater over a white undershirt. I wore my brand-new navy blue Brooks Brothers suit. I felt like an idiot. Again.

"Sean, good to see you again," he said, thrusting out a hand. "I'm glad you could cut loose and join me."

"Well, it was a tough choice. I was really anticipating another box lunch with a roomful of accountants."

"Really?

"They promised we could discuss debentures and currency in-dexing."

He laughed. "Rough down there, huh?"

"They're leaving no number unturned."

Even as we were chatting he was swiftly guiding me toward a glass table at the other end of the room. In fact, my ass was just hit-ting the seat when the black doors blew open and two waiters raced in shoving a cart. Amazing.

Jason said to me, "I hope you don't mind, I ordered for you. You strike me as a meat-and-potatoes guy."

I wasn't sure how to take that.

Anyway, we sat and studied each other as the waiters swiftly threw down placemats and silverware and dishes and condiments. It struck me that Jason was a time freak; one of those guys born with an amphetamine stuffed up his ass. It further struck me I wasn't really here because Jason thought I was a jolly good fellow he wanted to get to know better. His notion of deep, long-lasting friendships was probably an exchange of business cards.

Before the waiters could even back away from the table, Jason was cutting up his meat. Chop, chop, like in one of those Japanese steak houses. Incredible.

He glanced up and said, "I like your idea for dealing with this Nash thing, incidentally. It'll drive Sprint and AT&T nuts."

"Let's hope."

"Let's do. A lot's riding on it." He pointed his fork at me and added, "Funny that nobody else thought of it. Must be your back-ground in criminal law."

"How's that?"

"Make the prosecutor prove everything . . . isn't that how you guys think?"

"Sometimes . . . unless you suspect he can."

He regarded me a moment and then chuckled. He said, "Nash was completely out of the picture. But you can't prove a negative, right?" Before I could respond to that, he added, "Actually I didn't ask you up here to talk about Nash."

"Then what are we here to discuss?"

"You." He paused a moment, then said, "You impress me."

"Then I wish you'd put a word in with my boss. He hates me."

He chuckled again. "I'll do better."

"How's that?"

He stuffed two slices of steak between his lips and I've seen pythons chew longer. He said, "We'd like you to consider joining us."

"Us?"

"Us . . . Morris Networks. Jessica's been looking for a hotshot attorney for a year. She thinks you're perfect."

"Go on."

"It's simple. Jessica has never been completely satisfied with your firm. They do some things well, but she thinks their lack of criminal experience makes them myopic."

"If you live in the tropics, don't buy winter coats. What makes you think you need a criminal lawyer?"

He put down his knife and fork. His plate was completely empty. I was chewing my third bite.

He said, "Isn't it true criminal lawyers have a different mind-set?"

"I suppose."

Before he could say another word the black doors blew open and a waiter raced in, shoving another cart. A huge chocolate cake was on top.

Jason pointed at the cake. "Dark Side of the Moon. It's made by a bakery up in New Jersey called Classic Desserts. The guy who runs it's a genius. Genuine Belgian chocolate they make themselves. Try some. I have them fly down two a week."

As I mentioned, the rich do indeed have queer ways. How the waiter knew to enter at the precise instant when Jason put down his fork was mystifying. I searched for a hidden camera as the waiter swiftly cleared the table of dishes and threw a slice of cake in front of each of us. The world was rotating at 78 RPM inside this room. I dug into the cake, trying to get something in my stomach before Jason threw me out on my ass. He was right, incidentally— the cake was terrific.

He said, "Sean, it's your mindset we want. In house, we sometimes have to investigate criminal matters, embezzlement, petty theft, that sort of thing. You'd handle all that."

"And you need a full-time lawyer for that?"

"Jessica thinks it would be helpful." He tossed two more forkfuls into the furnace, and added, "What I want is your perspective on corporate matters and negotiations."

"I know nothing about either, and they don't interest me."

"You're doing fine so far. If your idea for handling this protest works, you will have helped make the company up to three billion a year."

The cake was history and he pushed away from the table. He said, "So, here's the deal. A thousand shares as a signing bonus. At today's market price, that's a hundred and thirty grand. Salary of five hundred grand, with a possibility of a fifty percent bonus. A three-year contract, and if I breach you get full pay, without bonuses, for the remainder."

My head was spinning. This was ten times what I made, unless you threw in the bonus, which took it up to fifteen times my salary.

He grinned and studied my face. He said, "In a few years you'll be a very wealthy man, Sean. You'd be a fool to turn it down."

I replied, somewhat lamely, "Law's not all about making money. I'll have to think about it."

He shook his head and chuckled. "You know, it's exactly that kind of values and principles I'm looking for." He glanced at his watch, and added, "Hey, I have to run. I'm supposed to meet with some customers, otherwise I'd love to spend a few more minutes chatting about this. I'm offering you a great deal . . . do think about it."

He was out of his seat and already headed back to the fleet of computer screens sprawled across his desk. Lunch, such as it was, had obviously ended, and I obediently got up and headed for the door. I glanced back over my shoulder and saw him pacing along the line of screens, surveying each of them, looking at . . . God knows what.

I walked out the door and discovered Tiffany awaiting me. She said, "Wow . . . five minutes. You two really hit it off. It's usually three minutes and you're out."

I shook my head. "Maybe you'd like to join me for lunch."

"Oh my God." She slapped her perfect hand on her perfect forehead. "I forgot to warn you to eat fast, didn't I?"

"Forget it. I never stood a chance."

"Nobody ever does." She laughed. Then she said, "Jason asked me to give you a tour. He said you might be joining us, and I should make sure you know what you're getting into."

I pinched myself. I mean, the almost surreal Miss Tiffany Allison shows up wiggling her extraordinary fanny, I speed-eat with a billionaire, get thrown an astounding offer, and now a guided tour by this wind-up Barbie doll. Days like this are why Sean Drummond gets out of bed in the morning.

As we headed back to the elevator bank, I asked her, "So Tiffany, what's with all those computer screens on his desk?"

"You know what we do, right?"

"Basically."

"Three of those screens are from the Bloomberg service. Jason is intensely concerned with what's happening on Wall Street. Our mergers are done with stock, and our employees are heavily vested, so Jason keeps a careful eye on the price."

"And would most of Jason's money be in company stock also?"

"Yes, there's that."

"Of course there's that. What's with the other screens?"

"Five of them track the traffic flow across our networks. Two are for Internet traffic, and the other three monitor special networks, like the Defense Department contract we got last year."

"Why would he care about that?"

"We're like road managers. We need to know where the traffic is coming from and where it's going. Watching those monitors we can divert buildups to other fiber-optic lines to prevent traffic jams."

"What is he, the Wizard of Oz?"

"Oh God, Jason doesn't do it." She laughed. "It's all done through routers and switches. He just likes to see that they're functioning efficiently. The last two screens are for video-teleconferencing. That's our big bread-earner and the future of our corporation, so he uses it for all internal business."

We had proceeded down ten floors and the elevator opened into a huge, darkened room. The temperature dropped about twenty degrees and about a hundred people were seated attentively behind consoles. Three large screens were on walls with lines of data blinking across them. Another wall was nothing but big gray metal boxes with wires coiling out the backs. Any second I expected Darth Vader to come waltzing out, ordering them all to destroy the universe.

"Operations room six," Tiffany explained, "where we handle our aviation contracts. Nine of the top airlines use us as their Internet and data backbone." She pointed at the machines against the wall. "Throw a bomb in this room and the entire U.S. air industry would stop running." I suddenly wished I'd brought a bomb.

She approached a console. "Mark here is a customer service rep. If American Airlines wants to know why a message they sent to a parts vendor was never answered, Mark traces the problem."

"You can read everybody's traffic?"

"Of course. Every customer and every message is coded, so Mark recalls it from the server. Usually, the message was sent to the wrong address, or the airline operator coded it incoherently."

I said, "How much business do you do?"

"Three billion last quarter. The same quarter last year we did two point six billion. Not bad considering the rotten economy. We have the best technology on the planet, and the most motivated people."

"Why are your people the most motivated?"

"Because we believe in Jason."

"I see." I asked her, "Why do *you* believe in Jason?"

"Well . . . he's just . . . extraordinary. For the past four years the entire telecommunications industry has been crashing. Dozens of companies have folded into bankruptcy. It's survival of the fittest, and we're not only the fittest, we've actually stayed profitable and growing. Jason's a genius." She studied my expression and said, "But you're skeptical, aren't you?"

"Reserving judgment."

"I have no problem with that. I'll have a packet delivered that contains our annual statement and a few articles about the company. Read them. If you're still 'reserving judgment,' or have questions, call me. We'll talk about it . . . perhaps over lunch tomorrow?"

It would be discourteous to not at least come up with a few questions to discuss with Miss Tiffany.

But we continued our tour, waltzing through more operations rooms and offices, and ended up at a product display that Tiffany explained was a revolutionary video compression and decompression system. This was a way of crushing billions of bits of information, like voices, or pictures, or whatever, a sort of digital trash compactor, converting it all into light and zapping it down a fiber-optic line, and then yanking all those crushed bits out of the compactor and restoring them all to their former, wrinkleless glory.

This was how I understood the lecture, anyway, but I ordinarily am bored to tears by these sorts of discussions. This whole digital age schmiel—I mean, it's a wonderful thing, right? Without it, I wouldn't get all those football games piped into my TV on Sunday afternoons. But spare me the frigging details, you know? But that offer of three-quarters of a million a year in salary and bonus did stiffen my interest in matters technological. Tiffany's presence sort of stiffened something else.

But all good things must come to an end, and she next deposited me back in the conference room. The packet she promised arrived shortly afterward and gave me something to amuse myself with as the accountants chattered and babbled.

At four o'clock the door opened again and I looked up, hoping to see my new friend. But it wasn't Tiffany, it was a receptionist from downstairs, escorting a nasty little runt who looked amazingly like Daniel Spinelli in a very bad mood.

CHAPTER NINETEEN

A MAJOR POLICE CONVENTION WAS BEING HELD AROUND A LONG, SHINY black limo. A platoon of Virginia state troopers, and scads of uniformed and nonuniformed locals, were being bullied around by short-haired, clean-cut guys in gray and blue suits who might as well have "FBI" stamped on their foreheads. Fifteen news vans and an army of reporters, cameramen, and photographers stood in a raucous pack being briefed by a good-looking Fed in a natty suit. Several news helicopters circled overhead.

Only two things draw reporters in such numbers—free booze and a particularly raunchy death.

I stood beside Spinelli in the small parking lot abutting the Iwo Jima monument, and it struck me that the statue hadn't attracted such a crowd since the day it was unveiled. Five minutes after we arrived, a taxi stopped on the road above us and Janet Morrow stepped out. I had followed Spinelli over in my leased Jag, which was really convenient because it meant I had an escape.

Anyway, I watched Janet walk down the hill, and I sensed from her expression that we shared the same deduction—someone profoundly newsworthy was experiencing rigor mortis inside that limo. Flies, after all, will flock to any corpse. Reporters are slightly more discriminating.

Spinelli stared gloomily at his own feet, jaw muscles bunching and unbunching, and I was left with the impression that he was annoyed with me, very annoyed with her, and his balls were really on fire about that limo. But I didn't press him. When one is standing beside a man who looks pissed and has a gun, patience tends to be a particularly worthy virtue.

Janet nodded politely at me and said to Spinelli, "Who died, Danny?"

He ignored her question and stiffly instructed both of us, "Follow me."

He led us directly to the limo, flashing his badge and cursing at a pair of naive state troopers who foolishly tried to stop him at the yellow crime scene tape. The front and rear doors of the limo hung open on the hinges. We went first to the driver's door, where I noted a heavy Hispanic man in a dark suit curled up on the floor. A small dribble of dark, dried blood ran down his forehead, and there appeared to be a swath of black electrical tape over the wound.

Next we peered inside the rear doors, where a young woman's upright, naked body was sprawled across the backseat. Her position, like Julia Cuthburt's, appeared to me to have been posed, her arms and legs spread wide apart—a bizarre display of complete vulnerability, and possibly another message to the police. Her ankles and wrists were chafed and raw, and a lipstick tube and hand mirror lay on the floor. As I mentioned, she was naked, and clothing articles were also on the rear floor, but were folded and stacked neatly, by her killer, the circumstances suggested. She had apparently been tied up and had struggled fiercely, yet no rope or other restraints were present that I could see. The killer, as before, was tidying up the loose ends and leaving no clues. In fact, I suspected the reason he had parked the car on the tarmac was to ensure there'd be no footprints for forensics to pick up.

I bent forward and examined the female victim more closely. Numerous bruises were evident on her torso, arms, and legs. Also, I observed some scorch marks on her arms and torso, made by something small and red-hot; possibly a lit cigarette, possibly a lighter. Her skin was waxy, and the inside of the car smelled awful, understandably, as her body had begun to bloat with gas. From these indications, she and the driver had been dead at least twelve hours. The female victim was brunette, quite pretty, and vaguely familiar, though I couldn't place her. Ending the description, and apparently her life, her head was twisted to the right at a wildly unnatural angle. Her death mask, if you will, was a snarl.

"Know her?" Spinelli asked Janet.

She failed to reply.

In fact, her head was still inside the car, inspecting the murder scene. It struck me that Spinelli had brought us here and arranged this viewing to elicit shock or astonishment. His expression indicated that he was now both angry and frustrated.

"I asked, did you know her?" he repeated.

Janet peered over her shoulder and replied, coolly, "Everybody knows her, Danny. Carolyn Fiorio."

Sounding quite annoyed, he repeated, "Do *you* know her?"

"I've seen her on TV and read about her in magazines. That's all."

"You, Major?"

"I've heard of her. The talk-show chick, right?"

Back to Janet, he asked, "Did your sister know her?"

"If she did, I wasn't aware of it."

He chewed on something, possibly his tongue. "Come with me," he ordered. So we did, following him to a clump of oak trees about fifty yards away from the corpses in the car. He looked around to make sure he wasn't overheard.

He picked at something on the tip of his nose and stared menacingly at Janet. "Fiorio was supposed to be at some big shindig last night at 7:15. The limo was ordered by her network staff and picked her up at the studio, about five after. The dead guy on the floor, that's Miguel Martinez . . . wife, three little kids, the regular driver. When she never showed at her gig, her studio was contacted, the studio called the limo service, and the limo service tried to contact Martinez on the car radio. About midnight, the studio called the D.C. cops and reported her and the limo AWOL. Three hours ago, the NBC and CBS D.C. affiliates got an anonymous call saying the car was here."

His tone as he described this hinted that we were high up on his shit list, or low on his popularity list, though in his case there might be no distinction.

Janet started to say, "I—"

His finger shot up to her face. "You listen to me, lady."

"I'm listening."

"You know things—I smell it."

"I don't know what you're talking about."

"My ass is on the line here. As the investigating officer of the first murder, I'm part of this task force, and I'm catching a world of shit. So quit fuckin' me around."

Janet calmly replied, "What is it you think I know, Danny?"

"Don't play that game with me."

"Game?"

"You *know* what I'm talking about."

"No, enlighten me."

He kicked a clod of dirt with his foot. We actually get instruction on this at law schools; how to piss people off. Miss Morrow, I suspected, got very good grades.

He was frustrated and said, "Don't you get it? There's been two more murders since your sister. We don't get this asshole off the street, there's gonna be more." He gave her a probing look and added, "Come on. You know somethin', don't ya? Tell me."

"Like what?"

"Ah, fuck."

So we stood like this, Spinelli, Janet, and I for thirty more seconds with nobody saying a word. An acorn fell from a tree and landed at our feet. A plane left a long contrail in the sky.

Janet finally said, "The same guy, right?"

"Yeah, yeah, same friggin' guy." He added, "We timed her death at around nine last night. Like your sister and Cuthburt."

I said, "And you think the killer was the one who called NBC and CBS?"

"That's what we think."

Janet said, "So he's deliberately turning up the heat on you. He chose Fiorio because she's a celebrity. He's drawing his own publicity to force you to publicly acknowledge that there's a monster on the streets."

He did not need to answer this, and he didn't.

"But why?" Janet wondered. She stared at the black limo and answered her own question. "Because he *wants* to sow panic."

Spinelli pointed a finger at the gaggle of reporters. "It's coming."

"What else?" Janet asked as I stared at her in astonishment. She now had Spinelli answering the questions. She said, "Come on, Danny, what have you not told us about?"

"The prick disclosed all kinds of shit to the press, so you'll hear about it anyway. Numbers were inked in on the victim's palms. Your sister was one slash ten, Cuthburt was two slash ten, and Fiorio is three slash ten."

She crossed her arms and asked, "Why didn't you tell us this before?"

He shrugged, but to be clear on this point, I asked, "He's numbering them?"

"Yeah. Also, he's whackin' the donkey on them."

Janet gave Spinelli a stern look and asked, "On Lisa, too?"

"On yer sister's trouser leg, we found sperm. But we got a big problem . . . and you won't be hearin' this one on the news."

"Go on."

"The DNA's different."

"Different? . . . explain *different*."

"Hey, I know. Weird." He added, "The sperm on Captain Morrow don't match the sperm on Cuthburt. And there's sperm on Fiorio's leg, too. We'll know by tomorrow whether it matches the sperm on yer sister or Cuthburt. But right now, we're assuming we got a pair of idiots."

Janet pondered this a moment, then said, "That doesn't make sense, Danny. The profiles for serial sex killers point to loners and social misfits. They regard these events as very intimate."

"I read the trade manuals. But it is what is."

She asked, "Any pubic hair at either scene?"

"Only the victim's."

She was shaking her head. "That doesn't make sense either."

"Tell me about it."

I suggested, "Unless the killers, you know, shave."

Spinelli gave me a startled look. "Yeah. We hadn't thought of that, you know, guys shaving down there. I mean, what kind of guy . . . ?"

I walked around a moment, trying to think about this newest development. I said to both of them, "So the killer knew Fiorio had this big event last night, like maybe it was publicized ahead of time?" Spinelli confirmed this with a nod, so I continued, "He probably tracked Fiorio for a few days and learned that she used a limo service. He waited outside her studio until the limo pulled up."

Spinelli pointed at a spot between his eyes and informed us, "Martinez got there about thirty minutes ahead of schedule, called his dispatcher, and waited a block or two from the studio. Our guess is the killer walked right up to the car window, like he needed directions or a light, and Martinez, not knowing any better, opened it. Probably the gun was silenced. The powder burns on Martinez's forehead indicate it was fired about three inches away. The barrel was pointed downward, like Martinez was looking up, and the killer wanted the bullet to go straight down the throat and into his chest cavity, but not exit, you know, so it didn't leave a big mess Fiorio might notice when she got in. He even slapped a piece of electric tape over the hole, to keep blood from seeping out."

"The type of pistol?"

"From the hole under the tape, we're estimating a forty-five."

"At point-blank range, directed straight down?"

"Right."

"Expert technique and expert choice of weapon. The slow velocity and large caliber assures catastrophic damage. Probably used a soft bullet, so it didn't ricochet off any bones, exit his body, and create a big mess." He nodded as I added, "He probably held the door as she got in the car." I asked, "Time of death, around nine, right?"

"Yeah."

"And we saw what they did during their two hours together."

Janet considered this, then suggested, "He apparently likes to get to know his victim. Or he likes his victim to get to know him."

Spinelli said, "Different things."

"Yes, they are . . . and I'd guess the latter," Janet replied. "That he ejaculates afterward indicates . . . what?" She considered her own question, then said, "Cuthburt and Fiorio were bound and tortured. God knows what he intended for Lisa, probably some variation of that treatment. He breaks their necks because it's manual, personal . . . the final domination. The climax must come right after he kills them. He never got to torture Lisa, and he still ejaculated."

"You keep saying he," Spinelli noted. "You doubt there's two of them?"

"I definitely do doubt it."

"Explain the DNA difference."

"I can't. But the whole act fits the silhouette and pattern of a killer who operates alone. The domination, time spent with the victim, the sexual release afterward, everything."

He said, "Maybe two assholes formed some kind of bond. They coordinate, but act separately."

She was shaking her head. "What are the odds of two of these maniacs getting together?"

He said, "Well, the FBI's got a coupla their profilers studying this thing. We'll have an assessment from the pros tonight."

I said to Spinelli, "Anything else?"

He regarded us closely, apparently concluded we were lost causes, yet could not resist one more shot. He said, "Yeah. If either one of you's holdin' back on me, I swear I'll fry your balls."

I nodded, then escorted Janet back to my car. Oddly enough, my respect for Spinelli was growing. Respect; not affection. Cops are trained to analyze the facts and reach conclusions. But the really good ones have a nose for the invisible and a sort of intuition about people, and Spinelli was right—Janet was withholding something.

But not only from him. And I'd had enough.

CHAPTER TWENTY

*H*e fingered the photograph of Anne Elizabeth Carrol even as he maintained a studious ear on the television coverage of Carolyn Fiorio's gruesome murder.

The coverage was pleasingly pervasive: constant chatter on the news channels; a jarring succession of those pesky special reports everywhere else. Cold shock was the general mood. Every station made note of the awful irony that mere minutes before her appalling death Fiorio had taken a bold stand against the death penalty. Two stations promised instantaneous documentaries that night on her life and many impressive accomplishments. The one at 9:00 P.M. sounded more intriguing and he made a mental note to catch it. He had been using the remote to switch back and forth. His thumb eventually got so damned tired that he settled on CNN for its fifteen-minute updates.

The FBI Director had looked huffy and pink as he had galloped through the crime scene, preening for the cameras and struggling to create the impression that he and his Feds would nip this nasty thing in the bud.

Pictures of that long black limo had been shown from every conceivable angle and direction. Knowing the cargo made it appear gloomy and funereal. The local limo companies were about to encounter a cruel drop in business, he was willing to bet. The news helicopters circled overhead, mechanical vultures that showed shot after shot of cops milling around, jotting notes, taking foot imprints, stuffing their heads inside the limo, trying futilely not to look as generally befuddled as he was confident they were.

It didn't help matters any when the FBI rolled out that smooth-tongued devil to spin the story. Hilarious really, watching him wriggle and squirm. He looked like he'd been kicked in the ribs when the reporters from NBC and CBS assaulted him with insights they just weren't supposed to know. The FBI spokesman had finally seen it was a lost cause and fled from their incessant cameras and piercing voices.

The journalists were infuriated and emotional. Fiorio was one of their own and had died cruelly. A journalist gets it and the damned apocalypse has arrived. The bunch of phonies. More than a few were calling their agents and begging for a chance to fill her spot, dreaming of that six-million contract. Damned shame what happened to poor old Carolyn Fiorio, but hey, the world must go on.

The face he was looking for popped onto the screen and he jerked the volume back up. Jerry Rosen, CNN's man on the spot, was peering into the camera, frowning grimly, and saying, ". . . and the police have only now admitted the connection between the three murders. Sources have told us that Carolyn Fiorio was brutally tortured and sexually assaulted before the killer broke her neck. The first victim, Lisa Morrow, apparently escaped the torture, perhaps because the killer feared detection. But the second victim, Miss Julia Cuthburt, was also tortured and sexually assaulted."

Rosen nodded as the anchorman began asking him questions. "Yes, Harvey," he responded, "the killer wrote numbers on their hands. One, two, three, and beside each number a slash and the numeral ten."

The anchorman said, "That sounds ominous, Jerry. Are there any hypotheses about what those numbers might mean?"

"Well, there are theories that he intends to kill ten young women and he's . . . well, he's checking them off as he goes along. That could be wrong, however. The FBI spokesman cautioned us not to jump to conclusions. He claimed the numbers could be some kind of code or talisman, perhaps biblical passages, or dates of some sort."

"Really . . . ?" the anchorman asked.

"Well, here's the odd thing, Harvey. A high-level source inside the FBI investigating team has informed us that, three years ago, a series of gruesome murders occurred in Los Angeles. They were remarkably similar to what we've seen here. That killer also numbered his victims one of five, and so forth."

"And was he caught?" the anchorman asked, deliberately leading his reporter.

"Never, Harvey." Rosen looked sad. "He killed five young women and eluded the FBI. Until now it was hoped that he had died, or simply decided he'd had enough. It now looks possible that he simply hibernated." He paused and stared melodramatically into the camera. "It now looks as if he's visiting Washington."

CNN shifted to the next story, and he pushed the mute button. Mistakes from this moment on would be perilous. The FBI weren't to be underestimated. They were the A-team of law enforcement for good reason.

He briefly reviewed his progress and was satisfied. The killings were coming at them fast and hard. Before the cops could even finish collecting and analyzing the evidence from one murder, they were inundated with a crop of fresh clues from the next. They were human. Each new murder drew their focus away from the earlier ones. They were conditioned to look for the similarities and peculiarities, to fit everything inside a neat pattern, to try to understand the twisted mind that manufactured them, and in the process were led even further away from the real connections.

He returned to Anne Carrol's photo and was struck again by how wildly out of proportion her nose was with her other features. It was huge and misshapen, had obviously been injured, the dominant feature of a face that was narrow and thin. That she'd never gotten it fixed mystified him. His most recent nose job had cost a mere three grand, done by a guy widely regarded as one of the best. For a thousand less she could have that bone shaved, those nostrils narrowed, and the woman would've spun necks. Lovely blond hair. Striking blue eyes. Lips a bit too thin and hard for his tastes, but she could've verged on loveliness.

She posed a considerable challenge, yet one he regarded as manageable. A solid six—the only warning flags were her background in law enforcement, thin as it might be, and her lesbianism. Subtract those factors and a full point would've been shaved off easily. Her lesbianism most likely accounted for her harebrained refusal to fix that damned nose, it suddenly struck him. He hated to generalize, but all those dykes seemed to feel they had a pass from the ordinary burdens of being female.

He had never done a lesbo before. This could prove knotty. Understanding his victims was his signature flair, the key to his success, he was convinced.

The thick textbook he'd hurried through the night before explained that women of her predilection tended to slip into two categories—the dominator, a male-like figure, and passive, doe-like types. He distrusted stereotypes of any form, though the textbook had been written by an expert in the field and deserved consideration.

Anne Carrol had been a soccer star in both high school and college, a bruising fullback to be precise. She drove a black cherry Jeep Wrangler, customized with silver mudflaps, no hardtop, and brawny, oversized tires. She climbed mountains for a hobby, having flown to Tibet the winter before for a two-week course on high-altitude Himalayan techniques. High pants, flannel shirts, and Sears work boots were her ordinary attire away from the office. She was a regular at the local health club, where she pumped some serious iron. He had stood in a corner, watched her bench 150 pounds, and was frankly astonished that a woman with her bony, birdlike build could pull it off.

She did not flaunt her lifestyle; nor did she make the slightest attempt to camouflage or conceal it. Two months before she had split up with a live-in girlfriend and moved on her own into a tiny efficiency in Crystal City, Virginia. She did not drink, and had stopped using drugs when she left law school and took a government job.

She had obtained a business degree before that, was analytical by inclination—in fact, was regarded as something of a prodigy at the Securities and Exchange Commission where she labored fourteen hours a day in its six-story headquarters. She was a registered Democrat, gave money to liberal causes, and corporate fraud was her passion and specialty. Unfortunately for her, she was also impatient, pushy, and sarcastic, the type who could and often did rub people the wrong way. The SEC kept her miles away from litigation. After an hour with her, juries would swoon for the defense, so her bosses wisely relegated her to the backroom, reviewing stock transactions and annual reports, picking and developing targets for the big buys upstairs.

He tossed down the photo and stared out the window into the courtyard of the Executive Suites. His room was in fact a suite, composed of a living room, an efficiency-style kitchen, and an expansive bedroom. The kitchen was a necessity, an enclave to hole up in complete privacy when he wasn't in action. The less traces he left the better. He paid cash for his groceries and toted them up to the room. All three of his rental cars had been picked up out of town and driven in. His last plane ticket showed him flying out of Washington to Philadelphia, where he picked up the last rental car and drove back. An associate was, in fact, at that moment using his real charge card and ID to spread a trail of evidence across northern New Jersey and New York City. Electronically, there would be no trace he'd ever been in or around Washington, D.C.

Pictures and reports and observation sheets detailing the habits of his victims cluttered the bedroom walls. Not much longer—the walls would soon be bare and every last piece of evidence would be incinerated. He would progress through each and every room with bottles of Pine-Sol and Windex, and scrub away every last fingerprint and fragment of evidence. He had rented the suite for the entire month and planned to be gone a week early.

He moved to the bathroom, undressed, and studied himself in the mirror. His head was completely bald, shaved down to the skin, yet he moved his large frame into the tub, and began spreading shaving cream over nearly every inch of his body and head. It had only been a day since his last shave, yet nothing would be left to chance. The only hairs he did not shave were his eyebrows and lashes, as their absence would be noticeable, and that was the last thing he could afford. The cops could search the murder sites with a vacuum cleaner and find no trace of his DNA or fingerprints.

By that night, the profilers at the FBI would inevitably conclude that he was the very same L.A. Killer who had turned that city upside down three years before. Victim profiles, flawless planning and execution, the tortures and method of death—they'd study it all and reach the inevitable conclusion. Every bit of it was identical, down to necks snapped to the right and the ejaculations.

The cop labs would note how none of the sperm deposits matched the sets they had collected in L.A. a few years before, but then none of the sperm deposits matched each other either.

They would add the L.A. murders to the total and assume Carolyn Fiorio was victim number eight, not number three, and would pull their hair out to understand his logic.

The FBI would recall that the L.A. Killer also had that an-

*noying habit of calling the press and offering them inside tips
that infuriated their investigators. Like it was all a big game and
he owned the board, which was exactly why he had called both
NBC and CBS, offering them the location of the limo and a few
very juicy details to taunt the FBI spokesman. Damned shame he
couldn't be there to witness the shock on the cops' faces when
they arrived at the murder site with the camera crews already
set up and waiting.*

*By midnight a planeload of Fibbies would be packed on the
red-eye to the coast, frantically rushing to get refreshed on the
particulars of that case.*

*He ran the razor across his chest and chuckled. Funny thing
was, long before two hours was up, Carolyn Fiorio had completely changed her mind about the death sentence. By the end
there, she was probably the most bloodthirsty advocate in the
whole damned country.*

CHAPTER TWENTY-ONE

THE SUN WAS GENTLY SETTING AS JANET AND I PEELED OUT OF THE PARKING lot, then through the wide boulevards of Rosslyn, toward Washington, and away from Carolyn Fiorio's crowded murder site. At the first red light I turned to her and inquired, "Did you get the impression Spinelli's pissed at us?"

She chose not to answer.

I said, more specifically, "Actually, he's pissed at *you.* I think he likes me, and he thinks you're jerking him off."

"Nobody likes you." She grinned. "And recall that he's the one who keeps calling me."

We both contemplated the road for a minute before I said, "What are you withholding and why?"

In reply, she asked, "Did you see the burn marks all over her legs and arms?"

"And the bruises, rope burns, and her broken neck. It was sickening. What's your point?"

"They're estimating he spent maybe thirty minutes with Cuthburt, and nearly two hours with Fiorio. The difference in ferocity was huge."

"Maybe the killer has a thing for celebrities. Maybe their different hair colors set him off. Maybe he gets a twitch in his ass on Thursdays. I'm not particularly fond of Thursdays myself."

"Don't you want to know how this guy thinks? Get inside his head?"

"No. Wackos live in a world of dark depravity and twisted impulses. That's a journey I'll leave to the pros. And so should you."

She stared out the window and said, "I just think . . ." and she let it drift off.

"What?"

"It . . . it doesn't add up. DNA traces that don't match. Lisa is simply murdered, Cuthburt's beaten, then killed, and now, Fiorio." She paused, and added, "The poor woman was brutalized, as though the killer had something to prove with her."

"Like what?"

"Like he wanted to generate publicity and excitement. He went over the top with her—a circus killing."

"Why would he do that?"

She ignored me and continued, "With Julia Cuthburt, he was inflicting humiliation and domination. The dog leash, the severe bruising on her butt, even the impertinent pose he left her in. Fiorio was tortured—methodically tortured. You see the difference?"

"Yes."

"The lack of consistency should indicate something to us. I think the killer is staging."

"Staging?"

"Not acting on impulses . . . staging."

"Why?"

"I don't know why." She stared straight ahead and asked, "Do you think there are two different killers?"

"Wouldn't it account for the differences? They match the generalities of the murder, but their individual pathologies creep to the surface and what they do to the victim before death appears different." I turned and asked, "Yes? No?"

"What about the pace? He's smart, and has to know that the faster he kills, the more likely he is to make a mistake."

"And doesn't that also point to two of them? Then they're only killing every four to six days."

"And how does he pick his victims?"

We appeared to be speaking at cross-purposes here—me trying to draw her out, her deliberately diverting me with these incessant mysteries. It's an old lawyer's stunt, you maintain control by asking questions.

And like Spinelli, I'd had enough of it. I swerved into the parking lot of the Orleans House, a restaurant on Wilson Boulevard, swung into a space, and parked. Janet asked, "What are you doing?"

I reached down into my briefcase, withdrew some printouts, and tossed them at her. She stared at the stack and asked, "What are these?"

"The sex cases Lisa was involved with."

I said nothing as she arranged them on her lap.

After several moments, Janet put her finger on a line and suggested, "Here. This looks interesting. Lieutenant John Singleton. Raped a woman and slashed her with a knife. Sex and violence, the same ingredients we're looking for, right? Also, he was an officer. Presumably he's intelligent and resourceful, like our killer."

I asked her, "Anything else?"

After a few moments, she plunked her finger on another sheet and replied, "Right here. Corporal Harry Goins, rape and attempted murder. Sex and violence again."

She read through the rest of the printouts, but apparently no other cases jumped out at her.

Clapper's executive officer had instructed Lisa's former offices to blindly forward every case she'd been involved with that involved sex in any shape, form, or variety. The result was an interesting mix of weirdness and oddities. Sex brings out the best and worst in people, and defense attorneys see the worst.

Janet eventually straightened up and said, "Singleton and Goins . . . they're the only two cases that appear to have a connection."

"You're sure?

"If these lists are complete, yes."

"They are complete, and I selected the same two."

"And did you run checks on them?"

I nodded. "Start with Lieutenant William Singleton. Lisa was his defense attorney. It was her second case, in fact."

"Go on."

"A girl from Fayetteville, outside of Fort Bragg, was jogging, someone pulled her into the bushes, cut her up a bit, then raped her. She gave the police a good description of her assailant: black, about six foot six, buck teeth, a nasty scar on his right hand. Some two weeks later, Lieutenant Williams was stopped for speeding through Fayetteville. The officer noticed a scar on his hand during the license exchange, that he was black, slightly bucktoothed, about six foot six, and he booked him."

"And what happened?"

"Lisa got him off."

"How?"

"Insufficient evidence. The semen swab taken from the victim somehow got lost. On the stand, the victim admitted it was dark, she was terrified, she wasn't wearing her glasses, and she couldn't be completely sure it was Williams."

"But it could have been, right?"

"It would seem so."

"So he's in the running."

"Not exactly."

"Why not?"

"Died in a training accident two years ago."

She shook her head. "We'll cross him off."

"Right. Now Harry Goins. He broke into the quarters of a Mrs.

Clare Weatherow, whose husband, a Special Forces sergeant, was on deployment to Bosnia. Goins raped Mrs. Weatherow, shot her in the head, and left her for dead. She wasn't dead. Ballistics matched the weapon he was carrying, the DNA matched, he was identified by the victim—open and shut. Lisa gave him the best defense possible, but he was found guilty and sentenced to thirty years in Leavenworth, no chance of parole."

"So he's still there?"

"Cellblock C."

I backed the car out of the parking space and said, "You got what you asked for, right?"

"Yes. Thank you."

"Good. I'm happy you're happy. It's been nice working with you."

She faced me and said, "What does that mean?"

"I quit. Or maybe, you're fired. Pick a term."

"Oh, stop this."

I didn't reply.

"Don't you want to find Lisa's killer?"

I still didn't reply.

"What's this about?"

Sometimes the best way for two people to communicate is to not communicate. Again, I declined to reply.

Well, the silence lasted a really long time, before she finally said, "Sean, stop this. I can't do this without you."

"Go on."

"I need you."

"For what?"

"Because . . . because I'm almost certain Lisa was murdered for some other reason than we know."

I'd already been there, heard that, and I frowned to signal we were back at square one.

"Lisa called two days before her murder," she informed me.

"And said what?"

"She was spooked. She thought somebody was watching her house."

"Go on."

"She saw a car parked in front of her townhouse one night. A few nights before, she had an eerie feeling somebody was watching her through her second-story window."

"A feeling?"

"Yes. But Lisa was very levelheaded. You know her."

Yes, I did, so I asked, "She had no idea who was watching?"

She shook her head. "I asked if she had anything to be afraid of. She said nothing specifically. I asked about grudges from old cases. She couldn't think of any. She said, if she had time to re-search it, maybe . . ." She shrugged.

"Which you and I just did."

"Right." She added, "She also mentioned there were things about the firm that bothered her. I asked her what. She told me she was still running it down and wouldn't be sure for a few days."

"And . . . ?"

"That was all."

"No hints . . . no clues?"

"I sensed she didn't want to talk about it. Either for client con-fidentiality or that it was just too vague. But it was her opinion that it had nothing to do with somebody following her."

"But that was conjecture on her part."

"Yes. But she sounded confident." Her face turned slightly flushed and she added, "I should have pressed her more."

And I should've been at the parking lot at nine, and the park-ing lot should've been better lit, and in a better world everybody would grow up happy and well-adjusted and there wouldn't be any sicko assholes murdering young women.

But the world was far from perfect, and I therefore considered what Janet had just told me. Over the course of her year at Culpert, Hutch, and Westin, Lisa had worked for a number of partners on a number of issues. The guiding idea of this screwy working-with-industry program was to get exposure to the full panoply of corporate legal issues; thus every month Lisa was shuffled to another case and client. Her final month had been spent on Cy's team, exclusively on the Morris Networks account. Assuming the firm was somehow involved, and I assumed no such thing, that left a wide breadth of cases she'd been involved with.

I recalled that Lisa had mentioned in our final conversation that she had things she wanted to share with me about the firm. But there was no sense of pressing urgency, nor any trace of fear or anxiety in her voice. I assumed then, as I assumed now, that she had intended to educate me about which piranhas and sharks I'd better not give a shot at my ass.

"I don't see it," I informed Janet.

"Maybe Lisa didn't see it either."

"Look, we just left our third murder site, where a woman was killed in an almost identical manner. Your sister was numbered, and spattered by sperm."

"Thank you. I know that."

"Then what's the point?"

There was another moment of silence before she said, "The night Lisa was murdered, what made Spinelli conclude it was theft?"

"Her purse was stolen."

"Was anything stolen from Cuthburt or Fiorio?"

"I don't . . . well, nobody mentioned it."

"Fiorio's purse was on the floor of the car. I saw it."

"Go on."

"Now think about this. Lisa was a lawyer. She always carried a briefcase. Where's that briefcase?"

"How would I know?"

"I searched her apartment. It wasn't there. I called her office at the Pentagon; not there either. I think her briefcase was stolen also." She added, "And her computer was stolen from her apartment, right?"

"There are many possible explanations for the thefts, assuming her briefcase was stolen." Then I asked, "Why didn't you bring this to Spinelli's attention?"

"Because, if I'm right, the police will blow it."

"How? . . . Why?"

"What will the police do?"

"Standard procedure. They'll start interrogating the firm to see what cases Lisa was involved with."

"And how will your firm respond?"

I was starting to see where this was going. "Like any law firm, they'll tell the cops it's all legally protected, confidential information, and tell them to stuff it."

"And if somebody in the firm is involved?"

"I've got it. A lot of burn bags will be carried out of the building over the next few days."

She had obviously thought this through, and she concluded, accurately, "There won't be a trace of evidence left."

I suggested, "And that's why you want me involved?"

When she didn't reply to that, I filled in the blank. "You want me to spy on the firm."

"Spy is a very ugly word." She stroked her hair and added, "Perhaps nose around a little. But not unless you want to."

"Want to? Excuse me, isn't there something in the legal canon that makes that taboo?" I added, "That wasn't a question."

"Murder is taboo, also."

"Janet, you've got a missing computer, and *maybe* a missing briefcase, with dozens of possible explanations, and you think that means there's a serial killer in one of the most prestigious law firms in the country."

"Did I say there was a killer *in* the firm?"

"You *implied* it."

"I did not. I suggested a connection."

"No." I emphasized, "I mean it—No."

"Well, I respect your decision." She paused, then said, "The stolen computer indicates her killer was concerned about an electronic message or file. Get me in to look at Lisa's computer."

"Sure. We'll walk in together, and I'll say, 'Excuse me, but my friend here wants to see who murdered her sister. So if you don't mind, she's going to log onto our secure computers, browse through our confidential information, and see if she can find which of you bastards did it.' "

"I think it would be more clever if you escorted me to your office and stepped outside for a minute."

"And if you're caught?"

"I'll say I need her e-mail addresses so I can invite her friends to the funeral. Okay?"

Definitely not okay. Every piece of evidence screamed that Lisa was the victim of a murderous maniac who chose her because the demons inside his head said she was the right flavor for that day. I looked her dead in the eye and said, "Absolutely not."

Well, Elizabeth the receptionist looked up when Janet and I entered, and she said, "Major Drummond, you haven't been around the past few days."

"I was in lockup."

"Lockup?"

"Yeah. Seems a guy who looked like me knocked off a bank three blocks from here."

"A bank?"

"A small local branch. Only ten grand was stolen. My lawyer got me sprung."

She reeled back into her seat.

I said, "But I was in Cleveland that day. I've got witnesses . . . a dozen of them."

She chuckled and in her stuffy English voice said, "Oh . . . you're making a silly joke."

Without smiling back, I said, "Elizabeth, this is Janet Morrow. I'm signing her in."

Elizabeth mumbled something as we headed down the hallway to my office. I walked to my desk, flipped on the computer, and neither of us spoke as it booted up. I wondered how I had allowed myself to be talked into this. What kind of exercise do you do to get a backbone?

The screen appeared and I mentioned, "I don't know Lisa's password."

Pointing at my chair, she said, "May I?" She settled in and studied the screen. She positioned the magic arrow, gave it a little tap, and two boxes appeared, one for the user's name, one for the user's password. She typed in Lisa's name, then tried a password. A bunch of stars appeared in the box, but whatever she tried caused an "Incorrect Password" message to flash onto the screen.

Janet sat back in her chair, thought for a few seconds, tapped a few more times, then six more tries without success.

I said, "Let me try," and bent over her shoulder. I typed in "J-A-G," and bingo, we had liftoff.

Janet said, "That's so obvious."

"No, it was brilliant. Simply brilliant."

She laughed. But the screen showed only three e-mails in Lisa's mailbox. Janet popped them open: administrative messages from the firm. Lisa was the fastidious type and it made sense that she had wiped the slate clean of her personal messages before she returned to the Army. Somewhere inside the belly of the server were probably electronic imprints of everything she ever wrote on the computer, but recovering those files was beyond our competence levels.

Janet maneuvered the mouse around and finally brought up Lisa's e-mail address book. If I failed to mention it, Lisa Morrow was a very popular girl. Janet scrolled down, and there were, I estimated, easily two hundred e-mail addresses.

Janet informed me, "I'm going to send a mass mailing that includes all these addresses to my personal computer. When we have the funeral figured out, I'll just mass-mail a blanket announcement to all these addresses."

It took her a few minutes to accomplish all that, and I then drove her back to the Four Seasons.

CHAPTER TWENTY-TWO

ANOTHER DAY IN HELL.

Late Sunday afternoon to be precise, a fine day, an Indian summer reprieve, sunbeams cascading through the windows, calculators clacking, and a trio of accountants at the end of the table heatedly debating the details of some obscure Bermuda partnership.

The city and suburbs outside these walls were experiencing a collective epileptic fit. The L.A. Killer, as he'd been anointed, had gone two nights without killing. Theories ran rampant. Maybe he'd had his fill. Maybe a broken-necked corpse was yet to be discovered. Maybe his next victim was among the many women who'd suddenly applied for panicked, unscheduled vacations, forcing him to stalk for a suitable replacement.

The D.C. phone lines were clogged with parents ringing up daughters and friends calling one another to make sure they were still alive. Police stations were inundated with requests to check on the safety of young women who failed to answer calls. A hotline had been opened and hundreds of sightings and scares were phoned in.

Serial killers are generally a phenomenon of the West. Californian and northwestern cities get them like clockwork. One week it's the ghoul in Seattle who lops off arms, the next it's the creep in San Bernardino who torches prostitutes. Ever since Charlie Manson struck terror into hearts, the citizenry react with a sort of tame horror and it's steady as she goes.

The occasional monster turns up in Philadelphia, Chicago, or New York. But Washington, D.C., aside from that freakish sniper case, has been mostly immune. We regard ourselves as the metropolis of crack wars, terrorists airplanes, Watergates and Monicagates. We have enough problems—serial killers aren't welcome.

The city was hysterical and the media was driving spikes through its heart. Retired FBI profilers were in huge demand on the news channels. The night before, *Nightline* had run an hourlong special with one who claimed he had worked on the L.A. Killer's case three years before, said he had no doubt this was the same guy, said he was the toughest killer he'd ever come up against, said he varied his patterns and approaches to match his target, that he got off on the terror, and was likely single, reclusive, and insecure. He added that two witnesses had gotten a peek at the L.A. Killer's back during one kidnapping; they described him as short, maybe five foot six, muscular like a former wrestler or gymnast, thick-shouldered and -necked, with dark hair worn in a ponytail.

But all that excitement and buzz was happening outside this room. Inside, flics were dropping out of the air, dead from boredom.

So I was seated in my corner chair, catatonically daydreaming about my options. Seven hundred and thirty grand a year. A hundred and thirty grand signing bonus. Nearly a million dollars my first year, and Tiffany had twice taken me to lunch to extol the company's "awesome" benefits—health plan, annual stock options, free lunches, all the best the private sector has to offer. By our second lunch she was putting her hand on my arm, batting her doe-like lashes, and slyly intimating there might be other fringe benefits as well.

Now she was talking.

In truth, I had mentally moved past the issue of whether, and was indulging in fantasies about *what—what* to do with that money, and *what* to do to Tiffany.

"Excuse me."

I looked up. A female accountant named Martha, who was the number-crunching ramrod, was holding forth a file and examining my face. She had a sort of mechanical voice, clipped, flat, and metallic, the way you'd imagine a female robot might speak. She asked, "How familiar are you with overseas partnerships?"

Was this a joke? Thus far, the accountants had brought me three issues for legal resolution. My contribution had been to compose short synopses of their queries and fax them to the firm to someone who gave a shit. Neither my alarming ignorance nor my complete apathy had gone undetected. Nobody in the room was taking me seriously, which was okay by me.

"Well, I dated a few German girls."

A gurgling sound erupted from her throat. "No, silly. That's not what I meant."

"Well, Martha, what did you mean?"

She replied, "A lot of firms engage in external partnerships to share access, or marketing efforts, or as joint investment vehicles."

"Go on."

"Morris Networks has a partnership with a Bermudan company called Grand Vistas. The partnership was formed two years ago."

"I've been to Bermuda," I replied helpfully.

"Then surely you know it's a very popular place for these partnerships." She adjusted her glasses, warming to the topic. "Liberal accounting policies, friendly banks, and no taxes make it an ideal business nexus."

"That's exactly why I vacationed there."

She was shaking her head. "Your firm did the legal work for this partnership with Grand Vistas. It's a joint investment vehicle."

"Of course it is. Now you know why we put it together." She looked impressed, until I asked, "What the hell does that mean?"

"It means that Morris Networks and Grand Vistas swap."

"Oh . . . right. I tried to swap spit with those German girls. From there, we could, you know, try some organ donation . . . but you're not really interested in this, are you?"

She rolled her eyes. "I'm referring to the swapping of shares and network capacities. Under the Generally Accepted Accounting Principles, capacity exchanges allow both companies to treat swaps as sales and book immediate revenues."

"And this is legal?"

"Yes . . . That's what I said."

"Oh . . ."

"Grand Vistas is apparently a holding company that has interests in several overseas telecommunications enterprises. Under a capacity swap, the two companies agree to exchange utilization of each other's networks."

"And the relevance of this is . . . ?"

"It's a very important relationship for Morris Networks. Last year, Morris booked three hundred million in revenue from Grand Vistas."

Well, this was very fascinating, but my mind had already drifted back to how Tiffany might look unencumbered by all those silly clothes they made her wear around the office. "Does this lecture last much longer?"

Martha shuffled her feet. "Morris Networks booked roughly eighty million in swaps with Grand Vistas the first quarter of this fiscal period. We're assuming the partnership remains in effect."

"Yes?"

"We need to know the expected duration. Your law firm prepared the contracts."

Well, this was annoying. It being Sunday, depending on their bent, the other members of the firm were probably off hitting the back nine at their country clubs, or sneaking into peep shows off Dupont Circle. I asked, "Can't this wait till tomorrow?"

"If you're willing to give us a two-day extension. Obviously, we can't complete the projected revenues unless we know the duration of the contract."

Well, obviously. I shook my head and walked to the bank of phones in the corner. My briefcase contained a list of the firm's home numbers and I dialed Barry's shiny house in the shiny suburb.

A woman's voice answered, "Jessica Bosworth. May I help you?" Her accent was northeastern preppy, a little whiny in my view, suggesting she was suicidally depressed about her lousy marriage and the fact her husband was a short-dicked bed wetter. But I sometimes read too much into things. Kids were hollering in the background. Who could blame them, considering who their father was.

I introduced myself and informed her that I needed to speak with her husband. It took nearly two minutes before Barry came on. He explained that he and his wife were hosting a kid's birthday party, and my timing was really lousy, and could we get this over with quickly. I said sure, explained what the accountants wanted, and he replied, "No problem. I prepared those contracts and negotiated the deal. I'm intimately familiar with the whole thing."

"I knew you were the man, Barry." I asked him, "So what's the nature of the contract?"

"Cross-investment, and they swap network utilization."

"Duration?"

"Four years, renewable. Since it was signed two years ago, it has at least two more years to run."

"Under what conditions can either party back out?"

"No conditions. There's no provisions for that in the contract."

"No conditions . . . isn't that unusual?"

A kid's voice was still hollering in the background. Barry reminded me, "Drummond, I'm in a hurry here." I heard an impatient sigh. "What are you, an expert in commercial contracts now?"

I just love having my own ignorance rubbed in my face. I replied, "I asked, isn't that unusual?"

"Both . . ." The kid's squeal got loud enough that Barry had to raise his voice to be heard. "Uh . . . look, both companies are very happy with the arrangement. Don't worry about it, all right?"

I wasn't worried about it. In fact, I didn't give a rat's ass about the contract. But it was Sunday afternoon and I was stuck in this room, with these people, because Barry put me here. And his kid probably had a stinky, barn-sized load of crap in his diapers, and was pulling frantically on his father's pants leg. With a little effort I can be a real pain in the ass. Actually, without effort. I said, "Right, so I'll just tell everybody to go home till tomorrow, when it's more convenient for you to answer my questions."

"Fuck off."

Boy, was this getting fun. A woman's increasingly indignant voice was screaming, "Barry . . . Barry . . . !"

"Hey, guess what?" I told Barry. "I just thought of a bunch more questions I need answered immediately. For starters—"

"Goddamn it, Drummond! Don't fuck with that contract. You understand? You don't know what in the hell you're getting into."

"I don't?"

"Uh . . ." The kid was now wailing and his wife was screaming at the top of her lungs, too.

He tried speaking over them, "It's perfectly legal. Bo—" He screamed, "Would you shut up!"

Back to me, he said, "Both parties agreed to the conditions. That's all you or the accountants need to know."

"What did you mean the contract's legal?"

"No. I, uh, I just meant the partnership is . . . ah, fuck . . ." He took a deep breath, then chuckled. "Hey, Sean . . . buddy, I'm trying to be helpful here." He paused again as the kid's voice moved up another couple of notches, and Barry must've slapped his hand over the mouthpiece, but not well enough, because I distinctly heard a loud slap and his muffled voice scream, "Shut the fuck up, you little monster!"

Geez. Time to reconsider the Daddy of the Year award I had planned to put Barry in for. A woman's voice began barking and I

could hear Barry bark back, losing not a single point on the nasti-
ness factor. I distinctly heard the words "bitch" and "asshole" before
a door slammed in the background.

Silence.

Barry then said to me, "Nobody held a gun to anybody's head,
Drummond. Everything's fucking legal, all right? Morris Networks
reports the partnership in a footnote with its annual filings to the
SEC. You got all that? Now, you tell the accountants to book the
fucking projections."

I had never expressed the slightest doubt about the *legality* of
the partnership. Barry raised that issue all by himself.

I said, "Hey, have a nice day."

The phone went dead.

So, this was interesting. Barry hadn't really confessed anything.
In fact, he'd denied everything. The problem was he hadn't been
asked to deny anything.

You have to wonder why. And while you're at it, recall that the
pristine name of Sean Drummond would be scribbled on the blame
line for this audit. If any part of it later proved false or misrepre-
sentative, the SEC and American Bar Association would come
trolling for moi's ass. Could it be that Barry wanted me overseeing
this audit precisely because of my incompetence?

Well, this was a great deal to surmise, and Barry had been
under considerable stress and pressure, and, as I mentioned, I
sometimes read too much into things.

But maybe not.

I walked over to Martha and informed her that she and her
buddies could safely assume the Bermuda partnership would last
the next two years.

She nodded and I went back to my corner and mulled this
over.

CHAPTER TWENTY-THREE

*A*nne Carrol was pedaling furiously and he hung back about two hundred yards behind her. The temperature was perfect, low forties, no humidity, no breeze. Fifteen miles and he had worked up barely more than a light sweat. A splendid evening for a long bike ride, in his view. She was averaging just under fifteen miles an hour, and he was confident he could pour it on and catch her at will.

Thirty minutes before, she had parked on a side street near Georgetown University, unstrapped her silver Cannondale eighteen-speed from the rack on the rear of her Jeep Wrangler, and spent ten minutes limbering up. All stretched out, she headed west on the old canal towpath that borders the brown Potomac River. The canal and towpath had been landmarks of D.C. for nearly two hundred years. At one time food and provisions were loaded onto shallow barges and hauled into the city by horses and mules. The towpath had since been converted into a trail for runners and bikers that stretched to the west for nearly twenty miles.

Traffic along the path had been thinner than normal, the result, no doubt, of the swelling paranoia about the L.A. Killer. The few young women he'd observed were biking or jogging with male companions or in packs. They were taking no chances. The killer was out there, they knew, and hungry.

As he'd been convinced she would, Anne Carrol ignored the warnings. She was too pushy and stubborn to let a killer alter her life in any way. She likely believed that sex maniacs wouldn't be interested in her or her type. Hetero girls get all that bad crap—the unwanted pregnancies, VD, and sex sickos. Lesbians were above all that.

She biked every Sunday evening, from March through December, till it got too cold and icy. He had trailed her the Sunday before, measured her tempo, studied the terrain, and plotted his takedown. Like the week before, she went at a leisurely pace for fifteen miles, hit her turnaround, and sprinted back.

They had hit that turnaround a mile back, and the time had come.

He glanced over his shoulder, saw nobody, and kicked up his speed to twenty. Inside three minutes, he had closed the gap to a hundred yards. He studied her back and pedaled harder. When he was thirty yards away she heard him coming. A brief glance over her right shoulder, no alarm on her face, and no change to her posture or pace. She courteously steered her bike to the left, giving him more room to pass on the right.

He drew alongside, she glanced at him, and he smiled, lifted his left hand for a friendly wave, and sped past. He kept pedaling furiously until he drew three hundred yards ahead of her. He went around a sharp bend in the trail, then squeezed hard on the brakes. The rear tire skidded out to the left and he put his right foot down to break the fall.

Anne Carrol came around the bend seconds later and had to steer hard to avoid a collision. His bike straddled the path, its tires spinning. Five yards away he was laid out, limp and still.

Anne pumped her brakes to a gradual stop. She climbed off

her bike and looked back at him. He squeezed his eyes shut and stayed still.

He heard her mumble, "Oh shit," then she walked her bike toward him.

"Hey," she yelled. "You okay?"

No answer.

"Hey, can you hear me?"

She was drawing closer and he remained rigidly still. He would wait till she was within feet of him before he would act. Too much distance and she would jump back on her bike and speed away.

He could hear her heavy breathing and footsteps. She couldn't be far and he emitted a soft groan so she'd know he was alive. Injured and desperately in need of swift help, but alive.

Twenty or so seconds passed and he groaned again. He had given her more than enough time. She should've been bending over him, checking his pulse, something.

He opened his eyes and lifted his head, affecting a severely pained expression. She stood back about seven feet, had her right hand inside her butt pack and was staring down at him.

He mumbled, "I'm hurt."

"What happened?"

"My . . . uh, my bike slid out. Please. Can you come help me?"

"Nope. Get up yourself."

"I don't know if — "

"Can you move your legs?"

"I, uh, I don't know."

She backed off another few feet, and said, "Do it. 'Cause I'm not helping you up."

So much for the Nurse Nightingale instinct women were supposed to have. It struck him that he may have misjudged his target. He had anticipated the lesbo thing might hold unexpected twists, but such a chilling lack of compassion unnerved him.

He let loose a few anguished snorts and grunts as he pushed himself up with his arms, and drew his legs under him. She was ten feet away, but he was quick and strong. If he could get enough balance and traction, he'd be on her before she could blink.

He stole one more glance at her before he made his move—and froze. Her right hand was no longer inside her fanny pack. It hung in front of her crotch, a snub-nosed .38 Special in her grip, not pointed at him specifically, just held there, casually, barrel pointed down.

He straightened up, and brushed dirt off his shirt and legs.

She said, "Can't be that bad, buddy. No blood."

He looked up. "I, uh, I came down on my head. I think I was knocked out there for a minute or two." He added, "Say, is that a gun?"

"Could be. How you feeling now?"

"Crappy." He moved his arms and stretched his legs, rotating his joints, as though checking for damage. "First time I ever took a spill."

"The price of bein' a dumbass." She added, "You were going too fast. Dirt trails, you don't go over fifteen. You sped by me, I'll bet, doing twenty."

God, she was preachy and nasty. Little wonder they kept her away from juries. He said, "Yeah, guess you're right." He affected a frightened expression and again asked, "That, uh . . . is that a gun in your hand?"

"Yeah, it's a gun. Ain't made of plastic, either."

"You're not planning on shooting me, are you?"

"Depends." She chuckled. "Behave, and we shouldn't have any problems."

"No kidding?"

"Lotta sicko assholes around. You never know."

He shook his head. "Yeah, well, you know you don't have to worry about me."

He saw her eyes taking him in, but distinctly not a look of sexual fascination—a cold physical assessment. He was wearing skintight biker's tights and a sleeveless shirt, and she would not be at all reassured by the sight of him. He was nearly six foot four, with broad, corded shoulders, thick arms, and legs that were carved with muscle. He looked like a middle linebacker.

She took another step back and asked, "And how do I know I don't have to worry about you?"

"Because I'm . . . well, I'm gay. Sorry, you're just not my type."

"Gay, huh?"

"Hey, it's not a crime."

She nodded. "Nope, not a crime." She pointed her jaw in the direction of his bike. "You go make sure it's not broken."

"Good idea." He walked over and hefted it up. "You ever take a spill?"

"Once or twice." She paused. "Not since I was four years old, though."

Bitch. He lifted the bike in the air, bounced the tires on the ground, and pretended to study the frame. "Guess I was pretty stupid, huh?"

"Guess you were."

He looked around and counted his luck that nobody had cycled past them yet. If that happened, this coldhearted bitch would get a pass for the night. He couldn't afford witnesses who might recall the big muscular guy who was with her on the towpath. He'd have to reschedule her, and that would be very inconvenient. Would his luck hold, though? Not much longer, he gauged.

"The bike seems okay," he said. "Not me, though. I feel real dizzy."

"Too bad." She nodded in the direction of Washington and added cavalierly, "Long walk back. Probably twelve miles or so."

An idea struck him and he asked her, "You wouldn't happen to have a cell phone in that pack, would you? I've got a friend, Dan, I could call and he'll come pick me up."

"Nope, no cell phone."

Shit— there went his excuse to get near her. If he could just get within three or four feet, he'd get his big hands wrapped around her skinny throat. Christ, was he looking forward to snapping her neck.

"Could you at least walk with me for a few minutes? Just enough to make sure I'm okay."

"You look okay to me."

"Please." He held out his arms and smiled. "Come on . . . give me a break. I'm gay and you've got a gun. What a combination. A few minutes?"

She coldly studied him. "What's your name?"

"Mike . . . Mike Nelson."

"Okay, Mike, here's the deal. You stay on your side of the path, and I'll stay on mine. You got that?" He nodded that he did, and she added, "Three minutes and I'm gone. The gun stays in my hand. I'm damned good with it, too. You're awful clingy, and I don't like that."

"Hey, like I said, you're not my type." Why wasn't she picking up on this gay angle he kept tossing out? Don't all gay people have some kind of warm-and-fuzzy solidarity thing? He cursed himself for not studying them more closely.

He moved to the right side of the path, keeping the bike to his right, so it wasn't between them. She moved to the left and very obtrusively positioned her bike to her right, between them. About eight feet separated them, and she held the gun near her waist where all she'd have to do was swivel her arm and drill him. He didn't doubt that she knew how to handle it. Damned lesbo probably wore a jockstrap.

They started walking, and very friendly-like he asked, "So, what's your name?"

"Anne."

"Just Anne? No last name?"

"None you're gonna hear."

"I don't get it. Why are you so suspicious?"

She looked straight ahead and said, "I was raped once. It was real unpleasant and isn't gonna happen again."

"Oh . . . I'm sorry."

"Why are you sorry? You didn't get raped." She then very matter-of-factly said, "Point is, Mike, we're out here all alone on this bike path. I don't know you from shit. You don't look like you took a hard spill, no blood, no scratches, and you claim you're gay, but how do I know you're not lying?"

He said, "Well, I—"

"Also," she interrupted, "there was a guy out here last week, cycling behind me, looked just like you. That was you, right, Mike?"

Damn, that explained it. He'd hung far enough back that he was sure she wouldn't see him. Must've happened after she hit the turnaround point. She could only have gotten a brief glimpse as they sped past each other in opposite directions. Most folks just aren't that sharp-eyed and observant. Shit, shit, shit. He thought furiously about how to handle this. Deny it? No, that wouldn't work. He could see in her eyes that she recalled him quite clearly.

He replied, "Yeah, I was out here last week. So what?"

"Well, I'm out here every Sunday night, and I never saw you before. Kind of an odd coincidence, right? One week you're following me, the next . . . well, here we are."

"There's a reason for that."

"I'll bet."

"I just moved to D.C. three weeks ago."

"Is that right?"

"From San Francisco. I was living with a guy, Paul, but we broke up." He paused and worked a little pain into his voice. "Actually . . . Paul dumped me. For a movie critic. I, uh, well, I had to move, you know. Everywhere I went reminded me of him."

She started to say something and he kept talking, sounding whiny. "And the guy he dumped me for was a queen, too. A goddamned queen. I never took Paul for the flaming queen type, you know?"

That should help, he thought. Just a big dopey guy troubled by a broken heart. Toss in a little fag jargon and sound like a real queer. Establish his credentials and get her to let down her guard.

Any minute and another bicyclist was going to come careening down the path and ruin this thing.

She shrugged. She glanced at her watch, apparently wishing the three minutes to end.

He said, "What about you?"

"What about me?"

"What do you do?" He scratched his head, as though struggling to recall, then guessed, "Cathy, isn't it?"

"Anne."

"Sorry."

"Well, you know, Mike, that's none of your damned business."

If he could only get her to put that damned pistol back in her fanny pack. Christ, she was making this hard. He said, "God, you're unfriendly."

"Yeah, well, tough shit. Guess you bumped into the wrong Good Samaritan."

"No. You're being very generous, and I appreciate it."

"Move back over, asshole," she ordered, noting that he and his bike had strayed toward the middle of the path.

"Sorry." He did as she ordered. "Geez, I'm woozy. I think I hit my head pretty hard. I can barely walk straight."

"Try harder, Mike." She glared over at him, and said, "My first shot, you'll be peeing out your asshole. You'll still be able to date, but the end of the evening's gonna be a big disappointment . . . 'cause you'll have no dick left."

His mouth hung open. "Wait a—"

"I wondered if you'd come for me, you fucking ghoul." Her pistol was now pointed directly at his groin.

"Anne, I don't—"

"Think I don't hear the news? Think I'm too stupid to put two and two together? You fucked up, Mike." She ran a hand through her hair, and said, "Though it's not really Mike, is it?"

A half mile ahead a bike was speeding quickly toward them. The bicycler was bent over the handlebars, cutting the drag and pedaling fiercely. Anne gestured toward the figure and said, "You got a real problem, now, asshole. Company's coming."

He stopped walking and faced her. She had been playing with him until somebody else came along, he realized.

He had badly underestimated her.

He smiled. "I am really looking forward to breaking your neck, dyke."

"Too bad."

"How did it feel to be raped, dyke?"

Her face reddened. "Up yours."

"What I have planned for you, dyke, you'll beg me to break your neck."

"God, you're disgusting." Anger was creeping into her voice.

They stood in silence and glared at each other with mutual hatred as the bicyclist drew nearer and nearer. The pistol barrel remained pointed at his groin.

The newcomer hit his brakes and his bike glided to a stop a few feet from them. The man was young, twenty-one or twenty-two, possibly a student at Georgetown or GW University, blond-haired with a frizzy goatee, goggle glasses, and the thick, trunklike thighs of a persistent biker.

He stared inquisitively at the gun in Anne's hand and asked, "What's going on? You need help?"

Anne's lips were just parting as Mike threw his arms up in the air and announced, "Boy, do I ever. I'm so glad you came along, man. This crazy bitch thinks I'm the L.A. Killer."

"What?"

"She's nuts. I'm riding along and I move up to pass her and she kicked me over. Could've killed me. Hurt like hell."

Anne said, "Shut up." Then to the stranger, "He's lying. He faked a spill. He is the L.A. Killer."

The newcomer studied him. Mike shrugged his big shoulders and shook his head at the sheer absurdity of the charge. "Bullshit. Complete bullshit. You know how women around here are right now. She's completely paranoid."

Anne was shaking her head, like she really didn't need this crap. She said, "Nice try, you murdering asshole. You're gonna fry."

Mike said, "See what I mean, man? The lady's gone over the edge. For Godsakes, please, see if you can talk some sense into her."

The newcomer appeared completely clueless. "I . . . uh . . . Christ, I've got no idea what's going on here."

Mike said, "Shit, look at me, man. You've heard the description of the L.A. Killer, right? It's all over TV and the radio. Short and stocky, with a ponytail, right? Do I look short and stocky? Where's my ponytail?"

The young man turned toward Anne and said, "It's true. The description's all over the news. Like he said."

She faced him. "I don't give a shit. This is the guy."

"Did he attack you?" the man asked, making no effort to disguise his skepticism.

"Not yet. But only 'cause I didn't give him the chance."

Mike's hands got a hard grip on the crossbar of his bike. The young man said to Anne, "Well, if he didn't attack you, how can you be so sure?"

Anne was becoming flustered. "I just know. I thought he'd come for me, and this is him."

"You thought he'd come after you?"

The young man and Anne were now facing each other.

Anne had just opened her mouth to explain, when suddenly Mike's bike flew through the air, an ill-shaped javelin hurtling straight at her. She turned and threw up her arms, but the twenty-four-pound rocket crashed into her torso and face.

Mike came right behind it. He leaped across the path and dove straight for the pistol. Her arm was trapped under the bike and he pried the gun out of her fist then bashed her forehead with it.

The newcomer was yelling, "Hey, man, take it easy! You don't have to do that!"

He threw the pistol aside. Anne was stunned and moaning,

and he climbed off her. He began walking toward the biker, say-ing, "Look, man, she gave me no choice. The chick could've shot me or something."

"Yeah, but—"

"No buts." Mike shook his head. "She's crazy. Jesus, I was scared."

He was two feet from the biker. He could've just shot him but the loud noise could draw more nosy guests. He swiped a hand across his forehead and said, "You see how it was, right? I couldn't take the chance."

Suddenly his fist lashed out and hit the biker on the nose. A spray of blood and the young man flew off the rear of the bike. Mike calmly walked over and easily lifted him off the ground. He yanked the helmet off his head and let it drop to the ground. The young man weighed about 160 pounds, but Mike was terrifi-cally strong and he held the howling man under his thick arms and sprinted full-speed toward a large oak tree beside the trail. Like the tip of a battering ram, the biker's head went straight into the bark and split open like a melon. His body went com-pletely limp, and Mike dropped it at the base of the tree. He bent over and checked the man's pulse—definitely dead.

Anne was just shoving the bike off her body when he re-turned. A deep gash on her forehead and another cut on her right shoulder were pouring blood. She looked at him and started to scream, when he leaped forward, slapped one hand over her mouth, and lifted her into the air with the other.

He murmured into her ear, "Hey, Anne, we got off on the wrong foot. No more lies between us. This is going to really, really hurt."

Her eyes bulged with understandable terror as he dragged her with one arm and began picking up the discarded bikes and hauling them into the thick underbrush.

CHAPTER TWENTY-FOUR

MONDAY MORNING—SEVEN O'CLOCK SHARP, INDIAN SUMMER HAD COME and gone, and I was seated behind my desk at the firm, booting up the computer. The numbers had been crunched and recrunched, the final audit was being drafted, and I was left with a few hours to kill.

So I thought I'd use the opportunity to make a more thorough examination of Lisa's file. I wasn't buying into Janet's suspicion, but the possible theft of Lisa's computer and briefcase did raise an eyebrow. We had searched her e-mail, and now I thought I'd check her general work file, noodle around, and see if anything struck a chord. It was this or spend the morning with the accountants. So it was this.

The two little boxes appeared, I typed in Lisa's name, then "J-A-G," and that pesky "Incorrect Password" message popped up. This was odd.

I was thinking about how odd it was when my phone rang. I lifted it up, said, "Drummond," and a voice curtly demanded, "Turn off your computer and come see me. Now."

"Who are—"

"Hal Merriweather. Ninth floor. Three minutes or I'll send a security officer to get you."

He hung up. I hate it when people do that.

I walked down the hallway to Elizabeth, who sort of blinked a few times as I approached. But I think she was starting to look forward to our occasional encounters. In the land of the blind, the one-eyed man is king, or whatever.

I smiled. "Morning, Elizabeth. You look stunning today."

She giggled. "Oh, you are a flirt, Major Drummond. Rob any banks lately?"

"Gave it up. Too many cameras and security guards."

"Found a new hobby, have we?"

"Not yet. But I'm looking into overbilling and corporate graft. The boys upstairs swear that's where the big bucks are."

She laughed.

I leaned across her desk and asked, "Hal Merriweather?"

"Hal, is it?" She diddled with something on her desk. "You haven't managed to land on his bad side, have you?"

"Who is he?"

"Our superintendent of administration. Not one to have mad at you, I should say."

"Why?"

"He's quite powerful, really. My supervisor. In charge of security, administration, personnel."

English people tend to speak in these odd half-sentences, like only an idiot needs a fully expressed thought. Well, I'm an idiot.

I tapped a finger on the desktop.

"Oh, let me see. He's youngish, early thirties I should think. Very efficient and quite competent, though I should say a bit difficult to get along with."

Subtlety is another English trait, and I translated this to mean Hal was a type-A asshole. I had reached this conclusion already. I told her, "I need the key to go up and see him."

"Ring you up, did he?"

"He heard what a great guy I am and wants to meet me."

She laughed. "Be on your toes, Major. Hal's manners could stand a bit of polish."

So she handed me the stairwell key, and actually, Hal's office wasn't that hard to find. His name was inscribed in gold letters on his doorway, like the partners', and happened to be located in the connecting corridor between the junior and senior partners. Given that all kinds of people downstairs with law degrees were killing themselves to get an office on this floor, and that the rest of the administrative staff were packed on the seventh floor, it struck me that Hal's stature within the firm perhaps exceeded his title.

The door was locked, so I knocked, a buzzing sound emitted, and I entered. Nobody was present, just two vacant desks in what appeared to be a narrow outer office. I walked to the next door and knocked again. Maybe this was like one of those dozens of boxes inside a box thing, and I'd keep walking into smaller and smaller rooms, and Hal was actually a midget who worked inside a tiny drawer.

But another buzzing sounded, and I entered what appeared to be the inner sanctum, where a guy who looked like he was named Hal was seated behind a desk. He was, as Elizabeth warned, in his mid-thirties, short and pudgy, with balding dark hair, flat black pig eyes, and a thick, imperious nose.

He also wasn't alone. Harold Bronson, the managing partner, and Cy, my titular boss, stood directly behind him. From Cy I was getting the old avoid-my-eyes routine. And from Bronson the-old-happy-guy-who-wasn't-happy act.

Hal was scowling and ordered, "Take a seat."

So much for pleasantries. I stood.

"Suit yourself," he said.

"I always do, pal." Regarding Hal's office, the desk, files, and bookcases appeared to have been purchased from an Office Depot sale. No paintings of ships or lush oriental carpets, nor was there any of the general clutter you associate with a real working office, suggesting Hal either didn't have much of a job, or was one of those anal neat freaks. Also of interest were the video monitors mounted on wall brackets. One showed the entryway, where sat Elizabeth, energetically buffing her nails. Another showed an empty stairwell, presumably the one that led to the partners' floor. And last, the interior of the elevator.

Among his other talents and duties, Hal appeared to be the partners' watchdog. He probably had a gun inside another drawer and would love nothing more than to cap somebody for trespassing, or farting in the partners' elevator.

Anyway, I smiled and reminded him, "You called me, Hal." I looked at my watch. "My time is billable. You've got thirty seconds and I go back to work."

It seemed clear that we were on the verge of a nasty little power spat, and I wanted to get in the first blow.

An eyebrow twitched, he flopped open a manila folder, and studied something with great care and interest. With no preamble, he mentioned, "At 5:46, on Thursday night, you signed a Miss Janet Morrow into the firm. Correct?"

"Does it say that on the sign-in form?"

"It does."

"Then why are you asking?"

"At 5:55 P.M. you logged onto the firm's server. Correct?"

"What form does it say that on?"

"The central server monitors all transactions. I receive a complete printout twice a day." He snapped, "At 5:55, correct?"

"You're sure it wasn't 5:57?"

The piggy eyes turned piggier. "The server is recalibrated every fourth second by the clock at Greenwich. It is accurate to within three microseconds. It does not make errors."

"But you do. Right, Hal?" I actually was starting to think I'd just been transported to a really bad episode of *Hogan's Heroes* with Sergeant Schultz saying, "Achtung, Herr Colonel Hogan, the commandant is mad zat zomebody drew pimples on Der Führer's picture."

And true to form, Hal continued, "Starting at 5:58 there were multiple attempts from your terminal to enter the e-mail account of Lisa Morrow. Seven fruitless attempts, followed by a successful effort."

"What time was the successful effort?"

He stared back at his form. "That would be 6:04."

"And how many microseconds?"

His face reddened. "It has been widely noted that you have an attitude problem. Don't try it in here." He set down the folder and informed me, "Breaking into another firm member's files is a violation of firm policy. That policy was included on the firm's associate exam you took and passed. You should also know it is a federal crime."

I suspected that having two partners staring over his shoulder was cramping Hal's style. This motorized, legalistic interrogation was too lawyerly and prompted for this chubby little buffoon. In fact, it struck me that Hal had been given a script.

He put his elbows on the table, bent toward me, and went on, "What were you doing in that file?"

"Ask your all-knowing server."

Again, Hal glanced at his file, and oops—apparently, the server could tell him. "You downloaded information and an e-mail was sent. We know Janet Morrow was present." He established eye contact and asked, "Did you in fact permit a non-firm member to access our confidential databases?"

"Did I?"

Bronson chose this moment to intrude. "Answer him, Drummond." He folded his arms and added, "Miss Morrow, we've learned, is a city prosecutor in Boston, and her office is currently involved in cases against two of our firm's clients."

Well, it suddenly struck me that Hal was the type of paranoid bureaucrat who liked burning people, and the presence of two senior partners implied that the firm took Hal's obsessive idiocy seriously.

I therefore addressed my remarks to the partners and said, "We looked up Lisa's e-mail addresses so her sister could inform her friends about the funeral."

Hal demanded, "But you logged on using Lisa Morrow's name and password?"

"Is there another way, Hal?"

"And Janet Morrow was present, wasn't she?"

"And she's Lisa Morrow's sister, and she only saw the e-mail addresses." I looked back at the partners and added, "Case closed, docket cleared, time to run up those billable hours."

Bronson looked annoyed. But apparently Hal wasn't finished, because he lifted up the folder again, withdrew a computer printout, and tossed it onto his desk. "Explain this, Drummond."

"This" turned out to be a long column of electronic scribbles with two phrases highlighted in yellow—"LF:BosVSParagon" and "LF:BosVSMurray."

I shrugged and he said, "Don't play dumb with me. You know 'LF' stands for legal file. And you know the entries are *City of Boston versus Paragon Ventures,* and *City of Boston versus William Murray.*"

I replied, "Do I?"

"And you know Paragon Ventures is under indictment by the Boston District Attorney's Office for fraud and overbilling the government on Medicare payments. And William Murray has been charged with mail order fraud and conspiracy. They are clients of this firm, and both files were downloaded from Lisa Morrow's e-mail file."

He leaned back into his chair and smugly rocked back and forth. I found myself wondering why a firm such as this would hire a putz such as this.

And I knew from his expression that he wasn't finished, and indeed, he then said, "How these files ended up in Lisa Morrow's e-mail is very mysterious. But she's no longer alive to explain, is she?"

"But a brain like yours has surely manufactured an explanation, Hal."

"In fact, I have. I surmise that Lisa Morrow intended to help her sister. You were her friend, possibly her accomplice. Alternatively, you might have planted those files in Captain Morrow's e-mail, foolishly assuming we wouldn't pay attention to electronic activity in a dead person's account. In any regard, both files contain confidential information that would benefit the City of Boston's case."

Cy's shoulders were slumped with disappointment. Bronson did not appear at all disappointed; he had that half-scowling, half-happy look of a high school vice principal who just caught the school hoodlum drilling peepholes in the girls' room walls.

"Why, Sean?" asked Cy. "I knew you were unhappy about this assignment . . . but why?"

Indeed, why? Had I failed to see those two files in Lisa's e-mail? I mean, Janet had been so hot-to-trot to see Lisa's files. But that theory only worked if Lisa was crooked also.

It was also possible the server had an electronic infarction and registered the wrong files in the wrong place. But unlikely.

Which obviously left a setup—a high-tech frame. But by who? And why? I recalled my conversation the day before with Barry. Was there a connection? If so, there's who . . . possibly why. But how?

The Law of Crappy Coincidences warns that when two really good things happen to you at once, that's probably a coincidence. But when two really shitty things happen, there's a direct connection—you just have to find it.

"What happens next?" I asked.

Bronson answered, "Our ethics committee will meet Tuesday evening to decide your fate and whether we should turn this matter over to the court system." He added, regretfully, "You'll be permitted to defend yourself, of course."

"Of course."

He further informed me, "Until then your electronic rights are suspended. If you enter the firm's facilities you must have an escort from Mr. Merriweather's office. Is that understood?"

"Fine."

He fixed me with his version of a nasty glare, lowered his voice, and ordered, "And now, you will return to Morris Networks and complete the audit."

Was he kidding? I'm not trusted enough to turn on a computer or walk through the firm without a watchdog, but I remain billable to clients.

On the other hand, the audit had probably set back Morris Networks a few million bucks, and it sure would suck to have to inform the client that the supervising attorney was too ethically challenged to perform his duties, and ask to have it done again. The client might very logically point out that since the firm picked me, the firm should now pick up the tab. Back to the Law of Crappy Coincidences—the audit was scheduled to be completed Tuesday and the disciplinary powwow was set for that night.

You see what I mean? These private-sector guys think we public-sector guys are too stupid to pee.

CHAPTER TWENTY-FIVE

As I DROVE TO MORRIS NETWORKS I USED THE JAG'S BUILT-IN CARPHONE to call Janet's cell phone. Five rings, and then a mechanical female voice offered me a series of options—dial one for voicemail and so forth. So I punched one, and said, "Drummond here. Call me. Pronto."

I took the elevator upstairs and went to the conference room, where I found Martha parked in a corner peering quizzically at a long spreadsheet. We exchanged brief pleasantries and I was struck by this really off-the-wall thought that she might be the one who recorded those phone messages for the wireless services. Same dull, flat monotone and . . . oh, who gives a crap.

"Yesterday," I reminded her, "you asked about a company called Grand Vistas."

"Yes?"

"What information do you have on it?"

"Is there a problem?"

"None at all. I need to inform them they're included in our financials. It's a standard legal courtesy."

She nodded, then went back into the room and returned with a thin manila folder. "The contact information is inside. It's a privately held foreign company. Surely Morris's normal accounting firm knows this company, but since we were only hired for this audit, we're completely unfamiliar with it."

I thanked her and retreated to the car.

Janet returned my call as I drove to my apartment. I gave her directions and told her to meet me there for lunch.

A mere two weeks before, my life had been simple, tidy, and largely pleasant. I had a job I liked and understood, in an organization I loved but nobody understood. True, my boss and I had something of a conflicted relationship, but, to the degree the Army allows any individual such latitude, I had been the master of my own fate.

Suddenly, I was inside the cat's paw of any number of parties. Janet, for one; manipulating me to investigate her suspicions. Spinelli, jerking me around every time a new corpse turned up. Barry, maybe lining me up as a future scapegoat. And now, somebody I didn't know, or maybe did know, was setting me up for something worse. The fates seemed to be handing out tickets for a piece of Sean Drummond's ass, and I wanted to know why.

I got to my apartment, flipped on my computer, went to Google.com, and typed in "Janet Morrow—Boston Globe."

Three direct hits, and a long list of partial hits. The first direct hit was a news story that concerned a murder conviction Janet had won for a Crips gang member who shot three goombahs from a competing gang. Janet was quoted as saying, "Justice has been served," and the defense attorney naturally swore the trial was disgustingly unfair and vowed to appeal. Next was more of the same, a life sentence for a bigamist who snuffed two wives for the insurance premiums, and then a conviction against a pimp who killed two of his girls in a murderous rage.

So this was both interesting and instructive—three murder cases within a seven-month period. District attorneys typically assign their top brawlers when the charge is murder, or, as we say in the trade, headline magnets. This suggested that Janet was a fair-haired girl when the big ones were in play.

I noodled past other entries till I found one titled "Janet Morrow receives Patriot Award," part of a newsletter from an organization calling itself "The Patriot League, Responsible Citizens Dedicated to the Preservation and Improvement of Law and Order in the Grand City of Boston and its Local Environs." Surely a worthy cause, whatever the hell it meant. Described in the article were the date of the dinner, who attended, and so forth—stuff people read only to see if they're mentioned. In a speech, the chairman of the Patriot League, Jack Something, exalted Janet's many legal accomplishments, her unparalleled conviction rate, and he anointed her the Avenging Angel of Boston. Cute.

Grand Vistas was next, and multiple entries popped up. It appeared to be the kind of malleable title befitting everything from a porn site "for lovers of big-assed Latino women" to a tourist agency. Eventually, I found a company Web site.

Your standard corporate logo popped on the screen, a huge Z, like Zorro, with a bunch of portals for everything from corporate information to job opportunities. I thought maybe I should start with the job openings. I might be needing one.

Grand Vistas described itself as an international holding company registered in Bermuda with extensive investments and interests in telecommunications, zinc, diamond mines, gold mines, shipping, and heavy equipment leasing. Sounded like a company with identity issues. Nothing about owners or investors. Nothing about the corporate structure or its corporate officers. A few pictures of ships and mines representative of the company's widespread businesses.

Geez. Trojan wrappers offer more information.

I dug the contact's phone number out of the folder. I studied a long string of numbers that started with 0011, an overseas exchange, though I didn't recognize the country code.

I was connected to one of those metallic voices that spooled me through ten options, none of which sounded like who I wanted to speak with, I suppose, because I had no idea who I did want to speak with. I was finally allowed to punch nine for a real human being.

"Grand Vistas. How may I help you?" answered a female voice, in English, but accented in some European flavor I couldn't discern. I informed her I wanted to speak with somebody who knew how the corporation operated. She pointed out that a number of offices knew how the corporation operated, and couldn't I be more specific. Accounting perhaps? Absolutely not, I replied. Legal? No, lawyers are assholes. Operations? Yes, fine.

A voice eventually answered, "Philippe Jardeau."

I said, "Hello, Philippe, do you speak English?"

"A leettle. Can I help you with sometheeng?"

"I hope so. Name's Bill . . . Bill Clinton, and I work for Morris Networks."

"Cleen—ton?" he asked with that odd way the French have of mistreating our vowels.

"Of all names, right?"

"I suppose."

"I always tell people I'm the one who *did* inhale."

"I'm sorry, I—"

"Hey, get this. My wife's name's Monica. Wow, she catches some shit." Well, enough with causing confusion about my telephonic disguise, I asked Philippe, "Hey, what's your position in the company?"

"I am the *aseestant* director for operations."

"Hey, I've got the right guy. Thing is, I'm working on a company audit, and the name of your conglomerate came up. I mean, we do all that swapping together every year."

"Swapping?"

"Yeah—exchanging shares and utilization on each other's networks."

"Ah . . . yes, I am familiar with *theeez*."

"This audit is critical to us getting a big Defense Department contract."

"Okay. I see."

"And we've booked a lot of revenue from you guys. Eighty million, last quarter."

"Yes?"

"Turns out our Defense Department has no record of you."

"And why is *theez* a problem?"

"It's a simple verification issue. Bureaucrats, right?"

There was a long pause before he said, "I am afraid I cannot help you."

"Hey, pal, nothing hard here. Just name the telecommunications companies that are swapping with Morris."

"I, um . . . one moment."

Philippe must've had his hand over the mouthpiece because I could hear muffled voices. The language wasn't English, but neither was it French.

He then informed me, "We are a private company, yes? We do not divulge our holdings to outsiders."

"You know, I'm always telling Jason he screwed up not staying private. Now we have to wear our underwear outside our pants."

"This is your problem, Mr. Cleenton . . . not ours."

"Good point." I asked, "Would you be more comfortable discussing this if I flew out and met with you? Tell me where and I'll be on a plane tonight."

"No, that w—"

"Philippe, this contract's worth two billion big ones. Jason's gonna get a big-time case of the ass if we lose it 'cause you guys are uptight about a meaningless confidentiality issue."

Another long pause, and I assumed Philippe was once again chatting with somebody in the background. He finally said, "What is your office in Morris Networks?"

"I'm with the audit firm. I work with Barry Bosworth. Know him?"

"Uh . . . no. A moment." When he finally spoke, he said, "Direct your questions to Mr. Bosworth. Do not call and bother us again." Abrupt tone, loud click, and an empty line.

Boy, he sure tidied up the loose ends.

I mean, in most ways, I knew nothing more than when I started. But in knowing that, I knew considerably more.

Some companies stay private and forgo public money because they're family firms and don't want anybody else messing with the family jewels. Others because it's an ego thing, and still others because they're owned by paranoid control freaks like Howard Hughes and regard public stockholders as nasty germs. But even those companies are willing to list their holdings. I mean, to some degree, the whole capitalist game is a big-pecker contest, and what's the fun if you don't post your inches?

So Grand Vistas was this mysterious holding company headquartered on an island known for no taxes and laissez-faire rules regarding business. Both employees I'd spoken to were foreigners. Yet the lingua franca of the company wasn't English, nor French, but nor did it sound Spanish or Asian. We were down to a hundred-some-odd languages, but good detective work often boils down to elimination rather than addition.

More intriguing was that way Philippe kept slapping his palm over the mouthpiece to confer with whoever guided him through our conversation. I mean, there's three kinds of folks with that kind of squeamishness—the military, spy agencies, and crooks.

I went to the kitchen, yanked two steaks out of the refrigerator, found two potatoes in the cupboard, and started preparing lunch.

CHAPTER TWENTY-SIX

*A*nne Carrol hadn't yet hit the news. Yet he was sure that within an hour her name would be the topic du jour in country stores, old ladies' knitting groups, and police stations nationwide. Unbelievable what that monster did to her, folks would say, wagging their fingers and looking plainly horrified.

If Fiorio garnered attention because of her fame and popularity, the pain inflicted on Anne Carrol's fiercely punished body would cause an entire nation to clench its teeth and cry for the murderous bastard to be caught.

Distasteful, but she had to be done in just that way. He sprayed another dose of Windex on the mirror and rubbed with enough vigor to purge every last trace of toothpaste or spit that might've splattered the surface. It was the sixth cleaning. But after all, he had spent a lot of time at the mirror, and there was no sense making a mistake at this stage. Modern techniques being what they were, DNA could be collected off a pinhead these days. The living room was done, every last surface scrubbed and rescrubbed with the best solvents money could buy. The closet—spotless. The kitchen sparkled. He had even rented a vacuum, for four hours running it back and forth and sucking up every particle and dustball. He had dumped the bags in a garbage receptacle at a mall three miles away. The clothes he'd worn over the past three weeks, the sheets he slept on, the pillows, everything had been hauled off and incinerated. The bicycle was buried in a seven-foot hole in some thick woods.

A spanking new briefcase rested on the spotless table in the living room, and the final two profiles were inside. His next kill wouldn't be done in this city, however. He had planned all along to ratchet up the heat here, and do her elsewhere. Her death would be different and no connection to the awful killer in D.C. would be imagined or construed. This wasn't her hometown anyway, was it? That she'd come here wasn't in his plans and he regarded it as a terrible inconvenience. Well, he'd just have to find a way to draw her out.

He'd heard on the morning news that the corpse of a twenty-year-old GW student named John Negroponte had been discovered twelve miles outside D.C. on the canal towpath. From the damage to his bike and the catastrophic dent in his head, the police were assuming he'd been biking too fast, lost control, and slammed into a tree. A tragic accident; he probably hit a rut and somehow his helmet slipped off. A memorial service was scheduled at the GW University chapel, and the public was invited to attend.

Two of the three rental cars were parked in the lot that bordered the hotel, freshly scrubbed and detailed, doors unlocked, keys tucked under the driver's mats. In three hours, two associates would appear to drive the cars back to Philadelphia and their rental agencies. He'd be long gone, on the far side of Baltimore, driving the last rental car north to Boston for the next kill.

The city of Washington would hold its breath for two or three days, and wonder where he'd strike next. After a week, *the FBI and cops would be scratching their heads. On the corpses' palms he had contracted for ten victims. The L.A. Killer promised five and delivered five. Their profilers had told them that he treated this as a wicked game of wits and would stake everything on winning.*

They conditioned themselves with their own procedures and techniques, and were always astonished when the killer didn't play by the very rules they'd assumed he'd set.

CHAPTER TWENTY-SEVEN

JANET ARRIVED AT NOON. SHE STEPPED INSIDE, DROPPED HER COAT BY THE door, and immediately began wandering and snooping. Why do women do that? We go to their apartments and maybe wonder what brand of beer they stock. Usually, that's something called "Lite" beer, which is really bubbly tap water, which is why I always bring my own. They'll claw through our underwear drawers if they think they won't be caught. And when they get caught, they say something silly, like, "Nope, no napkins here. Where do you keep them?"

Anyway, my apartment is very compact, having a tiny living room, efficiency kitchen, and bedroom with a cramped bath. I am fairly neat and tidy, though it has been suggested that an interior decorator might make a few minor alterations. I'm no expert, but I believe the style of decor is labeled "This Pit Needs F-ing Work," because some of my lady guests have mumbled words to the effect. It suits me and my needs, however.

I know, for example, that the guiding rule of interior decoration is the need for every living room to have a dominating piece.

Mine happens to be a sixty-inch big-screen TV, intravenously fed by a cable box. A few beaten-up bookshelves and a pair of reclining chairs strategically positioned six feet from the sixty-inch screen complete the decor. I have an obsession for bare white walls, and a thing against clutter, rugs, plants, side tables, lamps, and so forth. It took two men forty-five minutes to move me in, and will take probably less time to haul me out. Traveling light is practical when you're in the Army, and obligatory when you have trouble finding bosses that like you.

Janet was shaking her head. "You actually live here?" She swiftly said, "Oh . . . I'm sorry—you probably just moved in."

"Very funny."

She laughed. She said, "This pit needs work." Right.

Anyway, I wandered toward the tiny porch off my living room, where two steaks were grilling. She studied the mammoth TV a moment, then took the remote off the top, flipped it on, and asked, "Have you been watching?"

"Should I have been?"

"It's a bad one, Sean."

Well, the channel was preset on ESPN, so she had to surf around a bit for Fox News. A stunning female reporter stood with a mike pressed to her lips, a tall gray office building and banged-up green Dumpster as backdrops, saying, ". . . when the call came into our Washington studio, the building you see behind me, claiming that a body was inside the Dumpster outside. Leslie Jackson, our studio manager, and a security guard went to check, and then notified the police. Though local authorities aren't offering any details, we know from Leslie's description that the newest victim was horribly mutilated. Her corpse was naked, her limbs were shattered from repeated blows by a heavy blunt object. In a disturbingly gruesome step, her nose had been cut off her face."

She took a question from the anchorperson, and replied, "No, Mark, the body has not yet been identified, though the FBI expect to know her identity later today. They also confirmed that her neck was broken, just like the other vic—"

Janet abruptly hit the off button, then informed me, "Earlier they confirmed that four slash ten was written on her palm."

I flipped the steaks, and she joined me. She stood and stared off into the distance. The day was chilly and brisk. Dark clouds were sprinting and spiraling across the sky; a driving rainstorm appeared to be moving in, a typical mid-December day for Washington, and another woman would not live to see it.

I threw the steaks on a plate and Janet followed as I carried them into the kitchen. I withdrew the potatoes from the oven. A bottle of red wine was open, breathing, as they say, though exactly how dead grapes breathe is an enigma I'm sure I don't want answered. I filled a glass of wine for her and popped a beer for me. My kitchen was equipped with an eating counter and we both got comfortable.

I asked, "By the way, what are the odds of William Murray getting convicted?"

"What?"

"William Murray?" The question was meant to throw her, but I was getting a blank look. "Mail fraud and conspiracy?"

"I don't know what you're talking about." And she did, indeed, appear perplexed.

"Paragon Ventures?"

"The company accused of the big Medicare scam?"

"You know about it?"

"Yes—everybody knows about it. It was all over the *Boston Globe* for weeks. The Boston DA's office is handling it."

"Are you involved in the prosecution?"

"What's this about?"

"Are you involved?"

She shook her head. "Paragon Ventures is accused of committing a corporate crime. I work felonies, and I prosecute murders mostly. What's this about?"

"This morning I was dragged in front of a couple of the firm's senior partners. The server we logged onto the other day showed that we downloaded two legal files. It happens that Culper, Hutch, and Westin is handling the defense for both parties."

"Oh . . . and you—"

"Yes. I'm in very deep shit, accused of abetting your theft of confidential firm information that's very injurious to two of their highly valued clients."

"That is deep shit."

"Put on your hip boots. You're my accomplice."

She thought about this a moment, then asked, "And those files were supposed to be in Lisa's e-mail?"

"So the server says." I added, "And I was assured that the server does not lie. And did you know it's hooked up to some wildass clock in Greenwich that keeps it accurate to within three . . . whatevers?"

"What?" she asked, somewhat distracted. "It's ridiculous. You saw what I saw."

"I thought I did."

"You did. So . . . somebody doctored the files afterward. It's the only explanation."

"No, it's the most likely explanation." Then I asked her, "Barry Bosworth, did Lisa ever mention him?"

"Why? Do you think he's involved with this?"

"I have no reason to."

She stared at me for a few seconds, then said, "Over the course of the year, Lisa told me about a number of the people she worked with at your firm. I had the impression it's a very . . . an unfriendly environment." She added, "Bosworth was high on her list of people she didn't trust or like."

"His wife and children don't trust or like him. Specifics, please."

"Lisa complained about him several times. He gave her a hard time, took credit for some of her better work, generally tried to undermine her. He saw her as a threat, and tried his best to harm her."

"The same Barry I know and love. What about Sally Westin?"

"She was higher on the list than Barry."

"We're talking about the same Sally?"

She nodded, and she said, "Lisa mentioned several times that she thought something was strange and . . . No, actually, she said something was phony about her. I had the sense that her dislike of Westin was more personal than her feelings toward Bosworth. I think she regarded Sally as more dangerous." She added, "I don't know why."

I found this a bit confusing.

I mean, Sally struck me as a hopeless case—not overly bright, lousy client skills, one of those unfortunate people who kill themselves trying . . . literally. Every firm has them, that guy or gal who sweats too hard, stays too late, too often, and spends too much time on their knees sucking up to partners. They think effort and suction will be their own just rewards. Not so. Just not so. In the highly competitive field of law, talent and brains are the tickets to the brass ring. I had observed no inkling of either in Miss Sally Westin.

But regarding Sally, I also felt, as I mentioned, that something was odd, repressed, almost coiled. Knowing her tragic background, I supposed she was carrying around a bundle of confused emotions, bitter regrets, anger, guilt, and God knows what other poisonous attributes. The children of suicidal parents often have a heavy cross to bear, emptiness, unfulfillment, and confused destinies. But how that made Sally dangerous was a factor I had yet to figure out.

I asked Janet, "Anybody else I should be careful of, know about, whatever?"

She lifted her wineglass and stared down into the liquid. "Well, Cy Berger."

Now I really looked confused, so she asked, "You mean you still don't know?"

"Know what?"

"I thought you . . . well, I thought you knew." She put down the wineglass. "You recall that Lisa was dating someone for a good part of the past year?"

When I said nothing, she added, "I think I also mentioned that my father, my sisters, and I were very upset about it. He's much older, for one thing. But like everybody, we were also aware of his reputation, and that wasn't very reassuring."

"What did Lisa see in him?"

"He's charming and successful." But she contemplated my question further, then suggested, "I think partly it was the bad-boy image. Does that make sense?"

"No."

"Lisa's whole life she was very . . . what's the word here? Whatever she set her mind to, she always excelled at—first in the class in everything, track star, boys always calling. That can leave a woman vulnerable."

"Vulnerable?"

"Yeah, vul— You don't know women very well, do you?"

Well, I knew them well enough not to answer that.

She explained, "Some women . . . Lisa was one, maybe, they're very self-confident and that leads to a strong reforming instinct." Her eyes sort of wandered around my apartment as she added, "Possibly it's why Lisa liked you, too."

Hmmm. "Go on."

"Most women have a streak of it. Why do you think guys like Richard Gere and Vin Diesel are such big stars? Women watch them on the screen and dream of saving them from themselves."

Well, this was weird. Life truly is just filled with these little men are from Mars and women from Venus oddities. A guy sees a bad girl, does he even *think* about reforming her? No—he wonders, What are the odds I can get a piece of that action and sneak out the back door before she learns my real name and phone number? If I ever have a daughter, we're going to have a long chat about men. Pigs. Complete pigs.

But back to the subject. I said, "And how did it end?"

"This is Cy we're talking about."

"Lisa caught him cheating?"

"She did."

"With who?"

"Didn't say. Just that Cy and another woman started an affair." She added, "When Lisa confronted him, Cy actually tried to persuade her to enter a sharing arrangement."

"I'll bet that went over well."

"You can't imagine."

A piece of this made no sense, and I mentioned, "Cy said Lisa was offered a partnership in the Boston office. She accepted, and was preparing her resignation from the Army."

"He said that?"

"Yes."

"Well . . . I don't know about it."

"But you would know, wouldn't you?"

"Not necessarily."

"But I'd think—"

"This is the first I've heard of it."

I looked at her with confusion. I mean, Lisa would discuss where her boyfriend was tucking his ex-senatorial weenie, yet she failed to mention a job that would place the two of them in the same city? Weird. Just weird.

But there was a more pressing subject, and I said, "Have you ever heard of a company called Grand Vistas?"

"Should I have?" She then asked, "Is this another case the Boston DA's handling?"

"Not that I'm aware of. Possibly. It's an international company with holdings in everything from shipping to precious metals to telecommunications."

"Why would I have heard of it?"

"No particular reason." I refilled her wineglass. "I wondered if Lisa ever mentioned it."

"No."

"Do you know anybody who could maybe research it?"

She contemplated this and me a moment. "The Boston DA's office has a corporate fraud unit. It often works with the SEC. John Andrews, the head of the unit, is a friend."

"How good a friend?"

"He'd like to be more than a friend."

"So you could ask and—"

"And he'd want to know why. Johnny's in that job for a good reason. He bends the rules for no man . . . or woman."

"That would be problematic."

"I see." She took another sip of wine and asked, "A public or private company?"

"Private. And registered in Bermuda."

Just as she was on the verge of asking the next question, the phone rang. Daniel Spinelli identified himself and said I should meet him at the Alexandria police station as soon as I could get my butt over there. He further asked, Did I happen to know how to find the lovely Miss Janet Morrow? Indeed I did.

It wasn't hard to guess what this was about.

CHAPTER TWENTY-EIGHT

THERE WERE NO VACANT DESKS IN THE DETECTIVE SECTION OF THE Alexandria police station. All hands were on deck, to borrow a naval term, indicating that Lieutenant Martin and his grim flatfoots had escalated to full crisis mode. Phones were ringing, scores of people were being interviewed, detectives scurrying from desk to desk, trading tips and case notes and the odds on Sunday's Redskins game against the loathsome Dallas Cowboys. In short, all the trappings of a roomful of dedicated professionals working diligently to catch the bad guy before he struck again.

Anyway, Lieutenant Martin was in his glass cage, and appeared exhausted and wrung out; collar unbuttoned, tie loosened, sleeves rolled up, thick bags under bloodshot eyes—a man with a world of shit on his shoulders. Also I noted Spinelli and a stranger in a gray suit seated side by side against the back wall. Black-and-white photos of dead bodies in gruesome poses were everywhere, taped to the glass walls, spread around desks, piled in stacks on the floor.

It has been my experience that the more flustered the cops become, the more they make up for lack of progress by fabricating the signs of frantic activity. Cops are very good at faking it. These shots of dead girls were a sort of picturesque camouflage, or perhaps guilty reminders. In any regard, a guy was still free and running around town who would likely regard the gallery as a fine testament to his prowess and handiwork.

Janet nodded at Lieutenant Martin, then turned in the direction of Spinelli and the guy seated beside him, and she froze.

The guy got out of his chair, smiled, and said, "Hello, Janet."

"George."

Uh-oh—it seemed I had heard that name before.

He crossed the floor and planted a kiss on her cheek.

He said to her, "I am truly sorry about Lisa. I've been angling to get on this case since I heard. Of course, I had to wait till it turned federal."

She was staring at him like a corpse that popped out of a coffin. "You're on the case?"

"As of last night. But the Director decided that since two of the victims lived in Alexandria and the third was deposited here, the overall lead will stay with the locals. I've just been appointed the SAC for the Bureau's contingent."

SAC, if you don't know, is FBI-speak for Senior Agent in Charge. This is how Boy Scouts pronounce BMIC, Big Motherfucker in Charge, which would be more accurate, as the FBI tends to treat locals like idiots and leave lots of bruised feelings in its wake.

Special Agent George Meany, the guy who screwed his fiancée for a promotion, was tall and well-built, scrubbed and dressed like an overgrown choirboy, with clean-cut good looks and a John Wayneish way of moving and standing. Also, he looked remarkably like Eliot Ness, meaning a younger Robert Stack, right down to his cleft chin and scrunched-up forehead that seemed to convey eternal thoughtfulness and seriousness of purpose. Or possibly he had gas.

Anyway, he looked at me and held out a hand, which I took. He said, "I'm Special Agent George Meany. I assume you're Major Drummond."

"Well . . . somebody has to be."

He regarded me more closely and said, "Janet and I are old friends."

"Good for you."

"Very dear old friends."

I smiled at him, and in that instant we both, I think, concluded we weren't going to like each other. With men, it often comes down to a sort of dog thing, some quick, visceral sniffs, and bingo, watch your ass when you piss on each other's trees. But I knew why I didn't like him. He screwed, and then fucked, my friend, and that's disgusting. Plus, I didn't like the way he referred to Martin and Spinelli as "locals." It had a nasty, condescending ring, like he really meant yokels, and we should all kiss his angelic ass.

But why he instantly disliked me was the more intriguing question. The answer, I guess, was poised about a foot away, the tree, so to speak, who was still staring at George with her jaw agape.

And just to be sure we got things off on the right foot, I was about to say something really tart and nasty, when Janet intervened, saying, "George, I'm glad you're here. Really. This is a very tough case and it's obviously personal for me. I appreciate that you've asked to get involved." Janet looked at me and added, "George is one of the FBI's top field agents. We worked together in Boston."

She had already told me this, of course. So I interpreted this to mean, Keep your nose out of this, Drummond. Well, I'm a gentleman, and it wasn't any of my business, so I decided to comply with her wishes. I would behave perfectly toward George until I could think of a good way to stick my foot deeply up his ass.

Besides, Lieutenant Martin had suddenly begun apologizing for inconveniencing us again, and then flashed us photos of the most recently deceased. As Fox had reported, her nose had been hacked off, splattering the rest of her face with blood. A visual ID from these photos would have been difficult for her own mother. Regardless, Janet and I both said we didn't recognize her.

Next, a black-and-white photo was jammed in our faces—same

woman, pre-mortis, if you will, an office or passport photo, I guessed. A fairly attractive woman, I thought, but for her nose, a big knobby thing that overwhelmed every other feature. Again Janet and I confessed we didn't know her.

"Her name's Anne Carrol," Lieutenant Martin grimly informed us. "The victim was single, gay, and a hotshot attorney at the Securities and Exchange Commission."

So, this was interesting—two attorneys, an accountant, and a TV blabberperson. Roughly the same age, ranging from mildly attractive to very attractive, well educated, successful, single, and professional. Common threads, as we say in the trade. But was there some one thread in particular, some defining human essence that attracted a killer? Successful women? Attractive women? Right-handed women?

Well, it was a waste of time for me to hypothesize, because the FBI and local flatfoots were surely mulling the same comparisons, just as they were continuing to turn over every stone, judging by our presence here. I mean, here we were three murders away from Lisa's, and still bouncing in and out of the Alexandria station every time a new corpse turned up.

Anyway, checking the block, Spinelli asked Janet, "Is it possible your sister knew her?"

"Possibly." She thought about it a moment, then said, "She never mentioned her."

"Carrol was done last night, 'bout nine," Spinelli explained. "Shortly after ten this mornin' the ghoul called Fox and said to peek in the Dumpster out back. We still don't know where he did the job on her."

I asked Spinelli, "You're sure the killer made the call?"

"He said he tried to fix her nose."

"Oh . . . right."

Janet remarked to Spinelli, "The press are reporting that you suspect it's the L.A. Killer."

"That's the prevailing opinion," Martin confirmed. He then

glanced over at Spinelli, and informed us, "Although he doesn't agree."

Janet asked Spinelli, "Why, Danny?"

The question wasn't directed at him, but Meany bounced up and stated, "Janet, we're nearly a hundred percent sure it's him."

"But not a hundred percent?"

"You know that level of certainty's an impossibility. But I've looked at everything—it's him."

Janet glanced over at Spinelli and asked, "From the sperm on Fiorio's body, did you get a DNA match with the other victims?"

"The sperm on her thigh matched none of the other specimens," Spinelli replied.

"Well, isn't that odd?" Janet asked, or suggested. "Three different sperm types."

"It *is* a mystery," Meany said. "But don't read too much into it."

"I'm not, George." She then said to Meany, "I'm just curious. According to the news accounts, the L.A. Killer left his own semen."

"Right. That is what we thought, at the time. We figure he realized that was a mistake and is covering his tracks better this time."

Janet offered him an odd smile. "I'm confused."

"About what?"

"The sperm on the corpses . . . whose is it?"

"Whose? We have no idea whose. Not his, obviously. In fact, we think he's splashing specimens on the bodies."

"Specimens?"

"Yes . . . specimens. We think he carries vials around, most likely obtained from a fertility clinic or a doctor's office. Cuthburt's murder suggests this guy's an expert in B&E, and those types of facilities don't have a reputation for great security."

"But didn't the L.A. Killer ejaculate his own sperm?"

"As I said, that was our opinion. He was never caught, though, so we never got a DNA match. Maybe he was splashing, too."

"But you're suggesting this guy splashes different people's semen on the bodies. Why the difference?"

Meany crossed the floor and put a hand on her arm. "Look,

think back to that first case we worked together. Or any case you've ever prosecuted. There are always incongruous threads in these things."

I was about to ask Meany if by incongruous threads, he meant things like strong-arming witnesses, illegal wiretaps, and so forth. But before I could make that helpful point, Janet replied, "For the sake of argument, assume you've already got the L.A. Killer's DNA from the killings three years ago. Why would he hide it this time?"

Meany replied, "You said yourself, that's an assumption. In any regard, we know the man's a nut. Who can tell what twisted logic is driving him this time? The truth is, we won't know till we catch him." His hand was still on her arm as he informed her, "But we *will* catch him, Janet. Have no doubt about that."

Janet faced Spinelli and asked, "Danny, what's your view?"

"Mine?" He glanced pointedly at Meany and said, "We got a guy tryin' to act like the L.A. Killer."

"A copycat?"

He nodded. "That L.A. guy, he liked to squeal to the local news about the finer points of his handiwork, right?"

"So you're suggesting a copycat might have a profile to fit into."

"A fuckin' textbook."

"And what makes you think this isn't just the same guy?"

"The sperm thing. The L. A. wacko didn't toss somebody else's. This guy's jerkin' us around."

Meany, who was *still* holding Janet's arm, said, "We of course considered what Spinelli's suggesting. Look, the Director's directly involved and our top people are on it. We've carefully, blah, blah . . ." He launched into this incredibly long spiel about how his all-knowing and beloved FBI looks at everything, similarities, differences, and so forth, and computes them into its assessments. I tuned him out.

Not that I don't admire the FBI; I actually think they're a wonderful bunch and all that, but if these guys were *that* good, how come they didn't catch the Rosenbergs till after they gave the commies the blueprints for a nuclear device? I mean, you fry these two people *after* they already told the Sovs how to incinerate a hundred million folks? If there's such a thing as postmature ejaculation, these guys had it.

However, Janet's eyes never left his face, and, incidentally, his hand never left her arm. I found this annoying for some reason. The same guy who shoved a shiv in her back now shows up, all smiley and dimple-chinned, the white knight promising to slay the nasty old dragon. Give me a break—the only reason this jerk slapped on the kneepads and begged his bosses for this case was to wheedle his way back into Janet's knickers. Surely she saw right through him. Right?

But there was this moment after Meany finished his FBI-knows-all tutorial where everybody just sat and pondered what he'd said. Or maybe, like me, they'd all tuned out so long that they needed a moment to restart their motors.

Janet finally said, "Thank you, George."

Another moment passed before Janet suggested, "The theory was the L.A. Killer ejaculated. Either the torture or the act of killing got him off, right?"

Meany replied, "That's what our profilers concluded. The victim abuse and killing were sexual fantasies for him. We believe he experienced orgasm at some point during the torture, then snapped their necks." He added, "Roughly speaking, this case appears to follow the same model."

"Then shouldn't there be traces of his semen?"

"I know this is going to sound silly," Meany informed her. "Our profilers hypothesize that our killer now wears a condom."

Silly? I believe I mumbled, "Boy, it sounds so obvious now that you mention it."

Meany stared at me—three demerits.

Janet faced Meany again. "And what about the increasing ferocity toward the victims?"

"Not uncommon," he replied. "Success goes to their heads. We see it all the time. They start with certain inhibitions. The more they get away with, the more those inhibitions erode. Also, it gets harder to achieve sexual arousal. They push the envelope and experiment more."

Janet appeared to ponder this point, then said, "And you think that accounts for it?"

"There's a second theory we're wrestling with. He may see this as a competition . . . a game. The women are pieces on the board. The provocative postures of the victims, the calls to the networks, the splashed semen as a calling card, the whole process of physical escalation could mean he sees this as a match. He makes the rules, maybe even alters the rules, and we have to play."

Spinelli, I noticed, was hunched over, staring at the floor, feet tapping, a sort of sardonic expression pasted on his face. And it struck me that he and I, we had a few things in common. We both thought George Meany was an asshole. Also, this prolonged discussion about sperm and DNA made for great cocktail conversation—or possibly not—but nothing more. *Debates* about the queer habits of this ghoul weren't going to catch him. Maybe it made everybody feel better, but it was a substitute for actually dropping this guy. The score was Killer 4, Cops 0; they've got no tangible evidence to tie him to the crimes, no idea who he is or how they're going to catch him, and everybody's trying to figure out whether he slaps a poolie over his pudley.

Eventually, even they drew the conclusion that the subject had been exhausted, and after a few more closing comments, special thanks from Martin for coming in, and so forth, the group began to break up. Hands were shaken, fond adieus were exchanged, and then Meany escorted Janet and me back through the warren of detective desks and out to the parking lot.

In fact, we were at my car when Meany said to me, "Excuse us, Drummond. Janet and I need to talk about a few things. In private."

He then led Janet about thirty feet away. They squared off, about five feet apart, and faced each other. I had no intention of eavesdropping, because it was absolutely none of my business. I believe respect for others' privacy is next to Godliness. However, the hearing in my left ear happens to be better than my right, and if I kept my head twisted just so, snatches of the conversation did inadvertently drift into my aural cavity.

For instance, Meany, in a whiny tone, complaining, ". . . and you just disappeared out of my life, walked out . . . without giving me any chance to explain."

And Janet replying, "What did you expect, George? You shouldn't have gone to my boss on me. You betrayed me.

"I didn't. I swear I didn't. My supervisors in D.C. made that call. I swear that's—"

Well, the wind suddenly whipped up and there was a long exchange I couldn't catch. But I have a good eye for body language. And Meany was bending toward her, appearing earnest, that scrunched-up forehead pickled with sincerity, his hands roving all over her arms and shoulders. Also, Meany was one of those guys who closes the airspace, and the gap had narrowed from five feet to a few inches.

Then the wind died down and I overheard Meany say to her, ". . . and I *still* love you."

And Janet reply to him, "Well . . . I, uh, I'm confused about my feelings toward you."

I mean, please. Wake up, Janet. The guy was lying. From fifty feet away I could tell that—his lips were moving.

Anyway, the wind whipped up again, and they chatted for another few minutes, and you could tell it was getting pretty cordial before they finally concluded the discussion and headed back in my direction. I wouldn't say they were lovey-dovey or anything. But from their expressions and the relaxed, amiable way they moved, George had really twisted her ear and was back in some form of good graces.

In fact, Meany had his arm over Janet's shoulder and was whispering something.

Geez, somebody had to do something, so I interrupted and said, "Hey, George, you mentioned you were sure you'd catch this guy. How?"

As I mentioned previously, cops hate it when you try to pin them down. Plus, somebody needed to bring Janet back to her senses and show her this guy was full of shit.

In fact, Special Agent Meany appeared not to appreciate my inquiry, because his eyes sort of narrowed as he said, "Good detective work, great technology, and brainpower." He added, "Why? What business is it of yours?"

"Well, you know . . . curiosity."

"Great. I love curious witnesses. I've got seventy-five agents working around the clock, the media, public relations people, and my bosses jumping all over my ass, and I've got all the time in the world to answer questions from some clown like you."

Well, goodness. Janet gave George an odd look and said, "It was a perfectly fair question."

He shot me a curt glance and replied to her, "I'm sorry. You're right. I haven't gotten much sleep since I took over this investigation. I guess I'm a little irritable." He then leaned against the side of my car and said to me, "All right. You asked, so I'll fill you in on what I've discovered. I've reconstructed the murder sites and reviewed every element of the evidence and crime reports. You should always do that, right?"

"Right."

"Because sometimes . . . well, sometimes you pick up things others missed. Not that they're incompetent, but in the heat of battle, as you people call it, certain details can slip through the cracks."

I didn't want another long tutorial from this jerk, and I said, "Well, this is very interesting, but—"

"*And,*" he continued, "with a second look you pick up some of those things. Here's an example. Lieutenant Martin's log says that on the night of Lisa's murder you arrived at the Pentagon parking lot at 9:27 P.M. Martin's people estimate she was murdered about thirty minutes prior. You told Martin you were supposed to meet her in that parking lot. You see the problem?"

I was starting to explain what the problem was when he

added, with a nasty smirk, "Of course, I'm not blaming you, but I did wonder why Lisa was standing around in a big empty parking lot, late at night, vulnerable to this monster. She was well-known for being cautious, efficient, and punctual. Then I put two and two together. And, this is just a guess . . . but I concluded that her date didn't have the courtesy to be on time." He added, "In fact, had you been on time, it wouldn't have happened."

Janet was giving me a queer look.

I looked at her and explained, "I was late because I was getting a ticket from a cop."

He slapped a hand on my shoulder and said, "Don't make up excuses for my sake, pal. I told you . . . nobody's blaming you."

He turned to Janet and said, "Why don't I give you a lift back to your hotel? It'll give us a chance to catch up, and discuss our arrangements for dinner."

It struck me, as I watched them drive away, that I might have underestimated Mr. George Meany.

Did I get my ass kicked, or what?

CHAPTER TWENTY-NINE

THE ACCOUNTINGFEST WAS IN ITS DEATH THROES WHEN I POPPED BACK INTO the conference room. The two dozen accountants who had inhabited this room had disappeared back into whatever hobbit hole they crawled out of. Three guys in gray coveralls were feeding reams of now useless spreadsheets into shredders, and a techie was noisily disassembling the phones in the corner.

The end of an audit is a sad and ugly sight, and a tear of regret spilled down my cheek.

Right.

Martha, the head number-cruncher, was huddled in the far corner with Jessica Moner, Morris's beefy legal counsel and possibly my future boss, and beside her, to my surprise, was Barry, my backstabbing buddy and current boss.

They noticed me, and the conversation died. I mean, if Brutus and his buddies had been so ridiculously conspicuous, Caesar never would've had those shivs stuffed in his back, the Visigoths would've ended up a lost tribe, and we'd all be speaking Italian. But the lawyers, clever as they are in the arts of treachery, responded instinctively, smiled, and tossed a few innocuous waves. Martha stared at the floor and shuffled her feet, the picture of a troubled conscience.

I said to Barry, "Checking up on me?"

"What? . . . No, I, uh . . . I just dropped by to see how things are coming." He patted my shoulder and added, "And everything's great. Congratulations on making the timeline."

"Well, you know, Barry, it was a great team effort. Yes, my legal contributions were both brilliant and crucial, but Martha and her people deserve a little of the credit." I winked at Martha.

"Well . . . whatever." He said to Martha, "Why don't you get the audit?"

And Martha actually looked relieved as she left the room to retrieve it.

Jessica, still smiling, said to me, "We're glad you showed up. Great timing. This is working out perfectly."

"Why?"

"Your strategy concerning the Nash issue worked."

"Of course. Am I some guy, or what?"

She explained, "In fact, the Defense Department held a protest conference this morning. Silas Jackler from Fields, Jason, and Morgantheau led a joint team representing Sprint and AT&T. Barry and I were present on our behalf."

Barry chuckled and commented, "History was made this morning, Drummond. Silas Jackler developed a sudden case of lockjaw."

Jessica also chuckled and explained, "The Defense Department lawyers asked Jackler to specify his concerns."

I asked, "And did he?"

"He insisted it just *looked* suspicious. Apparently, he and his people were well aware of the legal risks."

Always one to get in the last word, Barry said, "He tried to throw a few peripheral jabs about Nash and we sat and acted dumb."

"That must have been very difficult for you," I said to Barry, tongue in cheek.

"So," Jessica summarized, "good work and we're proud as shit of you."

"Well, shucks."

"The best news of all," Barry added, "is that we persuaded the Defense lawyers to decide the protest by Friday."

"Wow . . . Friday . . . imagine that."

He added, "But we did have to guarantee the full audit immediately. And Jackler has until Thursday to submit any further documentation or the Nash issue goes away."

Jessica grinned. "Get it, Drummond? You sign the audit, we submit, end of fucking story."

The door opened and Martha hurried in, gripping a thin black looseleaf binder. She handed it off to Barry, who flipped it open, glanced at the cover sheet, and announced for my benefit, "Excellent. It all looks in order."

He then tossed it at me, whipped his Mont Blanc power pen out of his pocket, and jammed it in my face. "Bottom of the third page, scribble your name, and we'll get this over with."

I took the notebook, flipped it open, and read the three cover pages. Jessica and Barry smiled, crossed their arms, and patiently waited.

I knew what it said, but in situations like this you go through the motions anyway. It was all pro forma crap—I was confirming the legal sufficiency of the audit, a lofty assurance open to fairly broad interpretation. In street talk, if anything illegal or unethical was done, moi's ass was on Le Chopping Block.

I flipped shut the notebook and stated, "Boy . . . I'm guaranteeing a lot, aren't I?"

Barry and Jessica exchanged quick, anxious glances.

"Nothing to be nervous about," Barry assured me, before he swiftly added, "sign it."

"No."

"No?" Barry's smile disappeared. "God damn it, Drummond, do what you're told."

Jessica put a hand on his arm. "Drummond, what's the fucking problem here?"

"I'm not sure there is a problem." To her confused look, I added, "I haven't even seen the audit results yet. It wasn't completed before I left last night."

"Oh . . . you want to see the final results?"

"Well, that's what I'm assuring, aren't I? It shouldn't take long . . . maybe a day , , , maybe two."

Jessica was nodding at me and looking sharply at Barry, like, Hey asshole, wasn't it your bright idea to use this dunce for this job? Bang his balls together or whatever you need to do, but get the signature. *Now.*

And Barry very smoothly said, "Jessica, could you excuse us a moment? My associate and I need to talk."

"No fucking problem."

Wrong, Jessica—big f-ing problem. Barry and I went together out into the hallway. There was a fair amount of foot traffic, so he pointed at the men's room door and ordered, "Get your ass in there. Right now, Drummond." We stepped inside, the door closed, Barry shoved me against a wall and said, "What the fuck's going on here?"

"I don't know what you're talking about."

"The hell you don't. Your issues at the firm have no business here."

"My . . . Hey, word gets around, doesn't it?"

"You're on my team, idiot. Of course I was informed."

"Did you have to be told?"

"What's that mean?"

"What does it mean?"

"You lousy prick." He pounded my chest with his right fist. "You'll do what you're told. You better not be trying to blackmail me, Drummond."

I wasn't. I was trying to *extort* him. But you can't expect corporate lawyers to understand the fine distinctions of the criminal codes. I replied, "And if I am?"

He slugged my chest again and said, "You don't want to fuck with me, you punk. I'll—auugh!"

Well, Barry suddenly stopped talking. I suppose he was suddenly overcome by an abiding sense of shame and remorse for the way he'd been acting. Also, I think he noticed that my left hand was gripped tightly around his testicles.

I danced him backward until his butt was against the wall. Well, we then stared into each other's eyes for a moment, adjusting, as it were, to the terrible predicament we found ourselves in. Just to be sure that Barry fully understood that predicament, I informed him, "They say it only takes forty pounds of pressure to rip ears and nuts off a body. You believe that?"

I received a frantic nod. Personally, I didn't believe it. But what mattered was what he believed.

A quick jerk brought Barry up on his tippy-toes. "I should warn you I've done ears, no problems. But this nuts thing . . . it's kind of confusing . . . I mean, I tried it once and I don't know . . . I probably squeezed when I should've yanked . . . and, Jesus, they're sort of like grapes, you know? Very soft."

Barry's mouth opened, and I said, "Shhh."

Well, for once, he actually did shut up. Barry was being very reasonable. Maybe I had misjudged him after all.

I asked, "Did you insert those legal files in Lisa Morrow's e-mail?"

He shook his head, but it's important in these situations to be on the same wavelength, so I gave another hard tug. He babbled, "Ow, ow . . . I swear . . . I swear."

It looked like an honest response. "Okay, Grand Vistas. What is it?"

"You don't . . . I mean . . . please . . ."

"Do you think your voice will actually get higher?"

"It's . . . it's what I told you. It's a holding company."

"Who owns it?"

"I . . . I don't know."

Barry suddenly found himself another inch higher up on his tippy-toes. He'd better know how to levitate.

"I . . . I swear I don't know. God, ow . . . it hurts . . . please don't."

"Is it a front? What?"

"No . . . it's a . . . a real company. Like I tried to tell you, it's . . . auggh . . . it's a legal partnership."

I had to contemplate that for a moment. Barry, I thought, was being as honest as he knew how to be. I mean, you could only expect so much from a guy like him. But I was also certain he was scared out of his wits. The fount of that fear, however, was the interesting question.

So I asked him, "What are you afraid of?"

He studied my face, I think weighing which was worse— explaining to the Mrs. why there'd be no more tiny Barrys skipping around the suburbs, or exposing what he knew about Grand Vistas. Not a hard choice, in my view. But hey, that's me.

"I don't know who they are. I met with their lawyers and brought back the agreement. That's what I was told to do . . . and look . . . that's all I did."

"Told by who?"

"By Cy. And Jason."

"No due diligence?"

"No."

"Why not?"

"I was assured they were okay."

"What are you not telling me, Barry?"

"I, shit . . . I just, please, don't . . . auughhh."

Well, Barry somehow arched up another quarter inch, but I think he and I both knew we were down to the last millimeter.

"Ow . . . oh God, this hurts . . . ow, ow, ow . . ." Then he said, "All right . . . please . . . ow . . ."

So I let him down about two inches. He drew a few deep breaths, then blurted, "I swear, I don't know who they are. Not people you want to fuck with, though."

"Crooks? Spies? What?"

He was shaking his head. "I don't know . . . something. We met in a secret location in Locarno, Italy. They came with guards."

"Lots of rich assholes have private security."

"Not like that, Drummond. These guards were tough bastards. They were different, you understand?"

I suspected I did understand. I asked, "Nationality?"

"I only spoke with their lawyers. One French, the other German. The meeting lasted less than thirty minutes. They gave me the contract and told me to get it signed. No changes, no negotiations."

I released Barry's gonads and he slumped immediately to the floor. He was rubbing his crotch, and you could tell Mrs. Bosworth wouldn't have to fake any orgasms for the next few weeks. I walked to the basin and washed my hands. I said to Barry, "You will go out and inform Jessica that my concerns about the audit are reasonable and will be straightened out in a day or so. Understand?"

"You don't tell me—"

I took a step back in his direction and he slapped his hands over his crotch. I added, "Tell Cy and Bronson I'm completely unreasonable. Explain that I'm very pissed off. Put on your lawyer's hat and persuade them that I will not sign that audit if they take any action against me. Understand?"

He looked up at me. "You can't . . . This whole deal could go down the drain."

"Yes . . . it definitely could."

"Don't be an idiot. If we lose that contract for Morris, he'll drop our firm. It'll destroy us."

"Good point." I wiped my hands and added, "Be sure to explain that to Cy and Bronson also."

I left him blubbering on the men's room floor. I found Martha, got a copy of the audit, and departed.

Okay, yes, I had been very, very rough on Barry and his nuts. Sometimes I have no idea what gets into me. However, a string of ugly thoughts had begun dancing around inside my head. Right now, it was like one of those hyper-modernist, impressionist paintings with colors splashed everywhere, dripping down the canvas and running into one another.

But with a little elbow grease that picture would clarify.

CHAPTER THIRTY

A DEFENSE COUNSEL PRACTICING CRIMINAL LAW OWES HIS FEALTY TO HIS client—open and shut. It matters not that most clients are guilty, even when you *know* they're guilty. Unless the client wants to confess, it's ethical, in fact orthodox, to pretend innocence and try to hinder, smear, and obfuscate the search for truth and justice.

Corporate law is the same—but not. Morris Networks was my client and thus was owed my service and loyalty. Within limits. But where that line of loyalty is drawn is a murky province.

As I previously explained, corporate lawyers can actually become party to a felony. Therefore, if, for instance, an associate *knows* a client is up to its knickers in illegal muck he is expected to tattle to a partner. The partner then approaches the client, cautions its executives to amend their bad ways, and if the client refuses, then the partner should terminate the business relationship and everybody goes along their merry way.

More ticklish is what happens when the associate merely *suspects* something's amiss. The convenient thing, obviously, is to update your malpractice insurance and keep billing your ass off—actually *their* asses off, to get the possessive forms properly aligned. Investigating your own client isn't anywhere in the legal canon. And, obviously, as lawyers, we're expected to respect the attorney-client confidentiality to the bitter end.

This was the quandary gnawing at me as I drove away from the scotch-bottle tower of Morris Networks, my client, possible future employer, and partner of an international company that appeared shady—"appeared" being the operative verb.

Further complicating matters, I did not trust Barry, Sally, Cy, or Bronson. All four could be neck-deep in these shenanigans.

So. This was going to be tough. How to get to the bottom of it?

I needed someone I could really trust. Blood is thicker than water, as they say, and in fact, my parents had actually two children—the good-looking, lovable stud who is hung like a rhino, and my brother, John, a year older, a hell of a lot smarter, but, trust me on this very salient matter, shorter where short *really* matters.

If you're interested, my father was a career officer who made it to colonel before he was leading his brigade on a sweep in Vietnam, dropped his map, bent over to pick it up, and a Vietnamese peasant with an ancient crossbow and a wicked sense of humor plunked one up his ass. Colonel Drummond, however, was a tough bird and survived, though his organic garbage disposal had to be reconfigured, requiring hourly trips to the potty, further requiring him to trade his Army green for a medical disability discharge. Literally, his career went to shit.

But back to John, he and my father had that special bond that often exists between stern, ambitious, hard-driving military fathers and their eldest sons. My father wanted to mold John into his finest soldier; John wanted to mold my father into the parent of an orphan. But what was a bad deal for John was a good deal for me, since I got to hide in his shadow.

It was like watching one of those Greek myths and you knew tragedy loomed on the horizon. We got used to the MPs dragging John home drunk, high, zoned out, a menace to public safety and himself. And of course, John came to a predictably bad end. He started an Internet company, cashed out at the height of the boom in 1999, banked a hundred and fifty million, and now lives in a huge punchbowl of a house overlooking some Pacific bay. If he'd only had a better childhood, who knows how he might've turned out.

We exchange Christmas cards. He sends me postcards from exotic places he knows I can't afford to visit, and if I ever get married he'll be my best man. Other than that our lives have taken their separate paths.

What John has that I lack—setting aside money, a big house, and professional success—is the ability to interpret a spreadsheet. I called him from the carphone, got his answering machine, and warned him a long fax was coming. I then pulled into a Kinko's, employed a magic marker to darken out the name of Morris Networks, and faxed him the audit summary. Disclosing confidential corporate information to an outsider is a breach of ethics and law, but eradicating the company's name was a step back in the right direction.

But back to the past: When John and I were kids we had what psychologists would term a virulent sibling rivalry. At young ages, these things are determined by who can pound the crap out of the other. I was stronger and quicker, but he was more cunning and deceitful. He won most of the time, but my victories hurt more. Brotherhood is very primeval and it's a miracle any of us survive it. When you get older, you outgrow all that; not the rivalry, certainly, but how you measure victory. At this point in our lives, for instance, he was about one hundred and fifty million points ahead.

Anyway, I was seated in my apartment an hour later when my beloved brother called.

We got through the opening banter about Mom, Dad, his new Ferrari, the new waterfall in his swimming pool, and then he said, "Those were interesting spreadsheets you sent me. Morris Networks, right?"

"I can't tell you." I assured him, "But no, definitely not Morris Networks."

He chuckled. "I know the company, Sean. I've got money in Morris."

"Oh."

He chuckled some more. "Actually, my broker dumped the last share fifteen minutes ago."

"That bad?"

"Actually, the numbers look great."

"Then what's the problem?"

"What you don't see in the annual report, but you do see in an audit."

"Meaning?"

"I can't believe we have the same genes. Do I really need to explain this?" Well, he obviously did, so he continued, "Go to the bottom of the second page . . . put your right forefinger on the line that says operating profits." I did, and that line said $42,630,323.00. He explained, "That's what Morris made after expenses, write-offs, and a few other things you don't even want to understand. Now page eighteen, go down to the twentieth line."

I did that, too. He said, "Now put that same right forefinger on it. That's what Morris booked as swaps last quarter. Eighty mil . . . see the significance?"

"Nope."

"The swaps are keeping Morris Networks profitable and on target with its growth forecasts. Happened last year, too. Morris would've been in the red had it not booked three hundred mil in swaps."

"I don't get it."

He explained, "Swaps are like barter. Morris and whoever they're swapping with make up some artificial exchange rate for the value of each other's services, and then they both book it as revenue." He allowed me a moment to think about that, then said, "But it's not."

"And this is legal?"

"Legal . . . ? Yes. Nearly all telecoms do it."

"So what's the problem?"

"One, it's not necessarily real money. Two, it can be abused."

"How?"

"Take Morris—say it has excess capacity because it's not meeting its growth targets. Like, it built a highway that handles a million cars a day, but only half a million cars are paying tolls. Got that?"

"Go on."

"So it says to this other company, 'Hey, I'll give you space for a quarter of a million cars in exchange for space for a hundred thousand cars on your roads. The net value to each of us is eighty mil.' "

"That's what swapping is?"

"An idiot's interpretation of it." He paused, then asked, "Do you think you understand it?"

"Got it." *Prick.*

John went on, "They're purchasing each other's services but you have no way of knowing if there's any value."

"Why?"

"Maybe it's a paper exchange. Neither company actually ends up sending cars onto the other guy's network, so they're trading unused road space for unused road space, and it all stays unused road space."

"So it's a chimera?"

"It might be. It's even worse if they're round-tripping."

"Round-tripping?"

"Right. Usually this involves a hidden exchange inside the deal. Since they're both exchanging services, what happens is one or the other side inflates the value of what it's exchanging. For example, Morris might only provide twenty million in services but bill it at eighty, and book the other sixty as profit. Or vice versa." He added, "As an investor, I might be more comfortable if I knew who Morris is swapping with."

Wrong, wrong, wrong, big brother. I asked him, "Do you know Jason Morris?"

"Yeah, but not well. We met when he was still in an entrepreneurial firm and I was running around looking for investment money for my Internet start-up."

"What did you think of him?"

"A visionary—lots of smarts, lots of energy, and I'd trade all my riches for his poontang list. The guy only sleeps about three hours a night. The rest of the time he's making money or fucking." He paused, then concluded, "Pretty much what the press says he is."

"Is he honorable?"

He laughed. "There is no honor in business. There's law and how close you adhere to it." He paused, then added, "More relevantly . . . there's profit."

"Do you like him?"

"I bought his stock. Why?"

"No particular reason."

He laughed again. Then he said, "Regarding Morris, listen close."

"I'm listening."

"Three kinds of guys get into this biz. One, the techie who loves what he builds and can't wait for everybody else to love and admire it. Two, the money guy who's in it to see how much he can make."

He stopped talking. I reminded John, "You mentioned a third?"

"Jason—guys like him. His whole identity is wrapped up in his company. It's an extension of him. That company is his ego."

Left unsaid was that my brother had cashed out at the height of the boom, banked his winnings, and retired at the decrepit age of thirty-six. His company went bankrupt a year later. What did that make him?

Anyway, I asked, "Is it a good company?"

He replied, "Look, someday telephones will be collecting dust in museums. People will point at them and giggle . . . that people actually only *talked* to one another, without seeing their faces, they'll think that's quaint. Videophones, my boy . . . that's the next great big thing."

"But really, John, is it a good company?"

"You're not listening."

"Am too."

"Jason plans to usher that in. He's not just fiber optics, he's developing the compression and decompression systems that will allow moving pictures to work across phone lines. There's every possibility Morris Networks will be the AT&T of the twenty-first century. Jason will buy and sell Bill Gates a dozen times over."

"Quit exaggerating."

"Twenty times over."

"If his ass is attached to such a gold mine, why's he swapping?"

He replied, "Turn to page six, fifth line down." I did, and he continued, "R&D expenditures—forty percent of his revenue. Jason's in a race. He has to get the inventions and patents that can deliver videophones before his competitors. See his problem?"

"He has to stay in business long enough."

"And telecom CEOs are dropping like flies. Global Crossing, WorldCom, Qwest, and those are just the big ones. They miss a few growth targets, their stock tanks, the banks lower their credit ratings, then the lawyers show up for the Chapter 11 filings and stockholder lawsuits."

"And it's these swaps keeping Morris afloat?"

"You just got your business degree. Listen, I have to run. I just bought a new yacht and I'm dying to try it out."

It's great having a successful brother. Really.

So, what did I have? Jason Morris's business survival depended on a shady company that meets his lawyers in secretive, out-of-the-way places, that brings along a bunch of unsavory-looking goons, that dictates the terms of contracts. And the executives of that same consortium completely clam up when I ask them to name their holdings.

All of which added up to what?

A scene from *The Godfather* popped into my head, a corrupt old man with his daggerlike finger in Jason Morris's chest as he droned on about the deal he couldn't refuse, while Jason dreamed of the day he could buy and sell everybody on the Forbes 400 list.

Money, money, money—the root of all evil. Money tied to ego, the root of the most sublime evil.

CHAPTER THIRTY-ONE

Y ANSWERING MACHINE HELD THREE CALLS FROM CY BERGER. HE KEPT ASKing me to call him back as soon as it was convenient, and I assumed by that he meant convenient for me. But I didn't care what he meant; I'd call when I was ready. And I wasn't. Not yet.

Aside from my other growing problems, the firm was threatening me and Janet with charges serious enough to merit disbarment and even jail. But the firm needed my signature on the audit, which was leverage, albeit limited leverage. There surely was a plan B, which probably involved drafting some compliant associate to sign the audit. But there was a roomful of accountants who had witnessed my daily involvement in the audit, and legal niceties had to be met, so the compliant associate would have to go back and review every aspect of the process, and the timeline would no doubt slip beyond Friday. At the moment, I was a far more convenient solution, bordering on becoming completely inconvenient.

So I called Cy, and we exchanged a few phony pleasantries before he got around to it, asking almost nonchalantly, "So Sean, we had a difficult morning, didn't we?"

No, *we* didn't have a difficult morning, and it was so asinine to suggest otherwise that I decided not to reply.

The pause lasted long enough for Cy to realize that this tack would go nowhere. Finally, he said, "Well, I believe the ball's in your court."

"You mean, what will it take for me to sign the audit?"

"I'm going to be blunt here. That's what we're wondering."

"I'm innocent and I want to clear my name."

"Fair enough. Harold told you, you'll have that chance."

"And Hal implied it would be a kangaroo court."

After a moment, he said, "Hal is very protective of the firm. He has a tendency to be melodramatic."

"Is that a fancy word for being an asshole?"

He chuckled. "It will be fair, Sean." He then promised, "You have my word on this."

"But that still poses a problem, doesn't it?"

"What problem?"

"I need to get into your server to prove my innocence."

"Oh . . . I see you what you mean."

"And I'll need one of your computer people to guide me through the database."

"Even if I could allow that, it's too late. We need to get that audit into Defense tomorrow."

"No problem. I'll work all night."

After a considerable pause, he said, "All right. But Hal has to be there."

"Wrong. Hal will get a printout from the server in the morning. Remember, the server sees all and remembers all."

He realized that my request was a small price to pay and said, "Fair enough."

So I walked out of the paneled elevator an hour later and entered the seventh floor, where, with the notable exception of Mr. Piggy-eyes, the firm's entire administrative staff was crammed into a sprawling cube farm. Cy had told me that a computer expert named Cheryl would be waiting, and indeed, a skinny black woman of about forty was seated beside the water cooler, her nose stuffed inside the latest issue of *Glamour*. She did not look like a computer nerd, she looked like an overstressed, worn-down suburban mom, but I suppose they come in all flavors.

I introduced myself and she immediately complained, "I got a little boy bein' watched by my mama and don't want to be doin' this all night."

"If you're good, you won't."

"I'm good." She sized me up and asked, "So . . . what you wanta see?"

I explained that Lisa Morrow's active files had been wiped clean, and I needed to see if there was a record of her messages magnetically lingering in the wiry bowels of the server.

" 'Course there is," she informed me, and we then worked our way through the cube maze and eventually squeezed ourselves into her office carrel.

Cheryl fell into her chair, typed a few commands into her computer, then pointed at a chair and ordered, "Sit. And keep your mouth shut. I don't like being bothered when I'm workin'."

Fine by me. I moved a stack of manuals off the chair, laid them on the floor, and sat. Cheryl was already typing commands and long lines of incomprehensible code were flashing incessantly across the screen. She was really grumpy.

She asked, "What you say her name was?"

"Morrow . . . Lisa Morrow."

She nodded. "She the blond chick from the Army used to work upstairs?"

"Yup."

"Heard she died."

"She was murdered, actually."

"Uh-huh. I heard she was good folk." She studied her screen and said, "What you wanta look at?"

"Lisa's e-mail going back, say, three months."

She continued typing. "Everything's kept going back two years."

I watched what she was doing. In a way, I envy people who understand how the byzantine machine works, and in a larger way I don't. Most programmers are weird. When I was a kid we were told not to sit too close to the TV, or hair would grow on our palms—but maybe I've got my warnings confused. It strikes me today's mommies should warn their kids that too much time on your computer turns you into a dimwit.

She finally said, "Shit, shit, shit. Would ya look at this."

"What?"

"A firewall 'round her file." I suppose I looked a bit clueless, because she added, "Code protection. Single-layered, but it's a good one, very complex."

"What's that mean?"

"That somebody don't want us lookin'."

I studied the screen. "No way to get past it?"

"Hack past it."

"Yeah? How do we do that?"

"*We* don't." She spun around in her chair and faced me. "The server administrator can fix it . . . tomorrow."

Some voice in the back of my brain made me ask, "And that would be who?"

"Mr. Merriweather."

Wasn't that a surprise? Actually, it wasn't; so I took a gamble and asked, "He a pal of yours?"

"That fatassed moron? He got no friends on this floor."

That news was no surprise either. I said, "Cheryl, it's very possible something in that database will embarrass Merriweather, maybe even get him fired. But tomorrow morning, he'll know from the server printouts that we tried to enter Lisa's file, and he might find a way to block us forever."

"That's your problem. Wanta hear my problem? I got a kid with my mama."

"I'll buy your kid a shiny new bike, a baseball glove, whatever."

She stared into her computer screen for a long while. She finally said, "A BB gun. That's what he wants."

"Deal."

I took the stairwell upstairs, tried to fix us espressos, was foiled by the machine again, settled for two cups of regular coffee, and then returned to settle in and observe Cheryl in action. A stream of curses poured out her throat every ten minutes or so. I did not regard this as a hopeful sign.

She had started at ten, and at eleven I thought I detected a faint trace of a smile. It was nearly midnight when she mumbled, "Oh, baby," leaned back in her chair, ran her fingers through her hair, and announced, "Shit, I'm good."

I observed a long column of e-mails on the screen.

"Could I?" I asked. She climbed out of her chair, saying, "I gotta go pee. Don't you break nothin'."

I began with Lisa's oldest e-mails and worked forward. I checked incoming mail for the two files, and outgoing for any references to the Boston cases. Modern young executives, like Lisa, transact a lot of business electronically. I'm more old-fashioned, aka, a technological idiot. But even if my mastery were to extend beyond punching *off* and *on*, I prefer face-to-face and phone interaction, where a facial tic or a verbal nuance allows you to detect what's not being said, which often is more revealing than what is. Lisa had sent or received up to a hundred messages a day.

I felt unnerved, and actually a bit sad, rummaging through the messages of a dear but dead friend. Pieces of her—Lisa's intelligence, warmth, efficiency, and wit—jumped off the screen. I found myself stifling a sob or two.

Half her messages went to other firm members and concerned firm business, from her caseload to mundane administrative matters. I knew barely a handful of the firm's lawyers. Most of the names were just names.

Twenty or more times a day, Lisa e-mailed friends, associates, clients outside the firm, and I recognized the names of several JAG officers. She was popular and made a point to stay in contact with her chums, passing on jokes and anecdotes, but more often just brief, cheery notes, the high-tech version of a blown kiss. Cheryl returned from the ladies' room with two cups of espresso, and we sipped and chatted as I opened more e-mails, trying to detect anything curious or suspicious. A number had enclosures I made sure to open on the chance the legal files had been smuggled into Lisa's file in that manner.

I noticed several e-mails to Janet, and of course I opened those, too. Nothing too personal, though from the jovial, intimate tone you could tell that Lisa and Janet shared more than just sisterhood. Lisa updating Janet on her day, Janet updating Lisa about the family, about some mutual friends, and in one of her last e-mails from Lisa a promise that a package would arrive for her any day. I checked the date, about two weeks before Lisa's murder, and made a note to ask Janet about that package.

After another thirty minutes of this, the Jacks and Harrys and Barbaras and Marys of Lisa's life started running together into a big friendly blur. Once or twice I read an e-mail and something funny went off in the back of my head. But nothing went off in the front of my head.

By one-thirty, Cheryl was curled up in her chair and snoring. I was on an e-mail sent by Lisa to ANCAR@SEC.GOV that read, "Dear A., Meet at Starbucks at 7:00 tomorrow AM for package. Friends Always, Lisa."

Next was a message to DCOULTER@AOL.COM, something about providing an affidavit, when a bell went off inside my head.

I returned to the previous message and wondered what it was. I pondered this . . . and pondered this, and . . . nothing.

I moved on, and 122 messages later was one sent to JCUTH@JOHNSMATH.ORG that read, "Dear J., Appreciate your views and expertise greatly. I'll deliver package to your apartment tomorrow night. Friends Always, Lisa."

Ding, ding, ding. *What?* I studied it again. In every other e-mail Lisa referred to the recipient by their full name, not an initial. Actually, there had been another initial—A. So I went back to A., then back to J., and back and forth a few more times, and bingo!

I slapped my forehead hard enough that Cheryl suddenly shot up in her chair.

I had no idea what Lisa's messages to them were about, and in fact, didn't really care about the messages—the connection was the only thing that mattered.

J.—well, J. was Julia Cuthburt of Johnson and Smathers. And A.—that was Anne Carrol of the SEC.

Put the two together, and I was staring at the second and fourth victims of the L.A. Killer.

CHAPTER THIRTY-TWO

I T WAS NEARLY TWO IN THE MORNING, JANET WAS NOT ANSWERING HER cell phone, and I sat at Cheryl's desk and wondered, with monumental annoyance, why not. So I tried again, got three rings again, and then her throaty recorded voice again saying, "Janet Morrow. Please leave a message and I'll return your call."

I said, "Hey, it's me. I found the connection. Listen . . . Julia, Anne, and Lisa . . . they knew one another. This is big, right? Call me. Right now."

But I wasn't satisfied. Where could a beautiful twenty-nine-year-old single woman be at this hour, other than in her bed? Well, one just could not ignore the very revolting possibility that she and George the Jerk had completely mended fences, and her cell phone was turned off to avoid coitus interruptus. That suspicion, for some reason, *really* annoyed me.

So I dug out the Yellow Pages, looked up the Four Seasons Hotel, called the desk, and asked the operator to connect me to Janet Morrow.

In that flat impersonal tone affected by backroom help, she replied, "I'm sorry, that party checked out."

"What?"

"Sir . . . I said she checked out."

"But she . . . when?"

"Today."

"Why?"

"I'm sure I don't have that information, sir."

"What time today?"

"I'm sure I don't have that information either."

"But . . ."

"I'll put you through to the desk."

So she did, and the guy at the desk was both more human and more helpful, informing me that Janet had checked out at six o'clock.

Odd.

No—more than odd. She had never informed me she was leaving. And of course, I distinctly heard FBI-boy make a date with her for dinner.

"It's real late," Cheryl sleepily informed me. "I gotta get home and get some sleep."

"Sure. And Cheryl . . . thanks."

"Good. Okay. You got what you need?"

I stood up and pecked her cheek. "More. Much more." I whipped out my wallet and handed her a hundred-dollar bill. "Buy your son that BB gun."

"Don't cost that much," she informed me.

"Right. Get one for his mother, too. You can shoot at each other."

She smiled. "You a good man." She lifted up her purse and wandered out.

I remained at Cheryl's desk for five more minutes and tried to piece this thing together. There was a connection between Lisa, Julia Cuthburt, and Anne Carrol. The nature of their connection I didn't know, but the three women knew one another, and the fact that they were all three murdered strongly suggested they weren't picked randomly by a serial killer. It didn't eliminate a serial killer, but implied—no, not implied, it *established* that the killer chose them because of that connection.

So—where was Janet?

I rushed downstairs to the parking garage. My briefcase was in the Jag's trunk and I retrieved it. I dug around till I found the survivor assistance package that contained the phone number to Mr. Morrow, which I then dialed on the carphone.

Her father and I had spoken several times about various matters since our first encounter, so I knew it was a good number. It rang fifteen or twenty times, and I recalled that on my previous calls, after about six rings, a message machine answered. I tried again. Okay, yes, it was late, and Mr. Morrow was old and possibly his ears weren't what they used to be, but his youngest daughter, Elizabeth, lived with him, and geez . . . you'd think one of them would hear the damned phone.

Things were getting weirder. I mean, Janet is suddenly out of the loop and her father and little sister aren't in bed when, or where, they are supposed to be.

Coincidental? Possibly.

Maybe not.

I called the Boston operator, gave her Mr. Morrow's address, and told her I needed the number for the nearest police station. She connected me to a switchboard person.

The switchboard person said, "Officer Dianne Marino, how can I help you?"

"Major Sean Drummond, D.C. office of the Army's Criminal Investigation Division." Regarding this harmless little white lie, cops tend only to take other cops seriously, and I needed her to be responsive and helpful. I informed her, "We're working on the L.A. Killer murders down here. Perhaps you've heard about it, Officer Marino?"

"Are you kidding? I watched the *Nightline* special on it the other night. Gosh, that guy's some rotten bastard, isn't he?"

"Ad infinitum. Thing is, we have an emergency and need your help."

"Boston's Finest is here to serve, Major." You have to love that, right?

"A victim's parent might be in possession of critical knowledge. Problem is, we can't seem to reach him."

"Well, it's two-thirty in the morning. Other than us idiots on the night shift, that's bedtime."

"Officer Marino, the L.A. Killer knows no time."

"Uh . . . yes, right. Sorry."

"Let's keep our heads in the game here, shall we?"

"Sorry, sir. Won't happen again."

I might've been less officious and curt, but people have a certain impression about how military people have their lids screwed a little too tight and you have to validate that impression or they might think you're a phony.

I gave her Mr. Morrow's address and asked if she could have a patrol car run by the house, wake him up, and get him standing by the phone.

Can do, she replied, clearly on my wavelength now, and I told her I'd wait until she got confirmation from the patrol car. She put me on hold. Ten minutes passed, during which I tried to figure out all the buttons and controls in my fancy new Jag, even as I tried to mentally sort through the possible connections between Lisa and the other victims. It struck me that what I had not seen were e-mails to, from, or about the most famous victim, Carolyn Fiorio. Yet three of four murdered women knew one another, corresponded with some regularity, and Lisa signed off her e-mails, "Friends Always." Empty sentiments weren't Lisa's style and it seemed fair to presume the relationships were more than passing.

"Major, we . . . well, we have a problem," Officer Marino interrupted.

"Tell me about it."

"An incident."

"Go on."

"Mr. Morrow's house burned down yesterday evening."

While I tried to comprehend this, not to mention her dazzling gift for understatement, she added, "Sorry I didn't recognize it when you gave me the address. My shift didn't start till midnight. The fire happened earlier."

"How much earlier?"

"Just a sec . . . let me pull it up on my screen." After a few moments, she said, "A neighbor reported the fire shortly after five. Two alarmer. Those old houses up on Beacon Hill, they're ritzy, but firetraps. Wood-framed, none of the modern fire retardant materials. It's a—"

"Was anybody hurt?"

"Hold on." She read from the report, "One known vic, John Morrow, was severely burned. He was on the upper floor, and had to be pulled out by a fireman, and—"

"What about a young woman? Elizabeth Morrow?"

"Not listed." She then informed me, "But the inspectors haven't entered the premises to look for corpses inside. It has to cool down. Tomorrow, after—"

"Do you know the cause?"

"No . . . not yet. We'll of course dispatch an arson specialist with the inspectors in the morning. Do you think it's—"

"Thanks." I hung up.

The fire started around five, and Janet checked out of her hotel around six. What was going on here?

I started the Jag and left the parking garage without any particular idea where I was going, just sure I should be going somewhere.

The cold fresh air must have cleared my mind a bit, because I suddenly found myself wondering about that firewall around Lisa's file. I probably should've asked Cheryl if that was standard procedure for all departed attorneys. Law firms are more protective of privacy rights than most employers, and it would make sense to seal the files of departed attorneys. But say it wasn't. Answer: Somebody in the firm knew there was evidence in the server that showed a connection between the three deceased women, evidence that was technically impossible to eradicate, so the next best solution was to hide it and slap a firewall around it. Ergo: Somebody in the firm had to be involved in the murders.

Which triggered another revelation. Lisa had referred to packages in her e-mails to both Julia and Anne, and one message to Janet also referred to a package. Janet was sure she had never met and had no acquaintance with Anne or Julia. But all three had gotten packages from Lisa. Was that the connection?

Boston—I needed to go to Beantown pronto. Drive? Too long. And Reagan National Airport didn't spit out its first morning flight till six.

I was pondering my other options, and driving past the White House, when it hit me. I pulled over to the curb, dug through my briefcase, and withdrew a business card. I dialed the number and three rings later a groggy voice replied, "Spinelli."

"It's Drummond. Wake up."

"I'm on the fuckin' phone, ain't I?"

I would say he was being grumpy, but Spinelli's mood seemed inalterable. I said, "I'm offering you the chance to be a hero."

"Ah shit."

"So here's the deal. What if I told you Lisa Morrow, Julia Cuthbert, and Anne Carrol knew one another?"

"How do you know that?"

"I just do." I added, "And Janet Morrow might know why."

"No shit."

"But she's gone."

"Yeah?"

"The other shoe—her father's house burned down last night. He might be dead. She checked out an hour later, and we should assume she flew home."

He pondered this a moment, then suggested, "Then call her on her cell phone."

"Well, shit. Why didn't I think of that?"

"Not answering, huh?"

"And I don't want to think of why. Capisce? Now you earn your brass balls."

"What are you talking about?"

"Standby helicopters are always kept at Andrews Air Force Base and the Marine base at Quantico, fifteen minutes from the White House and Pentagon. Tell your bosses you need one—now."

"Fly to Boston?"

"My thought was we'd walk and pull the helicopter behind us. But now that you mention it, this flying thing, that might be better."

"Fuck you."

"You want to lose your key witness?"

"What the fuck are—"

"We know this killer has shown himself to be very clever and resourceful, don't we?" I allowed him a moment to think about that, and then said, "Hey, forget it. Sorry I bothered you. I'll call Meany and let the FBI—"

"Don't even think it." He paused a moment, then said, "Here's the deal. I handle this, I get credit for the collar."

"I don't care who gets credit."

"I do. I gotta promotion board comin' up."

"If she dies, I'll put that in your records."

"Thirty minutes, the Pentagon landing pad. And don't be fuckin' with me, or I'll—"

"What's this in my hand? Wow . . . George Meany's business card."

"Thirty minutes."

I tried Janet again and left another message to call me pronto. This was when it struck me that there were other possible explanations for what was going on here. Maybe J. stood for Jeanie, and A. for Alice. And maybe poor old Mr. Morrow came home from work, tossed a frozen pizza in the oven, forgot to remove the cardboard, and presto, a two-alarm blaze. We all know how forgetful some old people get.

But, as the French like to say, "L'audace, l'audace," which translates roughly to, "Attack, forget the risks, gamble, and win." Forget that the French haven't won a war in a couple of centuries.

CHAPTER THIRTY-THREE

WE LANDED AT 6:20 ON THE ROOF OF THE HARVARD UNIVERSITY MEDICAL Center, where Mr. Morrow had been rushed by ambulance after the fire.

Spinelli had remained busy the whole flight chattering into his headset, calling Boston to arrange police escorts, tracking down the whereabouts and condition of Mr. John Morrow—severe burns on 50 percent of his body, condition critical, in the ICU of Harvard Medical—and struggling to explain to his dubious bosses why all this was necessary.

I huddled on a seat in the back of the Blackhawk, stared out the window at the lights below, and tried again to piece the fragments together. What did Janet, Anne Carrol, and Julia Cuthburt have in common? After giving it great thought, I came up with nothing.

Anyway, a bored patrolman was awaiting us by the rooftop landing pad, and ushered us through an entrance and down a few floors to the ICU. We were led to a room with no doors. Inside, a body was laid out on a bed, covered with some form of burn sheeting, respirator on his face, IVs pumping liquids into both arms, two nurses and a young doctor huddled together and discussing something.

The doctor noticed us and came over. "Can I help you?"

I offered brief introductions and inquired, "How's our patient?"

"Touch and go." He glanced back over his shoulder. "The burns were quite severe. His legs and lower torso particularly."

Spinelli asked the doctor, "What are his chances?"

"Burns . . . they're tough." He frowned and pointed a finger at the patient. "He's stable for the time being. But he's old. And as I said, burns are tough."

In other words, John Morrow's chances were pretty good. Were I to paraphrase the young doctor exactly, he said, My malpractice insurance is killing me, and didn't one of you gentlemen mention you were a lawyer?

I explained to him, "We're here looking for his daughter Janet Morrow. Dark-haired, slender, very attractive."

He nodded. "She was here earlier. Two other sisters also. They were here all night, in fact. They left about"—he glanced at his watch—"about an hour ago, after we got him stabilized." For good measure, he added, "Of course, you never know with burns. They're tough."

I went to the nursing station and used the phone to inform Janet's cell phone answering service that I was in Boston, and I left her Spinelli's cell phone number.

I huddled with Spinelli. I said, "Okay, she's in the city. But where?"

He replied that he had already arranged for the Boston PD to dispatch a car to Janet's townhouse in downtown Boston, and another to her sister Carol's apartment located somewhere in Belmont. Had the sisters shown up at either location Spinelli would've gotten a call.

So that told us where they weren't. Not where they were. Janet made her living dealing with murderers, and maybe, after hearing that her father's house had caught fire, suspected something was amiss. But she didn't know yet about the connection between her sister and the other two victims, so maybe not. In fact, maybe she was at that very moment having her neck snapped.

All those maybes were giving me a headache.

I suggested to Spinelli that we should persuade the Boston police to issue an all-points on all three sisters. He suggested that was a dumb and unworkable idea, that APBs require legal authorization we were unlikely to get on such thin logic, that the sisters had been up all night and had to return to their apartments and townhouses to shower, change, eat, and so on. I responded that he had a good point, but if Janet *did* suspect something, she probably would be clever enough to avoid her own lair, as that was obviously the most likely place the killer would stake out. He noted that I had a good point also, except the Boston PD had a squad car parked in front of her townhouse. Well, yes, I replied, but maybe Janet and her sisters didn't know that.

Stalemate. We were both tired and our tempers were fraying. We were also hungry and thirsty, so we went down a few floors and found the cafeteria. We got a couple of bran muffins and cups of coffee and sat at a table.

Considering that we had become sort of partners, I decided I should get to know Spinelli better, and so I asked him, "So Danny, what brought you into the Army?"

"Poverty. You?"

"Nothing better to do."

He chuckled. I think he was starting to like me. I wasn't sure whether I was starting to like him.

I asked him, "You started out as an MP?"

He nodded. "Made it to staff sergeant, then went to the CID course."

"Like it?"

"There are days."

Okay, enough with these deep, probing questions. We now knew each other intimately, what made the other guy tick, and so forth. I asked, "You're the expert here. What do you think's going on?"

"Ain't got a friggin' clue."

"The other day you suggested this guy was a copycat."

"Yeah."

"Still think that?"

"Yeah. Why?"

"Curiosity." I added, "Incidentally, I saw no sign that Lisa knew Carolyn Fiorio."

"Maybe she didn't. Maybe there's some other connection or motive with Fiorio."

I thought about that. It made sense—possibly the killer knocked off Lisa, Cuthburt, and Carrol for one reason, and Fiorio for a different reason altogether. Then I gave a little more thought to that copycat idea.

Spinelli, I was coming to appreciate, was my kind of cop. The other law enforcement officials involved in this case so overintellectualized the problem, made it so fucking complicated, devised so many intricate theories and complex hypotheses that they ended up chasing their own asses. Spinelli was the meat-and-potatoes type.

I was sipping from my coffee and contemplating meat and potatoes, don't overthink, the answer is usually right under your nose, when it hit me. I slammed the cup down and said, "Follow me."

I raced back up the stairs, Spinelli sprinting behind me all the way back into the ICU and over to the nurses' station.

A heavyset black nurse was staring intently at some monitors, but glanced up when I said, "Excuse me. Were you here when Mr. Morrow's daughters left?"

"Yes."

"Did they leave a number for you to contact them?"

"They did." I explained that this was a police matter, Spinelli flashed his shield, and she gave us the number.

I smiled at her and asked, "Mind if I use your phone?"

"Go ahead. Just don't be long."

I dialed and a woman's voice answered, "Hello."

"This is Sean Drummond. May I ask whom I'm speaking with?"

"Ethel Morrow."

"I'm trying to contact Janet Morrow. Would you know where I can find her?"

"I'm her aunt. Of course I know where to find her."

"Right. Could you tell me where to find her?"

"Well . . . she's right here, young man. But this isn't a good time to talk with her."

I recalled Lisa once mentioning a spinster aunt, her father's sister, the dragon lady of the clan, who had helped raise the girls after their mother died. She was, according to Lisa, a nosy, eccentric, tart-tongued old biddy. But she was a parental figure of sorts, I guess. And it made sense that the girls went to see her at a moment like this.

I explained, "Listen, I'm standing outside your brother's hospital room. I flew up on a military helicopter. It's urgent that I speak with her right away."

"Oh, all right. But keep it short. She's quite upset."

A moment later, Janet came on the line. I said, "It's Drummond. I'm at the hospital. Where are you?"

"My aunt's house. What are you doing in Boston . . . at the hospital?"

"I'll explain later. Give me the address."

She did. And I wrote it down and handed it to Spinelli, who then dashed off in search of the patrolman who had met us on the roof.

I said to Janet, "Listen closely. Lisa knew Julia Cuthburt and Anne Carrol. She e-mailed them several times before they were all murdered."

"Oh my God."

"Spinelli's here, too. Don't leave your aunt's house. We'll be there soon."

CHAPTER THIRTY-FOUR

WE JUMPED INTO THE SQUAD CAR, A COP AT THE WHEEL, SPINELLI IN FRONT, Drummond in back. The cop punched his lights and siren, and we screeched out of the parking space. Then it struck me that this was wrong, wrong, wrong.

I ordered the cop to pull over and shut it down, then said to Spinelli, "What's this guy doing right now?"

"Who the hell knows? Watching her apartment, I guess." He scratched his nose, appeared briefly perplexed, and then commented, "Nah. He breaks into the house while the old man's at work, positions some igniters and fuel, and a few minutes after the old man gets home, he torches the house. Right?" I nodded, and he continued, "He finds a vantage and watches the fire. He sees the fireman haul out the body, then follows the meat wagon to the hospital, so he knows which one."

I suggested, "Where he picks up Janet's trail. He follows her when she leaves."

And he concluded, "He's probably watching her aunt's house right now."

We then spent a few moments batting this scenario around. Of course, there was a very good chance the killer wasn't behind the fire, that we were on a wild-goose chase, and Sean was earning himself a long session on a big couch with a very nice, very inquisitive shrink. But my instincts told me he was here. So did Spinelli's.

If we roared into the neighborhood, horns blaring, lights flashing, we'd blow this thing. The track record suggested that this guy was very, very good; we had no idea what he looked like; he'd see us; we wouldn't see him—end of story.

"We sneak in," Spinelli concluded.

"Fine."

"We need an unmarked car and some sort of disguise."

We batted that around awhile.

Plumbers or air-conditioning repairmen were the normal routines, but on short notice were out of the question. Then I got an idea and off we went.

Thirty minutes later, Monsignors Sean Drummond and Daniel Spinelli parked the beat-up Honda Civic we borrowed from Father Brian Mullraney of St. Mary's parish in front of Aunt Ethel's townhome in Cambridge. Charitably, the place was a pit: a small, two-storied clapboard affair, seedy and ill-tended, no front yard, just a five-stepped stoop that rose from the cracked sidewalk.

Aunt Ethel answered our knock. She was somewhere in her eighties, shrunken to less than five feet, wispy, white-haired, with a bony, scowling face and hard eyes that regarded us harshly.

I nervously fingered my collar and explained, "I'm Drummond. I called earlier. This is Chief Warrant Spinelli, a military police officer. Please . . . invite us in."

"Why are you dressed that way?"

I said, "Please. We'll explain inside."

She glowered at Spinelli and said, "I assume you have a badge or something."

He flashed his shield and we were inside, being led down a short hallway to the kitchen. The whole place smelled musty and airless, like lots of old people's homes, and was cluttered with old-lady junk; overstuffed chairs, doilies, figurines, and so forth. The kitchen was small and cramped, and looked like a mausoleum for ancient appliances. Aunt Ethel was a very strange duck.

Janet set down her teacup and calmly did the introduction thing, which, considering the circumstances, was sort of strained. The three sisters were huddled around the table, wrung out and glum.

There followed a moment of clumsy silence before Janet asked, "Why are you two dressed like priests?"

So I explained that, and what I had learned from Lisa's computer file, ending with our suspicion that the killer might be, and, in our view, probably was, hanging around the neighborhood, and he wasn't through.

My explanation came out a bit rushed, and understandably, the kitchen became very hushed and quiet. I mean, the Morrow sisters had just learned that their father's incineration was no accident, that one sister might be marked for death, and that the grim reaper might be lurking behind the garbage cans in Aunt Ethel's backyard. They were hardy women, and nobody got panicky or anything, but nobody looked drowsy anymore.

After a few moments, Janet asked, "Why burn down our house? Why try to kill my father?"

Spinelli replied, "To get you up here. Your old man's the cheese in the trap."

"Why? If he wanted to kill me, why not D.C.?"

Why indeed? Exactly the question I had been trying to piece together on the flight up. I wasn't sure, but back at the hospital, Spinelli had given me an idea worth exploring and I said, "Spinelli still thinks this guy is a copycat." I then asked, "Why do people copycat?"

Janet pondered this interesting question a moment, then replied, "The normal motives are envy, sympathy, or a perverted sense of brotherhood. Some want to feed off the fame and deeds of other killers, and some want to outdo famous killers, employing the same patterns and techniques, but excelling over the original. Emulation and ego enhancement."

I nodded. Her Harvard Law professors would be proud of her. This was a textbook reply, almost verbatim. But I'd had a little more time to consider this thing, and it had struck me that part of the problem was that everybody was too wedded to their textbooks. I suggested, "How about as a cover-up? He wants somebody else blamed. Yes? No?"

"That could make sense," Janet replied.

I continued, "And until now, nobody's found a link between the victims, thus the prevailing opinion is that there is no link. Killing you would cause everybody to rethink their theories and assumptions."

"Yes. But killing me up here engenders the same risk."

"He might think otherwise. Boston's outside of the scope and jurisdiction of the task force down in D.C. Also, the killer isn't aware of your . . . relationship to the head of the FBI field team. Or your entanglement in the investigation." This was obviously true, she nodded, and I continued, "So maybe he intends to kill you differently than he did Lisa and the others. Arrange your murder without any obvious parallels."

Janet thought about this, then pointed out, "You're making a lot of guesses."

"Look, I know this sounds odd, but . . ." I thought about how to couch this: "I'm starting to understand how he operates."

"You're right. That's completely off-the-wall."

"Humor me. Now, let's call the Boston PD and get out of here."

"Out of here?" Janet asked.

"Right. Away from this guy."

Janet exchanged looks with her sisters, then looked at me and Spinelli. She said, "Would you two step out of the kitchen? We need a moment to discuss this thing."

I glanced at Spinelli, and said to her, "There's nothing to discuss. Call the Boston PD."

She pointed a finger. "I think you'd be comfortable in the living room."

Well, what could we do? It was their house, so Spinelli and I shifted into the living room, where we began studying Aunt Ethel's very extensive collection of porcelain and crystal figurines, which, if you're into those things, was pretty interesting. There were several hand-painted ballerinas, and lots of tiny, delicate horses, and some unusual unicorns, and . . . who gives a shit.

"*We* should've called the Boston PD," I informed Spinelli.

"Maybe."

No maybes about it, pal. The four women in that kitchen were grieving over the murder of their sister and the attempted murder of their father. The shock of those events was not likely to lead to clear thinking or logical conclusions. I felt uneasy, realizing I had misplayed this, hoping they weren't convincing one another to do what I was sure they were trying to convince one another to do. After a time, Janet finally called us back into the kitchen. The four women were seated around the table, and I didn't like the pissed-off, determined set of their faces.

"Have a seat," said Janet.

Well, there were only four chairs, all of which were taken, so Spinelli and I brushed aside some clutter and hoisted ourselves up onto the linoleum counters, which earned us a really nasty glower from Aunt Ethel.

"We have a plan," said Janet.

I replied, "There's only one plan. Call the cops. *Now.*"

Carol, who was next oldest behind Janet, said, "First, let's talk about our plan."

And Elizabeth, the youngest, said, "This man murdered our sister and put our father in the hospital. We've paid for the right to decide what to do next."

I said, "That's not—"

"Also," Janet said, "he's murdered three other women and a driver. And there's every indication he intends to kill more. If you're right . . . if he's here, we have a chance to take him off the streets."

"So," Elizabeth agreed, "he thinks he has Janet in a trap. That gives us a chance to turn the tables and put *him* in a trap."

What they were thinking wasn't news. But Spinelli was nodding. And all three sisters and Aunt Ethel were nodding.

I drew a deep breath and said, "Thank you. That's a very noble gesture. It's also clearly a stupid idea. The odds are completely in his favor." I stared at Janet and added, "Don't even think of using yourself as bait. This guy will swallow you whole."

In retrospect, things might have gone better had I chosen a less provocative manner to state my objections.

Janet's nostrils sort of flared. Sounding somewhat pissy, she said to me, "I . . . Damn it, don't underestimate me. I can take care of myself. And don't you dare call me stupid again." She added, "Of course I plan to use the Boston PD."

Spinelli immediately said, "Good idea—slap up a cordon, and we got this guy by the balls. But be sure to tell 'em only plainclothes, and no closer than three blocks from here. This guy, he's good, and he'll ID 'em."

If I had had a gun, I would've drilled Spinelli on the spot. It suddenly occurred to me that his motive for rushing up here differed from mine. I mean, of course Spinelli wanted to apprehend the killer and become the Man of the Hour, but "Protect and Serve" means *protect* first. Also, you don't slap together bait operations on the fly. You take time to consider all the possible twists and eventualities, you handpick your best people, you plan, and then you replan, and then you rehearse, and even then, sometimes your bait ends up inside a chalk outline.

I tried again to explain my very reasonable objections, but it was clear I was the odd man out.

In any regard, Janet finally grew impatient and informed me, "Look, don't think we don't appreciate your figuring this out and rushing up here to warn us. But let me remind you, I'm a city prosecutor, and the local police are going to follow my lead." She pointed her finger at me and said, "You can be part of the solution, or you can keep your mouth shut."

Actually this was one of those cases where being part of the solution was being part of the problem. So I kept my mouth shut as
they tried to hatch a plot. Eventually, Janet stepped into the living
room and made the call to the Boston PD. Actually, this was the moment I had been waiting for. No doubt the cops would thank her
for volunteering, and then tell her she wasn't equipped for the job
and that would be it.

And when she finally stepped back into the kitchen, she said,
"I just spoke with Harry O'Malley, the commissioner."

Spinelli said, "Yeah, and . . ."

"Harry loved the idea. He said to give him thirty minutes to
arrange a cordon, and suggested we should use that time to refine
a plan."

Shit. In thirty minutes we would have both the killer and his
prey bottled up inside a tight cordon. The first problem with that
was, we had no idea what he looked like. The second problem was
he was very expert at this killing game. The old parable about the
two scorpions in the same box popped into my mind, and I recalled with a shudder how it ended—the scorpions stung each
other to death.

So they all sat at the table and batted ideas back and forth,
while I sulked on the counter, and outside, our killer paced
around, surely growing impatient and antsy. Eventually, he could
get tired of this waiting game and either depart or throw a murderous tantrum at this house. If he departed, this whole crazy
scheme would fall apart. Call that the best outcome. If he attacked,
he'd have to kill four women instead of one, not to mention the visiting clergymen. We might get him, and that would be good. He'd
probably get some of us also, and that would be bad.

Elizabeth and Carol kept proposing options, all of which entailed the three sisters leaving Aunt Ethel's house together and
sharing the risks and perils.

It was such a bad idea that even Janet knew it was a bad idea,
and she eventually advised her sisters, "He's here for me. We will
not put anybody else at risk."

Elizabeth and Carol shook their heads and began vigorously arguing otherwise.

So I broke my vow of silence and interrupted. "Janet's right."

"Of course I'm right," Janet replied. "He's waiting for me to separate. He'd prefer to avoid the complications and take me alone."

Spinelli remarked, "That would appear to be his modus operandi."

I said, "Really? With Fiorio he whacked the driver to take the limo. He's not squeamish about eliminating bystanders to get what he wants."

Actually, three sisters collectively exposing themselves lumped stupidity on top of idiocy. Three targets are naturally harder to protect than one. Protection is a game of risks and odds, and the more targets you add to the mix, the more those odds shift in the wrong direction.

So, while they argued back and forth, I sat and calculated those odds. On the plus side, like many Army CID agents, Spinelli was trained in bodyguard techniques. Among their many other functions, CID personnel are the ones who guard high-level Defense officials, and they are quite proud of the fact they have never lost an official. Very reassuring, *right?* Indeed, until you realized nobody had ever made an attempt. Still, CID received top-flight training, and from my days in black operations I had received similar training. My skills had atrophied, and I obviously wasn't the rip-snorting stud I was in my mid-twenties, but I hadn't forgotten everything I learned. For example, I recalled Lesson One—against a skilled assassin you have almost no chance of protecting The Package.

Eventually, Elizabeth and Carol backed off, and Janet and Spinelli settled upon the outline of a plan. Janet then called the commissioner's office again, and was switched to the office of the police captain who'd been designated as el jefe of this affair. They sounded like they were old pals, a few warm and friendly pleasantries were exchanged, and then Janet handed off the phone to Spinelli, who spent twenty minutes refining the plan with the Boston PD, settling upon a route, security arrangements, and so forth. I listened in, and considering what they wanted to accomplish, it was probably as good as it was going to get. But for the record, "as good as it was going to get" and "good enough" don't always match. So while Spinelli was hobnobbing on the phone, I drew Janet into the living room.

I got her alone and said, "I know you think you know what you're doing, but this is a very high-risk deal."

She nodded. "I'm aware of that. It's also the *right* thing to do. You know that."

Whether it was or wasn't the *right* thing was past being relevant. I replied, "But if you're going to go through with it, a few pointers."

"As long as they're constructive."

I pointed at her feet. "You and Carol appear to be close in shoe size. Trade your heels for her sneakers."

"That's a good idea. I will."

"He likes to kill with his hands. Don't let anybody get close."

"Right . . . nobody gets close."

"Your first choice is to run."

"Run . . . yes. I intend to."

"If you can't, tuck your chin into your chest and fall to the ground. That'll buy us time to reach you."

She nodded.

I said, "Get a knife from Aunt Ethel's kitchen."

"All right."

"Keep it in your coat pocket."

She nodded again, and I advised, "No more than a five-inch blade. Shorter blades are harder to block."

"A five-inch blade . . . right . . . good idea."

"Keep it in your grip at all times. Practice pulling it out a few times. If you use it, swing *up* and aim for his gut, not *down*. Amateurs swing down and end up dead."

She nodded again and then informed me, "I'm ready for this."

"No . . . you're not. You're an optimistic amateur going up against a ruthless killer."

"Stop trying to scare me. You'll make me so paranoid I'll blow it."

Well, I wanted her paranoid. Fear was her only hope of surviving this ordeal. I wanted her so skittish that the slightest threat would cause her to scream her lungs out and flee.

I mentioned, "One other thing for you to consider."

"What's that?"

"This guy, these killings, it's all, somehow, connected to the law firm."

Since she had suspected this in the first place, she did not appear surprised, but she still needed a moment to ponder this news. "How? Why?"

"I don't know yet. It might have to do with that company I mentioned to you. But it might not. Still, I think somebody in the firm is involved."

"Do you know who?"

"If I did, you wouldn't be doing this."

Then a fresh thought hit me. I said, "There were e-mails from Lisa to you, Anne Carrol, and Julia Cuthburt that referred to packages. Did you get a package?"

"When was this?"

"About . . ." I couldn't recall the exact date, but I remembered the general date, and said, "maybe three weeks ago."

"Yes, I did."

"And . . . ?"

"It was a birthday gift for my father. Lisa wanted me to include it with my gift." She glanced at her watch and said, "Look, I need to keep my mind on one problem at a time. Let's discuss it later."

"If there is a later." I added, "Remember, run; if you can't, fall down."

She nodded and returned to the kitchen.

CHAPTER THIRTY-FIVE

ONSIGNORS SPINELLI AND DRUMMOND WALKED OUT AUNT ETHEL'S FRONT
door, climbed into their beat-up Honda Civic, and departed. We
drove four blocks, parked by an intersection, then backtracked
two blocks.

Spinelli then led me to two unmarked cars and three Boston
detectives who were loitering outside a barbershop, blending
into their surroundings, though I thought they looked like sore
thumbs.

We approached on foot and one of the detectives, a freckly,
red-haired kid, beamed at us and said, "Good morning, Fathers."

Spinelli smiled back. "Up yours, dickhead."

I believe I mentioned that Spinelli has sociability issues. Anyway, he then flashed his tin, and explained, "If I were the killer,
you'd be dead as shit. Where's yer fuckin' radio?"

The young detective led Spinelli to his car, and they climbed in
together. Spinelli spent a few moments communicating to the captain in charge of this operation, tying down details and loose ends
and whatever.

I leaned against a lamp post. Having already scared the Morrow girls out of their shorts, I was now in the process of jerking the Boston PD through a major knothole. If I was wrong about the killer and his intentions, or he smelled a trap and disappeared, a bad day was going to become an incredibly shitty day. But, enough with happy thoughts; I switched to ruminations about the plan. In battle, you learn to think like the other guy, then use that to get one step ahead of him, even as he's trying to think like you. The Army euphemistically calls this getting inside an enemy's decision cycle. The one who gets a few synapses connections ahead of the other chokes on confetti at the victory parades; the other guy ships home in a body bag.

Our edge lay in the fact that we *were* trying to think like him. Because he wasn't aware we knew he was out there, he *wasn't* trying to think like us.

Anyway, while Spinelli wrapped up his explanation on the radio, I realized I was unarmed. So I attempted to sweet-talk the friendly, freckle-faced detective into loaning me a pistol. He informed me, somewhat frostily, that departmental policy strictly forbade the issuance of police ordnance to private citizens. I might've felt more secure having a weapon, but the truth is, I've never been able to hit shit with a pistol. In fact, Janet's chances of survival just went up a peg.

A few minutes later, an unmarked van pulled to the curb and another priest stepped out. Actually, the new priest was named Detective Sergeant Jack Pilcher, and he was the officer assigned by the Boston PD to escort Chief Warrant Spinelli, who lacked both jurisdiction and authority in this city.

In fact, his opening words to Spinelli were, "Listen up, soldier boy, this is my fucking city. You're along for the ride. Don't even think of using your weapon or trying to apprehend this butthole. We clear on this point?"

Despite his own sociability issues, Spinelli apparently knew to leave well enough alone. He replied, "You're the boss."

Then Pilcher noticed me, my priest's garb, my eager poise, and said, "Is this a fucking convention? Who the fuck are you?"

"Drummond."

"You CID, too?"

I overlooked that insult and said, "I'm a JAG officer."

"Great. What are you doing here?"

"I'm part of this show."

"The hell you are."

I glanced at Spinelli, who, I suddenly noticed, had stepped back a few paces, and with a perfectly innocuous expression was staring at something across the street. Had my partner somehow failed to inform the Boston PD that I was an inseparable member of the team here? If so, surely it was just a simple oversight, or a memory lapse.

I informed Sergeant Pilcher, "Actually, Miss Morrow specified that she wouldn't take a step out her front door unless I'm watching her ass." I added, more loudly, "Mr. Spinelli heard her demand. Right?"

Spinelli apparently had his mind on other matters and failed to reply. To help him focus on this issue I grabbed his arm and repeated, "Right, Spinelli?"

He replied, reluctantly, "Uh . . ." Well, I squeezed a bit harder, until he said, "Yeah. She said that."

"You see?" I informed Pilcher. "Hey, I'm not even armed."

Well, Detective Sergeant Pilcher still did not like this, and even frisked me to be sure I was both weaponless and harmless. He then spent two minutes briefing me on my role, which could be neatly summarized as stay the fuck out of his way.

We then waited five minutes, too keyed up to speak, staring off into the distance. Pilcher had a miniature mobile radio unit under his cassock, with a mike pinned to his chest and a tiny receiver in his ear. He used the wait to test his commo with his ops center. It either worked or he enjoyed talking into his own chest and nodding his head. But Spinelli's cell phone finally rang and he answered, "Yeah . . . Uh-huh . . . okay, good . . ." Then, "All right, we're moving."

Spinelli was conversing with Janet, and he didn't punch off, because from this moment on, he and Janet would stay connected through their cell phones. Jerry-rigged operations make me nervous, and I briefly wondered what would happen if somebody's battery died, or we ended up passing through one of those dead-space zones. Anyway, we began moving, Spinelli and Pilcher keeping their right hands tucked inside their cassocks, no doubt gripping their pistols. Pilcher moved down one side of the street. Spinelli and I cruised down the other, until we all ducked into doorways within sight of Aunt Ethel's house.

Pilcher must've informed the ops center we were in position, while Spinelli informed Janet that it was time to start the gig, because Aunt Martha's front door flew open and Janet stepped out. She hugged Aunt Ethel, kissed her sisters, and they all somehow managed to swallow their anxieties and make it appear like a natural parting scene.

Then Janet walked in our direction, her cell phone held to her ear with one hand, the other stuffed in her coat pocket, hopefully gripping a knife. I actually caught my breath. The day was cold and breezy, her hair was blowing behind her, framing her face, and she looked extraordinarily beautiful. Was I in lust, or what?

She passed Pilcher without a sideways glance and kept going. I looked around for anybody following her. Aunt Ethel's house was three blocks off Harvard Square, and Janet moved in that direction, then took a right and headed toward the Charles River that divides the obscenely wealthy College of Harvard from the obnoxiously wealthy Business School.

We trailed a block behind her until the streets suddenly became thick with Harvard students and pedestrians and window-shoppers. We lost sight of Janet for a few scary seconds, so we sped up and closed the gap to half a block.

This was the riskiest leg of her journey. The killer could blend in with the pedestrians and slip a knife into her ribs as they passed.

We had discussed this possibility at length but finally theorized that he wouldn't strike here because the street was too crowded. There'd been no witnesses in any of the other killings, making it fair to assume he took great care to avoid exposure. But the problem with assumptions and theories is they're only right until they're wrong.

Janet walked briskly past a large red-brick building. The sign by the road declared this to be the John F. Kennedy School of Government, which is where they train eggheads to screw up the government, but to sound really smart as they do it. She then hung a left onto the walking path that borders the Charles River.

We quickly reached the path and ended up walking side by side, a trio of thoughtful clerics contemplating the serene beauty of the heavenly river God created, or something like that. To our left was the Harvard Law School. I recalled that both Janet and Lisa had graduated from that school, and now we were hunting her murderer in the shadow of its walls.

I don't believe in fate, kismet, or cosmic coincidences, but I did pick up my pace and sharpen my senses a bit. In fact, I had this weird premonition that this guy possessed a sense of irony, or poetic symmetry, and wanted to whack Janet right here. The basic idea— the Massachusetts Institute of Technology is located some two miles downriver from Harvard in the direction Janet was walking. A bridge over the Charles River connects MIT's campus with Boston proper, and on the Boston side of that bridge is a subway stop. Janet had flown into Boston and been picked up by Carol, who had rushed her to the hospital. It seemed perfectly natural for Janet to leave her sisters with her aunt and catch a train to return to her apartment. If she survived the trip to her apartment, a more foolproof trap was being laid there by the Boston PD. It is a rule of thumb that protecting a stationary target is easier than protecting a moving one. We were sort of hoping to make it to that point without incident.

But clearly the choice wasn't ours. And therefore the Boston PD had sprinkled undercover cops from their narcotics unit at intervals along the route. Narcotics cops go the extra mile to look seedy and scummy, and while I was assured they were there, I hadn't detected any, which I regarded as a good sign. As long as it didn't mean there'd been a minor communications problem, and they were all on the *other* side of the river. This sometimes happens.

Anyway, it was a spectacular day for a stroll along the river; the temperature was cool, the sky clear and sunny, a nice breeze made the water ripple and sparkle. An occasional scull raced by on the water. A biker sped past us. Then a few more bikers, followed by a middle-aged, overweight male jogger. A minute later, a pair of chubby girl joggers wearing stretch pants huffed and puffed past us. The idea was, we would watch Janet's back, and she'd watch her front. Her cell phone was still at her ear, and she was chatting intermittently with Spinelli, appearing to all the world like a modern young executive, oblivious to the beauty around her, tied to her office, too driven and ambitious to stop and smell the roses, or whatever.

Two more joggers chugged past us, a guy and a girl. The guy was about six foot four, with long, dark hair, and in terrific shape. The girl was svelte with thick blond hair, and that bouncy run and well-toned body of the former cheerleader. They were chuckling and chatting as they sped past, the modern generation's version of foreplay. Ah, to be young, fit, and in lust.

Spinelli turned to me and asked, "See the sweet ass on that one?"

"Huh? . . . Oh yeah. But don't you think he was a little tall for you?"

He chuckled. "Fuck you."

I added, "He's a good match for Pilcher here, though."

Pilcher also replied, "Fuck you."

Obviously they were both pleased to have me along.

I watched Janet again. Three male joggers ran past us as the cheerleader and her big running partner passed Janet.

I studied the three men. The one in the middle, I noticed with a nasty jolt, was fairly short and very well built, with knotty shoulders and thickly muscled arms. But what really got my attention was the long, stringy ponytail bouncing off his back. He fit the precise physical description of the L.A. Killer and it struck me that Spinelli's copycat theory could be wrong. I mean, nothing I had discovered actually ruled out the L.A. Killer. Spinelli elbowed me in the ribs, indicating he also had noticed Mr. Ponytail and the possibility here. As the three men closed the distance to her, Spinelli said to her, via his phone, "There's three guys coming up behind you. Look around and keep your eye on the guy in the middle, the one with the ponytail."

Janet somehow managed to maintain her poise and glance casually back over her right shoulder. Pilcher's right hand was nearly out of his cassock pocket, ready to drill Mr. Ponytail if he made a wrong move.

When they passed right by Janet, I still kept my eye on Mr. Ponytail. So did everybody else, which was why we *all* failed to notice that the big guy who'd been running with the cheerleader had departed his partner, done a U-turn, and was sprinting straight toward Janet.

It was too late when I *did* notice. He was within feet of her. Without thinking, I yelled, "Janet!" Her head swung around to look, but the fatal mistake had been made, and she was on her own. The guy's approach was such that Janet was between us and him, and the odds of nailing her were greater than the odds of hitting him.

Janet was about five foot eight and he towered over her. His arm drew back and I saw a silvery glint that had to be a knife. Janet dropped the cell phone, her back to us, and she appeared to freeze in her tracks, too shocked to run or respond.

Just as his arm started to arc forward, he stepped toward her, twisted and moved sideways, and I heard a pop. Then he twisted again, and there was another pop. I was still forty yards away and sprinting, but I saw him bring his arm down, lower his shoulder, and slam into Janet like a middle linebacker sacking a wimpy quarterback. She flew about six feet through the air, landed on her butt, and somersaulted over backward from the force of the blow.

He then glanced at me and without a hint of confusion or hesitation sprinted immediately toward the four-lane highway above the pathway. He was incredibly fast, and was dodging around like a crooked Ping-Pong ball. Pilcher had dropped to a knee and was firing his pistol. Spinelli was standing upright and shooting. From the best I could tell, neither hit him.

I started sprinting after him, even as I knew it was useless. The guy had legs like pistons, and he was across the highway and dodging into the side streets of Cambridge before I could even reach Janet. Pilcher was screaming something into his microphone. A pair of seedy-looking bums who'd been loitering by the next bridge began running toward us. Presumably, these were the undercover cops we'd been promised.

Janet lay perfectly still. As I approached, I could see her pale blue eyes following me, which I took as a good sign.

I asked, "Are you hurt?"

She didn't reply at first, and I realized she was trying desperately to suck oxygen into her deflated lungs. I knelt beside her and performed a quick visual inspection. No blood. No cuts. The killer had failed to stab her. I saw a bullet hole in her coat, but she didn't appear to be wounded. She finally struggled into a sitting position and cursed a few times. That worked for me.

I said, "He got away."

"How?" She added, "I shot him. Twice."

That explained the holes in her coat. She apparently had a gun in her pocket and had fired right through her coat. But I'd seen the guy's moves and technique, and I was fairly certain she had missed him, and I was definitely certain I knew why. Then Spinelli jogged over and said, "The Boston PD is moving on him. We know where he ran, and he won't get out of the cordon."

I nodded, and then looked down at Janet. "Are you all right?"

"No. I'm pissed. I heard you yell and . . . and I shot him." She shook her head, and said, "From three feet away? How could I miss?"

Spinelli asked, "Where'd you get the gun?"

I reached out and helped her get to her feet. She brushed the leaves and dirt off her backside. She said, "I get death threats all the time, so I have a special permit. I even fly with it."

I asked, "What kind of gun?"

She reached into her pocket and withdrew a .?? caliber. She stared at the pistol and said, "Okay, it's a peashooter, but I'm accurate with it, and there's no kick."

That made sense. It also explained how even if she had hit the killer—which I strongly doubted—he could still run away. I hadn't seen his face, but I saw his size. About six foot four and perhaps 250–260 pounds of highly buffed muscle. A guy with that bulk could take a couple of .22 slugs and, unless they penetrated a vital organ, regard them as beestings.

I asked Janet, "Did you get a good look at him?"

"Yes, I . . . too good. Long, dark hair, a thick mustache, a goatee, and green eyes. Give me a good profiler and I'll give you a good picture."

Pilcher was talking rapidly into his microphone, and listening to his earpiece, saying, ". . . yeah . . . nah, she's okay." He listened for a moment, then said, "She says she pumped two rounds into him . . . uh-huh . . . ah, shit. Okay, lemme know."

He scowled.

Janet said, "What?"

"He just killed two of our guys five blocks from here. Came up from behind 'em, cut one guy's throat, and butchered the other one. This is one bad motherfucker."

I asked, "And did he get away?"

"Not yet. But he's out of the cordon. We got an all-points on him, and cops are converging from all over the city. We'll get this bastard."

Spinelli was staring at the ground, and commented to no one in particular, "Not a prayer."

CHAPTER THIRTY-SIX

Good news was in short supply at the Federal Building in Boston.

After murdering Detective Sergeants Phillip Janson and Horace O'Donnell, the perp had vanished. A thorough investigation by the forensics crew at the running path revealed that he wore size 12 shoes, and chose New Balance 715s for his morning jog. It further revealed no trace of blood, hair, or other bodily fluids, which was unfortunate, because a DNA trace would've been invaluable to tie him to one attempted and two successful murders.

A statewide manhunt was in full swing. Roadblocks were erected at various state border crossing points. Airports and bus stations had been faxed a copy of the facial composite constructed from Janet's description and ordered to detain anybody who bore the slightest resemblance. Hospitals in a two-hundred-mile radius were staked out for a big white man with one or possibly two bullet holes.

Still I think we all knew he was too smart for any of those steps to work. Of course the police and Feds had to go through the motions—to use a football analogy, the way a football team down

77-6 late in the fourth quarter kicks a field goal. Also, this guy had now added two cops to his ledger, and the blue brotherhood looks dimly upon that.

Four hours had passed since the screwup by the river. A planeload of puffy, red-faced FBI agents had flown up from Washington to interrogate all involved. Understand that FBI people, once they're drawn into a case, treat it as sort of a feudal setup, where they own the castles and playgrounds, and expect everybody else to grow their potatoes and kiss their asses. They felt jilted and mistreated. Their general mood was pissed.

Given that the FBI's public affairs office was handling the press releases regarding this case, everybody felt like it was time to play round-robin cover-your-ass.

The potentially embarrassing problem for the Boston PD was they had had the baddest motherfucker in the land in their sights. I overheard some of their conversations in the hallways and their line of bullshit was that they'd lost two brave men in the pursuit of this badass, who wasn't really their killer in the first place but a D.C. problem dropped on their doorstep. In short, they'd donated to charity—don't come knocking on their door. But of course, this was Boston, and in the event that that bullshit wasn't taken seriously, a few oily fixers from City Hall had showed up to work the hallways and discreetly remind the FBI that the two very influential senators from Massachusetts sat on both the Appropriations and Judiciary Committees; and if the FBI wanted their next budget request to pass, or their next fuckup to get generous treatment, this might be a prudent moment to sort of shuffle this thing under a rug. And it sure would be in the spirit of good fellowship to add a few adulatory words about the Boston PD in their press releases. Truly, you have to marvel at the way these things work.

Spinelli's line of defense was that I had contacted him and he'd taken every reasonable step and precaution to get this guy, including turning it over to the local authorities. That had the value of being true.

And Janet? Well, every story, especially a tragedy, needs a sexy, beautiful heroine, and she was made for the role, la femme fatale, the Beantown chick who kicked ass, the bereaved victim's sister who had risked body and soul to terminate a public menace. And then . . . well, then she had had the fortitude to stand in the dark shadow of the salivating monster and pour lead at his putrid guts. Books and movie to follow.

So, everybody had a good defense, alibi, or claim to glory.

Right . . . not quite everybody.

What every good government tale requires is a token scape-goat, and once everybody had spun their sides of the tale, all the black arrows sort of pointed back at the guy who lacked either beauty or an institution to cover his butt. I began to figure this out as more and more sour-faced Fibbies trickled into my interrogation room. When it hit twenty, it became standing room only, and a guy was posted at the door to issue tickets and bathroom passes. George Meany, incidentally, was front and center, and in off mo-ments, when he thought I wasn't looking, I caught him smirking.

My interrogator, Special Agent Arnold, was at that moment say-ing to me, ". . . and because you had everybody jump the gun, we've lost our only chance to apprehend the killer, Drummond. This was amateur hour. God knows how far you set us back . . ." Blah blah blah.

This particular lecture wasn't improving the third time around, but I was listening intently and hanging my head in shame. Also, I think I must have been unconsciously drumming my hands on the table to the beat to "In-A-Gadda-Da-Vida," and carrying it really well. This was brought to my attention when he suddenly reached out and pinned both my hands to the table.

"Do I need to slap your ass in manacles?" he inquired.

"Does your wife enjoy that?"

"You leave my wife out of—"

"She liked it when I did her." I smiled. He didn't smile back.

Anyway, interrogators are never supposed to lose control of the situation, and he obviously had a large crowd, so after a few huffy breaths, he said, "Major, would you explain again, you know . . . how you decided the killer had left D.C. and come here?"

For the fourth time, I replied, "When I saw the names of two of the victims in Lisa Morrow's e-mail, the implication struck me as clear. Lisa, Cuthburt, and Carrol were friends or acquaintances."

"This would be J. and A., right? Isn't that what you claimed?"

"No. That's what I stated for a fact." I added, "I then tried to get hold of Miss Morrow, was notified about the fire, and put two and two together."

"You, uh . . . —Gee, I hope I'm not being repetitive here, but, boy, that's speculative. Certainly, there's a few things you're not telling us." He leaned back in his chair and straightened his lapels. "What are those things?"

"I had a hunch."

"Did the killer call you? Leave a note? Somehow make contact?"

Of course, the FBI, filled as it is with lawyers and accountants, and backed up by the world's best scientific labs, considers the whole notion of hunches and instincts silly. And I could hear a few murmurs from the gallery. Also a few derisory snickers. I was getting really annoyed.

He bent forward. "This Sherlock Holmes bullshit isn't selling, Drummond. We're the good guys here. Tell us."

"Okay, okay . . . you're right."

"I am?"

"Wow . . . I can't fool you guys, can I?"

"I'm glad you're coming around."

"The truth is . . ." He leaned toward me. "When I was with your wife, she said, well . . . she said you've got a tiny dick."

He howled and slapped the table. I did hear a few distinct chuckles from the boys in the third bleacher, however. Trust me, it's not easy when you're playing to somebody else's home crowd.

I said, "You're pissed. I didn't call you. I'm sorry, I lost my head."

"Why didn't you call us?"

"Army lawyers call CID."

"Bullshit. Special Agent Meany informed us that he gave you his business card." He added nastily, "Had you called us, this entire disaster would have been avoided. Think about that, wiseass."

Okay, I thought about it. The two dead Boston PD detectives and the escaped felon were on my shoulders because I called the wrong kind of cop? Did I need this nonsense?

In truth, two hours of this bullshit had convinced me that had I gone to the Fibbies instead of Spinelli, Janet Morrow would be a chalk outline beside the Charles River. They wouldn't have believed a word. Despite my arguments, and the corroborating physical descriptions of four witnesses, they continued to insist this guy was the L.A. Killer.

However I had surmised he would turn up in Boston, they were convinced I had reached the right conclusion from completely idiotic assumptions. Go a step further, and Spinelli and my theory about this guy being a copycat contradicted the very public assurances the FBI had given John Q. Public. Obviously, this was inconvenient, and nobody in that room, and Mr. Meany particularly, wanted egg on their face by admitting they fingered the wrong guy. But also, in a big bureaucracy like theirs, everything has to be run up the flagpole before anybody knows what they think.

Mysteriously, another gray suit slipped into the room, walked over to the interrogator, whispered something in his ear, and then stepped back. A lot of these guys had those earphone thingees, and suddenly a lot of hands were adjusting their volume or getting them better seated in their ears. It looked like a Twenty Stooges skit.

Special Agent Arnold stood and straightened his suit. He informed me, "This interrogation is over. You plan to return to D.C., correct?"

I indicated I did.

"We know how to reach you. We'll pick this up there at a later time."

And on that ominous note, bodies began racing for the door. What the . . . ? I mean, one moment I'm the Man of the Hour, ticket scalpers are in the hallway making a fortune off me, and suddenly I'm in an empty room. I finally got up and walked out.

Janet and Danny Spinelli were waiting in the hallway, sipping from paper coffee cups and looking mildly anxious.

Janet pushed off the wall and said to me, "You were in there almost two hours. Is anything wrong?"

"Wrong? No, it just took a while for them to, you know, tell me how much they admired the brilliant way this was conceived and conducted, and how swell it all turned out for everybody."

She rubbed her temples and groaned. "I'm sorry. I know you were right." She then said, "They . . . well, they found another body."

"Whose? Where?"

"Ten blocks from the two dead officers. A man named Harold Boticher. His throat was slashed, and his wallet and car keys were stolen. His body was found in a Dumpster, like Anne Carrol's."

The implication was obvious. "Did they get the make of his car?"

"Make, model, and tag numbers." That explained why the room emptied.

Spinelli commented grumpily, "It's a fuckin' waste of time. He's already got himself another."

He was right, of course. Perversely, Spinelli and I both appeared to be getting a bead on this guy. The FBI was still running everywhere he wanted them to go.

And right on cue, Dudley Do-Right came cruising around a corner, trailed by three of his stooges. Special Agent Meany was waving his arms and barking instructions, and the three agents were scribbling notes and nodding obsequiously. I mean, it was just *too* frigging obvious that this jerk was trying to impress his former belle with what a busy, roundly admired, take-charge kind of guy he was.

He suddenly glanced in our direction, like he had just noticed us, then sent his three aides scurrying. He approached, shaking his head, oozing with concern, and said to Janet, "My God, honey, that was a very dumb thing you did. You're lucky to be alive."

Honey? Had I missed something here?

Janet replied, "That's not the way it looked at the time. We had him, George. He was within three feet of me. I fired two shots at him."

His hands were all over her arms again. "I understand. And I admire your courage. Really . . . I don't blame you." He glanced at me and said, "I blame the idiots who let you expose yourself. You were responding to your grief . . ." Still looking at me, he said, "Why didn't you call me? You needed advice from someone you could trust. Don't do anything again without checking with me. That's an order, honey."

Well, fuck you, George.

"There wasn't time," Janet said. "We had a narrow window of opportunity, and we didn't want to lose him."

"I understand." His hands moved to her shoulders and he looked into her eyes and added, "But I don't want to lose *you*. Not now . . . not again. Now that we've resolved our little problem, I . . . well, I'm glad you're okay."

Yuck. I mean, there's a murderous maniac out on the streets, and I'm stuck with this asshole in a live episode of *Days of Our Lives*. Turn the channel, please.

But Janet appeared to buy his malarkey, and replied, "Well, I'm fine, George." She then asked him, "What are the odds of catching him?"

"Hard to tell. I've put out a multistate alert. I'll be directing the search from the Boston Field Office. Also, I've distributed the composite sketch you provided—that's an edge I didn't have before." He paused a moment, his expression turned all oozy and charming, and he said, "You know, I can't believe you had the coolness and presence to study him that closely. You are really something, babe."

Geez. I've had tiffs with some formers, and of course you have to work it a little if you want to get back into their good graces and panties. But there's a point where you give your whole sex a bad name. Meany was working her *too* hard. And I wondered why.

And as if that wasn't enough, his expression turned grave, and he added, "Honey, I don't want to worry you, but there's a chance he'll come after you again. We think he fled the city, but you can never be sure. You're the only living witness who can ID him in a courtroom." He paused, like this pained him greatly, then said, "You know the standard procedure in these things."

Janet was already shaking her head. "I'm not going into protective custody, George."

"But—"

"No. Don't even think about it."

He studied her face a moment. "Oh, come on. It would make things easier for all concerned."

She stared back at him.

As much as I hated to agree with George on anything, I said, "Do what he says. He's right."

She said to both of us, "We all know I cannot be forced into this program. This asshole is not going to chase me into protective custody."

I opened my lips, but she cut me off: "No—Subject closed."

I looked at her and tried to figure out what was going through her head. Playing Parcheesi with a bunch of Fibbies in a hotel room for a month or two was bad, but dying was very, very bad. Unless . . . well, unless Janet *wanted* this guy to strike again. To draw him back to her, she had to remain accessible and vulnerable.

Anyway, Meany was shaking his head, saying, "I knew you'd say that."

"Well then, you're right."

"But you will be guarded and protected until the picture clarifies. Refusal is not an option." She did not say yes; nor did she refuse.

He continued, "Remember Bob Anderson from my old office? He'll stay with you until I can spare more agents. But at the moment, with this search, I just can't."

Janet said, "Thank you, but I'll be fine, George. Sean and Danny are here also."

He smiled knowingly. "Right. I'll get Bob to ask the Boston PD to back him up."

Boy, George was racking up big-time points.

Then his beeper went off, he yanked it off his belt, studied the screen, scrunched up his forehead, and said, "Got a fast-breaking emergency here, babe. The New York State Police think they've just spotted the stolen car on the New York Thruway. They're initiating a chase." And off he raced.

Something about George really bothered me. Well, a lot about George bothered me, but something, I don't know, something I couldn't put my finger on, *really* bothered me. I was sure he was very smart, and all those awards and promotions implied some level of professional competency, right? But why couldn't Meany and his people see the astounding brilliance of the detective work Spinelli and I had done? False modesty aside, maybe he had such a hard-on for me, he couldn't admit I was right.

Or maybe the answer was simpler. The FBI is a bureaucracy—which is both its strength and its Achilles' heel—and when the powers that be have publicly stated that the killer is the same ponytailed runt who was such a big hit in L.A., ambitious guys like Meany know it's a bad career move to contradict the big guys. What they do is wait for their bosses to change their minds before they can change their own minds.

Anyway, we all three walked out together, and, lo and behold, we were met at the building's entrance by a young, gawky-looking kid in a lumpy gray suit.

I guess he recognized Janet because he approached her with a big smile, and said, "I don't know if you remember me . . . Special Agent Bob Anderson. I worked on that Shelton case you prosecuted a few years ago."

Janet smiled, too. "Of course. I had you on the stand, didn't I?"

"That was me." He looked thoughtful for a moment, then said, "I'm really sorry."

"Don't worry about it."

"Well, I . . . gosh, that defense attorney . . ."

"I remember," Janet said. "That can happen."

Bob looked down at his feet. "The way he peppered me with all those questions . . . and kept misquoting me—"

"Put it behind you, Bob." She glanced at me and added, "Sometimes, mistrials just happen."

Bob said, "I guess."

Spinelli's eyebrows were ever so slightly raised. We were both staring at Bob, and sharing the same thought.

I suppose it was possible Meany had picked his best and brightest to go after the killer on the theory that the best way to protect Janet was to eliminate the threat. A less charitable interpretation might be that Meany wanted to bag the country's most notorious asshole, become famous, and jump another peg up the career ladder. If that meant his former lover got whacked because the biggest fuckup in the Boston office had been assigned to protect her, success sometimes requires sacrifice. Right?

"Call me Bob, by the way," the kid said to Spinelli and me. "I like to keep things loose and informal. But make no mistake, I'm in charge. Do everything I say, and everything's going to be just fine."

Spinelli rolled his eyes.

Anyway, Janet directed Bob to Aunt Ethel's house. The traffic was heating up, and Bob was an overcautious driver, which is lousy tradecraft when your passenger's a target, not to mention it dragged out our trip to nearly forty minutes. But as we climbed out of the Crown Victoria in front of the house, I looked up and down the street, for some reason bothered by something. *What?* Janet and Spinelli were already up the steps and opening the door, Bob had his hand stuffed inside his jacket, and I couldn't shake the feeling.

Janet turned around and asked me, "What is it, Sean?"

"Uh . . . nothing." But there was something.

Anyway, we entered the house of Aunt Ethel, where Elizabeth, Carol, and Aunt Ethel mobbed Janet, and, predictably, there was a

lot of hugging and kissing, which is another of those Men are from
Mars, Women from Venus things. And then they drew Janet into
the kitchen, where they made her recount how it went, which I
really didn't want to overhear.

Spinelli, Bob, and I loitered in the living room, while I tried to
put my finger on what bothered me. Also, I needed to find a way
to chat with Janet regarding the firm of Culper, Hutch, and Westin,
but without Bob listening in.

Incidentally, Bob had moved immediately to the window, and
was standing full-square in the middle of the plate glass, hands on
his hips, and his jaw thrust forward. This was for the benefit of the
killer, I guess, like he'd see this badass profiling in the window and
jump on the next flight to Brazil or something. I hoped Bob was
wearing his bulletproof vest.

I said to Spinelli, "Hey, Danny, you see Aunt Ethel's porcelain
collection yet? As a porcelain aficionado yourself, I'm sure you'll be
impressed."

"What? . . . I'm not interested in the old broad's fuckin'—"

I jerked him toward me. "Check the unicorn with a dick on it."

Well, my hint was subtle enough, but he did pick up on it, and
he followed me until I got him out of Bob's earshot, where I whispered, "Occupy the kid. I need to slip out back with Janet."

He looked at me curiously. "Why?"

"Later."

"Nah. You'll explain now."

I noticed Bob looking over his shoulder at us, and I said, "Don't
screw with me on this."

He rubbed his chin. "You know somethin'. I smell it. And you
ain't sharin'."

"Look, Spinelli . . . help me out here."

"You owe me. You promised I get this guy. I wanta know everything."

Well, what could I do? I promised, "I'll tell you everything." But
my fingers were crossed.

He stared at me a moment, then sauntered over to Bob, saying, "So, kid, how long you been in?"

Content that he would keep Bob occupied with cop talk, I slipped into the kitchen. I told Elizabeth and Carol to keep chattering, and then drew Janet out the back door.

We ended up on a tiny back porch, where Janet said, "What's this about?"

"It's time for our discussion." But I was being cautious, and I looked around for a moment and saw the cars parked on the street, and I suddenly realized what had been niggling at my brain. I said, "The killer . . . he stole a car, right?"

"It appears so."

"How did he get to Boston in the first place?"

"Plane, train, boat, car, swam, hiked, parachuted in. Have I missed anything?" I shook my head and she said, "At this moment, they're showing his composite at every terminal in the city."

"So they should."

Janet was sharp, though, and quickly concluded, "You're suggesting he came in a rental car?"

"And he would've parked it nearby . . . for his getaway."

She finished that thought, saying, "But after what happened at the river, he couldn't come back here."

So we began walking, through the backyard, then out to the street, where we started checking license plates. Rental cars tend to be fairly new, well-kept, clean, and shiny. Plus, if he'd driven up from D.C., the car should have out-of-state plates.

I moved to the other side of the street, and Janet stayed on the near side. We walked swiftly up the block, then took a right and did the cross street. We did the next block over, and the next. It was a residential neighborhood and early afternoon, and there weren't that many cars. Also, Janet reminded me that because of Boston's car theft rates, the smart citizens respond by buying inexpensive, crappy eyesores, which are cheaper to insure and less attractive to thieves. And in fact, most of the cars I saw were junkheaps.

We were moving quickly and we marked a few cars as possibilities, but they all had in-state plates. The third block over, I spotted a fairly new, forest green Ford Taurus with Pennsylvania plates. Virginia or D.C. plates seemed more logical, but this car was parked within twenty feet of a street corner, in fact, forward of the legal parking distance. If it was a getaway car, this was a smart stunt, because nobody else could park in front and hem it in. But this is America, where every privilege comes with a price—like a ticket on the windshield. I yanked the ticket off and noted it had been issued five hours before.

So, the right kind of car, in the right kind of place, *and* it had sat there the right amount of time. I waved at Janet and she jogged over. A swift inspection revealed a thin valise lying on the rear floor of an otherwise empty car.

The right and proper thing to do in this situation was call the Boston PD and have them dispatch a squad car. We'd have to wait for the cops, they'd have to call the DA's office, legal cause would have to be established, a lawyer would have to go see a judge, the judge would have to be persuaded to issue a search warrant, and around and around we go.

In any regard, the .22 in Janet's pocket apparently had a mind of its own. It was really weird, the way it somehow leaped out of her pocket, and then flew through the air and slammed its own butt against the driver's side window, which shattered inward. Well, what can you do?

Janet appeared shocked. "Damn it, Sean, I'm a city prosecutor and you just broke the law." As she issued this warning she was eagerly unlocking the doors and scrambling into the backseat.

I clambered in behind her. She already had the valise open and carefully withdrew two manila folders, pinching them with her shirt sleeves to avoid fingerprints. She dropped the first folder on the seat and the contents spilled out.

"That's me," she said, pointing at a large black-and-white photo.

"Good picture, too," I replied. And indeed it was, as were three more shots of her, taken from various angles, in different backgrounds and lighting, with her wearing a variety of outfits. Janet had obviously been under observation for a period of at least several days.

"Do you recall when you wore those clothes?"

She studied the photos and pointed at one. "Incredible. I wore that pantsuit before I went to D.C." She paused. "The same day Lisa died."

We jointly pondered that fact a moment.

Beneath the pictures were three or four printed sheets, and we spread them around using our elbows and shirt sleeves. The pages were neatly typed and paginated, with proper spelling, flawless punctuation, and so forth. The killer appeared to be one of those anal-retentive assholes who always did three more pages than the teacher asked for. I never trusted that type. Future serial killers—all of them.

Two pages were filled with carefully organized personal data about Janet: home address, phone number, automobile type and license number, family members, historical information, and so on. Nearly everything on these sheets could be obtained from public sources, though the sheer quantity of information indicated somebody who knew where to look and how much he could get.

But the next page did not appear to have been taken from public sources.

I pointed at a list of names and asked her, "Who are they?"

"Close friends." She looked horrified. She pointed at a few entries on the bottom of the page. "My dry cleaner . . . my gym . . . my doctor . . . the deli where I usually get lunch."

Janet swept her file sheets aside, then allowed the contents of the second folder to drop onto the seat.

The first item to spill out was a photograph of an extraordinarily good-looking man in a gray pinstriped Brooks Brothers suit, climbing into a green Jaguar sedan.

CHAPTER THIRTY-SEVEN

A LONG MOMENT PASSED WHERE JANET AND I AVOIDED VERBAL AND EYE CONtact. It was somewhat of a jolt to discover my name on this asshole's to-do list. It was unexpected, for one thing. Also, I'd seen this guy in action, and while I'd like to say I handled this news with my normal aplomb, in fact I felt a rumble of fear in my chest.

But shock aside, all kinds of pieces suddenly began tumbling into place. We both needed a moment to think about this.

She rifled through two more pictures, graciously allowing me a moment to think about updating my life insurance. I was wearing the same gray pinstriped suit, so presumably all the photos were taken on the same day. There was a mere half sheet of personal data: address, phone number, car type, license number, place of employment, and so on. The information on me was notably skimpier than her sheets—nothing about family, personal habits, or favorite haunts.

"I wore that suit only two days ago," I mentioned after I got my emotional sea legs back.

"You're a starter project. He's building his profile on you."

"I see that, but why am I on his list?"

"Before we get to that, I'll tell you what this confirms—he's not the L.A. Killer. Nor a sex maniac. At least, not *just* a sex maniac."

"Agreed. But why me?"

She correctly understood that my question wasn't rhetorical, that we had stumbled onto something very important, if we only knew what. She leaned back against the seat and hypothesized, "Sean, I make my living convicting murderers. They come in all stripes, and are driven by countless motivations. Sometimes they don't know why they're killing. A voice inside their head tells them to, it's a rite of passage into a gang, or the Mafia. Sometimes it's a response to boredom or rage."

"None of the above apply. You specialize in murder—now, what kind of killer compiles lists, creates files, methodically organizes his assaults, *and* makes sure someone else gets the credit for his handiwork?"

"I've noticed his . . . uniqueness." Actually, I was sure she had noticed considerably more, and probably knew exactly what I was getting at. But like a good prosecutor she wanted to hear it from my lips. In fact, she asked, "Do you think *you* know his motivation?"

"I think I do."

But Janet was putting the materials back into the briefcase, and she asked, referring to the contents, "What should we do about this?"

"Good question." As lawyers, we were both aware that we had created a sticky problem here. All right, I had created the problem, but Janet charitably did not mention that. I hate I-told-you-so women, incidentally. She was really nice. We smiled at each other.

But evidence illegally obtained—for instance, by breaking into an automobile without a warrant—is impermissible in court. Ironic as it might sound, Janet and I could be charged with breaking and entering, and destruction of property, even as a key piece of evidence was ruled as too contaminated for use. Well, we couldn't allow that to happen.

I said, "Slide it under the front seat. We'll report the car as damaged, let the cops tow it to the impound, and at least our killer won't be able to recover it. If we ever get this guy into a court, we'll figure out some slick way to have it discovered and introduced as evidence." That is, if we live through this, I failed to add.

She nodded. "I'll call the Boston PD on my cell phone." She added, "I won't give them my name—just that I saw somebody break a car window, and I'll tell them where to find it."

"Good idea."

She made the call and we then began walking back to Aunt Ethel's. Back to the other matter, I said to Janet, "Look, this guy . . . Down by the river, I formed a few impressions."

"I'm listening."

"Before I became a JAG, I made my living in special operations. You develop an eye for the talent and the type."

"What's his type?"

I wasn't ready to get into that yet, so I said, "Review what happened this morning. He selected a partner to jog with, a very attractive young lady who would draw the attention and make him less noticeable."

"I already figured that one out."

"Remember how he and the young lady first ran by you?"

"Yes . . . so?"

"Reconnaissance. He was sizing up his target, looking for surveillance, plotting where to take you, and where and how to make his escape. A mental rehearsal."

"Okay."

"He chose his approach to keep you between us and him. He'd seen us and he used your body as a screen, so we'd be lousy witnesses."

She thought about this a moment, then asked, "You think he was that calculating?"

"There's more." I then asked her, "What was he doing when you fired at him?"

She thought back, then said, "I . . . yes, it was some kind of strange weaving motion."

"He stepped closer to you?"

"Yes. He did. Then he started weaving."

"Because you communicated that you had a gun. It was the look in your eye, maybe, but I'd bet you jammed the barrel against your coat, and he detected it. Certain self-defense courses teach that in close-quarters situations, you move right up to the shooter, then start a quick shifting of the feet and midsection, intended to throw off a shooter's aim."

"You think I missed him?"

"I do." She appeared disappointed as I added, "Now, think about the way he aborted the mission, then rushed you and knocked you over. Or afterward how he dodged around like a broken Ping-Pong ball, moving unpredictably from side to side. That's another technique taught in certain specialty courses."

She thought about all that, then asked, "So you think he's former military?"

"Maybe. They're not street skills. And it was reflexive—no confusion, no hesitation, he just responded, fluidly and automatically. You understand what I'm saying? Eye-to-synapse-to-muscle coordination like his is extraordinarily rare. He's a natural. Also, he trains constantly to have that edge."

Janet considered all this, then said, "Sean, he's not a machine. He's human, and therefore fallible. He fell for our trap."

"That won't happen again."

She considered this, then asked, "He is coming again, though?"

"Guys only get that good if they invest a lot of ego into their work. They don't regard failures as failures, just notices to do better next time."

She cracked a faint smile, confirming my earlier suspicion. She definitely wanted to go another round with this guy. Also it confirmed she was a selective listener—we should have both been on the next flight to Mongolia.

But I knew she wasn't going to be *talked* out of it, and I said, "So, what do you conclude?"

"He's hired help. But was he hired by somebody in your firm?"

"Somebody in the firm is connected."

"Somebody Lisa worked with obviously."

"Yes. And now we know it has to be somebody I work with also."

I then spent a few minutes updating Janet on everything I had learned about Morris Networks and Grand Vistas. I was careful to couch it just right; these are the things I know, these are the things I only suspect, and these are the harebrained meanderings of a paranoid mind. Unfortunately, the latter outweighed the former, but in our business circumstantial cases are often the best you can get.

When I finished, she said, "It makes sense. Money and scandal—those are the motives."

"Maybe."

"Do you have another idea?"

"Well, I'll share a random theory. Morris Networks has a clutch of Defense contracts, and it's about to win a contract with DARPA, the organization that handles most of our most secretive projects."

"Go on."

"Morris Networks can read all its customers' e-mails and listen in to their traffic."

"Really?"

"So, here's this big company that hocked its soul to a secretive foreign conglomerate. And through its networks runs some of the most sensitive secrets in this country. War plans, top-secret technologies, troop movements, you name it. What if this foreign conglomerate is a front? What if it *actually* belongs to a foreign intelligence agency?"

"And is eavesdropping on sensitive information?" She considered that a moment, then said, "Is that possible?"

"During the cold war, we found out the Soviets had underwater cables running through some of its military harbors. We learned those cables were used by the Soviet military to carry some of their most sensitive information. We sent in subs to tap those cables. For years, we moved subs in and out of the harbors, right under their noses, tapping into the traffic. It was a gold mine."

"And we got away with this?"

"Right to the end. What I'm suggesting is the possibility that Grand Vistas might be a front operation. Maybe they have some kind of deal with Morris Networks—money for the Defense Department's mail."

"Sean, this is big."

"I know."

"If those are the stakes, the murders make even more sense."

"Right. But it is only a theory, not a fact."

She then said, "I'd better call George and inform him."

"Not yet."

"I sense you and he have . . . issues. But don't underestimate him."

When I failed to respond, she insisted, "He knows his job."

"The guy who sent Bob knows his job?"

"I . . . look, George has his hands full right now. I've seen him in action. Believe me, he's very good."

"I'm not debating his competence. But what will he do about it?"

She thought about this and swiftly drew the right conclusion. Our earlier problem hadn't disappeared—we had no evidence linking the firm to the killer. The instant Meany and his Boy Scouts started flashing their Fed badges, the disaster would play out—the firm would clam up, the culprits would be spooked, hard drives would start crashing, and reams of paper would start disappearing into shredders.

I said, "Nor can I divulge what I know about Grand Vistas without violating attorney-client privilege, right? It would be both unethical and legally inadmissible, right?"

"Okay, you make a good point."

I let her think about that a moment, then I said, "However, the law permits me to inform my attorney about these matters. So you're my attorney."

"You can't afford me." She peered at me curiously. "You're serious?" I nodded and she asked, "Why do you need an attorney?"

"To threaten Culper, Hutch, and Westin with a lawsuit."

"A lawsuit?"

"To use the law to fight the law."

"I don't want to throw a wrench in the works, but I think the legal code insists that you have grounds."

I glanced at my watch. "I have grounds. We'll discuss it on our way back to D.C."

"What am I getting into?"

"I've got a disciplinary hearing tonight at the firm. You'll represent me. So go inside and tell Bob to pack his bags."

Before Janet slipped through the back door, I said, "By the way, could I borrow your cell phone to call my office?"

"Sure."

I waited until she was inside before I called Northern Virginia information and got the number for the Rosslyn office of the Associated Press, which I then dialed. I asked the switch to put me through to Jacob Stynowitz, whose byline I had noticed on several stories regarding the serial killer. Actually, his stories were really good.

When he picked up, I said, "Mr. Stynowitz, I'm Major Drummond, a JAG officer. I've been following your stories about the L.A. Killer. Hey—they're excellent."

"Thanks. I try my best."

"It shows. Gripping stuff." I didn't want to lay it on too thick, so I said, "You've heard about the two cop killings this morning in Boston?"

"Yeah, sure. It's on CNN right now."

"I was there."

"You were there?"

"A few feet away. Saw the whole thing. The guy trying to kill the girl on the running path . . . the cops rushing around."

"Well, that's interesting. Is that the reason for this call?"

"Yeah. See, I thought . . . if you're doing a story on this Boston thing . . . I could maybe give you a few colorful quotes. I know how these things work, the FBI controlling what's put out, and they only tell you what they want you to know . . ."

There was silence on the other end for a moment.

He asked, "Is there a way I can confirm you were a witness?"

"I just spent the morning in the Federal Building with the FBI. Ask them."

"I will. Now, Mr. . . . I mean, Major . . ."

"Drummond."

"Right. I'm required by law to inform you that I'm recording this conversation."

"Fine."

He started asking questions, all of which were pretty general in nature, and I answered truthfully, though not completely, as you might imagine. He wanted a little local color, a general description of the event, and so forth.

After a few minutes of this back-and-forth, he'd spent his nickel, and he said, "Anything else you wanted to add?"

"Well, you didn't ask me to describe him."

"You mean you saw him?"

"I got a great look at him."

"Uh-huh. A short guy with a ponytail, right?"

"No."

"No?"

"About six foot four, maybe six-five, nearly two hundred and fifty pounds, and he didn't have a ponytail."

The line went silent for a moment. He finally said, "Uh . . . that conflicts with the FBI's description of the L.A. Killer."

"Yes, I noticed that." I suggested, "Draw your own conclusion."

"You mean . . . you mean, they've pinned the wrong guy?"

"Consider that a good conclusion." I swiftly added, "And another thing . . ." I paused a moment, then said, "Well . . . ah, no, forget about it."

"What? Come on."

"A lot of people are terrified of this guy, right?"

"You could say that."

"And I guess . . . well, what I'd say, having watched him in action, is his reputation's way overblown."

"How so?"

"It's pretty stupid to attack that woman right there in the wide open, police everywhere. And Miss Morrow definitely outfoxed him. You had to see this big idiot running away from this tiny woman."

Mr. Stynowitz was beginning to sound very excited, and he suggested, "You're saying he's not only not the L.A. Killer, but he's also not competent?"

The string of double negatives aside, I replied, "That's what I am saying." I added, "Look, I know this sounds crass, but what I witnessed this morning was stunningly stupid. This is a really sick, perverted idiot who has managed to murder a few women because he sneaks up on them. But when it's face-to-face, he runs like a jackass. Essentially, he's a gutless coward."

Well, we did a little more back-and-forth, but I'd gotten the quotes I wanted in, and he ended by making sure I didn't mind being openly named, which was really ethical of him, because a lot of his colleagues don't do that, and he promised he'd play me square, and then we signed off.

The Associated Press, you have to understand, are sort of the hacks of modern journalism, trained to compose and file their stories quickly, which are then distributed to multiple news services. Given Joe Q. Public's prurient interest in this case, by evening, Sean Drummond's commentary about America's most famous killer would make it into a lot of news channels.

The files in the rental car placed Janet ahead of me in the killer's queue. Had she obeyed Meany's very sound advice and retreated into protective custody, her odds of living a long and fulfilling life would be excellent. But even the President's security detail couldn't protect her out in the open—against this guy, nobody could.

I had held back on the throttle a little in my talk with Janet. I mean, there's what you see—what we *all* saw—but to really get inside his head, it helps when you once walked in his shoes.

So, back to what we all saw—his physique. A build like that is the product of thousands of hours in the weight room, careful dieting, probably steroids, and colossal willpower. He probably had a teeny weenie and was compensating, but the shrinks could nail the tail on that particular donkey. Also, nobody gets that expert at the killing game without abnormal drive, discipline, and a vicious competitive streak.

But psychotic minds are individualistic, distinguishable by their unique fetishes and idiosyncrasies. Thus, back to his signature style. It had been his intention to arrange Janet's murder without drawing parallels to the other victims, right? So why not snuff her with a drive-by shot? Or whack her with sniper rifle from a distance? Atomize her with a bomb? All of these options offered less chance of witnesses *and* less risk of failure. Also, given her public profile as an ADA who messed around with mob cases, both the torching of her father's home and her murder could easily be blamed on the goombahs. No—he used a knife and you have to ask, why? My guess was because he wanted *her* to see him, and *he* wanted to see the fear in her eyes. This guy drew sustenance and satisfaction from fear. For him, killing *had* to be personal, a contest where triumph depended on the victim having some chance of winning, but ultimately losing.

All of which suggested an outsized ego driven by a particularly twisted narcissistic complex.

Inside my head I could picture this guy jerking heavy iron bars over his head and gazing adoringly at his own sculpted image in the mirror. By extrapolation, I was betting he followed his own publicity compulsively. He fed on the public fear and outrage. It made him feel oh so fucking smart and superior to outsmart the

FBI and the great American public. At risk of getting too wrapped around the twisted metaphysics of this thing, for him, the public image, the way he shaped that image, the way he manipulated that image, that was another mirror.

So, back to *my* motive. He would understand *why* I was shooting off my mouth. I was alerting him that I was aware I was on his list, and in a visceral, machismo, one-badass-to-another way, I was pissing on his mirror. Here he had gone to all this time, trouble, and effort to copycat, and I was tearing off his disguise, yanking down his drawers, and telling the world he had a teeny weenie. Metaphorically speaking. Three points on the board for Drummond. He would now feel the *need* to recoup those points. Also, he would assume I *wasn't* guarded, whereas Janet *was* guarded, and every professional killer knows to go after the low-lying fruit first.

I truly didn't really want this guy coming after me. I used to be quite good at this game, a long time, a few serious wounds, and too many cheeseburgers ago. He was clearly still at the top of his game, in tip-top shape, a creature honed and sharpened to a murderous edge. But I definitely didn't want him coming after Janet. In fact, what I really wanted was to convey to George Meany that I had no hesitation about going into protective custody, especially if the FBI had a safe house in Bermuda. In the interest of the federal budget, I'd even agree to shack up with Janet.

But Janet wouldn't go, so I couldn't go. I was therefore telling myself that Janet's odds of stopping this monster were less than mine. Also, I was developing a very deep crush on her, despite the fact that she was once actually engaged to George the Dork.

I withdrew my wallet and pulled out Lisa's picture.

The calculus had just changed. This guy had snuffed out a beautiful life, actually, several beautiful lives, and when I thought that was the product of madness, I could live with the state meting out whatever penalty twelve of his peers thought he deserved. Now that I knew he had murdered my beautiful and talented friend for filthy lucre, I wanted to strangle him with his own guts.

CHAPTER THIRTY-EIGHT

Predictably, George Meany threw a monumental hissy fit when Janet informed Bob, and Bob then unhappily informed his boss, that she had insisted on returning to D.C. for business. After what sounded like a fairly good tongue-lashing, an ashen-faced Bob handed Janet his cell phone.

She said to Meany, "George, let's not get into an argument about this."

He said something, and she nodded, and replied, "That's right. My mind is made up. I have work to do, and I'm going to do it." And they went back and forth like that for a while, sounding like an old married couple.

But apparently, experience had taught him that with the lady in question he wasn't going to win this, or any, argument. A compromise of sorts was reached; he would have two more special agents meet us at the Delta departure gate, to be reinforced by two more agents when we arrived at Ronald Reagan National.

Janet and her aunt and sisters then spent some time doing the emotional good-bye thing, and I used the occasion to draw

Spinelli out to the back porch. We had a deal, and to show I honored my word, I gave him a swift rundown on our suspicions about the firm, what we'd found inside the car, and so on. He got the sanitized version, of course. Daniel Spinelli was motivated by self-interest, and to protect *my* self-interest I carefully held back a few key issues I might need in exchange for later favors. He seemed to really appreciate my confidences, however, so I exploited his good mood to arrange another deal.

In fact, two guys in nondescript clothing were cooling their heels by the curb when we pulled up to the Delta entrance at Logan International in Bob's black sedan. From the look of them, Meany had apparently concluded that the search for the killer was going nowhere; or his boss had ordered him to move Janet's safety up a few pegs on his priority list, because these two were clearly members of the A-team. Grim-faced, hard-nosed, and well-built, they had already completed the paperwork to fly with their guns, and in fact had persuaded Delta to whisk us through the ticketing procedure and allow us to cool our heels in the VIP lounge until three minutes before takeoff.

I like guys who take no chances when my safety is at stake. Also, I was really hungry, and I stuffed my pockets with free peanuts.

But they obviously had been prebriefed that we were difficult cargo, because they put up almost no fight when Janet insisted they sit no closer than six seats forward or aft, so she and I could have a discussion about confidential legal matters. It wasn't like this guy was going to come running down the aisle and whack us, anyway, so they obliged us, and we had two hours to jointly ponder our dilemma and plot our strategy.

The dilemma was fairly straightforward—somebody in the firm was an accessory to murder. Janet commented that this was like one of those old closed-room mysteries English people go nuts about, where somebody killed the host—but who? The shortlist included Harold Bronson, Cy Berger, Barry Bosworth, Sally Westin, and Hal Merriweather. I *wanted* it to be Hal, or Barry, or Harold.

The trifecta would be Hal, *and* Barry, *and* Harold. I believe I mentioned I have a vindictive streak, and the beast demanded to be fed. I could live with it being Sally, though I'd be very surprised. I'd be disappointed if it was Cy, but only mildly surprised.

Anyway, I informed my new attorney about the basis for my lawsuit, and we efficiently worked through the details of how we would shape and present it. The legal fine points and elements of proof were meaningless anyway—it was all bluff and bluster.

There's a saying in our biz: If the law is on your side, pound on the law; if the facts are on your side, pound on the facts; if neither is on your side, pound on the table. We lacked the law and facts, and they owned the damned table, which meant we had to pound on them. The basic idea was to infuriate, insult, and threaten everybody and see who got all sweaty about it. Somebody in that room had important things to hide. The time had come to find out who, and what.

By the way, not two, but four more agents met us at Reagan National Airport. Spinelli had had enough of us, and he left alone in a taxi. Janet and I departed a few minutes later in an inauspicious caravan of three shiny black Crown Victorias; a lead car in front, us in the middle, and a chase car behind. We traveled at high speed, straight to 1616 Connecticut Avenue. Janet informed our bodyguards that we were attending a confidential legal conference, so they would have to wait in the downstairs lobby.

At 7:30 P.M., the elevator door opened on the eighth floor. Hal Merriweather was perched stiffly beside Elizabeth's long wooden desk. Standing freeform, he looked like an egg on stilts.

I said, "If it isn't my man. Hal, this is my attorney, Miss Janet Morrow. Janet, this is the idiot who claims we stole information from the firm."

The supercilious grin on Hal's face disappeared. "Janet Morr— Are you stupid, Drummond? What in the hell is she doing here?"

"Don't let his appearance fool you," I told Janet. "Hal's even stupider than he looks."

She laughed.

Hal's face turned a nice shade of off-pink. "Watch your mouth, asshole. You want more trouble? Just fuck with me." Hal's manners and charm apparently took a turn for the worse when his minders weren't around.

I laughed. "Janet . . . save me from this guy . . . please."

"Smart people don't ignore my warnings, Drummond."

"Smart people ignore *you,* Hal."

"Fuck you."

I said, "Move your ass, errand boy. Your bosses are waiting."

"We'll see who's laughing in an hour, asshole."

"Every time I see you, I laugh, pal."

He unlocked the doorway to the stairwell and led us up the stairs to the next floor. I couldn't resist informing Janet, "No, that's not the Goodyear blimp, that's Hal's ass."

Hah-hah. Boy, I was hot. I had Hal worked into a nice frothy fury, which was exactly how we wanted him.

We entered the ninth floor hallway, where Hal led us to the big conference room in the center of the floor. He banged open the door and stomped inside. The room was large, thirty by fifty feet or so, expensively furnished with leather-backed chairs around a very long, carved conference table.

Cy, Harold Bronson, and two other gentlemen were seated side by side at the far side of the table, the picture of intimidation. Barry, but a lowly associate, was hunched over in a chair along the wall. Hal tromped over and joined him. They made a lovely pair of matched idiots.

For the benefit of the two other gentlemen, Cy said, "Major Sean Drummond, if you haven't met him." He said to me, "Sean, we'll have to ask your friend to leave. This is a private hearing."

"Wrong. She's my attorney . . . Miss Janet Morrow."

The other three partners stared inquisitively. Cy squirmed uncomfortably in his seat. I mentioned to Cy, "You were *well* acquainted with her sister Lisa, weren't you?"

Given Janet's unexpected presence, he understood the underlying context.

"She was a friend," he replied innocuously. I did notice, however, that my comment drew nosy stares from the other partners, who were inevitably aware of Cy's reputation with the ladies, though apparently not with the particular lady in question.

Of course, the purpose of this little repartee was to dry-fire a warning shot across Cy's bow that I knew about his affair, a serious breach of professional ethics in the workplace. And regarding his behavior in a session that concerned my professional ethics, he might want to balance my needs with his own. But what's a little blackmail among friends? Though, actually, we weren't really friends. And in any regard, what is blackmail to one man is often insurance to another.

Cy recovered his composure and said to Janet, "Miss Morrow, I'm truly sorry about Lisa's death. We all thought very highly of her. And I . . . well, I intended to send the family a card expressing my condolences, but things have been very busy."

Janet nodded coolly. "We look forward to getting it."

Cy seemed to have gotten the point, so I said, "I'm afraid I haven't met the other partners."

One was middle-aged: dark, thinning hair shot with gray, gold-rimmed glasses, and a fleshy, pugnacious, pockmarked face. He looked like a Mafia cutthroat in a gray wool suit. He said, "I'm Marcus Belknap, managing partner at the New York office."

The other was older, silver-haired, sort of a patrician face, heavy-lidded eyes, probably went to Harvard Law, married a millionaire's daughter, enjoyed racquetball, fast Porsches, and three-martini lunches. He said, "Harvey Weatherill, Philadelphia office."

Their names and titles were irrelevant to me; they were outsiders brought in to lend this thing a patina of fairness and balance it clearly did not merit. The outsiders would vote however Cy and Bronson told them to—assuming it got to that stage. The important point was that the other side of the table was stacked with corporate attorneys accustomed to the silky, elbow-rubbing environment of conference rooms and protracted debates over where to put a comma in a contract clause; Janet and I were hard-eyed criminal brawlers accustomed to kneecapping our opponents.

We all spent a moment sizing up one another before Bronson opened the bidding, saying, "We will begin this session with a briefing and presentation of evidence from Mr. Hal Merriweather. Then we will move to a more disturbing matter of atrocious misconduct, and testimony on that matter will also be presented." He took a theatrical pause, as if to underline the gravity of this session, then said, "Mr. Merriweather."

Hal bounced out of his chair and spent ten minutes detailing with great gusto my egregious burglary of confidential firm information, the several laws and several firm policies I had violated, the irrefutable evidence, and so forth. I rocked back in my chair, closed my eyes, and let him drone on.

But I guess he finally wrapped it up, because I felt Janet's elbow in my ribs and heard Bronson saying, "Well, Drummond?"

"What?"

"Again, what do you have to say in your behalf?"

I looked at Janet, and she looked at me. She replied, "We'll wait until the second charge has been fully aired."

Cy looked curiously at Bronson and said, "What is this second charge, Harold?"

He enjoyed the attention as he explained, "In the office complex of a client, Drummond assaulted his supervising attorney."

The other partners all looked properly aghast.

I asked Bronson, "Who did I assault?"

"*Whom*, Drummond. And you know damn well." But he explained for the benefit of the others, "Barry Bosworth."

"How?"

"You grabbed him . . . well, you know where you grabbed him."

Janet clarified. "By the balls, gentlemen."

I chuckled. I love this stuff.

Cy said to me, "Sean, these are very grave matters. Conduct yourself accordingly."

Bronson snapped. "You're being offered a chance to defend

yourself, which I, personally, consider a complete waste of our time."

"Of course you do, Harold."

Sensing the decorum needed to be brought up a notch, Cy said, "For the edification of the partners who haven't been briefed on the altercation, Barry, describe what happened."

So Barry cleared his throat, sat up a bit straighter, and explained, "The incident occurred three days ago, at the headquarters of Morris Networks. The audit was complete and I had gone over to supervise the final steps. I explained to Drummond the great importance of getting it to the Defense Department right away, asked him to sign it, and he told me we needed to talk. He led me to the men's room, I thought for privacy. The second we entered, he shoved me against the wall, grabbed my . . . well, my testicles, and threatened to rip them off."

Cy asked, "Unprovoked?"

"Well . . . yes. It was a complete surprise, Cy."

When no further questions were raised, he continued, "He told me he wouldn't sign unless the firm dropped all charges against him. I told him we wouldn't be blackmailed. He told me how much he detested the firm. Harold, he called you a phony, pompous ass." He looked at me and added, "These are his words, mind you—he said the partners of this firm are all limp-wristed assholes who lack the backbone to stand up to him."

Cy looked at me. "True?"

"Parts of it." For instance, it was true the partners were assholes.

"What parts aren't true?" Cy asked.

Janet replied, "Are we done describing my client's purported crimes and offenses?"

The partners all looked at one another. Cy replied, "I believe we are."

Bronson informed Janet, "If you have something relevant and factual, we'll hear you out."

Janet acknowledged his patronizing tone with a smile. "Relevant?"

"You're an attorney, young lady. You should know the definition."

"If my client discovered a massive fraud involving your firm, would that be relevant?"

"No, it is not. I will not allow you to turn this into a circus."

"Have it your way, then," Janet replied. "I'm filing a civil suit in the morning for the vicious and unprovoked assault on my client by Barry Bosworth."

"What?" Bronson exploded.

Janet said to me, "Please show these gentlemen your wounds."

I obediently unbuttoned my shirt and pointed at a massive bruise on my left chest. It looked awful. In fact, it *should* look awful. I had invested a lot of time, trouble, and pain in the bathroom on the plane from Boston, using my shoe to reinforce and expand the mild bruise Barry had actually inflicted.

Janet explained, "These hideous wounds were inflicted by Mr. Bosworth in his attempt to coerce my client into signing a legally flawed audit." Janet then said to me, "Explain the full extent of your injuries."

It is axiomatic for lawyers to spice up a conversation with emotive adjectives and pronouns, and Janet had done her part, so I appeared appropriately distraught. "Barry ordered me into the men's room. The moment we entered, he brutally shoved me against the wall, resulting in a severe concussion. He then assaulted me with his fists, inflicting these serious wounds. I now have short-term memory loss, blurred vision, difficulty breathing, severe whiplash, and mental trauma. I've developed a sleeping disorder, appetite problems, mental anguish, and self-esteem issues."

They didn't know whether to laugh or howl.

Janet added, "These injuries have been photographed, a doctor has examined my client, and we have statements from two renowned psychiatrists. Sean will require years of expensive therapy. His sterling military career is through, as is his ability to lead the happy, well-adjusted life he experienced before his employment here."

Well, we hadn't actually accomplished any of that on the plane ride down, but it is also axiomatic for lawyers to exaggerate, and indeed, they were all staring at Janet now, fully attentive, as she further explained, "Your firm placed my client in the grip of a sadistic bully, and Bosworth committed his heinous, unprovoked assault at the behest of your firm's tawdry financial interests." She allowed a moment for the shock to settle in. Then she said, "We'll be asking for one hundred million in damages."

"This is preposterous," Bronson exploded, leaping out of his chair.

The two outside partners were shaking their heads and trying to make sense out of this circus. Cy's eyes, though, were examining us—apparently, he was the only one in the room with enough sense to take this farce, and us, seriously.

He asked Janet, "You're claiming Barry attacked Drummond?"

"No question about that." She nodded in Barry's direction. "It boils down to who had the motive. His partnership comes under review next month, and clearly relies on his ability to maintain Morris Networks as a client. Your firm is notorious for its treatment of associates. All that pressure . . . he simply snapped."

Janet peered up at Bronson, who, incidentally, appeared livid, and she instructed him, "Sit down and act like an adult."

Unaccustomed as he was to being talked down to, he huffed and puffed, while Cy tried to restore order, and Barry insisted, "Cy, Harold . . . it's a travesty. I never touched him."

Janet was handling this really well, and she sat patiently and waited for the noise and emotion to subside before she continued. She said, "Our case will obviously require us to expose the filthy scheme Bosworth was trying to keep hidden, a conspiracy involving a company named Grand Vistas that has been indulging in fraudulent activities with your client Morris Networks. We will show that Barry Bosworth put the scheme together, that he met with executives from Grand Vistas, that he arranged the appropriate contracts, that he and, by extension, the senior partners of this firm were knee-deep in bilking thousands of investors."

Cy looked surprised and said, "Don't be ridiculous."

Janet replied, "Morris Networks and Grand Vistas will necessarily be included as litigants. The assault occurred on the improperly policed premises of the former, to cover up the illegal activities of both litigants."

Janet stood and I followed her lead. She stared down at the partners and warned, "When the Pentagon hears about this, Morris Networks' contracts will in all likelihood be canceled. I suspect Mr. Morris's response will be to start shopping around for a new law firm."

Cy appeared frustrated and implored us, saying, "Please, sit down. Let's talk this out."

Barry yelled, "He's lying!"

Bronson said, "Young lady, you're a fool if you think you can blackmail this firm."

Well, we'd gone as far as facts and suspicions would allow, and before we snatched defeat from the jaws of victory, I announced, "We'll be filing at 10:00 A.M. at the Arlington courthouse. Shortly thereafter, we'll issue a press release to the *Wall Street Journal* and the *New York Times*. I'd advise you to contact your clients and warn them."

CHAPTER THIRTY-NINE

THE MOMENT WE STEPPED OFF THE ELEVATOR AND INTO THE LOWER LOBBY, George Meany moved about a foot from me, shoved a finger in my face, and said, "Drummond, I've had enough of you and your shit."

I was a little surprised to see him, and a lot pissed over his finger in my face. In fact, I was just reaching out to stuff the finger up George's ass when Janet stepped between us and said, "Knock it off, George. If you've got something to say, say it to me."

He leaned back, surprised. "This doesn't concern you, Janet. It concerns me and Drummond."

"If it's between you two, it concerns me."

"No, it doesn't," he insisted. But of course it did. Still, he paused briefly before confessing, "No, I don't appreciate this asshole convincing you to fly down here and putting you at risk this way. But that's not why I'm here."

"Then why are you here?"

He studied her face. He said, "The Director called me an hour ago. He's furious. The Director, God damn it . . ." He paused and poor Georgie did look a little stunned, and my guess was that the conversation hadn't been all that pleasant. He said, "All because your friend here was shooting off his idiotic mouth to some AP reporter."

Janet glanced at me, then back at Meany. She asked, "What are you talking about?"

"The news, Janet." In response to her blank look, he explained, "It's being carried everywhere. This idiot, Drummond, told some reporter the killer is a dimwit, that the Bureau is bungling this case since we've failed to stop him. He also informed the reporter that the FBI is focused on the wrong suspect, that the man who attacked you clearly isn't the L.A. Killer." His eyes shifted to me. "Do I need to explain how much the Bureau appreciates having its nose rubbed in shit by this clown?"

I didn't recall couching my comments exactly that way. But you see what happens when you do a favor for a reporter?

Now Janet also was looking at me, and she asked, a bit sharply, "Sean, please tell me you didn't say all that to a reporter."

"I sure did. All those women looking over their shoulders for a short, stumpy guy with a ponytail. It might even save a life. Did you or your boss ever think about that, George?"

"He's lying," Meany said. "Drummond called the reporter to humiliate me and harm my career."

Not true. Just not true. But I kicked myself because I should have.

He stared at me and added, "Well, guess what, smart guy. The Director made a call to *your* boss. General Thomas Clapper, right? You're the one who now has career problems."

I was hoping Janet was seeing what a grouchy, vindictive dickhead this guy was.

But at the same time, it struck me that I might be in serious trouble here. In fact, I was having disturbing visions of Johnston Island Atoll, of Sean Drummond choking on leftover anthrax or mustard gas, or something.

Then again, with a world-class killer hunting my ass, and a roomful of pissed-off lawyers upstairs who would also like to murder me, this was the least of my problems. In fact, I had a lot of balls up in the air, and my life depended on remembering which were catastrophic and which were merely disastrous.

Anyway, Meany began briefing Janet about all the things he'd done to catch the killer. And it all sounded really impressive, unless you listened really closely, in which case it amounted to a lot more of Meany sniffing his own ass.

Also, it went on for a while, because Meany was one of those guys who mistake words and action for results. But he finally wrapped it up, saying, "So, that's where we're at, honey."

Janet replied, "Good. What's next?"

"Next is you. We need to get you out of here, to someplace safe. The Director authorized a safe house. We're also beefing up your security detail to ten men."

Janet said, "George, that's excessive."

He smiled and touched her arm. "I'd make it twenty if the Bureau would let me. You're the most important thing in my life, babe. I'm taking no chances."

Even the other agents were coughing into their hands and rolling their eyes, which I guess George noticed, because he swiftly mentioned, "Actually, the Director was very expressive about taking every precaution concerning your safety."

Well, which was it, George—love and lust, or orders from on high?

Understand, though, that I really didn't give a shit about his motives, and I was actually very pleased with this arrangement. I actually wanted—no, I actually *needed*—Janet tucked away in a safe and faraway place.

So we bid each other adieu, which in Janet's case meant a kiss on my cheek, which surprised me a little and annoyed George Meany a lot, before he whisked the damsel away to his mountain fortress.

But I now owed George big-time.

And, as if I didn't have enough problems already, I suddenly recalled that my leased Jag was still parked near the Pentagon heliport, all of Meany's guys had just left in a cloud of shiny Crown Vics, and I was fairly certain nobody upstairs was in the mood to give mean old Sean a lift back to his apartment. This really got on my nerves. I called a cab.

I actually knocked on my own apartment door, which I don't ordinarily do. But I was glad I did, because it was opened by Danny, who wore a bulletproof vest and, coincidentally, was directing the nasty black barrel of an M16 assault rifle at my face.

He said, over his left shoulder, "It's all right. It's him."

He stepped back and I entered. I noticed two other men in the middle of my living room, also wearing bulletproof vests, and both were at that moment lowering their weapons.

Spinelli waved an arm in their direction and said, "Chief Warrants Bill Belinovski and Charlie Waters."

We all nodded at one another. I said to Spinelli, "Problems?"

"None. The provo owes me a few. I told him you was a witness to the murder of an Army soldier and needed protection."

His reference was to the provost marshal of Fort Myer and the Military District of Washington, a full colonel by rank, military police by branch, who had the unenviable task of overseeing law and order for the entire Army community living around the Capital area. This entails some thirty thousand people, so this is a guy who survives on aspirins and hemorrhoid suppositories. And after signing this authorization, I was going to have to send him my firstborn child, or, considering my romantic prospects, somebody else's firstborn.

Understand that I'd done everything I could think of to draw the killer to me. But Mrs. Drummond didn't raise an idiot; no sir. While there's a certain gallantry in solitary combat—you know, the knights of old, mounted on their trusted steeds, swords at the ready, charging one another in a celestial contest of courage, skill, and wits—the Infantry Manual clearly states that if you show up for the fight, and it turns out it's an even match, you planned wrong.

Anyway, I faced the three of them and asked, "Did anyone, by chance, happen to remember to bring a flak jacket for me?"

Spinelli lifted one off the floor, tossed it at me, and said, "No weapon though. No authorization for that." He then asked, "How sure are you he's coming?"

"Enough so that I just took out a million dollar term life policy."

We all chuckled, which is the right and manly thing to do in such situations. Everybody knows Army guys are steadfast, hard as nails, and brave to a fault, so that was the act we were trapped in.

But Bill, who incidentally was about six foot two, about 220 pounds, and about as well acquainted with weight machines as our killer, asked me, "What can you tell us about this peckerhead, Major? Strengths, weaknesses."

"I'm glad you asked. You've studied the composite?"

"Danny showed us the shots."

"Then we all know what he looks like"—I reconsidered that— "well, we know what he looked like this morning. He might be into disguises. But I'm expecting a blind date to drop by. So if a tall, really ugly, fat broad with big tits shows up . . ."

"Yeah?"

"And she asks for me . . ."

"Uh-huh."

"This guy is pretty clever . . . and, well . . . there's only one way to really know. You know what I'm saying? That's your job, Bill."

Yuck, yuck.

But we were all, I think, feeling tense and keyed up, and it's important to get past that, because cool thinking and settled nerves were our only prayer of success.

So everybody stopped laughing, and in a more serious vein, I continued, "Here's what the composite doesn't show, that he can't disguise. He's about your size, Bill . . . slightly bigger, perhaps."

Spinelli commented, "Bigger. The bastard's built like a tank."

I cleared my throat and continued, "He's racked up eight kills we know of, but his skill level suggests he's killed more. Possibly many more. In fact, we suspect he's a professional for hire."

Charlie, I noticed, was shifting his feet.

"He prefers to kill with his hands." I continued, "His proficiency with other weapons is an open question, but he's been well trained by somebody, and prudence dictates we assume he's qualified with all weapons. I'd give him a good-to-go on reflexes, speed, and mental agility. I wouldn't exactly say he's a candyass." How's that for a soaring understatement?

But Spinelli said, "The guy's a murderous motherfucker."

Not helpful, Spinelli. Bill's eyes went a little wide, so I awarded both him and Charlie another reassuring look, and continued, "Yes, well . . . why don't we move on to some of his weaknesses?"

Charlie nodded, eagerly. "Great. What are this guy's weaknesses?"

"Well, for one, he . . . uh . . . well—"

"He's got no weaknesses," interrupted Spinelli. "The guy's a perfect fucking killing machine."

Bill and Charlie sort of swallowed.

I said, "You're very funny. For one thing, the killer is *not* expecting four of us. Also, he may be resourceful, clever, and skilled, but his technique to date indicates an overreliance on surprise. This worked for him in the past; I doubt he'll discard it. Remove the element of surprise and he'll lose some of his edge." I allowed them to think about that before I suggested, "In fact, we should expect him to try some unorthodox way of getting in here."

Charlie grinned at this remark. I grinned back, but Charlie was the one who worried me. He appeared to be somewhere around thirty, was prematurely balding, black, and slender. What concerned me was his face: too wholesome, too youthful, and too innocent. In fact, he reminded me of a frisky puppy I had as a kid, who ran in front of a truck and became a pancake. Bill also looked wholesome, because all soldiers *look* wholesome, but there was a hardness in his eyes that dispelled any sense of softness. Unless Charlie was one of those guys who could drill holes in dimes flying through the air, I was sort of anxious about him, and sort of wondering why Spinelli brought him to the party.

But Charlie said, "No problems on that account. I hope he does."

"Is that right?"

"Sure. That's why I'm here, Major. My specialty is facility protection."

This is a fairly important field in an Army with lots of tanks and missiles and things that go boom, because Uncle Sam would get very annoyed at the Green Machine if Abdullah the Jihadist filched an Abrams tank or an Apache gunship and used it to put a few dents in the White House. I therefore gave Mr. Waters the benefit of the doubt. At least, I hoped he was competent. For my sake—for all our sakes—he better be.

The phone rang, I excused myself, and went into the bedroom to take the call. It was Jessica Moner, Jason's legal brawler, and in her typically brassy, abrasive way, she said, "Drummond, you asshole, what's this shit about you launching a lawsuit tomorrow morning?"

"Who informed you?"

"Bosworth informed me. And now I'm informing you, stop the bad joke—now."

"You sound angry."

"I could kill you." I pondered how literally to take that sentiment as she added, "I don't know what the bad blood is between you and your firm, but don't drag us into your shitpile."

"Sorry, Jessica, my lawyer says it's the only way."

"What the fuck are—"

"Maintaining you as a client was Bosworth's motive. You're the casus belli of the dispute."

"No, you're adding us because we have deep pockets. Bad idea, buddy boy . . ."

"Blame Barry. He pounded the crap out of me. I never realized what an animal he is."

"Bosworth can barely lift his dick to pee."

"He practices at home, on his kids."

She paused for a moment, as it was obvious this track was leading nowhere.

She then asked, "What is it you *think* you have?"

Nice try. "All of it, Jessica. Come to court in the morning, and you'll hear all about your sweet arrangement with Grand Vistas. Make a deal with the devil and you go to hell."

"Are we forgetting legal confidentiality, Drummond? You can't expose what you learned working as our attorney. I'll get an injunction, sue your ass off, and have you disbarred, you stupid shit."

"Read the statutes on whistleblowers."

"Whistleblower? You're an attorney, asshole."

"You know, that's what my attorney thinks will make it a particularly intriguing case." I paused, then said, "Hey, we both might get our names on a famous precedent. Think about it . . . *Drummond versus Moner*—nice ring, right?"

There was a long pause before Jessica, suddenly friendly, said, "Sean, look, the offer to work here's still open. I like your style. You'll like it here, and you'll get rich. Don't fuck this up."

"You won't hire me if I sue you? That's small-minded, Jessica."

"Okay . . . sure, I'm hearin' you more clearly. It's about the money, right? Make your offer and I'll try to clear it with Jason."

"Fine. Two million a year."

"What?"

"Three million a year."

"Don't try to blackmail me, Drummond, or I'll—"

"Four million a year."

"Damn it, you asshole, I'll—"

"Five million."

There was a brief sputter, followed by another pause, while Jessica contemplated how much her floppy tongue was costing.

"Think, Jessica. What it's worth to you and Jason to keep the partnership with Grand Vistas out of the courts and out of the news?"

"I'll . . . all right. I'll talk to Jason about three million. Okay?"

"Wrong answer. Ten million."

"Listen, you pinheaded fuck. Don't screw with me. I'm giving you your last chance to be rich and healthy. Piss me off, and I swear I'll make you regret it."

"See you in court." I hung up.

I sat on the bed and contemplated our conversation. Clearly Jessica was in on it. But connected to the killer? Or was she just part of the scam?

Before I could finish that thought, the phone rang again. It was Cy and he said, "Sean, you and I need to talk."

"We already talked."

"The firm is willing to drop all charges against you and Miss Morrow."

"Should've done that yesterday, Cy. Actually, never should've brought charges in the first place."

"Perhaps you're right." Cy obviously had better bargaining skills than Jessica, but a career on the Hill does tend to round out one's heels. He said, "I'm confused, Sean. What is this case of fraud you referred to?"

"Nice try."

"You mentioned the partnership with Grand Vistas. Barry handled that."

"Because *you* told him to."

"Yes. Because Jason asked me to send him. What's happening here?"

Cy sounded his usually sincere, earnest, and above-it-all self. He had a real gift for silky bullshit and was probing to find out exactly what I knew—how little or how much—so they could assess the potential damage.

In truth, I knew very little. As I explained earlier, the idea was to push and see who pushed back, how hard they pushed back, and from there, maybe to understand why.

For instance, the firm was now willing to drop all charges. That wasn't the mood when Janet and I left the conference room—so A must've called B, and B must have told A to make this thing go away. But who was A? And who was B?

Also, I now knew Morris Networks would pay me three million a year to keep my yap shut—more, probably, if I dealt with someone less peppery than Jessica Moner.

Anyway, I said, "What's happening, Cy, is corporate graft. Without Grand Vistas, Morris Networks would be vulture bait. Come to court and you'll hear about it."

"Hear me out, Sean. Morris is a very profitable and honest company."

Yes, and Cy was working overtime to establish his ignorance, and, along the way, his innocence.

"Prove that in court."

"Look . . . don't do anything till we get a chance to talk."

I replied, "Tomorrow, 10:00 A.M.," and hung up.

For some reason, I recalled the old joke: What do you call a lawyer who's gone bad?—Senator.

I went into the kitchen and fixed a pot of coffee. Charlie was stringing electronic security systems around the windows. My door had acquired two new deadbolts and my bedroom dresser was shoved against it. Spinelli and Bill were seated in front of the big screen, watching a rerun of *NYPD Blue*, Spinelli scratching his nose with one hand and cradling a pistol with the other. Just another hum-drum day at the Drummond homestead.

I had just poured a cup of coffee when the phone rang again. I rushed back to the bedroom and caught it on the fourth ring.

"Sean, it's Jason."

"Oh. Well, I hope I'm not keeping you from something important."

"Not at all. What the hell's going on here?"

"What's going on is, I was brutally assaulted in your office building, by an attorney representing your firm, who was being pressured by Jessica Moner."

"That's outrageous. I'll fire him."

"That won't cure my nightmares."

"Oh, come on." He chuckled. I remained silent.

He stopped chuckling and said, "Sean, you're a businessman. Think like one."

"No, I'm an Army officer."

"Then . . . try to think like one."

"Gee, I'm a fish out of water here, Jason. How do you busi-nessmen think at moments like this?"

"You ask yourself one question—what's the most advanta-geous thing for you right at this moment?"

"Oh . . . Well, help me out here. What would that be?"

"A settlement. That's how you lawyers handle these things, isn't it?"

"When the offer's sweet enough, yeah."

"Okay. Let's see what that takes." You could hear the confi-dence and thrill in his voice. This guy made his living off deals; I was a fattened calf of the public dole. He was just tickled pink that some novice thought he could joust with him over money. Was this going to be fun, or what?

To get the ball rolling, I asked him, "What terms are you proposing, Jason?"

"I hadn't really thought about it."

"Well . . . suggest something."

"How about ten million?"

"How about thirty?"

"Get serious."

"Serious? Fifty million."

"I . . . look, that's a lot of money."

"Ooops . . . seventy million. Keep flapping your gums, Jason, and it'll hit a hundred. In fact, that's the number in our civil suit. It could be that's an unrealistic figure, but compounded by the sweet satisfaction that you personally will lose a few billion in stock value, it works out okay for me." I couldn't resist adding, "*You* think like a businessman, Jason."

There was another long pause. I mean, this guy experienced no qualms about throwing away a few hundred grand for a fine piece of ass. Blow *this* deal, and thousands of lawyers and stock-holders would scramble to get a piece of *his* ass. Also, he had to be thinking about all those recent corporate chieftains being led away in Fed bracelets.

He suggested, finally, "Seventy million is possible. I'd have to find a way to structure it, though. I can't just hand over a check . . . taxes, SEC filings, notification to my board . . . I have to consider these things. The money, I need a way to explain it. Maybe if . . . well, maybe if we worked it as a stock transfer . . ."

While Jason rambled on, I contemplated the stakes and sums here. I mean, seventy million big ones.

This was a dangerous number, an intoxicating number, and I knew if I thought about it, I mean really took a moment and thought about it, everything it could buy . . . I slapped myself and interrupted him. "Jason, I've reconsidered."

"Good, Sean. I don't like this, I really don't, but I've got eight thousand hardworking employees to consider. Wall Street is a treacherous place these days. I've done nothing wrong, but these days, a rumor of impropriety . . . Christ, stockholders pull the trigger over a whisper."

I was tired of this guy, and I was really tired of this game, and I said, "I mean I changed my mind about the money. See you in court, pal."

I hung up on him.

I called Janet on her cell. When she answered, I said, "How's it going?"

"Lousy. I feel left out."

"Don't. You did your part, and it's working."

"Tell me about that."

"Jessica Moner called, then Cy, then Jason. We're up to seventy million to drop the suit."

Janet was a cool cookie, but I heard a sharp intake of breath.

I added, "I probably shouldn't tell you this, but as my attorney, I was going to cut you in for half."

"Well . . . That's *very* generous."

"I have a soft spot for lawyers. Of course, we never would've lived long enough to spend a dime."

"That's a consolation." She paused a moment, then asked, "Sean, what's going on here?"

"I still don't know. More than just bookkeeping sleight of hand, though."

"You're right. That much to hide a simple financial impropriety?"

I suggested, "So, let's start back at the beginning."

"Good. What happened in the beginning?"

"It begins with Lisa, like me, being assigned to work on the Morris Networks account."

"And they probably chose you two because of your lack of competence in corporate finance."

"A good assumption."

"Because they're lawyers and because Barry definitely—maybe Cy, possibly Bronson, and perhaps others—knew that Morris was cooking its books. None of them wanted their fingerprints on it. They wanted a patsy to take the fall, in the event a fall ever needed to be taken."

Following that line of thought, I said, "And if it came to light, the firm could shovel the crap in our direction. The partners would say they had patriotically volunteered their services for this Army program, and never realized how stupid and incompetent JAG officers are."

"But like you, Lisa probably discovered it, and she had to be eliminated."

"Right."

"But how did they get onto her?"

"Well, when I became curious, I faxed the audit to my brother, who's a business wizard. He interpreted the spreadsheets and told me what I should worry about."

"Back to Lisa, please."

"We've never left Lisa. The other victims, what were their jobs?"

"A TV news personality, an accountant, an SEC attorney . . . oh, shit."

"Right. Lisa stumbled onto something suspicious, something she didn't understand, and she gave financial data to Julia Cuth-

burt, an accountant, and Anne Carrol, an SEC attorney, for interpretation."

"But how did the firm find out?"

"Hal Merriweather, I think."

"Why?"

"Hal gets printouts from the server twice a day. I'd guess that
when Lisa e-mailed Cuthburt and Carrol, Merriweather recognized
the SEC and Cuthburt's accounting firm from their Internet addresses."

"What about Fiorio?"

"Maybe Lisa was using her to expose this thing. I don't know
what her role was, or why she was murdered."

And of course, Janet then asked, "And me? Lisa and I never discussed a word about this."

"Well, I've thought about that."

"Go on."

"In Lisa's e-mails to you, Cuthburt, and Carrol, she mentioned
packages. I think the packages were the audit, and I think Merriweather presumed you got one, too."

In fact, I was speculating wildly. I was connecting dots in
midair. But the dots did connect.

After a moment, Janet said, "So they sent a hit man after Lisa,
and the rest of us, to bury it."

"Yes." Then I said, "Incidentally, did you call your friend in
Boston and ask him to check on Grand Vistas?"

"I did. I should call him back now, shouldn't I?"

She should, and we agreed she'd call me right back. I returned
to the living room, where Spinelli and his buddies were seated on
the couch, shotguns in their laps, eyes glued to an old rerun of
Miami Vice. Cops love their cop shows.

We spent a few moments surveying the preparations. This
began with an incisive dissertation by Charlie about the vulnera-
bilities and ports of entry to my home. My apartment complex had
been built some fifty years earlier, when construction techniques
included heavy steel girders, cinderblock walls, and super-thick

layers between floors. Were the building newer and less sturdy, he informed me, intruders might blow their way through walls or ceilings, but that wouldn't happen here. I informed Charlie that this was exactly the selling point that drew me here. He thought that was very funny.

He next showed me an electronic device he had installed on the floor of the tiny porch off my living room: a dark pad that operates like a dog fence, except the current is triggered by touch and vibration. Were I to, say, accidentally wander out onto my porch, Charlie assured me, I'd be fine. I'd get some fried hairtips and loose teeth, but the voltage was designed to be incapacitating, not lethal. My windows were covered with dark paper and wired with motion sensors. A miniature camera in a filament had been run underneath the door, displaying the hallway. Four metal shooter's shields of the variety favored by SWAT teams had been erected in the living room, facing the door.

After we inspected all these little treats and nasties, Bill asked me, "What makes you think he'll come soon?"

"A hunch."

Charlie asked, "How does he even know you're here?"

"Because they've been following Janet and me for days."

"They?" Spinelli asked. I guess I had failed to mention this part to him.

"Yes, they," I responded. "Inside the files in the rental car were multiple photos of Janet and me. Janet, for instance, was photographed the same day Lisa died. The picture was taken in Boston. Think about that."

"No shit."

"He's not acting alone. He has an accomplice who handles the research, probably handles logistics, and helps set up the kill."

He shook his head. "That's how the asshole kills so many, so quickly."

"We should assume they saw me leave the firm and come here."

The phone rang and I returned to the bedroom.

It was Janet, and she informed me, "I caught John at home. He says there's nothing in his database about Grand Vistas."

"Is that odd?"

"For privately owned internationals that do little business in the States, no. So he called the U.S. consulate in Bermuda. The consulate found an address and sent a man over to check. Grand Vistas occupies a small office on Hamilton Street. The consulate man spoke with the landlord and was told Grand Vistas has rented the office the past four years. The landlord says he rarely sees anybody enter or leave."

"Meaning what?"

"John was guessing, but the office might contain a phone switch. The office fulfills the residency requirements; calls come in and are rerouted somewhere else."

"Isn't that odd?"

"Not according to John. Corporations that want the tax benefits of Bermudan registration set up these empty shells fairly frequently." She added, "He then called the SEC and asked some contacts there if they have anything on Grand Vistas."

"Did they?"

"They never heard of it."

"Anything else?"

"One more thing. The SEC sent an open inquiry to their counterparts in every European country. It was marked expedite, so hopefully they'll respond soon."

There was a long silence, then Janet said, "Sean, it's time to tell George about this."

"Is he there? . . . With you?"

"No. He dropped me off and immediately left to attend to some business. He left me his cell phone number."

"We will not tell him. Not yet."

"What are you worried about?"

"Did I mention who runs the backbone of the FBI's data and Internet needs? Morris Networks."

"This is scary."

She was right. It was scary.

But I was also pleased that the pieces were finally falling into place. It was all coming together—the killer, the motive, the accomplices—all the who, what, and how stuff that solves a crime. Right?

Wrong. I couldn't shake the feeling that I was missing something, something big, that in making everything fit together, I was looking the wrong way.

CHAPTER FORTY

So WE WERE HUDDLED IN MY LIVING ROOM IN OUR BULLETPROOF VESTS, swapping stories, watching the big-screen tube, munching popcorn, the usual routine when you're expecting a hit man to drop in.

The Army expends a lot of energy and money trying to understand things nobody but soldiers give a crap about. For example, the best time to attack somebody. The general theory holds this to be somewhere between 3:00 A.M. and 5:00 A.M., when sleep cycles are heaviest, alertness is dullest, moonlight is dimmest, and, in our case, TV shows are worst. After Jay Leno, it's a bottomless pit. Sometimes, before Jay Leno.

We were reduced to infomercials after about 2:00 A.M., and I was out of gas, as was Spinelli, since we'd both spent the previous night playing masked crusader and rushing to Janet's rescue.

Charlie kept his nose tucked inside a small cathode-ray screen that led to the tiny camera that peeked out into the hallway.

By 4:00 A.M., I began entertaining the notion that this guy would try to hit me on the way to the courtroom that morning. For a variety of reasons, moving targets are easier to take down than stationary ones. But perhaps I was just looking for an excuse to nap.

The more unsettling notion I tried not to dwell upon was that nobody was coming after me. I had guessed right about Boston, but guesses are like coin tosses: fifty-fifty every time.

At 4:05, Charlie popped his nose out of the monitor. He said, "Somebody's out there. Near the end of the hall, too far to see clearly."

Bill helpfully suggested, "Could be a neighbor going for a jog or leaving for work."

Yes; could be. But they all grabbed their rifles and shotguns, we adjusted our vests, and we crouched behind the shooter's shields. I was beginning to wish I had a weapon.

Spinelli whispered to his partners, "Shoot to kill."

The proper advisory was "employ only reasonable force," and as an attorney, I should have swiftly corrected and clarified this point. I let it slide. People who try to get fancy in situations like this often get dead.

A few minutes passed during which Charlie kept his face pressed into his monitor. In fact, so much time passed that we were all starting to unwind and relax, when out the blue there was this loud, awful scream on the porch. At the same instant, the TV shut off and the lights went off, apparently from the energy surge on the porch.

Spinelli immediately spun around and began pumping rounds through the glass porch door, which showered outward.

Bill was beside me and he suddenly doubled over. Then Charlie flew backward off his feet and landed with a thud. Spinelli screamed, "Shit!" and kept firing his M16 through the destroyed porch door, where three dark figures had suddenly materialized, dangling off ropes, pointing silenced weapons inside, spraying my apartment with bullets.

A second later, my apartment door exploded from a huge blast that blew wooden splinters through the air.

Enough of this no-weapon shit—I scrambled around the floor, found Bill's shotgun, rolled backward, and aimed it at the door. A dark figure came diving through, and I fired twice but couldn't be sure I hit him. Then another figure dashed through, I fired again, caught him in the midsection, and he flew backward, right back into the hallway.

Spinelli had emptied his M16 and now resorted to his pistol. He was still firing at the porch, although when I spun around and looked, the figures on the ropes had vanished.

Then there was silence. I said, "Reload and stay down."

Spinelli said, "Something's stickin' out my fuckin' shoulder."

I felt around the floor for Bill and Charlie. My hand crashed into a body, then a full head of silky hair—Bill, apparently, and I felt his neck for a pulse. The pressure brought a moan. His ticker was still pumping; faintly, but that's all you need. I kept moving my hand around until it came up against Charlie; I could feel no pulse. Shit.

My ears were ringing, but then I thought I heard sirens. I tried to picture what just happened—three guys were hanging off ropes outside the porch, and at least two more had tried to make it through the door. Not one guy; five guys. I mean, what the . . . ?

The phone suddenly rang. I crawled over and answered.

A male voice ordered, "Put Drummond on."

The voice was baritone, but this weird mechanical baritone, as though it had smoked a million cigarettes, or was being distorted by some high-tech disguising device.

I said, "Who the hell's this?" I mean, maybe I didn't know who, but I did know *what* the call was about—roll call. Was I dead, or did I still need to be whacked? I'm not completely stupid, and I had no intention of confirming anything.

There was a weird laugh before he replied, "Tell Drummond it's the dimwit from Boston. Stop wasting my time and put him on."

I replied, "Can I take a message?"

"Heh-heh. You're very funny, Drummond."

Shit. "And you're an incompetent fuckup. This is twice you missed. First Janet Morrow, now me. Your bosses know about this one yet?"

"I didn't do this one. I just dropped by to, you know, observe."

What an asshole. This guy's ego was even bigger than I imagined. I said, "I forgot. You only do unarmed women."

"I do who I want." He added, menacingly, "For example, I'm going to do you."

"Before or after I mount your slimy ass on my wall?"

"You have a wall left?" He laughed. "I heard a big explosion."

"The place was in need of a redo. Thank your pals for me."

"I'll pass it along. But forget the redo. Waste of money."

"I'm out of your league, asshole. You do unarmed girls."

"You'd be surprised, Drummond. I kill guys all the time."

"You're right . . . I'd be surprised." We both let a moment pass, then I said, "You're probably telling yourself the ghoulish things you did to those women were necessary to mislead the cops. Truth is, you're a sick little pervert, and deep down, you enjoyed it."

"You're a shrink now? Stick with law."

I laughed. "Hey, truth is, I'm looking forward to meeting you."

"You'll never see me coming."

"I've already seen you. Big, dopey-looking jerk-off who's taken so many steroids your tiny dick's stopped working. Maybe that's why you enjoyed doing the women."

He paused a moment, then said, "*The priest* . . . you were the one who yelled?"

"Confess to me, jerk-off. Tell me all how your mother mistreated you, how you saw her diddling Daddy, and how much that screwed up your head."

"I'll do better. I'll tell you my life story as I cut body parts off you."

"I'll be looking for the big pussy in ladies' undies."

"Look all you want, Drummond. I never look the same twice."

"Discuss your identity issues with someone who gives a shit."

We both paused again, then I asked, "Incidentally, who trained you?"

"Self-help books and practice. Who trained you?"

"My little sister. That's all I need to take your ass down."

We both chuckled, a couple of adolescents trading dopey insults and playground threats. But we meant every word of it. And we both, through however we learned it, could deliver on our threats.

Then he said, "But in the interest of accuracy, Drummond, you don't have a little sister. A brother, John, and a mother and father who also live in California, but no little sister. In fact, I have their addresses in my pocket."

I felt a sudden chill. "Don't even think about it, asshole. Go near them and I'll make your death indescribably painful."

He laughed. "Well, this has been really fun. I enjoy getting to know my victims. It makes my work so much more meaningful, and memorable."

But before he could hang up I thought of something else, and I said, "Hey, don't you owe Morris Networks a rebate? Weren't you supposed to ice me before I figured out and exposed the scam?"

"I don't know what you're talking about."

"Morris Networks, bozo. The assholes who overpay you for your screwups and mishaps. I know all about Jason Morris, and about Hal Merriweather and about . . . well, about the lawyers working with them."

"Drummond, you're starting to annoy me."

"Wait'll I kill you, sport."

"And I'll be sure you have the opportunity to tell me how much you regret your taunts." He paused a moment, then said, "Ah . . . one last thing, please be sure to pass my regards to Miss Morrow. Tell her I haven't forgotten her." Then he hung up.

At that very instant the cops rushed through the door and all hell broke loose.

CHAPTER FORTY-ONE

THEY CAME IN LIKE A SWAT TEAM, ROLLING THROUGH THE DOORWAY, YELLING and hollering. The lights were still out, so I yelled, "Just friendlies in here."

A voice replied, "Drummond?"

It was a familiar voice, though I couldn't place it. Spinelli, however, yelled, "Who the fuck did you expect, Martin? . . . It's his fuckin' apartment."

Then a pair of flashlights popped on and somebody yelled, "Weapons down, and stand with your hands over your heads!"

I put the shotgun down, placed my hands over my head, and stood. Their flashlights and weapons were pointed in our direction.

One cop yelled, "Hey, asshole, I said put your hands up."

Spinelli sourly replied, "Shut the fuck up. I've got a chunk of wood in my shoulder."

I said, "Everybody relax."

And everybody did. Somewhat.

Once the cops had collected all the weapons and determined

that everybody was either disarmed, unconscious, or dead, two
more figures came through the doorway.

A medical technician came rushing in first, and was directed
toward Bill, who obviously needed more help than Charlie, who
unfortunately was dead. Then in sauntered George Meany, sporting
one of those nifty dark blue FBI windbreakers, an FBI cap, an FBI
shirt, and for all I knew had "FBI" tattooed on his ass.

Nor had it escaped my notice that Meany waited until Martin
cleared and secured the place before he decided to join us. George
was smarter than I gave him credit for. Just a little chicken.

But there was something else that didn't escape my notice. I
glanced at my watch, and I recalled that the shooting started a little after 4:05, and while I didn't know how long the firefight
lasted, or even how long I chatted with Mr. Asshole on the telly,
Martin and his guys got here awfully damned fast. I mean, it was
only 4:15, and Supercop Meany is up and about at this hour, playing Johnny-on-the-spot.

But before I could ponder these facts further, the lights
popped back on, and my eyes were drawn to the carnage. Two
bodies were by the doorway, one inside the door, and one plastered like a swatted fly on the hallway wall. I was going to have to
invest in new furniture, wall repairs, carpets, and so on. The guys
hanging from the ropes had employed silencers, and until this moment I hadn't fully appreciated how much lead they squirted
through my porch door. The walls were peppered and my big-
screen TV was a big-screen mess. It was a miracle only Bill and
Charlie had been hit.

Also, I noticed that about three-quarters of the cops were
dressed like Meany, so they were Feds.

Lieutenant Martin also looked around and said, "Jesus, what
the hell happened here?"

I replied, "I fucked up. I let Spinelli spend the night."

Spinelli and I both giggled, and everybody stared at us like we
were weird.

But we were both, I think, nervous and jittery, not yet recovered from the aftershock of being ducks in a shooting gallery. Lieutenant Martin, particularly, appeared not to appreciate my dark humor and pointed at the gun shields and the pile of spent shotgun and M16 shells on the floor. "Whose are those?"

Spinelli said, "Mine. Tell your dickheads not to touch them." Danny, characteristically, was finessing the situation.

I mentioned to Lieutenant Martin, "You might want to get some people up to the roof. Three of the shooters hung down on ropes."

While he shouted at a few officers to get upstairs, George Meany, I noticed, had moved into the corner, where he was talking quietly into his cell phone. I did not like the look or smell of this.

The nearest shotgun was a mere five feet away from my foot. Could I pick it up and blow George's ass into the kitchen without anybody noticing?

But Martin was peppering me with questions—whose corpses were on the floor, why were there corpses on my floor, that kind of thing. So I ignored George Meany and informed him, "Before I say a word, I need to confer with my attorney."

He shook his head. "But you are a damned lawyer."

He appeared slightly frustrated as I pointed at Spinelli and added, "Yes. I'm his lawyer, and he's got nothing to say."

Meany overheard this exchange, snapped shut his cell phone, and moved toward me. "Forget it, Drummond."

"Forget what, *George?*" I mean, Meany had obviously stepped forward to show the idiotic locals how a real pro handles a recalcitrant witness.

But we were off to a bad start already. From his expression, he did not like my response or my tone. He said, "You have a lot of explaining to do, Drummond. And you must think I'm stupid if you believe I'll allow you to conspire on your alibis."

Actually, I *knew* he was stupid. But I resisted the urge to tell him that, and instead asked, "Would you happen to have a law degree?"

"An accounting degree. So what?"

"Yet, as a federal officer, you've surely been taught that I cannot be deprived of legal representation?"

"This . . . well, this is different."

"Why?"

"Because you were involved in this . . . whatever the hell it was."

"Crime?"

"Yes . . . maybe."

"Am I a suspect?"

"Maybe."

"And what felony did I potentially commit?"

Thinking he was capable of playing this game, he smiled. "Possibly none."

I said, "You heard him, Danny. We're free to leave."

In fact, I was walking toward the door when Meany yelled, "Don't you fucking move!"

"But you said no crime was committed. I'll leave if I want."

"There is the possibility of a crime."

"Really? Then you're required by law to inform me of the exact nature of that crime. Read Miranda, pal."

"Possibly manslaughter, discharging firearms, disturbing the peace . . . I won't know till we fully interrogate you and get to the bottom of this."

I looked at Martin. "You heard the man and the charges. He suspects me of being a suspect. That suspicion obviously extends to my accomplice, Mr. Spinelli. We demand to speak with our lawyers."

Martin was staring at Meany and realizing, I think, that he really was an idiot. I was just brokenhearted that Janet wasn't here to witness what a putz this guy was. Not only was I slick and brilliant; he was stupid.

But back to Lieutenant Martin, whom I actually liked, and whom I felt a little sorry for. This whole affair was fairly confusing.

But he was smart enough to appreciate that Meany had just

blown any chance of an on-scene interrogation, so he rolled his eyes and nodded.

Actually, I was being a prick on the general legal principle that you should always be a prick. Also, I wasn't sure whether I had a legal problem or not. Whoever they were, the shooters had invaded my home. Virginia law stipulates that homeowners may take reasonable steps to protect themselves and their property. When your door blows down and a firing squad starts emptying clips through your porch door, reasonable steps cover a lot of territory.

Spinelli and his fellow agents were all properly licensed to carry firearms—kosher on that front. Also, we had that helpful authorization provided by the provost marshal. But I didn't mention that yet, because somebody was bound to wonder why there was a need for such an authorization. And why three armed agents of the United States Army were camped out with loaded guns in Sean Drummond's apartment.

Martin and his boys weren't stupid. After inventorying our arsenal and finding the shooter's shields and burglar detection systems, they'd start scratching their furrowed brows and pondering what the hell was going on here.

George Meany *was* an idiot, and even he knew something was fishy.

But fortunately things suddenly turned chaotic. Five extendable stretchers had been brought up, and six medical technicians and a covey of cops and detectives were huddled around corpses. Some of Martin's guys were scraping chalkmarks, Bill was being wheeled out with an IV poking out his arm, and a medic was trying to coax an ill-tempered Spinelli onto a stretcher. Spinelli was right, incidentally—there was a big splinter of wood poking out of his shoulder.

Just then two guys in gray suits appeared in the doorway. A cop blocked them from entering, and Lieutenant Martin glanced in their direction and yelled, appropriately, "Crime scene, gentlemen. Turn your asses around and get out."

Meany said, "Let them come in."

What?

The one in the lead, the older of the two, walked confidently up to Martin, flashed a set of credentials, and said, "How about a word in the hallway, Lieutenant."

What bothered me most about this was that he had deliberately positioned himself so *I* couldn't see the credentials. But they must've been pretty good shit, because Martin shrugged and obediently joined him in the hall. The second guy remained by the doorway and kept his eye on me. But I did notice that he and George exchanged brief nods. Not good. Really, not good.

Also, I noticed that the two gray-suited gentlemen had failed to sign in with the cop who stood by the door, a legal requirement for all visitors at an active crime scene. Nor did Lieutenant Martin make a stink about it. Also not good.

After a minute or so, Martin walked back inside, followed by the other gentleman. He said to me, "These gentlemen are going to take you to a suitable location for a debriefing."

For the record, semantically speaking, cops interrogate; other kinds of agencies debrief. It sounds more polite and genteel. It's not; it just sounds that way.

As though the choice were mine, I said, "Whatever."

I looked over at George and smiled.

For once, George smiled back.

I said, "Hey, George, I think one of the attackers left some spent cartridges on the porch. Did you check there yet?"

"What? No . . . I'll, uh . . ." He turned around, stepped onto the porch, and then said, "Auuggghhh."

I walked out between the two gentlemen in gray suits, who, incidentally, had forgotten to offer me their names or show me their credentials. And of course, I noticed that they also had arrived awfully damned fast, which added another notch to my curiosity.

Well, good things come to those who wait.

But so do bad things.

CHAPTER FORTY-TWO

IMAGINE MY DELIGHT WHEN I FOUND MYSELF IN A BLACK GOVERNMENT sedan, speeding down the George Washington Parkway. Or my utter surprise when we took the exit to Langley and were soon waved through a guarded checkpoint, and then pulled to a stop in front of the sprawling headquarters of the Central Intelligence Agency.

A word here about that "debriefing" thing. The list of the proliferating species of Feds who do spooky things, and carry variations of law enforcement credentials, has gotten to be as long as your frigging arm. There's the DEA, the NSA, the DIA, guys from several counterterrorism agencies so new they don't even have recognizable initials yet; and these days, even the IRS, U.S. postal inspectors, and Customs Service are elbowing their way into national security turf.

Still, think foppish, secretive, uptight assholes and you end up with . . . who?

Anyway, my lockjawed escorts and I climbed out of the sedan and then loitered by the entrance until three black Crown Vics pulled up and Janet stepped out. I was pleased to see her; just not pleased to see her *here*. However, she pecked my cheek and squeezed my shoulder, which I liked. We had only a brief moment to speak, during which she informed me that George the Moron had phoned and told her about the little problem back in my apartment. I didn't really think it was a good idea to discuss this in front of our two gray-suited escorts, and I promised we'd talk more about it later.

But regarding this building, the Army and the Agency are on the same team, and in my line of work, as you might imagine, I often come into contact with CIA people. I have found them to be almost universally loyal, patriotic, intelligent, and courageous. But if you ever, say, end up in the shower with one, keep your hand on the hot water knob and, for Godsakes, don't drop the soap—it's sort of instinctive for them.

Our mute escorts directed us inside, got us building passes, then led us swiftly to an elevator that sped us upstairs to the fourth floor. Janet's expression was one of surprise and awe, and in fact, she looked like Dorothy after the twister dropped her tush in a strange land filled with odd people, wicked witches, and wizards. That metaphor fit really well, incidentally; inside this building nobody was what they appeared to be, hearts and sometimes brains are in short supply, and all kinds of weird crap occurs behind impenetrable curtains.

Anyway, we were led to a briefing room, sort of a mini-theater, and asked to take seats. Which we did. But when I looked back over my shoulder for our escorts, they had vanished, probably through trapdoors in the floor or something.

Janet examined the room and whispered, "What are we doing *here?*"

"First time?"

"Of course."

"Keep your legs crossed, don't take any IOUs, and I hope you're on the pill."

She shook her head. Apparently, she thought I was trying to be witty or melodramatic. I wasn't.

The door behind us opened. A man and a lady entered.

The man looked like your typical CIA field operative type—ordinary build, indeterminate weight, facial features, and age, a guy you could spend a long weekend skiing with and not remember what he looked like, his name, even that you skied; just that some-body humped you in the shower and stole your ID and charge cards.

The woman was older, close to seventy, I think—white-haired, thin, soft-featured, in fact grandmotherly in appearance, dress, and manners. But as I mentioned, nothing in the CIA is as it appears—she probably stuck firecrackers up puppies' butts for fun and frolic.

The two of them sat in the row in front of us. The man spun around and said, "I'm Jack MacGruder. And this is Phyllis Carney. I'm in charge of Operation Trojan Horse. Phyllis is my boss."

It suddenly struck me that my suspicion about Grand Vistas being a foreign intelligence front of some sort had to be correct, that this guy and this lady were somehow onto the gambit also, and now it was time for us all to play a little truth or consequences.

But before I could say a word about that, the man who called himself Jack MacGruder said to the thing masquerading as a rear projection booth, "Dim the lights and start."

The CIA is really into mind games, and the idea here was to create psychic shock, and build on the momentum.

Well, the lights cooperatively dimmed and there were a few bright flickers on the screen, then a slide that said, "Operation Trojan Horse, TOP SECRET, L-5 Compartmentalized."

Without further preamble, Mr. MacGruder began speaking. "In 1995, President Clinton signed a Top Secret finding ordering the Central Intelligence Agency to form a task force for the purpose of tracking illegal funds worldwide. His order grew out of a general frustration with the drug lords in Latin America. A number of methods were employed to stamp out their business, influence, and power. All failed. By 1995, Colombia had been turned into a charnel house by cocaine barons who were literally stronger than the state. We were warning the President that the balkanization of Colombia threatened to spill over to other Latin states, to destabilize newly democratic governments that lacked both the police power and wealth to resist cocaine money."

A new slide appeared—your basic map of the world with hundreds of little boxes filled with tiny initials in a number of countries. I should mention that nobody makes slides like the U.S. government. I even have this quirky theory that we won the cold war because their slidemakers couldn't cram as much shit onto an eight-by-eleven page as ours. But let's save the full explanation for another occasion.

Anyway, the guy known as Jack MacGruder continued, "But we in the CIA were also concerned with other rising international groups, like the Mafiya who had seized control of much of Russia's economy, and terrorist groups like Al Qaeda, led by a fanatic millionaire who was receiving millions in illegal donations and investing his own wealth to subsidize his growing organization. What you see here is a country-by-country listing of criminal and terrorist organizations we regard as threats to American interests."

Well, this was a very long list, but you expect that from the CIA. Not that anybody was padding the rolls of bad guys or anything, but I noticed one group called GSA. I guess I just ate my last Girl Scout cookie. I love my country.

Phyllis interrupted at this point, saying, "You can see we have a large and diverse problem. You would be surprised at how much illegal money washes around the world every year. We estimate it's over a trillion dollars. And that's a conservative figure. It could be two, possibly three times as much. Chinese triads, Japanese Yakuza, Burmese generals, Balkan warlords, African rulers who loot their national treasuries . . . The list is endless."

"You see our problem?" MacGruder asked.

"Money?" I answered.

"*Illegal* money," Mr. MacGruder corrected. "In around two hun-

dred different currencies, shuttling through banks, moving electronically, so invisibly that it's become impossible to segregate and
track. Every time we find a new way, the crooks get a little smarter,
and invent a new scam. The world's best bankers in Geneva and
New York work with them. They employ MBAs from Harvard and
Penn. They're sophisticated and, believe me, they're ingenious."

"And," Phyllis added, "they use it to buy bombs, guns, nuclear
materials, political influence, and, ultimately, death. Shakespeare
had it right—money truly is the root of all evil. Every year a hundred thousand Americans die from drugs. Entire nations—Mexico,
Russia, much of Central America and Africa, and of course, Colombia, as Jack mentioned—are virtually run by criminal cartels. A recent Russian poll suggests that ordinary Russians pay half as much
in bribes as they pay in taxes. Criminal power has grown exponentially in the past forty years. Capitalism may be the best conceivable economic engine, but the greedy and wicked thrive in it."

MacGruder stood up and walked up to the stage to be near the
screen. A new slide appeared; another map of the world, but certain countries had cute little red stars. He tapped a pointer at the
screen, and informed us, "These are the countries and territories
with banking and financial regulations that virtually encourage
criminal elements and illegal groups—like terrorists—to use their
financial institutions. There's a lot of money havens, aren't there?"

Janet and I nodded to acknowledge that indeed there were. So
what?

"The so what," Phyllis Carney said, somehow reading our
minds, "was, how were we to accomplish this mission the President gave us? So many strategies and techniques had been tried
and failed. Intriguing question, don't you think?"

"How?" Janet asked.

MacGruder said, "Money is their lifeblood. So we started by
hunting their money. The dilemma with making dirty money is you
have to get it cleaned before it has real value. Laundered, in the vernacular, and then safely invested. And the more you have, the more
difficult this is to accomplish. You expect your money to lose fifty

percent of its value in the process, sometimes as much as eighty percent. The middlemen and the launderers take great risks and demand prolific rewards."

Phyllis spun and asked us, "Any questions at this point?"

I thought she was joking. We obviously had questions, starting with, Why are we here? But they'd get to that in their own good time, so I traded a glance with Janet, and we both shook our heads.

She continued, "It was Jack's brainchild, actually. We decided to pick one of these hidden money laundering organizations. And about four years ago, our DEA found one for us. It was well established in Europe, and was making impressive inroads into the drug trade in Latin America. We made a cursory examination of the organization. An impressive group—smart people, good systems, a very sophisticated understanding of banking, commerce, and . . . goodness, I hope this isn't too boring for you."

"Not at all," I replied.

She nodded at MacGruder, who continued, "It was just what we were looking for. We cooked up a plan. We would protect this syndicate from the DEA, from the Treasury Department, and from the prying eyes of our counterparts in Europe and Asia. We would, in effect, invisibly nurture it, help it grow and succeed. We would try to put other money launderers out of business, creating market forces that drove the customers toward this syndicate. We would try to turn this syndicate into a powerhouse, the Microsoft or GE of money laundering."

"Grand Vistas?" I asked.

"That's the name it uses in its partnership with Morris Networks. Grand Vistas is a subsidiary, if you will. It has many other subsidiaries that go by many other names. The syndicate really does own diamond mines and shipping companies and equipment leasing companies. Also banks and steel mills, and it even has significant ownership of a foreign car manufacturer that's very popular with modern yuppies. It's a remarkable money machine."

The lights suddenly flicked back on. MacGruder said, "Do you sec why we can't let you expose Grand Vistas and its relationship with Morris?"

I looked over at Janet, who appeared horrified. She said, "You *nurtured* the organization that murdered my sister?"

MacGruder and Phyllis obviously knew this moment was coming, had even anticipated it. Phyllis smoothly replied, "Well, we're not sure they were even implicated in your sister's death."

"Not sure?" Janet snapped. "You mean hope. When this blows up, your asses are going down, too."

MacGruder calmly said, "Miss Morrow, if we thought they were implicated, you would never have been brought here, would never have heard this briefing, and would never be able to point an accusing finger at this Agency."

Which I guess was his sinewy concept of a reassurance. Only a CIA person would tell you, on the one hand, to trust him, because he's letting you in on a secret, while confessing that if he thought it would land him in hot water, he'd never tell you.

And I think even Phyllis noticed MacGruder's faux pas, and she added, "We're very sorry about your sister's death, but we can find absolutely no link or connection between Grand Vistas and her murderer. Our people have looked quite hard."

Phyllis continued explaining to Janet the Agency's all-encompassing pursuit, turning over rock after rock, looking for a tie-in. It was such patent bullshit.

Anyway, when she finally paused to catch her breath, I asked her, "And could you tell us how Morris Networks and this money laundering syndicate are connected?"

She nodded at MacGruder, who explained, "The past three years, as you know, stock markets around the world have been tanking. Thousands of companies, like Morris Networks, have found themselves overextended, deeply in debt, credit ratings destroyed, banks refusing to make more loans, their revenues shrinking so drastically they're on the verge of cratering."

Phyllis said, "The money launderers haven't been blind to the rich possibilities. Many of these distressed companies are desperate for capital. The companies face bankruptcy. Their executives confront professional ruin. Grand Vistas was created to be Morris's white knight. This syndicate has dozens more Grand Vistas, operating in tandem with other corporations. Some are targeting American companies, some are infiltrating other stock exchanges."

MacGruder said, "What Phyllis is saying is that the criminal cartels, through this syndicate, are making a massive investment in the American and European economies. Through these interlocking relationships they are getting in at fire sale prices, and when the global economy recovers, their wealth will expand exponentially."

They both paused, and their eyes flicked back and forth from Janet to me. They weren't sweating or anything, because CIA people get some kind of gene injection that makes them permanently cool and reptilian. But their sphincters were probably the size of pinheads.

Janet said nothing. She appeared either mesmerized by the big empty screen, or so mentally stunned she was left speechless. Having bumped against the CIA before, nothing, I mean really *nothing* they do or say surprises me.

But the pressing question was, what if Janet and I, or Janet, or I, didn't want to take a vow of silence? Obviously, we were brought here to have so much bullshit thrown at us that we'd agree to a gag order of some sort. Would we be pumped full of drugs and awaken on the Agency's version of Johnston Island Atoll? Every month or so a plane would fly over and parachute food.

Perhaps I'm too cynical, but I also sensed something was missing. I mean, when it's the CIA something is *always* missing; too often, that something is the truth. But the CIA treasures it secrets. It takes a root canal to get them to admit their real names. Yet here we were, and they were letting us in on a very big secret. Why?

There had to be more. I was sure there was more. But what? Were they trying to cover up an operation that went sour? A rogue operation? Had some of their people failed to keep their fingers out of this syndicate's cookie jar?

You can go crazy trying to second-guess the CIA, which is so compartmentalized, salami-sliced, and balkanized, it can't even second-guess itself. I wondered if Phyllis and MacGruder even knew what they were hiding.

"Well?" Phyllis asked.

"Well, what?"

"I think you know."

"I believe I do." I suggested, "You'd like us to stop looking for the killer because it might expose or compromise your operation. Did I miss anything?"

"Not a thing." She smiled. "I think you've grasped the issue quite well."

Janet said, "And also forget about the brutal murders of four innocent women? Including my sister."

Phyllis reiterated to Janet, "I told you, we're not sure there is any connection."

"Up yours."

"There's no need for that. I'm trying to be helpful."

"Then drop dead."

I think we knew what Janet's answer was.

It seemed appropriate for me to add, "I'm with her."

And that's the exact moment when the door flew open and two new gentlemen entered.

CHAPTER FORTY-THREE

Jᴀᴍᴇꜱ Pᴇᴛᴇʀꜱᴏɴ ʜᴀᴅ ʙᴇᴇɴ Dɪʀᴇᴄᴛᴏʀ ᴏꜰ ᴛʜᴇ Cᴇɴᴛʀᴀʟ Iɴᴛᴇʟʟɪɢᴇɴᴄᴇ Agency for six years, a long time in any appointed job in Washington—an eternity for the head honcho of the cosmically accident-prone CIA.

He was short and stout, dark-haired, with intense dark eyes, thick, blubbery lips, and, like many powerful men, he exuded great doses of competence and self-confidence. What was surprising for someone with his dark title, complexion, and responsibilities, this was combined with a look of openness, candor, and even friendliness. Of course it was illusory.

His eyes were directed at Phyllis as he entered and asked, "Well, how's it going?"

"I'm afraid not well," she confessed.

He nodded at her and MacGruder, and then said, "This is Tom."

There was no need to introduce Tom to me, the second man, if you will, who I wouldn't call Tom anyway, because he was General Thomas Clapper—at that precise moment, the last person I expected, wanted, and needed to see.

But Clapper moved straight toward me, held out his hand, and said, a bit too formally, "Major Drummond, how are you?"

"Okay, General. You know, considering."

His eyes indicated that he did know. Also that a serious career counseling session lay in my near future.

From their timing, it wasn't hard to guess there was an observation port into this room.

He smiled at Janet. "I'm Thomas Clapper, Lisa's former boss." He smiled harder and asked, "May I call you Janet?"

As I mentioned, Clapper is a bona fide southern gentleman. He can be quite charming, even captivating, when he's not pissed at you. Or so people tell me.

Janet replied, "Yes . . . please do."

"Janet, I'm very sorry about Lisa. I've spoken with your father, and now I'd like to convey my sympathies to you. I've spent almost thirty-five years as a JAG. I thought the world of her. She was both a wonderful person and one of the best lawyers I ever saw."

This sounded perfectly sincere and probably was. Janet replied, "Thank you."

"I was the one who sent Drummond up to Boston to be your family's survival assistance officer."

"Thank you, again."

He glanced at me. "Don't thank me for that."

She mistook this for humor and politely chuckled. He didn't. She said to him, "He saved my life. Perhaps you've misjudged him."

"No chance of that." He smiled at her, though. Not at me; at her. Bad sign.

But speaking of bad signs, I noticed that Peterson had used Clapper's little diversion to gather his lieutenants in the corner and whisper a few directions. He who called himself Jack MacGruder did not appear to like or approve of the directions. Peterson leaned closer to him and whispered something. MacGruder shrugged, backed away, and apparently lost the debate, whatever it was.

Peterson then joined us, shook hands with Janet, then me,

then ordered everybody to get reseated. He remained standing and looked down at us. Short men know all the tricks.

To Janet and me, he said, "I've instructed Jack and Phyllis that it's time to let you in on the rest of the story." He stared at both of us as he added, "You realize that nothing said here will ever be repeated outside this room."

Janet said, "I won't agree to that."

"When we're done, I'm sure you will."

"I'm sure you're wrong."

"Oh, you'll come around." The poor fool obviously didn't have my experience with her.

But there's a thin line between confident expressions and polite threats, and I wasn't completely sure which I had just heard from his lips.

Now that he had made his point, though, he turned to Mac-Gruder and ordered, "Tell them, Jack." Gosh—maybe Jack *was* his real name.

And Jack, a bit sourly said, "Operation Trojan Horse—the cover name conveys exactly what's happening. The syndicate we've been discussing has become the largest money-washing conduit in the world. Success breeds success in this occupation as in others, and what's happening here is criminal organizations and terrorist groups have been lining up to let this syndicate wash and handle their cash."

Phyllis put a hand on MacGruder's arm and asked us, "Do you understand why we did this?"

"Tell us," Janet replied.

"We've fostered this growth to allow our people, and the National Security Agency, to dissect the pieces of this sprawling syndicate. It is quite large, and highly fragmented, but we track a fair amount of its phone calls, e-mails, and wire transfers. We don't have every piece of it mapped out yet, but with each day it operates its filthy business, we learn more."

MacGruder amplified on her thought, saying, "Most important, we learn where its money comes from, how much, and where it goes."

I suggested, "Then seize it and shut it down."

Peterson replied, "That's the last thing we want to do."

"Perhaps it should be the first."

"It's not about the money," Phyllis responded. "That never was the point of this thing."

"What is the point?"

"Money is just paper, printed by governments. Our interest lies in the syndicate's customers. We care about the people and organizations who make this money, how they make this money, where it's coming from, where it's going, and what it buys. We learn where they deposit it and where they pick it up, once it's been freshly laundered. We've been exploiting this information to roll up terrorist groups and criminal gangs worldwide. We pick off their people a few at a time, so they don't become suspicious. We drag in those people, sweat them a bit, and learn more. Sometimes we do it, sometimes other U.S. government agencies do it, sometimes we cue our foreign counterparts to handle it." She paused to let us absorb this, then commented, "It's become a virtual Yellow Pages to the nastiest organizations on earth."

MacGruder added, "How do you think we've been able to roll up so many Al Qaeda cells these past few years? Al Qaeda uses our syndicate extensively. We've mined this piggy bank for intelligence we could never hope to get any other way. We've been able to plot Colombian money, Mexican money, terrorist money—"

Peterson suddenly said, "That's enough, Jack." And just when it was getting really interesting, Jack stopped.

Looking at Janet and me, Peterson said, "Do you understand what you've been told?"

But he wasn't really inquiring, he was emphasizing, and he further amplified, "Trojan Horse is the most lucrative intelligence operation we've ever run. It's the modern equivalent of Venoma, when we broke the Soviet code, or when we broke Japan's and Germany's codes in the Second World War. In this fragmented new world order of ours, this operation, this syndicate, this is our key to the bank."

I glanced at Janet. It was a good thing she was studying Peterson's face, not mine—I seemed to be experiencing a massive attack of moral claustrophobia. Understand that Clapper was here to jar my memory about my profession, to counter the concern, I guess, that after a few weeks of wearing civilian suits and hanging out with the rich and privileged, my brain had turned somewhat mushy toward the entire concept of Duty, Honor, Country. Also there was the matter of the signed oath required of all Special Actions attorneys. If my memory served, something about protecting national security secrets upon penalty of God knows what.

So I was sitting there, weathering a crisis of guilt, conscience, and conflicted loyalties. I could see absolutely no way for this to be resolved to everybody's satisfaction—even to *anybody's* satisfaction. Whichever side I chose was going to cause me great personal angst and loss.

Janet finished mulling and, of course, asked Peterson, "So who murdered my sister?"

"I don't know."

"You really don't?"

"I really don't."

"You have suspicions, though, don't you?"

"Remember where you are, Janet. This building is a vault of suspicions. My day begins with suspicions, my day is filled with suspicions, and the worst of those suspicions keep me awake at night." He snapped, "Yes—I have suspicions."

"All right. Help me get my sister's murderers."

Sounded like a good solution to me.

But Peterson scowled and said, "The CIA isn't permitted to engage in operations inside the United States. I'd like to help; I can't."

"You mean," Janet said, "you don't want to risk having your precious operation compromised."

"Of course it's a factor," he confessed. "The killer is not my concern, however. It's a domestic matter, not international. My interest is this syndicate, with protecting millions of lives from international terrorism, drugs, and other criminal mayhem."

And like that—bang, something went off in the back of my head. *What?*

Janet said, "That's too bad. My sister is my concern. And if you think . . ." and so on, and so forth. I hadn't slept in two nights. I was forgetting something, and I was groggy, and the temperature in the room wasn't helping. Yet . . . *what?*

I sat up. "Wait a minute."

Janet stopped talking. Peterson stopped talking.

I said, "The cops, Meany—how did they get to my apartment so fast this morning? And what the hell was Meany doing there?"

Peterson shook his head. "Who's Meany? What are you talking about?"

MacGruder coughed. Phyllis sat and looked ladylike and grandmotherly, like she should have a sewing kit in her lap and should be knitting something; like a handmade garrote, maybe.

"Who's Meany?" Peterson repeated.

Only after a long pause did MacGruder inform his boss, "I believe he's referring to Special Agent George Meany, sir. He's the SAC of the FBI task force hunting the serial killer."

And like that, another piece fell into place in my head, and I said, "Tell us about the cover-up, Jack."

He did not respond to that. In fact, aside from some squeaky seats and feet shuffling, the room went completely quiet.

Peterson said, "Drummond, I have no idea what you're talking about."

I nodded in the direction of Phyllis and Jack. "They do."

So he regarded Phyllis a moment. And then Jack.

After a moment of this, Phyllis suggested, very suavely, "Director, perhaps we should have a word with you . . . in private?"

Janet was staring at me.

But I broke eye contact with Janet, and I established eye contact with Phyllis. I asked her, "When did *you* know?"

She was still making eye contact with her boss, who said to

her, "Answer him, Phyllis." He then added—actually, he empha-sized—"I'd like to know, too."

Well, all this asinine eye contact stuff came to an abrupt end, because Phyllis turned back to Jack and said, "You explain it." Shit really does roll downhill.

Jack stammered, "We weren't . . . I mean, when Captain Mor-row was murdered, we had no idea . . . we never put two and two together . . . she'd left the law firm, weeks before. The police con-cluded it was a robbery."

"What about after Cuthburt?" I suggested helpfully.

"No, no . . . not then either. We made no connection between her and Captain Morrow. Not really until Anne Carrol was . . . well . . . she was SEC, and the FBI discovered the link, actually . . ." He paused, then said, "Only then was it brought to *our* attention."

Janet fixed him with a frosty glare and asked, "Why?"

MacGruder's eyes darted at Peterson, who nodded. He said, "Trojan Horse is a joint operation between us and the FBI. We handle the overseas parts, the FBI handles the domestic pieces. Our FBI counterparts have an operation inside Culper, Hutch, and Westin. A lot of work went into setting it up. It's critically im-portant and must be protected."

"What kind of operation?" I asked.

"You'll recall that I mentioned the syndicate is exploiting dis-tressed companies. In fact, Morris Networks was one of the first"—he shook his head—"actually, it was the first we *detected*. That discovery made us nervous."

"About what?"

"How the syndicate knew."

"Knew what?"

"Understand, corporations experiencing financial turmoil, that are hemorrhaging cash, they are extremely secretive with this in-formation. If word leaks, their competitors know and jump on them, their stock tanks, and bankruptcy becomes virtually un-stoppable. Consider Exxon, WorldCom, Global Crossing, or any of the others that have been in the news in recent years. Their CEOs knew . . . their chief financial officers and legal departments knew. The rest of their people had no clue they were teetering toward bankruptcy. Even Wall Street and their bankers were kept in the dark." He added, "So, how was our syndicate cherry-picking these companies? How did it know to target them? It had to be acquiring insider information."

"Go on."

"We gave that a lot of thought. It's very sophisticated, really. You see, when corporate officers know a financial train wreck might be unavoidable, what do they do? They face a legal nightmare, lawsuits from bondholders, from stockholders, from banks, possibly SEC investigations, and so on. Many corporate officers and board members confront personal liability. Their risks are enormous. Those risks have to be scrutinized, managed, even minimized, and, hopefully, well in advance."

I said, "So they consult lawyers with expertise in these matters."

"Precisely. In advance of a bankruptcy declaration."

I thought about this a moment. I asked, "You're saying the firm is . . . what? A talent scout for the syndicate?"

"That's what I'm saying. Troubled companies approach your firm for advice and preparations, and the syndicate is notified."

"Who's notifying it? The whole firm? Everybody?"

He chuckled. "Only in a John Grisham novel, Major. No, not everybody."

I didn't chuckle. "Who?" I asked.

"We're not sure."

"But you said—"

"I said the FBI is running an operation."

"Meaning what?"

"Meaning the FBI has a mole inside the firm."

"A mole?"

"An undercover agent."

"I know what a mole is. Who?"

"That's considerably more than you need to know."

There was a long pause before Phyllis explained, "We have to *know* what companies this syndicate is getting involved with. Consider your friend Jason Morris. The precise details are cloudy, but we've been able to speculate how it happened."

Jack picked up on her cue and explained, "Several years ago, Morris found himself in dire trouble. His personal fortune, all of it, was invested in company stock. His business was sharply contracting, the entire telecom sector was suffering an overcapacity crisis, and the banks turned merciless. He therefore approached your firm for preparatory bankruptcy advice."

"Why my firm?"

"We don't know. But somebody in the firm informed the syndicate of this, Jason Morris was approached, and he made his deal. The money exchange works through capacity swaps. It's a shell game, of course. Grand Vistas ships him cash, and he ships them stock. Because the transaction occurs under the accounting rubric of a capacity swap, it escapes the scrutiny of an outright loan or sale."

There was silence for a moment as we all considered what this meant.

As though we were too stupid to figure it out, Phyllis commented, "Really, it's brilliant. The money gets laundered every time Grand Vistas sells the stock. Very large amounts of money. And if Morris Networks' stock rises in value, Grand Vistas and its clients make scads more money."

Well, the realities were ever-shifting inside this room. The floodgates were open, and Janet and I were being deluged with disclosures and information—just, notably, not the specific information I had very clearly asked for.

In short, we had their balls in our hands, just not all their balls.

I said, "Explain *why* George Meany was at my apartment so fast this morning?"

Phyllis replied, "You'll have to ask George that question."

"I'm asking you."

"I don't have that answer."

"I think you do."

"You think wrong. We're teamed with the FBI on this matter, but we don't share everything." She added, "And neither do they."

No kidding. The CIA and FBI not talking to each other? Could that be? She was probably lying, but the best lies are always grounded in the best truths.

I looked up at Peterson. A minute before, he had realized that his subordinates were withholding information not only from us, but from him. Phyllis and Jack probably now had a few career issues to sort through with him.

But he had either concluded that we'd already heard enough, or that we really did not need to hear the next big revelation, because that next big revelation was very bad—that it was illegal, and completely indefensible. Or perhaps *he* didn't want to hear that next confession because he'd lose his plausible deniability. Nobody survives six years in his job who doesn't know when he's heard enough.

Changing the conversation, he faced Janet and asked, "Tell me what you think I can do for you. How can we resolve this?"

Janet said, "I want the killer and the people responsible."

"You're asking too much."

"I am not. I want justice for my murdered sister and my father. The murderer *and* the people who sent him."

He looked at me. "Can you reason with her?"

Shit—there it was. The Choice; do I screw Lisa's memory and my friendship, or whatever my exact relationship was with Janet; or trample on my oath of service and my sworn duty to safeguard and preserve what was obviously a dire national secret?

I could feel Janet's eyes looking into my heart, and I could feel Clapper's eyes boring into my soul.

I said to Peterson, "The hit man has sworn to kill me, Janet, and our families. You understand this, right?"

"I have no problem with getting the killer. He's a cold-blooded murderer and deserves to be brought to justice."

"Define justice."

He had anticipated this question and replied, "Don't be premature. We'll define his justice when we find him."

And at just that moment, Clapper, who'd been silently witnessing this affair, said, "Director Peterson, I think you should answer Sean's question."

I glanced at him, but he wasn't looking at me.

"All right," Peterson said. "I won't pretend or deny that it wouldn't be hugely convenient if the killer were to resist apprehension and force the issue. There are alternatives, however. *If* we take him alive, the Director of the FBI and I can classify him as a terrorist, and a security risk, and seal his trial. Are you satisfied?"

No—I wanted this bastard dead and buried. But I was satisfied the legal technicalities were being met.

Clapper asked, "And if we learn the names of his direct accomplices?"

"I can't, and I won't, bend on that," Peterson replied. "His accomplices need to feel secure and stay in place for the continued success of Trojan Horse." He added, "At some point, indeterminate at this stage, their day of reckoning will come. You'll have to be satisfied with that."

Janet's lips were just parting, so I swiftly said, "We won't expose the connection to Grand Vistas. But until the killer is stopped, I want protection for Janet, for me, and our immediate families."

"We can arrange that."

MacGruder said, "Let's not forget the matter of this lawsuit he's threatened his firm with."

"How do you know—"

He smiled. "The FBI's person inside the firm keeps us well-informed. You have that firm up in a lather, Drummond. You have to find a convincing way to withdraw your threat and let things get back to normal."

"We can do that." I glanced at Janet. She looked shocked, disappointed, but more than that, also disillusioned. At the outcome, most certainly, and, I suppose, in me. I swallowed and said, "Janet, there's no other way. Half a loaf is better than—"

"Shut up."

"Right."

Peterson regarded her a moment, then said, "And do I have your agreement?"

"And do I have a choice?" It wasn't a question, it was a statement of bitter resignation. She then added, "I'll do what I have to do."

"Thank you. I mean that. This is hard to stomach, but it's for the good of the country." He then paused a moment before he said, "Now, this is distasteful for me, but I have to warn you both that if there's a leak, if this operation is compromised in any way, I know where to look. We don't have an official secrets act, like the British, but there are certain punitive measures that can—and I assure you, will—be brought against you. You understand."

I nodded, and Janet stared at him a moment, before her chin dipped also.

But Peterson had good intuitive instincts and appeared to recognize that I had just paid a very dear price to seal this bargain.

To make amends, he leaned back on his heels and said to me, "Major, I must compliment you on your remarkable detective work. How you discovered this operation . . . how you unwrapped this mystery, it's a great tribute to your integrity and your intelligence."

Clapper commented, "Before Sean became a lawyer, he used to do a lot of work for your people."

Peterson nodded, like that explained it. He added, "Well, when this is over, Drummond, maybe you should think about working over here."

I smiled. "I might like that, Director."

Of course, I was lying.

And in this building, it made no echo.

CHAPTER FORTY-FOUR

IT WAS NOON WHEN JANET AND I STEPPED OFF THE ELEVATOR ONTO THE twelfth floor of Morris Networks.

I had called Mom, Dad, and brother John, and explained to them that life was going to be a little different for a few days, that stupid Sean had stirred up some stupid shit, and the nice boys and girls of the Federal Bureau of Investigation were going to be hanging around and watching over all of their asses for the next few days. I suggested to John that this might be a good time to visit Mom and Dad—this was easier for the Feds, and cheaper, a point I had been asked to stress by my new government pals.

Mom told me to be careful, Dad snorted that he'd watch after his own ass, and John said he thought that instead of visiting Dad and thirty years of grudges, he would just take a private jet to Tahiti or somewhere obscure like that.

Janet called her family also, but she had become very uncommunicative toward me, and did not inform me how it went.

We had driven over in my car, and while I did not observe any coverage, I had been assured that at least ten federal eyes would remain on moi and Janet wherever we went.

But Tiffany Allison was not smiling as the elevator door opened. In fact, Miss Allison looked positively stunning: coiffed, manicured, and buffed to a fine shine, but indeed, she was not smiling.

Without any welcome or ado, she coldly escorted us to Jason's door. Perhaps I was imagining things, but her ass, and it truly was a world-class ass, appeared to be wiggling and swishing more erotically than usual. Good-byes and fuck-yous take many forms.

She opened Jason's door and ushered us inside, offering me one final, frosty look, and then shut the door behind us.

Jason climbed out from his circular desk and walked toward us. Jessica Moner remained seated at the glass conference table with an expression of icy hatred. Sean Drummond was not having a very good day with the ladies.

Jason approached Janet and said to her, "You must be the lawyer I spoke with this morning."

"Janet Morrow," she reminded him, curt but businesslike. "Frankly, I'm happy we were able to work this out. I hate going to court."

"You should be glad. Jessica says you wouldn't stand a chance. She's not happy with me."

"Don't listen to her. You made the right choice."

Jessica growled something that sounded like "my ass," but maybe she was just complaining about having to lug that big thing around all day.

Jason, however, wanted to keep things cordial and professional, so he smiled at Janet and said, "Please . . . call me Jason." He swung his arm to indicate our seats. "Let's get started, shall we?"

So we sat at the glass table, and Jessica pulled a lump of papers out of her legal case and spread them around.

Jessica looked at Janet and me and said, "This is the agreement Drummond has to sign before we pay a fuckin' dime to you assholes . . ." and so on, as she continued in her pithy way to lay out the basic terms and conditions. It was all fairly boilerplate—a long-winded, legalistic way of saying that in return for not launching a suit, and keeping my mouth shut, the corporation of Morris Networks hereby pays me seventy million dollars.

Still, it was surreal listening to her babble on. Having already faxed Jessica's office my checking account number, in mere minutes, seventy million dollars was going to start flowing across a thin copper wire and end up mine, all mine.

Actually, after Janet's cut, half mine.

After Uncle Sam's cut, a quarter mine.

After the fine Commonwealth of Virginia took its bite, less than a quarter mine.

What a country.

She finally finished her spiel, saying to Janet and me, "Now . . . read the fuckin' contract and be sure you agree to our terms and stipulations."

I glanced at Janet and she glanced back. The ice was thin under my butt, but she had to tolerate me, and for the greater good of Western civilization, we had to get through this. Also, one, or possibly two people at this table might have played a hand in her sister's death and putting her father into intensive care, not to mention adding both our names to the killer's social register, so this was tough going. But as I said, we had to play our roles, and we had to read through the agreement to be sure Jessica hadn't slipped any nasty willies into the small print.

Thus, for the better part of the next ten minutes, we browsed and parsed the text like the good lawyers were both were. Jason acted like his usual caffeinated self, and he fidgeted, fiddled, and twitched. Three times, he trekked to his desk and inspected his beloved monitors. I caught him, once or twice, gazing curiously at Janet, perhaps calculating whether she was a candidate for a weekend in Bimini. Not a chance, pal.

Jessica sat and steamed. I caught her eye once or twice, and found myself wondering, not at all absently, or charitably, if she was the one who ordered the hits.

She certainly fit *a* profile. She had serious anger management issues, as my New Age friends would say; a big bone up her ass, in my words. Also, she liked to come across as a badass, and one has to wonder where that act stops. Talk shit, and pretty soon you have to act like a shit, my mother always used to warn me. Jessica was clearly Morris's consigliere in matters of law and business. But did that also extend to matters of life and death?

Or was it Jason himself? It was hard to believe a guy with his moolah and fame would take such risks. But he had taken his bath in corruption, and crime tends to be a greased slope. One step nearly always begets another. The human conscience is funny— once subjected to the concept of elasticity, it never completely snaps back into place. Also, Jason had the most to lose, and nearly always that's where you locate the greatest guilt. He was a visionary with grand ambitions, and so were Hitler, Stalin, and Mao. The vision consumes the soul, and the innocents who stand in the way get trampled and buried.

Janet finally announced, "Everything looks in order."

"Then it's acceptable?" Jason asked her, and then me, and we both nodded.

He said, "Then, I'd like to say a few words, if you don't mind."

I replied, "You're buying the podium."

I had the sense he did not find me funny. He studied my face. "I'm very disappointed in you, Sean. I thought you and I had bonded."

"Not half as disappointed as I am in you, Jason. I never realized what an unsafe or crooked workplace you run."

"I trusted you."

"And I'm doing you a big favor, keeping this out of court."

"I'm not so sure," he said. "You look perfectly healthy to me."

"Internal injuries are tricky, Jason. Beneath the surface, I'm shattered, a shambling wreck, horribly scarred and disfigured."

Jason did not reply to this. But his eyes narrowed. I would've taken it for anger or exasperation, but it was more likely frustration. Jessica had obviously put him up to making one last stab, and we had to play this out for whatever recording device she had hidden in this office. If I admitted, if I even intimated, I was blackmailing his company, or faking my injuries, I'd lose the grounds for the civil suit, and, with it, the threat of exposure. And of course, seventy million frequent-flier miles would at some point in the future end up back in Jason's vault.

I scribbled my name on three copies of the settlement, then shoved them across the table at Jason. He sighed, and then scrawled his name. Then our lawyers added their signatures, and the agreement was stamped by Jessica with the certified seal of the Commonwealth of Virginia.

I said, "I believe we get one copy of that."

Jessica threw it across the table.

I did make a point to say "thank you" before we left.

CHAPTER FORTY-FIVE

Aᴄᴛ Tᴡᴏ ᴏғ ᴛʜɪs ᴄʜᴀʀᴀᴅᴇ ᴡᴀs ᴏɴ ᴛʜᴇ ᴇɪɢʜᴛʜ ғʟᴏᴏʀ ᴏғ Cᴜʟᴘᴇʀ, Wᴇsᴛɪɴ, and Hutch. Elizabeth looked up with a cheery smile when I entered. "Morning, Major. Do I hear properly that you're back to work?"

"Work? Ooops . . . I must be in the wrong place."

She laughed. "The halls are adrift with rumors. Personally I was rooting for you."

"Thank you."

"Well, the place would be terribly dull without you."

I leaned on her desk. "Those days are over. I've learned my lesson—I'm reformed and purified, another gray, lifeless suit." I paused, and then asked, "Could I have the key for the ninth floor? I need to have a word with your fatassed idiot of a boss."

She tossed me the key and laughed. "That's the spirit."

I looked up at the camera and stuck my tongue out.

More chuckles.

A few moments later I pushed the button to Hal's office. It

buzzed, I entered, and two nerdy-looking types were seated behind desks, focusing intently on their computer screens.

I explained, "I'm Drummond. I'm here to see Lord Hal."

"In there," one answered.

He pushed a buzzer and I pushed open Hal's door. Merriweather was seated behind his desk, typing something into his computer.

He glanced up. "Oh . . . it's you."

"I thought I'd stop by and say no hard feelings."

"Oh, fuck off."

"My sentiments exactly." We exchanged brief yet meaningful glances of mutual hatred. "Cy told you I'm back with the firm?"

"He told me."

"That all the charges have been dropped?"

"I heard."

"That I'm allowed to roam the halls at will, turn on computers, and so on?"

"I heard. And I'll be watching you, Drummond."

And I'll be watching you, too. I leaned against his desk. "Hey, Hal, a question I've been meaning to ask. Do you recall my friend Lisa Morrow?"

"What about her?"

"Well, I have this really oddball theory that—oh, hell, you don't want to hear it."

"What are you talking about?"

"Oh, okay. I know this going to sound funny . . . weird, really . . . but, okay, here it is. I think her murder had to do with her work here."

"You're so full of shit. Try listening to the news. That serial killer got her."

I leaned closer. "See, Hal, what I think is that the serial killer is a phony. He's actually a hit man sent to get Lisa."

He looked me dead in the eye. "I have no idea what you're talking about."

"No?"

"I didn't even know her," he insisted. But his piggy eyes did get a little piggier.

"But she knew you."

"It's a big firm, Drummond. Are you accusing me of something?"

I chuckled. "Gee . . . Hal, you're a hard guy to have a friendly chat with."

"Think you're a smart guy, don't you?"

"It is a heavy burden having an IQ of 200. Am I letting it show?"

"You done, Drummond?"

"Definitely not with you."

I could feel his eyes on my back as I walked out. The two guys in the outer office were still staring into their computer monitors as I passed.

I got a cup of coffee and then returned to my luxurious office. In fact, I had just flipped on my computer when there was a light knock. Sally Westin stuck her head in, saying, "I hope I'm not bothering you. Elizabeth told me you came in."

"Not at all. How are you doing?"

"Fine." She smiled and entered. "Tired and overworked."

"The wages of sin."

She shuffled her feet. "Uh, Barry asked me to stop by as soon as you got in." She held up a black notebook and added, "The Morris Networks audit . . . your signature . . ."

She walked across the floor and laid the notebook in front of me. I flipped it open and reached into my pocket for a pen.

Sally said, "We've been hearing disturbing rumors."

"Nasty ones, I hope."

"Something about you assaulting Barry, or Barry assaulting you?"

"Ridiculous. We're thinking of getting married. Anything else?"

"That you were having problems with the audit."

"More nonsense. It was such fun, I just signed up for a CPA night course."

"I mean, the accuracy of the audit. You're sure you're okay with it?"

"Would I sign it if I wasn't?"

She pulled up a chair and asked, "May I?"

"Be my guest."

"Thanks." A moment passed, then she said, "Listen, Sean, I think you and I got off on the wrong foot."

I finished signing the audit and glanced up. Sally looked like crap—saddlebags under her eyes, droopy-lidded, limp-haired. Excessive ambition is hard to hide, even with makeup.

"What makes you think that?"

"I know you think I'm stuffy, driven, and uptight."

"You?" I smiled and she smiled back. I suggested, "You know, you might give thought to maybe jumping naked out of a cake at the firm Christmas party."

She chuckled. "Would it get me a partnership?"

"You'll get invitations to more parties."

She grew serious again and said, "You need friends in this firm. I've been remiss. I was supposed to be watching out for you." She stared at the floor. "I didn't do a very good job."

"I'm a tough patient. We'll both try harder."

She stood and collected the notebook. "I *am* your friend, Sean. Remember that. Confide in me. If you have problems, call me."

"I will. Thanks."

I checked my e-mail. A long line of firm correspondence was queued up, administrative crap, summaries of important cases—so many e-mails, in fact, that it took nearly five minutes to delete it all. Feeling better, I tackled my phone messages. Since there were none, that didn't take long.

It was late afternoon, and having not slept for two days, I decided that Act Two had wound down, and I shut down the computer and left.

At the reception area, Elizabeth asked, "Sneaking out a bit early, aren't we, Major?"

"Shhhh." I pointed at Hal's monitor and whispered, "Don't tell anybody."

She giggled. I leaned on her desk. "Elizabeth, how long did you say you've worked here?"

"Fourteen years."

"Like it?"

"What I like is the paycheck's not too rubbery."

"Good point. Uh . . . what about Hal? When did he get here?"

"Two, possibly three years ago."

"I see."

"Do what I do . . . about Hal, I mean."

"What's that?"

"Simply pretend he doesn't exist."

I laughed and turned toward the elevator. Then another thought struck me. I turned back around and asked Elizabeth, "When I came in, did you notify Sally I was here?"

"No. Should I have?"

"Yes. And don't ever forget to do it again."

She laughed again. Why didn't anybody take me seriously?

CHAPTER FORTY-SIX

I PARKED IN THE UNDERGROUND GARAGE BESIDE THE MADISON HOTEL, EN-
tered the lobby, and headed straight to my suite on the third floor,
which happened to be right beside Janet's suite, and the suites
next door and across the hall were all filled with security stooges
to safeguard our health and welfare. In fact, our hallway was like
an armed camp, with security cameras, motion detectors, and
enough explosives that I hoped nobody lit a match.

The Madison, incidentally, was not really a bad joint to hide out
in until our killer was found. It's a five-star inn, outfitted with all the
luxury stuff—nice rooms, great restaurants, and so forth. Thank
God the FBI wasn't in charge of this show, or we'd be holed up in
some dive out on Route 1, eating stale pizza, and the piped-in cable
would be modified so we only got Lifestyle Network. The CIA, you
have to understand, has a totally different take on these things. It
helps to have classified budgets, which are the nearest thing to a
blank check from Uncle Sam. Also, there's a big cultural gap between the FBI and CIA, like the difference between an adult Scout
den and a Machiavelli fan club, which is maybe why they don't like

or trust each other very much, and maybe why they don't share things very well.

Anyway, I had just entered my room when there was a knock on my door. It was Janet, and she said, "You're back early."

"The early bird gets the drink."

"Buy me a drink, too."

So I dutifully went to the minibar, got a beer for her and a scotch for me. She got herself a chair by the window And, well, here we were, all alone and together.

I really did need this drink.

She asked me, "How did it go?"

"Fine. They're happy I signed the audit and happy I dropped the suit against them. In fact, I was getting high fives from everybody for fleecing Morris for seventy million. They're thinking of offering me a partnership."

"So they bought it?"

"Yes. Cy said I'm off the Morris account, though. Jessica apparently called him and said I'm not a nice person."

"Too bad. They're such nice people."

"Also, the money's in my bank. And I'm serious about you getting half. After the ten-day lock, I'll arrange it."

"Keep it."

"I don't think you—"

"It's blood money. Keep it."

I checked my watch—it was definitely time for a drink.

She took the beer from my hand, sipped, and said, "By the way, that woman who met us at the elevator seemed particularly upset with you."

I scratched my head. "Oh . . . you mean Miss Allison . . . Jason's executive assistant."

"Forget it." She rolled her eyes. "It's none of my business."

Of course it wasn't. That's why she raised it.

I said, "We had lunch together. Once . . . maybe twice. I found her selfish, and not the least bit interesting."

"She's gorgeous."

"I didn't notice."

"No wonder things never worked out between you and my sister."

"What's that mean?"

"Nothing . . . absolutely nothing."

I kicked off my shoes and fell onto the bed. Two sleepless days, gun battles, FBI grillings, CIA briefings, and now this—geez. I was feeling a little under the weather, and, I guess, a little hot under the collar.

"You took a dive on me," Janet finally said.

I cleared my throat and replied, "I did *not.*"

"Oh yes you did."

"No. I took the best deal we were going to get."

"How do you *know* that?"

"Because I know Washington. Because people here think differently than they do in Boston. 'Inside the beltway' is not a geographic euphemism, Janet, it's a mindset. Stop me if I get too metaphorical, but Peterson and his people spend their lives weighing the greater good against lesser wrongs. It's a dirty business. They don't like it either. But they do it, and we're all the better for it."

"But the killer is just a hired gun. The responsibility for Lisa's death lies with the people who paid him."

"We all know that."

"If you know that, how could *you* let them off?"

"Because I was being ordered to. Why do you think Clapper was there?" Some impulse made me add, "And I've got news for you—were Lisa, your sister, my friend, my sister in arms . . . were she in my shoes, she would've made the identical choice. Think about that."

So she sat there a moment, looking into her beer, and I sat there unknotting my tie. I wished I knew what was going on inside her head. The truth was, I had become a bit smitten with her. Maybe very smitten.

Which I guess accounted for my hurt feelings and tantrum. I

felt like I had lost something very precious, although the truth was, I never really had it. It probably would never have worked anyway, between George, her sister's murder, the whole artificiality of what brought us together. But after that morning, all doubts were dispelled.

She said, "You mentioned the word 'cover-up' this morning."

"Did I?"

"And I had the impression Peterson and his people side stepped it."

"Was that your impression?"

"What were you talking about?"

"Nothing. I was making a stab in the dark."

"No, you had a very clear sense of something."

"Ask your friend George."

"Is George . . . I mean, do you think he's involved?"

I finished my scotch. "Ask *him.*"

Well, the next word was on the tip of her tongue, but a loud knock rattled the door. I went over and opened it, and two gray-suited thugs stepped inside, followed by Jack MacGruder, the honcho of Operation Trojan Horse, which was a shitty title, in my view. A code name is to supposed to hide the purpose of the operation, right? And if the bad guys ever heard that name, they'd be scratching their heads, saying, Trojan Horse? . . . Trojan Horse? . . . These CIA people are so bright and devious . . . what could that possibly, possibly mean? You know?

Anyway, MacGruder pointed at Janet's drink and asked, "Got any more of those?"

I went to the minibar and retrieved a beer. The thugs stood by the door, MacGruder sat in the chair opposite Janet, and I returned to the bed.

His eyes strayed around the expansive room. He smiled pleasantly and said, "It's a fairly nice hotel, don't you think? You two could be here a long time. We want to be sure you're comfortable and happy."

I replied, "We've got a killer who wants our asses, my career's in the shitter, Janet's father is in the hospital, and her sister's in the morgue. Spare us the happy hospitality bullshit, Jack. Tell us what's going on, and get the hell out."

MacGruder drew a deep breath. Had he thought we were going to be cheerful and polite passengers, he now knew better. He said, "Fine. You recall that the killer escaped from Boston in a car. The latest update from the FBI is they found the car stolen from a Mr. Harry Boticher in Boston. It was discovered in the parking lot of the Maryland House, which you might recognize as a roadside stop along 95. Another car was reported stolen there, and that one was found this afternoon, parked, of all places, illegally, one block from FBI headquarters." He chuckled. "This fellow has a great sense of humor, doesn't he?"

Screw you, Jack. But Janet said, "Any prints, hair, or fibers?"

"Fibers from a cotton shirt. But the cars were wiped down clean. He even used a solvent, if you can believe it."

I asked, "And the bodies in my apartment?"

He shook his head. "Not helpful. One Caucasian male, and the other was of Latin extraction. No IDs were on their bodies, their prints aren't on file, their photos were run through the FBI's database and there's no record. Both were carrying modified Uzis, and we're unable to trace them. Also, there were some blood splatters on your porch, but nobody's turned up in any area hospitals."

I asked, "And our families?"

"The FBI has established clandestine surveillance nets around all of them. Everybody's fine and healthy, and we'll keep them that way."

I asked, "How's Spinelli?"

"He'll be in a sling a few months. He was released from the hospital about an hour ago."

I stretched and yawned. I knew I needed to hear all this, but I didn't trust Jack MacGruder and I wanted him to disappear. I trusted and liked Janet, and I wanted her to disappear also.

I guess Janet read my mind because she said, "Jack, he's exhausted. Why don't I walk you out?"

"Uh . . . okay, fine."

I drained my scotch, fell back onto the bed, and the next thing I knew it was morning.

And Jack was back.

And he brought George.

CHAPTER FORTY-SEVEN

I LET THEM INTO MY ROOM, AND WHILE MEANY CALLED ROOM SERVICE AND ordered breakfast, I slipped into the bathroom to shower, shave, and dress. Just knowing MacGruder was nearby, I didn't even bend over to wash my little toes.

When I walked out of the bathroom, I was squeaky clean, I felt rested, I still had my charge card and virginity, and was looking quite debonair in my blue serge Brooks Brothers rags. Meany was seated at the table with MacGruder, and somebody had obviously gone next door and invited Janet, who now sat beside George. A cart piled with plates of steak, eggs, bagels, pancakes, donuts, and so forth was parked next to them.

Meany smiled at me. "Thanks for breakfast, Drummond. It's delicious."

"What the hell did you order?"

"Everything on the menu. Relax. You're rich."

Hah-hah. Prick. The Agency was paying for it.

Meany pointed at a chair. "Why don't you join us?"

"Yeah. My room, my food . . . I should definitely join you."

So I sat. I filled a plate, and then Meany and MacGruder made me recount everything that happened the day before, and peppered me with questions about whether I'd been convincing, and was everybody buying my baloney. This went on for twenty minutes, and I must've made a pretty good case, because neither Meany nor MacGruder expressed any arguments, nor offered any suggestions.

Still, when I finished, Meany just had to say, "It's just too bad we had to go through all this. If you hadn't stuck your nose where it doesn't belong, Drummond . . . none of this had to happen."

"What does that mean?"

"Simple. You nearly compromised a very important operation that we worked a long time to build. You nearly exposed one of our agents. We really don't appreciate ignorant clowns messing around in our business."

Of course, Meany was posturing for Miss You-know-who. Also, I guess, that little incident on my back porch had left some bruised feelings. He was chewing his breakfast a bit gingerly. So maybe he couldn't stop himself, but I'd had enough of him, and he'd called me a clown once too often, and I knew I shouldn't but I said, "Did I make your job hard, George?"

"Damned right you did."

"What is your job?"

"You know damn well what my job is."

"I know what you *said* your job was. But in fact, that wasn't your job, was it?"

"I don't know what you're talking about."

But for a guy who was merely confused over semantics he did in fact look nervous.

I asked him, "Are you still telling the public you're hunting the L.A. Killer?"

"Is that what this is about? You're still trying to second-guess us?"

I now had Janet's attention, and she said to George, "Is that true?"

George ignored her and said to me, "In a case of this scope and importance, the choice of suspects is out of my hands."

"Is it really?"

"Yes."

"Do *you* believe it's the L.A. Killer?"

"I might have a few doubts. In murder cases, I always have doubts. As an attorney, I would expect you to understand that." He added, "The Bureau's position is that the similarities between here and L.A. remain persuasive."

"What about the differing physical descriptions?"

"I'm glad you raised that issue. Had you read the morning paper, you'd know that one of the two witnesses who *claimed* she saw the L.A. Killer three years ago recanted. She admits the man she saw could've been much taller."

"Or maybe he gained a foot since then?" I suggested.

"He was bending over, shoving the victim into a car, and she admits she probably misjudged his height."

"How convenient."

"What are you implying, Drummond? I don't control what witnesses say."

It was time to switch tacks, so I asked, "How did you get to my apartment so fast yesterday?"

"How did I . . . ?" He paused, then said, "I work around the clock. I was at Martin's office, coordinating, when one of your neighbors called and reported gunfire. We checked the address, saw it was your building, and I thought I'd better be there."

George had just made his fatal mistake. And I think he knew it. He had to know, as a cop experienced in interrogation, that the whole trick is to prod that first unsupportable lie from the suspect's lips.

"Who called?" I asked him.

"I . . . I don't remember. Actually, I never knew. Martin's people took the call."

"Odd. The Alexandria station is over fifteen minutes away. You were at my apartment inside three minutes. Account for that."

"I'm not going to account for it. I'm not here to be interrogated by you. You're way out of line."

Janet suddenly bent forward and said, "Answer him, George. I'd like to know, too."

He stared at her. "Honey, I can't believe you're taking this jerk's side. I . . . are you forgetting *us* . . . what you mean to me?"

But Janet had put two and two together. She leaned back and studied George. She said, "You're supposed to cover this up. You're supposed to mislead the public . . . to hide the true identity of the killer."

"That's not true, honey. I—"

I said to Janet, "I wouldn't be surprised if George was the one who tipped off the press, and made the connection with the L.A. Killer. Not only that," I added, "I'll bet George was supposed to make sure the killer wasn't captured, to make sure this guy died with the secret of who he worked for."

Meany sat back in his chair. I couldn't tell what he was thinking, but if I had to guess, it would start with putting a bullet through my forehead. And it would end with the realization that the gig was up.

Never one to leave well enough alone, I continued, "So, you're a bright guy, George. And you figured out I was taunting the killer, that I was setting myself up. So you and Martin . . . you what? . . . you set up a stakeout around my building?"

He had not yet made up his mind to be cooperative, so I further suggested, "Your guys had the killer's composite, and if they laid eyes on him, they had orders to shoot to kill. Right?"

"Don't be an idiot. We were there to protect you. You owe me your thanks, Drummond."

"And a fine job you did. I'll remember to call you the next time my life's at risk."

When he failed to reply to that, I asked, "How did they get past you, George?"

"You're such a smart guy, you figure it out."

So I did. I said, "They didn't. They were already inside my building."

He nodded. "Good guess, Drummond. There was a vacant apartment down the hall from you. They broke into it the day before and set up shop. We hadn't anticipated that, nor that outside contractors would be brought in to handle you."

He turned to Janet and said, "Stop looking at me that way. We both wanted the same thing here."

"Did we?"

"Yes, of course. When I went to the Deputy Director, I told him I wanted this case. I wanted Lisa's killer. I told him about us, and he said I could have this case, but on one condition. I had to handle it this way."

Possibly George was telling the truth. In fact, he probably was. But both Janet and I could fill in the rest of the void. George was perfect, because of his relationship with a victim's sister, and as it became more and more clear that Janet and I needed to be reined in, he became more and more perfect.

Janet's eyes moved from George's face, to MacGruder's face, ending up at my face, and I think she concluded that she wasn't really in the best of company, that all her breakfast partners had, in our own unique ways, betrayed her trust.

She stood and said, "If you'll excuse me, I'm going to return to my room." She paused, then said, "And I'd like to return to Boston, today." She took another step, then stopped and said, "I would appreciate it, Agent Meany, if your people would make the proper arrangements."

Did I mention that Janet looked absolutely stunning in a scarlet sweater as she walked out?

CHAPTER FORTY-EIGHT

THE FIRST THING I DID WHEN I ARRIVED AT THE FIRM WAS ASK ELIZABETH FOR the key to the ninth floor to make another visit to my pal Hal. His two assistants again had their asses parked at their desks, and were staring intently into their computer screens. Maybe they had X-rated videos in their hard drives, or something.

The same one who had spoken to me the day before looked up and said, "Yes?"

"I'm here to see Hal."

"He's not in yet."

It was ten o'clock. I said, "When do you expect him?"

"He's usually here at seven. Maybe he had a dentist appointment or something. But I'll tell Hal you came by."

His face was stuffed back in his terminal when I said, "Do that."

I next went to visit Cy in his office. The partners' suites were set up like Hal's office, but with a paralegal or secretary parked out front, and considerably more elegant furnishings inside. Cy's paralegal appeared to be about twenty-five, a great body and nice face, though a bit slutty-looking, if you want my personal opinion. I wondered if Cy was doing her, too, as she buzzed him and told me to go in.

Cy was seated in a leather lounge chair, leisurely sipping coffee and reading the *Wall Street Journal.* He carefully folded the paper in his lap and said, "Good morning, Sean."

I explained that everything was going well, that I was back in everybody's good graces, which brought a twisted smile to his lips, because I'd never been in anybody's good graces. But Cy was too much the politician to point that out.

I said, "So what's my next assignment?"

"It's under discussion. I'm afraid Harold still has hard feelings. Actually, I'm afraid he's thinking of notifying Tommy that the firm no longer wishes to participate in this program. That would mean you go back to the Army. I'm sorry. I might not be able to block it."

"Boy, that would be a shame. I'm learning a lot." I then said, "Tell me about Hal."

"You already know he's a bit of a jerk. But, Sean, he's good at what he does."

"Well, who does he work for?"

"Why?"

"In the event I stay, I think he's still got a grudge, and I'm wondering what I'm in for here."

"He works for Harold."

"And did Bronson hire him?"

"He did."

"Do you recall the circumstances?"

"The man before Hal was killed in an accident. It was very inconvenient for the firm and we were in desperate need of a replacement. Somebody recommended Hal."

"Do you recall who?"

"Somebody at Morris Networks, I think." He added, "Sean, I know you don't like him, but he's a hardworking son of a bitch. He rarely leaves before midnight. Same with his people. The associates appreciate that they're always here to help when a hard drive crashes or they need instant administrative help."

I said, "What about Sally?"

That question for some reason drew a funny look and he replied, "What about her?"

"Do any of the older partners remember her father?"

"A few. Melvin Sperling worked with him. Jimmy Martino, Jack Clatterman . . . maybe others. Why?"

"Do they remember her?"

"No. She wasn't born till after her father moved on."

I thought that over and asked, "Where's her mother?"

"Is there a reason you're asking?"

"We're working together. I'd like to know more about her."

He replied, "I don't know where you're going with this, but I'm certain I don't like it."

We stared at each other a moment, and then it hit me. I mean, wow. I said, "Jesus, Cy, you're screwing her, too?"

"That's none of your damned business." Which is how veteran politicians say yes.

Well, it was suddenly an awkward conversation. And neither of us spoke for half a minute or so.

Until I said, "She's less than half your age."

"Who seduces women who are my age?"

Good point. And in any regard, lecturing Cy on sexual morality and discrimination was beyond a waste of time, so instead I asked, "Did Lisa catch you with her?"

He smiled, though it was a strained, uneasy one. "More or less."

"Uh-huh." The lecture he really needed to hear had to do with his tastes in women. I repeated, "Tell me about her mother."

"Her mother?" He looked at the far wall and asked, "I told you her father committed suicide?"

"Yeah."

"The police found him in the garage, hanging from a rafter. Her mother was in the bedroom. He shot her in the head before he killed himself."

"That's bad."

"Yes . . ." He cracked a knuckle and added, "He left a will stipulating that his daughter would become a ward of the state. Under no conditions would she be given to his detested father to raise. Sally was two at the time. She grew up in orphanages and foster homes."

Cy then asked, "Sean, what's going on here? Why are you interested in Sally?"

"I just like to know who I'm working with."

He toyed with his cufflink and stared at the wall. I let him draw his own conclusions. There's an old saying that a wise man never gets between a man and his girlies. It can be hard to comply with when it's a man like Cy who screws half the city. Yet it's still sage advice.

I left him there and returned to my office. A secretary brought me a cup of espresso, I turned on the TV, and I waited.

CHAPTER FORTY-NINE

THE CALL CAME AT TWO, EARLIER THAN I EXPECTED, BUT GIVEN HAL'S AB-sence, I can't say the call itself was unexpected.

The voice belonged to Jack MacGruder in a tone that was anxious and strained, which was also expected. He identified himself as Thomas Pemberton, because Jack was tried and blue and really into all that smoke-and-mirror silliness. He reminded me of our appointment for a late lunch, and said he would be anxiously waiting my arrival: code word for get your ass here right now, Drummond.

So I left the firm and drove back to the Madison Hotel. But in fact, when I got to my room, not only was Jack there, so was his boss, Phyllis Carney, and of course, George Meany. They all shared a common expression, which is to say, a mixture of confused, angry, and very worried.

Meany seized the opening honors. He waved an arm and said, "You sit at that table."

They remained standing. I knew the name of this game, and I replied, "I'll stand."

Well, they all looked at one another, the way lions look at one another when there's only one carcass to go around.

Phyllis finally said, "You have a great deal of explaining to do, Drummond."

"About what?"

"About what?" Meany repeated, and he looked at the other two. "You hear that?—*about what?*"

MacGruder said, "Hal Merriweather's body was found in his apartment this morning. There was a suicide note beside his bed, a Glock pistol in his hand, and a very large hole in his head."

"Oh my God! Hal? . . . you're sure? . . . suicide?" I shook my head. "Boy, you can never tell, can you? He seemed so happy . . . so, well, I guess, optimistic the last time I saw him."

"Exactly when was that, Drummond?" asked Meany.

"Yesterday. We'd been having a few issues, minor tiffs really, and I stopped by his office to, you know, bury the hatchet." I paused and then said, "Hey, wait a damned minute. You're not thinking . . . I mean, you're not accusing . . ." I shook my head. "Aw, Jack, you tell them. I didn't do it. I couldn't do it. I was here in my room all night, under your surveillance. Your people even followed me to work. I'll bet you guys even have my phones tapped."

Meany started to say, "Drummond, you damn well—"

But Phyllis jumped in, informing me, "Also, Jason Morris was scuba diving off the Florida Keys early this morning. He went on a dive, and an hour later, his body was found."

"Jason, too?" I shook my head again. "You know, I tell all my close friends, stay away from the risky stuff. I mean . . . sure you want the thrills, but is it really worth it? See what I'm talking about? Here's this guy, so much to live for, big bucks, nice house, the ladies drooling all over him, and now he's compost, right?"

Jack MacGruder said, "Stop the goddamn games, Drummond. Don't treat us like idiots."

"But Jack. I saw Jason just yesterday—healthy, full of life and promise. Okay, our meeting ended on a bit of an adversarial note, but in an odd way, you know, I liked Jason. I really did. But, you know what they say about accidents." Obviously nobody replied to that, so I said, "Fate fears neither money nor power."

Meany, a little put off by my bullshit, demanded, "How did you do it?"

"What, George?"

His finger shot up. "Don't . . ." He drew a deep breath. "How did you arrange their deaths?"

"Am I a suspect again? Do I need a lawyer?"

Once burned, once learned, I guess, because George began making a really tortured effort to act circumspect and sly. He said, "Morris was murdered. Somebody cut the line to his airtank and held him down till he drowned. There are bruises on his arms, clear evidence he put up a fight."

"Don't assume it was done by a human. Jason liked to swim with sharks, you know."

They all got my metaphor. But I can't say anybody appreciated it.

MacGruder said, "You went back on our deal and you exposed these people, didn't you?"

"Jack, I fully complied with the pact I made with Mr. Peterson. You have my word on this."

But Phyllis was pretty smart, and she suggested, "What about *before* your bargain?"

"Good question."

"Then answer it."

Meany shook his head and said, "You lousy, lying son of a bitch."

Phyllis looked impatient, and said, "Drummond, we must know what you did, how much you exposed. For Godsakes, we have people inside this syndicate. We have to know whether it's time to get them out and collapse this thing. We have to know whether you've caused us a huge disaster."

"I understand your needs. But do you understand my needs?"

"I don't care about that."

"I do."

We stood there for a moment, frozen, watching each other.

Phyllis said, "What are you proposing?"

"A deal. Your word there'll be no legal problems, and I'll tell you everything." I added, "I broke no laws. But if you decide otherwise, prosecute me."

George said to his CIA counterparts, "No deal. Absolutely not." I think George was carrying a grudge, incidentally.

Phyllis replied, "What's your argument against it, George?"

He faced her and said, "This guy could be an accessory to murder. No deals." After a moment of further thought, he mentioned, "And jurisdiction of this matter resides with the Bureau, not the Agency. Murder is a domestic crime and the decision of whether to prosecute rests with me."

She said, "Then what do you propose?"

"He'll break when I throw his ass in a cell and charge him."

I said, "Charge me with what, George? I've got witnesses. Tell him, Jack." For good measure, I added, "And there's a bit of a time crunch, if I'm not mistaken. Arrest me, and I'll keep my mouth shut till hell freezes over."

Poor Jack MacGruder clearly did not enjoy being put on the hot seat. He did admit, however, "It's true. He was watched and tagged this whole time."

Well, we'd reached a stalemate, and a moment passed, then Phyllis said, "If you'll excuse me, I need a moment to discuss this with Director Peterson." She was really classy and well-mannered, that lady. And she went into the bathroom and closed the door, where I guess she had one of those souped-up Batphones in her purse that she used to have a secure and confidential chat with her boss. This lasted a few minutes, as you might imagine. And I guess Peterson had to talk with Meany's boss, who maybe needed to talk to the Attorney General, and around and around it goes. MacGruder, Meany, and I stood around with our thumbs up our butts, staring at walls, and so on.

But finally Phyllis emerged, and after a moment, she said, "All right. There'll be no problems, *if* you're telling the truth. But if I find out you're lying, or if you're playing games . . ."

I said, "I wouldn't dream of playing games." But, as you might imagine, nobody in the room at the moment swallowed that. Anyway, I said, "Yesterday morning, right after the gunfight, the killer called me."

"He called you?" Meany asked.

"Right. He was checking to see if I was still on his target matrix. So we talked."

"About what?" Phyllis asked.

"What he was going to do to me, what I'd like to do to him, that kind of thing. But our conversation turned a little testy, and I suggested to him that I knew who sent him and whose asses he was sent to protect and why. Jason Morris and Hal Merriweather."

There was a stunned silence for a moment.

Meany spoke first, and said, "My God, Drummond. You marked them for execution."

Yes, I had. I definitely had. But I'd be really stupid to confirm that, so instead I informed them, "Merriweather was the syndicate's inside guy."

"Merriweather?" Phyllis asked. "How do you know that?"

"He was in charge of the firm's information management systems, and was therefore authorized to mess around in the server. When he caught me sniffing around, he tried to set me up to be thrown out of the firm. He also slapped a firewall around Lisa's electronic files to prevent intruders from seeing the connection between her, Julia, and Anne."

"Go on."

"Twice a day, he got server printouts that kept him informed of every case and client in the firm. It's right there in their manuals—the instant you speak with a potential client, you're required to notify the firm's management committee through e-mail, so they know what the emerging opportunities are, and case teams can be formed. That's how Merriweather learned who approached the firm for bankruptcy advice."

Meany's face had become incredulous, and he said, "Then a lot of people in that firm would know. Did it ever cross your mind, Drummond, that you might have just marked an innocent man to be killed?"

Phyllis, who really was very quick on the uptake, was apparently becoming just as annoyed with George's malicious attitude as I was, and she informed him, "Don't be an idiot. The syndicate knows who its inside man is. His death just confirms it."

I nodded that this was so, because it obviously was so. But to further amplify her point, I added, "The irony is that the killer no doubt informed Merriweather that I fingered him and Morris, Merriweather informed the syndicate, and in so doing, he made himself expendable. He signed his own death warrant." Phyllis nodded, and even smiled, struck, I think, by this turn of heavenly justice.

But Meany was by no means finished or defeated, and he said to me, "But Morris is a different story, Drummond. Isn't he? The only suspicion we have on him was his possible implication in corporate graft. You gave him a death sentence."

I said, "He set up the relationship with Grand Vistas."

"You know this for a fact?"

"Yes. He was the guy who told Cy Berger to send Barry Bosworth to Italy for the contract."

"That's circumstantial and inconclusive."

"No, George, it's ironclad. Morris knew his company's condition and turned to the devil for salvation. Open and shut."

"That doesn't justify a death sentence, does it?"

I could sense Phyllis studying my face throughout this little exchange. She said, "He's right, Drummond." She regarded me more closely and asked, "You have no proof about Morris, do you?"

"He set up the partnership."

"Of course. But regarding the murders . . ."

"Look, he set this thing up, and—"

"And you gambled," she suggested. "You assumed he had knowledge about the murders, so you pulled the trigger. Isn't that correct?"

I wasn't going to answer her. But, yes; right on the money. In the split second I had to decide which names to give the killer, I threw the dice and included Jason Morris. I was not sure Morris had been behind, or was even knowledgeable about, the murders. My instincts told me he was, and I went with them.

Everyone was looking at me now and trying to see what I was thinking. I had actually considered this issue a great deal over the past twenty-four hours. Agonized over it, really. I knew I could have, at any point, stopped the wheels I put in motion. I could have informed the CIA or Meany about my little plot, and they would have jumped through their asses and found some way to put up a wall of protection around Morris and Merriweather. But the man who plotted Lisa's murder would've been spared.

Genghis Khan was once supposed to have advised, "Kill them all, and you know you get the guilty ones." American law does not operate that way, nor should it, nor should individuals. The most basic tenet of American law is the presumption of innocence. The protection of innocents is sacrosanct and is what separates civilization from savages.

I had reasoned and rationalized that Morris was the grand architect of the crimes that had caused the deaths of innocents. At the least, his guilt was indirect, and that was enough. But it wasn't enough. And so I had accepted the bald fact that I was going to spend the rest of my life knowing I might have sentenced an innocent—or, actually, a corrupt man—to death, but for a crime I did not know for certain, and definitely could not prove, he committed.

"Christ, you're no better than them," Meany said.

It was an overstatement, but it was not an inaccurate one.

After a long and awkward moment, Phyllis glanced at Jack MacGruder. She said, "Well?"

MacGruder said, "He deserves to live with his decision."

She said, less certainly, "Do you think so?"

He replied, "I'm not sure that's a good idea. We don't owe him anything."

"It will cause no harm, Jack. Morris Networks is an artifact of history at this point."

I had no idea what she was talking about, but clearly Mac-Gruder was your typical CIA type, secrets to the grave, tight lips save ships, and all that shit. He did not like her decision and somewhat spitefully confided, "We were tracing Morris. Phone taps, e-mail taps, you name it." He paused, and then said, "He knew."

"He knew?" I asked.

Phyllis said, "I'm afraid we had to fib to you and Miss Morrow the other day." Her spindly fingers toyed with a lovely spider brooch on her collar for a moment, then she added, "In an e-mail about a month ago, Morris was informed by his contact in Grand Vistas of a serious leak that had to be plugged. That was the precise phrase, incidentally." She then observed, "Don't you find it peculiar the way all these criminals use plumber's language that way?"

MacGruder said, "It was too generic to know what it meant. Only after the second death—"

And Phyllis interrupted to say, "I mentioned before that the syndicate is very sophisticated, and cautious about its communications. It would be fair to presume that the matter was discussed in more detail with Morris. Later, of course. And probably at his home in Florida."

MacGruder explained that comment, saying, "Our FBI friends occasionally see men passing in and out who are part of the syndicate." Another moment passed, then MacGruder said, "Really, Morris had gotten himself into a tricky pickle."

I assumed he was referring to the baseball predicament of being trapped between the bases, rather than the ex-cucumber. I said, "You mean, it was him or the women?"

"Indeed. The syndicate could not allow him to survive if this thing became exposed. There would be an explosion of publicity, a trial, and Lord knows what Morris would have confessed."

I wouldn't say I breathed a sigh of relief. In fact, I had suspected as much. However, with that confirmed, I could continue walking through life with a halo. Right. I said to Phyllis, very sincerely, "Thank you."

She replied, "Think nothing of it."

So I thought nothing of it, and said to her, "I owe you one, and here it is. I'll bet you're also wondering why Sally Westin didn't figure out it was Merriweather."

Okay, yes, I was showing off. But sometimes it's a good idea to let the other side know you're still ahead of them in the game, and this was one of those times. Also, I had one more point I needed to get on the scoreboard.

Phyllis shrugged. "I don't know what you're talking about. Who's Sally Westin?" But I guess she realized from my expression that it wasn't selling. Plus, I had piqued her curiosity, so she cleared her throat, then asked, "All right. How do you know about Sally?"

"One, she's a lousy lawyer. A for effort, F for effect, right? Two, Sally arrived at the firm about three years ago, about when your investigation started, right? And if you're wondering why Sally wasn't able to pinpoint Merriweather, go back to point one." I let them ponder that, and then asked, "Who is she?"

Phyllis nodded at Jack, who then said, "Not Sally Westin, if you're wondering. The real Sally Westin became a nun and lives in a convent north of Denver. Go figure, right. The woman you know as Sally is a Bureau special agent, and that's all you need to know."

Jack studied the carpet a moment, then commented, "Jesus, I thought she had a foolproof cover. We invested a lot of time studying that firm. That whole thing with the Westin family, when we discovered that, I mean, how often does a legend like that land in your lap? We even had her graduate from Duke, because the firm has no Duke grads."

"It's a great cover," I told him. "She's got them completely fooled." Then I let the shoe drop. "But for that one little slip, the girl's a real pro."

Phyllis's lower lip twitched. "Little slip?"

"Her affair with Cy Berger. But you already know about that, right? I mean, surely an agent of her caliber would've informed you that she was sleeping with a possible suspect."

Phyllis's left eyebrow shot up at that one. She said, "You're sure about this?"

"Ask her."

"Oh, we will. Most definitely, we will."

Lisa was surely smiling down on me for that one.

The way I figured it, Sally's bulletproof legend had one flaw: She was drastically out of her legal league in a top firm. But if she slept with Cy then all her problems were solved. In return for all the free poon he could stomach, he'd slide her past her annual reviews, and she wouldn't have to return to the FBI with her tail tucked between her legs. Or maybe Cy was just irresistible to the ladies. How would I know? I appear to have a few problems in that department.

Anyway, Phyllis then said, "Do you have anything else to add?"

"No. I've told you everything."

She searched Jack's face and asked, "Well?"

He rubbed his jaw a moment, then suggested, "My guess would be the syndicate realized the Grand Vistas–Morris Networks connection was getting out of hand, its people were exposed, and decided to terminate them. By tomorrow, they'll have cashed out their stock in Morris Networks, Grand Vistas will be history, and they'll move on to the next thing."

"I agree with that assessment, Jack." She then asked, "Any further damage we should be concerned with?"

He shook his head. "Not unless we treat Morris's and Merriweather's deaths like murders. But if we handle them like unrelated events, exactly as they were orchestrated to appear—a suicide and a diving accident—the syndicate will have no reason to think they've been further compromised."

Phyllis also seemed to agree with that assessment. She looked back at me and said, "You had already thought that through, hadn't you?"

"Maybe."

Meany said to me, "Jesus, you are one cold-blooded bastard."

"Maybe I am, George. But Morris and Merriweather made their own choice. Make a deal with the devil, and you're on his time."

They all thought about that a moment.

But Phyllis had started playing with that spider brooch again, and she said, "But there's one problem left, isn't there?"

"You mean me."

"Yes . . . you."

Jack pointed out, "The syndicate should not be concerned with him. As far as they know, he's unaware of their existence, or their connection to Grand Vistas. If they collapse that connection today or tomorrow, Drummond should be free and clear."

Phyllis nodded. She asked me, "Is that your assessment?"

"Jack's right. The syndicate won't worry about me. I'm no threat to them."

She said, "Then why that anxious look on your face, young man?"

"The killer, is he syndicate, or a local hire?"

Jack replied, "We assume he's a local. For obvious reasons, it's their habit to employ locals when it's called for. They did a thing like this in Pakistan a year ago; all local hires."

But again Phyllis showed her intelligence. She said to me, "But it's gotten personal between you two, hasn't it?"

"I know it's personal for me. I think it's personal for him."

"That's unfortunate."

"Tell me about it."

"You've really got yourself in a fix, then." After a moment, she asked, "What would you like us to do about that?"

"Don't remove your security from Janet, or from either of our families. This guy is vindictive."

Meany, who'd been quietly licking his wounds, chose this moment to state, "The Bureau's position, as you know, is the killer must be brought to justice. He has brutally murdered eight people and his case is on the front page of every newspaper in the country. We have to get him, Phyllis. Our image with the public is on the line."

So they all looked at me.

Well, one did not need to be a genius to know what they were all thinking.

CHAPTER FIFTY

A DRIVING WINTER RAIN WAS FALLING OUTSIDE THE CLASSROOM WINDOW, and my students were daydreaming, doodling, flirting, making fart jokes—anything but listening to me.

It had been three very long and considerably tense days since our meeting in the hotel.

In fact, we had departed the Madison right after that talk, and moved straight to the Pentagon, to Room 2E535, General Clapper's office. Phyllis explained to my boss that I needed to be yanked out of the firm, toute suite, and immediately reassigned to other duties—duties that would leave me exposed and vulnerable, just not too exposed or vulnerable. I wasn't at all sure what that meant, but Clapper promised to handle it, then very cordially asked Phyllis to wait in his outer office while he and I shared a few thoughts.

So our thought-sharing turned out to be one-way, and it began a bit stiffly, with a long talk about proper legal procedures, and the need for flawless professional conduct when operating in the private sector, not to mention other federal government agencies, that kind of thing. Clapper actually made some very good and valid points and I dutifully noted those areas where I badly needed improvement as I stood rigidly at attention in front of his desk.

Well, he got all that off his chest, then said, "Major Drummond, you may now be seated."

So we adjourned to the same leather chairs over in the corner where all this started a few short weeks before. I sat across from him. He crossed his legs, smiled, and asked, "I believe there's one other matter we have to settle."

I replied, tongue in cheek, "I thought you covered everything fairly well."

"The money."

"Money?"

"Seventy million dollars."

"Oh . . . *that* money."

"Refresh my memory. How did it come into your possession?"

"The fruits of a legal settlement."

"I think you're confused, Major. It was the fruits of a criminal investigation."

I said, "No, General, I was assaulted and pursued a very common legal remedy."

He replied, "Perhaps we're having a terminology issue. You *extorted* the money from a public company. This extortion was authorized for a criminal investigation. The vernacular term is 'sting,' and the money therefore belongs not to the agent, but to the government that authorized the agent." He gave me a guarded look and added, "I've already asked the JAG School for an opinion on this matter and they assured me the odds are one thousand to one in the government's favor."

But that was three days ago, and I'm not one to dwell on the past. He got a piece of my ass, but as things turned out, I got a piece of his, too. I had strained his long and amiable friendship with Cy, who, oddly enough, did not appreciate that his old buddy had sent Calamity Sean into his very fine firm. The firm did not appreciate that Cy had extended the offer to the Army, and around and around it goes. The day after I left the firm, the management committee invited Cy to change his status from active partner to "of counsel" status, which is a polite term for "you're retired," though in his case it meant "you're fired." Barry got the same treatment, except in his case, there was no "of counsel" about it. He was simply fired.

But never think Clapper lacks a sense of humor. In response to Phyllis's request, he assigned me to temporary instructor duty at Fort Myer, teaching JAG officers, of all things, a seminar on corporate accounting. JAG officers are JAG officers precisely because they want nothing to do with corporate law. Right? And it always makes for a lively classroom experience when the instructor shares the sentiments of the students.

Like my protégés had been doing the past hour, I checked the clock on the wall—three more minutes till happy hour. I paused from my truly invigorating and riveting explanation about currency hedging, and thought we'd end on a high note. Of course, this means a good joke. So I yelled at them to shut up. And they did.

I said, "Okay, these three guys are being interviewed by the CIA for jobs. The CIA recruiter takes them into a room, one at a time. He says to the first guy, 'Here's a gun. Your wife's inside that door. Go in and shoot her.' The guy takes the gun, he gulps, he goes into the room, ten minutes pass, then he comes out and confesses he just can't do it. The recruiter informs him he lacks the acceptable level of commitment, and sends him away. The next guy comes in, same routine, but he's in there only three minutes before he emerges and is sent away. The third guy takes the gun, and enters the room. A moment later there's the sound of three shots. Five more minutes pass before the guy finally emerges. He throws the gun at the recruiter and says, 'You stupid son of a bitch, some idiot put blanks in that gun. I had to strangle the bitch to death.' "

I was pelted with paper and laughter.

I said, "Class dismissed," and they all fled.

So I began gathering my teaching materials and cramming them into my legal case. Happily, I was teaching this class in the

Post Community Center, so I only had a short walk through the rain, across a parking lot and a grass field to the Bachelor Officers' Quarters, more commonly called the BOQ, where I had a small, cramped room.

My stay in the BOQ was supposed to be temporary, until the killer was apprehended, and/or the repairs were completed on my apartment. But temporary was now looking to be a very long time. Do you believe the management company that owned my apartment building actually submitted a motion to the claims court to have me evicted? Personally, I thought their grounds were a little specious and shaky, but their lawyers appeared quite confident that an explosion and gunfight justified a forced relocation.

Still, all in all, I was happy to be back in the Army, happy to be back with people who dress and think like me, and really happy to be out of the firm. I would miss Elizabeth; I had a sort of Mrs. Robinson crush on her. The Jaguar truly was a devastating loss. But I at least had a nice wardrobe even Clapper couldn't take away.

There was a knock on the door, and a soldier stuck his head inside. He asked, "You done here, Major?"

"Yeah. A few more minutes to pack up," I informed him.

"Hey, sir, if you don't mind, I've got cleanup detail. I'd like to get an early start. Got a hot date tonight."

"Be my guest."

I turned around and began removing the slides from the projector and putting them into my case. He began straightening the chairs and desks behind me.

I said, "How long you been in?"

"Too long. Enlistment ends in two months and I'm not reupping. No sir, I've had enough."

"Yeah? Think twice, pal. I have to tell you the private sector's not all it's cut out to be, either."

"No?"

"Nope. Let me tell you—"

I don't know how long it was before my eyes popped open. But I found myself seated in a chair, dripping wet, and the back of my head ached terribly. So I reached up to massage it, and wouldn't you know, it turned out my hands were inconveniently tied behind my back.

He was looking down at me, holding an empty jar in his hand. He smiled and said, "Surprise."

What an asshole. This was not good. It was after five, Friday, the community center was about empty, and surely the door was locked. So I spent a moment studying him. He was dressed in an Army battle dress uniform, in fact, with the rank of buck sergeant on his collar. His nametag said Smith, and obviously that was phony.

Also, the guy was really huge, big-shouldered, thick arms, thick legs, and a linebacker's neck. No wonder none of his victims managed to fight him off. He was quite good-looking, actually, strong jaw, straight-nosed, and startling blue eyes. He did not look at all like a murderer, which I'm sure helped him get close to his victims. His head was completely shaved, although that's not uncommon on Army posts. Also, resting by his left foot was a green duffel bag, and I found myself wondering what was inside it.

I said, "Hey, you don't want to kill me, pal."

"No?"

"I'm a great lawyer, and you're the kind of guy who's going to need one."

"Is that the best you can do?"

"Well, what can I say? You cheated. You took me from behind."

"Oh, now, Drummond. I promised you I'd come."

"I thought you left."

"Left for where?"

"Whatever shithole you crawled out of."

He laughed. "That will cost you one finger."

"Fine. Middle finger, right hand." I smiled.

"You've got a deal." He smiled, too. We were really getting along well.

I asked, "Incidentally, who are you?"

"I go by many names. Bill, Tom, Jack, call me whatever you like."

"Asshole?"

"Well . . . there goes another finger."

"Right. Middle digit, left hand."

"Hey, I admire that. It's hard to keep a sense of humor in a tense situation like this."

"Tell me about it."

He bent closer and studied me. He said, "I promised you could hear my life story, but didn't I also say I'd be slicing off body parts as we spoke?"

"Yeah. But maybe you should rethink that. I mean, I'll try my best to be an attentive listener, but if you're cutting and chatting, I might be a bit distracted."

He dipped his head to acknowledge this obvious wisdom, but pointed out, "Yeah . . . but time is sort of an issue for me. Tell you what. You get five questions before I begin."

"Just five?"

"Yup, just five." He laughed. "Ooops . . . now four."

"Shit."

"Was that another question?"

"Uh . . . no." He laughed again, and I really wanted to get my hands around his thick neck. I said, "Why?"

"Why what? Why do I kill? Why did I kill the women? Why can't Oliver Stone make a halfway decent movie?" He frowned and added, "Specificity, Counselor. Don't they teach you assholes that in law schools?"

"Fine. Why did you kill the women?"

"Money. It's how I make my living. Like you, I used to be a soldier. I was trained to kill for ideology and idiotic political decisions. Well, shit . . . it got old. The empty wallet got old. So I shifted to the private sector, and set up my own shop. Travel, adventure, great kicks, and the money . . . you wouldn't believe the money . . . it's great. I offer good, speedy service, reliability, and a guarantee on my work. And you know what?"

"Wha— Uh, no. I don't know what."

He laughed. "Nice catch. Two points."

This was almost comical. I mean, I'm stuck with a psychopathic idiot who thinks he's Jay Leno. But I knew his type. He *had* to tell me how smart he was, how very fucking superior, how good he was at the game. Because, like any standard psychopath, for him this was a game. He needed to domineer, to win, at murder, and, I guess, at being a wiseass. I couldn't touch him at the former, but I could bury his ass at the latter. Yet it struck me that I'd better start pulling my punches—as long as he stayed good-humored and chatty, he wasn't cutting me into pieces. Right.

I said, "Okay. Why did you kill the women that way?"

"Aw, I knew you'd ask that next. Okay, the deal was Merriweather found those e-mails about Morrow sending them packages. So Lisa had to be first because if I killed Julia or Anne before her, she would've known. You see that, right?" He paused, then said, "Hey, smartass, you ever figure out how those three knew each other?"

"No. But I don't want to waste a question on that."

He smiled. "You're learning. But here's a freebie. They were all in some young women's professional group. You know, where a bunch of stupid feminist bitches get together once a month to complain about glass ceilings, male-dominant environments, and how hard it is to get ahead without spreading your legs. If a bunch of white male assholes got together and did that, they'd call it discriminatory behavior. What a fucking country, huh?"

I wasn't really interested in this idiot's sociological opinions, so I said, "You're getting away from my question."

"No, I've saved the best for last." He laughed. "Janet's last. I figured, she's not an accountant, or an SEC attorney, so even if she understood the spreadsheets, it would take her the longest to figure out what to do with it."

I said, "Hey, I've got good news."

"Yeah?"

"Her package was a birthday gift Lisa wanted her to give their father."

"Yeah?"

"No kidding. A complete misunderstanding. So it ends with me."

When he did not respond to that, I said, "She's under tight security, you know. And now there's no reason to kill her."

He appeared to be swallowing this, so I added, "You don't have to add the risk. Good deal for her, good deal for you."

He shook his head. "Nah, she dies." He studied my face and asked, "Hey, you got a thing for her?"

"Review the deal, jerk-off. I didn't say I'd answer your questions."

He chuckled. "Ah, now you're pissed. Well, I'll be sure to tell her you said hi in a few days."

Shit. Then he said, "Hey, we forgot all about Fiorio, didn't we? Aren't you wondering about her?"

"No."

Of course I was. But I knew he *had* to tell. And he did.

"Mind games, Drummond." He began ticking down fingers. "Fiorio had nothing to do with this. But she was famous, the cops and FBI would flip over backward to solve her murder, and get more totally misled and lost." He paused a moment, then confessed, "And, hey, I was a little starstruck. I was nuts for her show. I really wanted to meet her. But I regret it now. There's a real hole in my life at six-thirty every evening." He laughed. "Do you believe, I got her autograph before I killed her?"

He glanced down at his watch, and somewhat cavalierly said, "Hey, I hope you don't mind if I start making preparations. I'm sure you understand." He bent down and starting pulling items out of the duffel bag. He said, "Next question, please."

I looked at what he was pulling out of the bag, and given the situation and all I probably should've asked him to read me *War and Peace.* But instead I asked, "Who hired you?"

"You don't know already?"

"Maybe I do."

"Merriweather, initially. He didn't say who he was working for, and in this business, you don't ask. But he offered big money. Ten million up front, five million bonus if the job was done to complete satisfaction. He explained his problem, I briefed him on my plan, and he loved it."

"Hal was impressed by a cheese sandwich."

He frowned at me. "You're *still* pissed at me about Morrow, aren't you? But see if you can look at this professionally. Four victims in a chain, and they had to be done quick. I thought about arranging four accidents, but arithmetically, you know, it's a loser. The accident thing, you know the problem with that? It's high risk, never a sure thing. When you have to do multiples, the copycat thing's the only way. Someone else gets blamed, no suspicion about ulterior motives, and the cops end up chasing their own asses."

I said, "Who hired you to do Merriweather and Morris?"

He laughed. "I don't know, and I don't care. It was all handled over the phone. Five million to do him and Morris."

He had stood up and started stripping out of his uniform. Uh-oh. The game plan, obviously, was he'd get naked to do his slicing and dicing, and you could tell he'd really planned it out in advance, and remembered all the little things. A pile of tools lay on the floor, several sharp knives, a hacksaw, wirecutters, and so forth. Also three fluffy towels and four boxes of babies' Handi Wipes he'd use to clean up, before he got back into the uniform, packed everything back inside the duffel, marched out of the building, and disappeared.

By this time he was totally naked, except for a pair of shower clogs he had slipped onto his feet. The guy made even my brother John look like a stud stallion. Why is it guys with tiny pudleys always feel like they have something to prove? It's not the size that counts, it's the technique—any woman will tell you that.

So what if they're lying.

And I had a really juicy dig about that I wanted to get in, and this was really a nuisance, but I couldn't, because the second I finished asking about Merriweather and Morris, Mr. Asshole had reached over and slapped a tape gag over my mouth. I think this meant our conversation was over and it was time for the real fun to begin.

As you might imagine, I found this both frustrating and very annoying.

He bent over, picked up a serrated knife, and studied me. He said, "I believe we agreed that I would start with the middle finger of your right hand." I nodded. He said, "I don't want to upset you, Drummond, but I lied. I'm doing your dick first."

He reached forward and undid my zipper. He was bent over, and just about to pull Mr. Willie out, when a shotgun blast ripped into his ass. He stood up straight and dropped the knife. He looked quite surprised, actually.

Then came two more blasts in quick succession that nearly blew the guy in half, and splattered his blood and viscera all over me.

Then a voice said, "Military police. Please drop your weapon and place your hands over your head. Don't make me shoot."

By this time the big asshole was standing somewhat precariously on his stout legs, teetering and wobbling, and staring down at his abdomen, very surprised to see his entrails oozing out of some fairly large holes. His eyes shifted to my face. The tape over my mouth kept me from smiling. But I did put forth my very best effort to make my eyes look really, really happy.

His legs collapsed beneath him.

I looked over at the window where the shots had come from, and Danny Spinelli was peering in at me and smiling. The next moment, the door to the classroom crashed open and two MPs with a SWAT battering ram rushed in, followed by Feds in their windbreakers and then more MPs.

Well, it took a few minutes before everybody got organized and settled, before I was untied and ungagged, and before a team of medics provided the official verdict on Mr. Asshole's medical condition—definitely dead. But frankly, I was a little peeved; and in fact, they immediately regretted untying the ropes before they undid my gag, because within seconds, you could see they all wanted to slap that tape back over my mouth. I was howling at everybody in sight.

Finally, the pair I really wanted to talk to, Spinelli and Meany, showed up. Spinelli I was particularly annoyed at. I mean, the deal I'd made with Phyllis was that I'd be bait for this guy, but on one condition. The Army had to be involved, and Spinelli had to be in charge of the Army contingent. Not that I completely trusted Spinelli. I didn't. I just *definitely* did not trust George Meany.

Never put your complete faith in a man with a score to settle. I didn't think Meany would deliberately leave me hanging in the wind or anything like that, but these matters often come down to split-second timing, and a little voice in the back of his head might have said, *Okay, George, wait one more second . . . look, he's about to cut off Drummond's dick . . . his dick, George . . . remember what he did to you and Janet, George . . . now, one more second,* and before you know it, Sean doesn't need zippers for his pants anymore.

So I looked at Spinelli and said, "That guy was two inches from altering my life, you asshole."

He said, "Ah, Jesus, you're such a friggin' ingrate."

"What took you so long?"

"How the fuck were we supposed to know the guy made it in here?"

How about because the guy wasn't supposed to have made it in here in the first place? They had stakeouts set up around this building, and around the BOQ. Make sense? Sure did to me.

But an MP, who was studying the array of tools on the floor, looked up and said, "Chief, the guy wore a uniform. No wonder he got past us. It's right here. He's an Army guy, and his name's Smith."

Spinelli looked at me, and said, "You see what I got to work with here?" He shook his head and repeated sarcastically, "Says his name is Smith." Then he asked, "Hey, think this will get me promoted to chief warrant five?"

I shook my head.

Meany, looking not at all apologetic, said, "When we saw your class depart, we decided to give you fifteen minutes. We thought you were packing your materials, maybe a student stayed after to talk, whatever."

Right. And I'll bet George was out there arguing to give me thirty minutes. But I left that one alone.

Well, it had been damned close, and my legs were still a little shaky and wobbly, but I stumbled to the window, where I stared up at the sky for a while. Everybody sensed I needed a moment of privacy and left me alone.

As I mentioned, I'm Catholic. Yet, I have to confess I harbor a few visceral doubts about that heaven and hell thing. If God had a criminal lawyer's soul, it would make sense, Saint Peter at the gate with his ledger of sins, the whole pattern of eternal justice, the blessed and the damned, good people in one chamber, evil people cast into another.

It has a nice ring, but it's a little too pat. But I most definitely do believe in a spirit that exists after death, and I hoped Lisa had seen this bastard get his due.

CHAPTER FIFTY-ONE

THE DAY WAS BITTERLY COLD, AND THE SNOW WAS COMING DOWN IN SHEETS of frozen white tears.

The chapel ceremony was blessedly short. Lisa would have appreciated that—it wasn't her way to overstate her case to a jury, or to dwell too long on a point, or to overstay her welcome. Her killer had been stopped, the investigation was ended, so the coroner finally released her body for the funeral. The Episcopalian minister who had flown down from Boston had known her from birth, and interspersed his eulogy with tales of her childhood, of her steady progress through life, of her goodness and her spiritual loveliness. There were no dry eyes when he was done.

The Army's Old Guard did their usual splendid job, and we all fell into step with the steady clomp-clomp of the horse hooves dragging the caisson, and her body.

And so I looked out at all the souls who had gathered here, who had all, in some way, large or small, been touched by Lisa. I picked out Clapper and a large retinue of JAG officers in Army greens. I saw Imelda Pepperfield, my hard-bitten legal assistant, who tried to appear stoic and miserably failed. I picked out the faces of Jack MacGruder, and his boss Phyllis, and she was looking at me in a way that worried me a bit. I think I had impressed her with my slyness and my ruthlessness. I had gone into that room and strangled my wife, and the CIA doesn't forget people like that.

I saw Lisa's family, of course, Mr. Morrow in a wheelchair, Aunt Ethel glowering angrily at the skies, and Elizabeth, and Carol, and of course, Janet. I had picked up Felix, Lisa's apartment manager, on my way over. I couldn't see him, but he was there. Cy had sent flowers, but he was not there.

And I looked out at them all, a quiet, huddled mass, and I then looked at the black casket poised over the rectangular hole. I said, "I have the great honor to say the last words. I promise to be brief, because Lisa would not want me to be otherwise. Seneca once warned, 'Men do not care how nobly they live, but only how long they live, although it is within the reach of every man to live nobly, but within no man's power to live long.' "

I paused and we all examined the snowflakes bouncing off Lisa's casket. I said, "She lived nobly—as a soldier, and as a lawyer, she epitomized the best of both. She was my friend, she was all our friend."

I turned to the captain in charge of the honor guard and said, "Begin." Two sergeants stepped forward, removed the American flag, and folded it into a compact triangle. The flag was handed to the captain, who presented it to Janet, Lisa's shadow, as her father had requested.

The shots rang through the air, and the crowd jumped a little, as they always do. The bugle sang its mournful song, and we all cried and watched the black casket descend with painful solemnity into the dark hole a ruthless killer had made her destiny.

I lingered and stared down into the grave as the crowd of mourners slowly trickled past and then made their slow trek back up the hill of Arlington National Cemetery where so many have trod. I had finally put together all the pieces of this, the last secret, if you will. Lisa had known something was seriously amiss in the firm. She had accepted their offer of partnership, because she wanted their trust, because she wanted to expose them, because it was in her nature to rid the world of evil things. But she had not understood the evil thing she was toying with, and that had cost her her life.

I would return here in a few days, and we would have a long and friendly chat. I would tell her how it all ended up, and I would tell her how much I missed her. I reached into my wallet and withdrew her Army photo, which had become crinkled and creased. I kissed it, and then dropped it in the hole.

When I finally looked up, Janet stood directly beside me.

She was staring at me, I think trying to figure out how to break this gently. We had been thrown together by murder and the tumultuous events that grew out of it, that had obviously led to weird emotional currents. Fear, desperation, love, jealousy, and great tidal waves of greed. But all that was over, and who knew what remained.

She said, "That was beautifully said, Sean. Thank you."

I said nothing.

She stared down at the casket. "The news reported the L.A. Killer was killed, resisting arrest."

"Live by the sword, die by the sword."

"And that Jason Morris died in a diving accident."

"I read that."

"And Hal Merriweather committed suicide."

"A fitting end for a miserable little man."

She looked up at the sky, then back at me. "How did you do it?"

"I have no idea what you're talking about."

"Yes you do. I want to know."

"You should believe what you read in the newspapers, Janet." But after a pause, I said, "Qui facit per alium facit per se."

After a moment, she said, "He who does through another does through himself."

"Is that what it means?"

She smiled. She then said, "Lisa once told me the thing she liked most about you was your loyalty."

I shrugged. "And what do you most like about me?"

"Who said I like anything about you?"

"Right."

She put her hand on my arm. "I'm joking."

After another pause, I asked, "How's George?"

"He wasn't invited to the funeral."

"Right."

She said, "Thank you for the money, by the way. We decided to give it to charity. Twenty-two million dollars to the Old Soldier's Home, in Lisa's name and memory."

Oh, yes, the money. Remember when I mentioned Clapper and I had that little chat? Well, I agreed to turn over my loot, but insisted that my lawyer, Janet Morrow, had earned her cut for fair and valid legal services rendered. She was not a federal employee, I had hired her for her services, and no law in the land could deprive her of that cash. He got back on the horn to the JAG School, and they agreed I had a good point. But half the money was out of the question; I'd been overly generous, they insisted. Well, I couldn't argue with that, and I didn't try. The generally accepted legal fee was one-third, approximately twenty-two million.

I informed Janet, "She would've liked that." I saw old Felix up at the top of the hill, waiting patiently. I said, "She had a thing for old soldiers."

"Yes, I think you're right."

After a quiet moment, I said, "Well, listen, I better get back to work. I'm back to working criminal cases, incidentally."

I started to walk away, and Janet said, "Can I ask you something?"

"What?"

"Do you think . . . would Lisa . . . would she be upset if I became involved with you?"

"She'd tell you you're nuts."

"I suppose you're right."

I took three more steps before I turned around. "What hotel did you say you're staying at?"

"The Four Seasons again."

"Nice place."

She nodded.

I took three more steps and turned around again. "Seven o'clock sharp. I swear I won't be late."

She shook her head. "Take your time, I've still got my gun."